*Inheritance*

*from Mother*

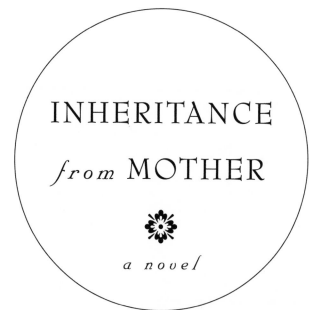

# INHERITANCE *from* MOTHER

❀

*a novel*

# MINAE MIZUMURA

TRANSLATED FROM THE JAPANESE BY
JULIET WINTERS CARPENTER

OTHER PRESS
NEW YORK

Copyright © 2012 by Minae Mizumura
First published in Japanese as 母の遺産—新聞小説
[Haha no Isan—Shinbun Shosetsu]
in 2012 by Chuokoron Shinsha, Inc., Tokyo.
English translation copyright © 2016 by Juliet Winters Carpenter
and Minae Mizumura
English translation rights arranged with Minae Mizumura
through Writers House/Japan Foreign-Rights Centre

Production editor: Yvonne E. Cárdenas
Text designer: Julie Fry
This book was set in Albertina with Bernhard Modern
and Benton Sans by Alpha Design & Composition of Pittsfield, NH.

10 9 8 7 6 5 4 3 2 1

Library of Congress Cataloging-in-Publication Data

Names: Mizumura, Minae, author. | Carpenter, Juliet Winters,
    translator.
Title: Inheritance from mother / Minae Mizumura ; translated from
    the Japanese by Juliet Winters Carpenter.
Other titles: Haha no isan. English
Description: New York : Other Press, 2017. | Previously published in
    Japanese as Haha no isan : shinbun shosetsu. Tokyo : Chuokoron
    Shinsha, 2012.
Identifiers: LCCN 2016034277 (print) | LCCN 2016046176 (ebook) |
    ISBN 9781590517826 (hardback) | ISBN 9781590517833 (e-book)
Subjects: LCSH: Women college teachers—Fiction. | Middle-
    aged women—Fiction. | Mothers and daughters—Fiction. |
    Marriage—Fiction. | Self-realization—Fiction. | Japan—Fiction.
    | Domestic fiction. | Psychological fiction. | BISAC: FICTION
    / Contemporary Women. | FICTION / Literary. | FICTION /
    Cultural Heritage.
Classification: LCC PL856.I948 H3413 2017 (print) | LCC PL856.I948
    (ebook) | DDC 895.63/5—dc23
LC record available at https://lccn.loc.gov/2016034277

## PART ONE

## PART TWO

This novel, an homage to the dying tradition of serial novels, was itself serialized in the newspaper *Yomiuri Shimbun* from 2010 to 2011.

# Part One

## THE LONG TELEPHONE CALL IN LIEU OF A WAKE

"So how much do we get back from Golden?"

Before answering, Mitsuki, on the phone with her sister Natsuki, glanced once again at the numbers. On this late-fall night the window by the desk was closed, but instinctively she lowered her voice in reply. "Around seventeen million yen."*

"What?" said Natsuki. "You mean they keep a whole ten million even though she was there such a short time?"

"Looks like it."

"Golden" was the private, exclusive nursing home where their mother had been living. Its full name was Golden Years, but everyone always called it Golden. The home had charged an initial deposit of 27 million yen, far more than their mother's dwindling savings would have covered. Funds for the deposit and the high monthly fees had come from selling the land in Chitose Funabashi, the Tokyo suburb where the family home had been. Their mother had actually lived in Golden just four and a half months before coming down with pneumonia. They had kept her room throughout her three-and-a-half-month stay in the hospital, making a total of eight months.

---

* $170,000, at the rate of 100 yen to the US dollar.

Once she saw that her mother's death was imminent, Mitsuki had taken to opening Golden's pamphlet and studying the page with the refund scale. Residents forfeited one-third of the deposit on moving in and the rest on a monthly basis over a seven-year period. She checked her calculations repeatedly, punching in the numbers on a desktop calculator until she was sure.

"I spent all that money, thinking she'd live another ten years," said Mitsuki. "What an idiot."

Pleated French lace curtains embroidered with a delicate floral design, two and a half times the width of the window: that had been one folly. Their family was particular about beautiful things. Whatever mixed feelings about their mother Mitsuki and her sister may have had, they took pride in this inclination that was theirs by birth and upbringing. Mitsuki had poured herself with zeal into decorating her mother's final home, a tiny room of just twenty square meters, and her sister had supported her in her every whim. Still, looking back, Mitsuki thought her zeal had bordered on the pathological.

Natsuki comforted her. "Yes, but back then we were positive she'd be there a long time."

Based on the average lifespan of women in Japan, who enjoy greater longevity than women anywhere else in the world, their mother in her mid-eighties could have expected to live another eight years. Plus she came from a line of women who lived long, even for Japan.

"True."

"Besides, compared with how much she's leaving us, you didn't spend all that much."

People whose parents are indigent must provide for them in old age out of their own pocket. Their mother had had enough laid by to provide for herself and also leave them each an inheritance which, although surely below the amount that would require them to pay inheritance tax, would still be a tidy sum.

In addition to the pamphlet showing the refund scale, on the desk in front of Mitsuki was a heap of items from the filing cabinet in a jumble of colors and shapes: savings passbooks, new and worn, decorated with stripes or gradations of different hues; bank seals of black lacquer or ivory, some round, some oval; documents from securities companies; a memo pad covered with scribbled figures; and various notes, sorted by denomination. On top of them all was an estimate from the funeral home.

"I wonder how much she left us altogether," Natsuki said, as if to herself.

Natsuki's relationship with their mother had been strained. At one point their mother had washed her hands of her elder daughter and ingratiated herself instead with Mitsuki, the previously neglected younger daughter, entrusting her with everything, including her finances. Natsuki was never good at managing money anyway and, while resenting their mother, had used this treatment as an excuse to sit back and do nothing. As a result, she had little grasp of the flow of their mother's funds.

"Altogether, including the money due back from Golden, I figure it should come to about thirty-five million apiece."

For Natsuki, who had married into wealth, this probably wasn't a lot of money. As Mitsuki was about to mention this, her sister sighed and said with feeling, "That's a lot of money."

To keep her husband and daughter from overhearing the conversation, Natsuki was undoubtedly calling from the soundproof piano room where she liked to retreat with her two cats.

Earlier that evening, after leaving the body at the mortuary, Mitsuki, her sister, brother-in-law, and niece had all gone out for dinner at a nearby chain restaurant specializing in *shabu-shabu* hot pot; they had parted at around eleven. Even after returning home, Mitsuki had remained exhilarated, knowing that her mother was finally dead—and Natsuki must have felt the same way, for before going to bed she had called, wanting to talk to the one person she knew would fully share her excitement and listen to her with infinite understanding. The sisters each had had a very different relationship with their mother, so they felt liberated in different ways, but their excitement was identical—keen and palpable.

Mitsuki's professor husband was on sabbatical and had been in Vietnam since the end of March, ostensibly to do research. Natsuki could therefore call late at night with the assurance that she would disturb no one. The phone had rung just as Mitsuki was in the midst of recalculating how much their mother had left them.

"It's hard to believe I've suddenly got so much money," Natsuki said. "For the Shimazakis that might not be much, but for me it is."

The Shimazakis were Natsuki's in-laws; her husband, a cellist, was their second son. Yet even after decades of marriage, even after her falling-out with their mother, Natsuki remained at heart a Katsura. As did Mitsuki, for that matter. But a woman marrying into wealth was somehow under greater social obligation to become steeped in the ways of her new family. Despite this pressure, Natsuki had remained stubbornly herself.

"What'll you two use the money for?" she asked.

Natsuki uttered the words "you two" with complete innocence. She meant Mitsuki and her husband, Tetsuo, but the words gave Mitsuki momentary pause. In her reply, she ignored the "two" of "you two" and spoke only about herself.

"Not sure. First off, I want to get my strength back. Go for all the acupuncture and massages I want, soak in a hot spring. If I can, I'd like to quit teaching, too."

"That sounds good. Tetsuo will be happy too, won't he? Now he can afford the high-rise condo in the city center he's always wanted."

Tetsuo had never even been told her mother was in the hospital, but this her sister did not know. Instead of responding, she asked a question of her own. "What about you, what'll you use the money for?"

Natsuki and her husband, Yuji, owned a spacious apartment of more than 150 square meters in an exclusive old residential area in central Tokyo. Not only were they not saddled with a mortgage, his parents had built them a villa by the family summerhouse on the coast, next to one for his sister and her husband.

"I'm not sure either. I've always felt…small, you know? I've never earned more than a pittance. It's such a relief to think that finally I'll have some money of my own. I could trade my Yamaha in for a Steinway. Hey, with thirty-five million I could even buy myself a little condo and get a divorce!" After this bit of flippancy, she went on seriously, "You know what the best part is? Getting free of her while I'm still in my fifties. All those years, I struggled to put the idea out of my mind, tried not to think of anything so lucky."

"I know."

"Watching her, all I could think was that I didn't want to live to be so old. Life lost its appeal in a way."

"I know what you mean."

Burdened by their mother's constant needs and wants, Mitsuki had felt the joy of life wither and fade. And then one summer night just when her menstrual cycle was becoming irregular, she had sat for hours with her bare back exposed to air-conditioning. Before she knew it she'd developed a syndrome known colloquially as "air-conditioningitis." Her nervous system was affected, and she developed what the doctor called "autonomic dysfunction," a kind of neuropathy that dragged on and on.

To top it all off, their mother had fallen and fractured her shoulder and hip just before New Year's, a catastrophe that aggravated the sisters' own ailments. Natsuki, though strong since childhood, now had a chronic and worsening eye condition, and Mitsuki, weak since childhood, suffered increasingly from her nerves. Then too, although her sister didn't know it, she had her husband to fret about.

As they continued to chat, Mitsuki thought of their mother's body lying in the mortuary—in a freezer, to be precise—turning steadily to ice from the outside in. Eventually the internal organs would freeze, every last one. Even the eyes, which had stayed wide open, staring, until a nurse had gently closed them, would freeze solid. What of her white hair, full and wiry to the last? What would become of it?

*Aujourd'hui, maman est morte.* Today, mother died. The opening line of the first novel she had ever read in French, long ago.

By rights, this should have been the night of the wake. A night when, according to Buddhist tradition or still more ancient custom in Japan, newly bereaved family members would stay up all night, keeping candles lit and incense burning as they bade the departed farewell. Now that so many people died in the hospital, how many families took the body home to hold a proper wake anymore? Customs were fluid, changing year by year. What others might do she had no idea, nor did she—or her sister, she felt sure—much care. She felt no guilt about leaving their mother's body unattended in the mortuary freezer while chatting on the phone about how to spend their inheritance. She even felt no guilt about not feeling guilty. And she had no intention of revisiting the funeral home till two days later, when the body would be put into its coffin.

"Anyway, tomorrow we've got to get some rest."

Mitsuki hung up the telephone and switched off her computer. She wasn't going to tell Tetsuo that her mother was gone. The time difference between Japan and Vietnam was two hours. Right now, he might be setting out nightcaps and snacks for two. He felt at ease in the kitchen, and she had always liked watching him putter there. Now he was showing that homebody side of himself to some young woman. He didn't deserve to be told about her mother's death.

She prepared for bed as usual and slid under the covers. Light from the lamp on her nightstand fell on a French novel, the one she had started reading at her mother's bedside during those last few days, while waiting for her to die. She switched the light off.

Even in the dark, tears did not come. Her excitement was mingled only with fatigue from having sat all day with her dying mother. It occurred to her that long ago when her grandmother died—back when Mitsuki was a child—her mother, too, had not wept.

Only decades later did her mother show a trace of emotion. One afternoon as they walked along the beach at Atami, the setting for a famous scene in an old serial novel of tragic love, her mother had laughed derisively. Referring to the novel's hero and heroine, she'd said, "There never was any Kan'ichi in your grandmother's life. How silly...her thinking she was O-Miya!" Her voice quavered as she fought back tears, perhaps at a sudden memory.

Mitsuki had walked on in silence, fearing her mother might turn maudlin.

Her mother had struggled to keep pace, jabbing her cane into the sand.

## 2

## THE FLOWER-EMBROIDERED POCKET TISSUE CASE

Like many educated women, Mitsuki believed she had no call to consider herself unfortunate. Whether you looked back through history or around the globe today, human misery was so extreme and so widespread that the Buddhist term "a world of suffering" seemed truly apt. The world was awash in wretchedness. For her to think herself unfortunate was a sin.

Of course, a golden-haired, blue-eyed woman raised by nannies in the Sixteenth Arrondissement of Paris, say, or on Manhattan's Upper East Side, might well think it a great misfortune—even if she couldn't say so aloud—just to have been born in the rural wilds of France or America, let alone in the Far East. But Mitsuki had always thought that if she had to be born in the Far East in the latter half of the twentieth century, at least she was fortunate to have landed in Japan. She had been brought up in fairly privileged circumstances, and had even spent a year studying in Paris, thanks to her mother. Her husband was a college professor, and she herself taught college part time. Even now, her circumstances were fairly privileged. She had no call to consider herself unfortunate.

And yet one day she realized that she could no longer consider herself happy either. As the years piled on she had come to feel a sense of wrongness about her life, a sense that it wasn't supposed to turn out this way. Eventually that sense of wrongness had entangled her in heavy, sticky filaments that dulled her skin as well as her heart. Her step lost its bounce, her smiles grew infrequent, the luster faded from her eyes. She found it hard to believe that she had ever been a happy little girl who would burst into song at the drop of a hat and twirl on her toes.

Just when the change began, she wasn't sure. It wasn't the time she first discovered her husband's infidelity (looking back, she realized there had been ominous signs even midway through their honeymoon). No, she became aware of the sticky meshes of woe only after her father was consigned to a dreary extended-care hospital. Or no, it was still earlier, when That Man first entered her mother's life and cobwebs began to show on the ceilings of their house in Chitose Funabashi, where her father was left to sit alone, hollow-eyed.

In these last few years, the heavy, sticky filaments had wrapped around Mitsuki with ever-increasing momentum—especially after she came down with that strange syndrome.

That night, after sitting directly exposed to air-conditioning for hours, by the time she reached home she'd been ready to drop. After a night of restless sleep, she found that far from having recovered, she shivered with cold at the mere touch of her bedsheets. Her temperature usually registered on the high side, but in the morning it was quite low.

She went to the hospital, where a young doctor in his thirties unsympathetically informed her, a middle-aged woman struggling to endure the hospital's air-conditioning, "People don't die even with a temperature lower than yours." He didn't write her a prescription.

After coming home, she did some checking online and learned that the Western medical establishment dismissed sensitivity to the cold as "poor circulation." The word and indeed the concept of air-conditioningitis seemed not to exist in the West. Yet on the Japanese Web, any number of women reported suffering from exposure to air-conditioning: their hands, feet, and lower abdomen turned to ice; their shoulders and back stiffened; they felt chronically fatigued. By far the most complaints were from women her age. Whether the syndrome was uniquely prevalent among Asians she didn't know, but she began to take an herbal remedy prescribed by a woman specialist in traditional Chinese medicine, and she also started acupuncture treatments. She discovered that if she saw a specialist in psychosomatic medicine, she could get prescriptions for anti-anxiety drugs, antidepressants, and sleeping aids.

As a child, Mitsuki had frequently caught colds and run high fevers, and as an adult she tired easily. Now there was never a day when she felt well. Added to her physical ailments was the ever-increasing burden of her aging mother, whose treatment of her late father she found impossible to forgive. Meanwhile, she went on dealing with her wayward husband as if nothing were wrong, trying not to think of her marriage, even as emptiness spread inside her.

Her small misfortunes had resonated together like notes in a symphony, quickening and surging in a crescendo that reached a climax late last year. Or, to use the jo-ha-kyu terminology of the Noh master Zeami (she was, after all, Japanese), her troubles had built up to the frenetic kyu pitch.

From the end of the year until her mother's death eleven months later, life had been something of a nightmare.

Wretched: as the nightmare progressed, Mitsuki had begun to think of herself this way. She remembered reading a fairy tale as a child about a princess who never laughed. A semi-invalid middle-aged woman who rarely laughed anymore should be allowed to consider herself wretched.

It had happened last December 28 at two in the afternoon.

Both Mitsuki and her husband were on winter vacation. He was supposed to be interviewed for a magazine and have his picture taken, so he set off at ten-thirty wearing a starched shirt with a mandarin collar—a style so popular among cultural commentators on TV that she referred to it privately as the "literati shirt."

That day she'd felt fine.

Normally a short trip to the supermarket wore her out, and she would come home and lie down on the bed afterward, but that day she was energized from doing the New Year's shopping. She quickly put the various delicacies, auspicious even if ready-made, in the refrigerator, then got on the stepladder and brought down a set of antique ceremonial lacquerware—a sake decanter and cups, a tiered box and plates, and a tray with legs—all packed in old cardboard boxes. She carefully wiped each piece and placed the set on top of the wooden cabinet that housed the TV. Though the lacquer was worn in spots, the utensils were exquisitely decorated with a pine pattern in raised lacquerwork, and the box lid bore a flying crane in mother-of-pearl inlay. The set was a family heirloom, but her mother hadn't wanted it and her sister had no use for it, having been provided with a new set by her in-laws, so it came to Mitsuki by default.

Next she got out a tall vase that she and Tetsuo had chosen together in Okinawa and placed in it a ready-made arrangement of green pine, silver branches, and red berries that she'd picked up at a flower shop on the way home—a miniature version of the traditional *kadomatsu* (gate pine) New Year's decorations, scaled down to the needs of condominium residents. She placed the arrangement next to the lacquerware set, and the entire room took on a festive air.

Every year on the last day of December, she and Tetsuo always went to his parents' house in Toride, Ibaraki Prefecture, one of the most remote suburbs of the sprawling Tokyo metropolis. Mitsuki would stay two nights, New Year's Eve and January 1, and come back January 2 for a celebration with just her mother and sister. Previously her mother had seemed to care little about "Katsura New Year's," but after That Man finally vanished from her life this had become a major event for her as, anxious to maintain ties with her daughters, even Natsuki, she was glad of an excuse for the three of them to get together. They still gathered every year in Mitsuki's place, where Mitsuki used to bring her father from the hospital for New Year's to feast on his favorite dishes and listen to his favorite Christmas music, even though he responded less and less as the years went by...

But today, the twenty-eighth of December, was no time to sit idle, lost in memories. There was far too much work to do.

She gave the pine branches a final touch and then went to her room. She had a rush translation job to finish, and the year-end housecleaning was waiting, not to mention the laundry. But before anything else, she wanted to see to some correspondence. She had just received two notices from old college friends saying they were in mourning after the loss of a parent and so would be refraining from offering customary New Year's greetings. Having already sent out her New Year's cards for delivery the morning of January 1, she needed to quickly get off letters of condolence.

Was December a month when many old people died?

Vaguely envious of her friends' bereavement, she took out several sheets of handmade rice paper saved for just such occasions and wrote a few lines, using a fountain pen to make her writing as presentable as possible. As she took out matching envelopes, she recalled that the only postal stamps left in her drawer were inappropriate, featuring either bright flowers or ukiyo-e paintings. For letters of condolence, neither would do. She went into her husband's study-cum-bedroom to look for some plain stamps.

Usually she stayed out of his room. A large computer monitor sat on his desk, surrounded by a slew of books and papers, as befitted a scholar's study. She knew that if she tidied his desk he wouldn't be able to find anything, so when she cleaned she did no more than dust lightly and run the vacuum cleaner. She rarely had occasion to open his desk drawers.

Now when she pulled open the top drawer, something colorful and pretty caught her eye. She picked it up to find it was a pocket tissue case of pink silk, embroidered with tiny flowers of blue, green, and yellow—the sort of thing sold in Asian goods boutiques catering to young people. A tiny flower garden. Tetsuo may have had his feminine side, but in the end he was a man. Generally he made do with packets of pocket tissue with advertising inserts that people handed out on the street for free, or with whatever she brought home from the supermarket. This embroidered tissue case had lain hidden in the drawer like a dainty fairy, yet its very daintiness was full of menace.

He was seeing a young woman. She knew it in her bones.

Usually if a person needed to borrow tissues, someone would hand him one or two. Could he have taken a whole packet like this, stuck it in his pocket, and brought it home without thinking, case and all? Impossible.

As she stood there frozen, holding the menacing object in one hand, the telephone rang. She picked it up with her other hand. The caller was a woman whose voice she didn't recognize.

"Is this the residence of Ms. Mitsuki Hirayama?"

The emergency notification card in her mother's wallet listed Mitsuki's name as the first contact.

The woman identified the hospital she was calling from. "Your mother, Noriko Katsura, was brought in by ambulance with multiple fractures."

The tissue case in Mitsuki's hand seemed to glow, as if mocking her.

She immediately called her sister with the news. Natsuki responded in a fed-up tone, "Whaaat, not *again*? Well, I can't always leave everything to you. I'll go too."

Her sister never said, "I'll go. You stay." At a time like this it was always "I'll go too." Mitsuki checked her watch. Tetsuo would be in the middle of his interview, his cell phone switched off. He was punctilious about such things. She left a voice message for him: *My mother fell and broke some bones again. I don't know what's going to happen tonight so please get something to eat on the way home, okay?* And then rushed off to the hospital.

While she sat waiting on a bench in front of the emergency treatment room, the pink tissue case rose to mind—only to yield to totally different thoughts that began racing through her brain like fire:

*Mother is dying.*

*My mother is dying.*

*Finally she's going to die.*

But no. It couldn't really be happening.

The nurse on the telephone had been short on details, but she did explain that Mitsuki's mother had slipped and fallen in front of a laundry shop near her house, breaking her hip and shoulder. The woman who ran the shop had called the ambulance.

People didn't die of broken hips or shoulders.

"Is she conscious?" Mitsuki had asked.

Yes, fully alert, the nurse had said.

If she hadn't hit her head, then there was even less chance she would die. Even as Mitsuki told herself this, a voice inside said, *Still, she's in her mid-eighties, you never know, she could die from the shock of the fall. Or maybe she did hit her head and there's bleeding in the brain . . .* Her mind produced one fatal scenario after another.

In half an hour, the doors swung open and Mitsuki's name was called. She went in and found spaces marked off by cream-colored curtains to the right and left. She was directed to one of them, and there was her mother lying faceup on the bed, looking quite herself, foundation and lipstick meticulously applied as usual.

"Mitsuki!" she burst out as soon as she saw her daughter. "I'm sorry! I'm so sorry!"

# 3

## PORTABLE TOILET

Mitsuki had constantly begged her mother not to fall, not to cause any more trouble; that must be why she sounded so mortified. From the moment she slipped and fell, during the ambulance ride and all the time she was receiving treatment in the hospital, she must have been waiting apologetically for Mitsuki to appear. Her mother's contrition would soon fade, Mitsuki knew, but she softened at this heartfelt appeal.

The X-rays showed fractures to the right shoulder and the femoral neck of the right hip. The shoulder was shattered beyond repair. Both injuries would require surgery, followed by a month in the hospital and another two or three months of rehabilitation.

"Will she be able to walk?" she asked the doctor.

"That depends on her. If she makes the effort, then yes, I think she can walk again."

Her mother was lying down, her dark eyes wide open, looking from the doctor to Mitsuki and back. She was hard of hearing, so she had difficulty catching other people's conversations. The doctor gave off an unmistakable air of being terribly busy, and Mitsuki refrained from asking further questions. After he was gone, she knelt at her mother's bedside and repeated what he had said, then asked, "So how did you fall?"

"I don't know, it must've been the wind. Before I knew it I was flat on the ground."

She'd begun using a cane years ago, after a youth speeding on his bicycle had run into her, knocking her down. In time the cane was no longer enough, and when out on errands by herself she would push a wheeled walker with a basket. That day as she left the laundry shop and was trying to put some freshly starched and ironed sheets into the basket, a sudden gust of wind had knocked her to the ground.

Natsuki finally showed up, looking as if she'd rushed over. Without so much as a ring on her finger, she somehow projected an aura of wealth.

"Oh, Natsuki!" Their mother stretched out her left arm—the right arm was immobilized—for her elder daughter to grasp, which Natsuki did, looking faintly flustered. "I broke my bones again."

Natsuki seemed moved by this simple declaration. "It's all right, Mother, you couldn't help it." Her tone was uncharacteristically gentle.

Mitsuki took advantage of her sister's arrival to make a quick telephone call to her mother's "care manager," filling her in about the accident and asking her to cancel all visits by home helpers for the time being.

"Oh, I'm terribly sorry to hear that," said the care manager. "But I know your mother. She's got magical strength. She'll bounce back!"

The woman's usual bright tone helped Mitsuki to accept the situation, and it was comforting to know that home helpers would be on hand when her mother returned home.

She had always been grateful that medical expenses for the elderly were virtually free. The primary burdens of caregiving, however— everything from grocery shopping to changing diapers—tended to fall disproportionately on female family members, so several years ago when the Long-Term Care Insurance system was finally introduced, she'd lost no time in putting in an application. A government-assigned care manager had soon appeared at her mother's door, and ever since, this bright-voiced woman had seen to it that home helpers came by regularly.

After the quick telephone call, there was some paperwork to do for admission to the hospital, and then the sisters set off for the family home to pick up various items their mother would need.

When they returned, they found her in a double room in the bed by the window. Mitsuki, though she hated to deplete their mother's savings, had requested a double room rather than a ward. Their father had spent seven long years in a ward and never once had a bed by the window; even in such small matters, their mother's luck held strong.

Then she spotted a urinary catheter and drainage bag hanging below the bed.

No sooner did their mother see them than she wailed, "Oh, this is the end of the line for Noriko Katsura!" She had a habit of referring to herself in the third person when using a self-mocking tone. On her wrinkled face, with the makeup starting to come off, self-mockery was writ large.

Mitsuki too thought this latest mishap would be the end of her mother, and no doubt so did Natsuki. Exactly how it would play out, she wasn't sure. As their mother aged, and one by one the things she enjoyed fell away, her familiar cry of "I've got to have some fun while I still can!" had only intensified. She had continued her frantic search for any sort of gratification, however small. In any case, today marked the beginning of a stage of her life certain to contain far less gratification than ever before.

Yet there was a long way to go before her life would be truly finished.

"Come, come!" Mitsuki said aloud with forced cheerfulness. "You're not the type to reach the end of the line so easily. If you exert yourself, you'll be on your feet again in no time."

She felt uncomfortable having this exchange in the hearing of the room's other occupant, a woman separated from them only by a thin curtain, but she needed to speak loudly to make herself heard. The woman was around seventy. If she wasn't stone deaf, she would soon realize that there was something a bit odd about the way this family talked among themselves, at times overly dramatic, at times drily cynical. They were not exactly your typical Japanese family.

Her mother sighed. "I'd rather be dead."

"Well, you're not dead," Mitsuki replied. "You'll just have to pick yourself up and go on. What else can you do?"

"I should have died."

"You'll have surgery and rehab. They'll get you up walking again."

At the time, Mitsuki had still believed that her mother was likely to walk again. She would have a far harder time of it than before, but for the past few years she had been living downstairs anyway, and she should be able to totter around well enough with her cane.

Her mother ignored Mitsuki's assurances and looked about her. "Even if I run up a bill here I won't go broke, will I?"

"You'll be fine." Mitsuki sounded confident, but as she spoke she couldn't help envisioning her mother's shrinking savings balance.

"And did you call my care manager?"

"Yes, first thing."

"Good girl." She turned to Natsuki, who had been silently putting things away. "Did you get all my medicines?"

Whenever the three of them were together, Natsuki, always a bit sulky, let Mitsuki do the talking. Now in answer she held up a Ziploc bag with the medicines in it.

Their mother nodded in satisfaction—and then launched rapid-fire into a list of things for them to do: Cancel the newspaper and the twice-weekly meals Mitsuki had arranged to be delivered to her door. Tell the neighbor who helped her dispose of recyclable trash that she was in the hospital, and give her a box of cakes. Go back to the laundry shop to retrieve the sheets and give the lady there a box of cakes, too, to thank her for calling the ambulance. Get back two DVDs she had lent out—Nureyev's *Romeo and Juliet* to a home helper named Shirakawa and Pavarotti's *Aida* to "the flower-nutty man" at the beauty shop. Notify everyone who needed to be notified and tell them not to come see her in the hospital. Her bank seals were in the back of the refrigerator—Mitsuki knew where—in a red leather cosmetics pouch, one Grandpa Yokohama gave her years ago. Her passbooks were in a stack of towels under the sink, her cash cards in the cabinet by her desk. Also, she had several thousand yen tucked away in the pockets of her long silk coat, her half-coat, the cashmere coat with shoulder cape, a cheap raincoat, and various slacks and handbags. Go through them all and take the money out. And on and on.

Clearly, she had spent the entire time they were gone pondering what she needed to tell them to do. She rattled on like one possessed, as if she knew that her already diminished faculties would soon fade away. Natsuki went on sorting and putting things away while Mitsuki scribbled notes.

Then the surgeon stopped by, having heard that they were there. After making clear that he wasn't the attending physician, he explained their mother's situation. She had previously fractured her wrist, left shoulder, and left hip. Had she broken only the right hip this time, she could probably have gone on managing her cane with the right hand, but as luck would have it she'd shattered the right shoulder as well. He could give her a new shoulder using artificial bone, but she would no longer be able to support her weight with a cane. Not only that, the shoulder would be vulnerable to dislocation. She would need to walk with the aid of a railing.

22

To demonstrate what he meant, the doctor grabbed an imaginary railing and pulled himself along sideways with a crablike gait.

As Mitsuki listened, she mentally reviewed the layout of her mother's room, wondering if they could put in a railing between the bed and the bathroom.

"It might be a good idea to keep a portable toilet beside her bed," the doctor said.

Mitsuki flinched.

"And since she's getting on in years, the worst-case scenario is that she might be confined to a wheelchair. Keep that in mind—you might want to get started looking at nursing homes."

Things were progressing so quickly that Mitsuki found her imagination hard-pressed to keep up. She sensed her sister frozen in astonishment behind her while their mother, dark eyes opened wide, keenly watched. Mitsuki's wish for her mother to die was abstract—tinged with poetry, even. By contrast, the words "portable toilet" had a stark reality that caught her off guard.

After they saw the surgeon off, Mitsuki went over and knelt at her mother's bedside. Slowly rubbing her mother's upper arm, she repeated in her ear more or less what the doctor had said. There was no point in letting her own shock show, so she left out the part about being confined to a wheelchair. "It seems like you'll have to walk by holding onto a railing. So he says it might be a good idea to put a portable commode next to your bed at night."

"A portable commode?" Her mother too was thrown off guard. "You mean a portable toilet? I won't have any such thing in my room." She glared up at the ceiling, incensed. "I won't have it!"

"He just mentioned it as a possibility, that's all."

"Forget it! I. Will. Not. Have it. Period."

## 4

## A HUSBAND SIPPING AGED SAKE

"It just never occurred to me that she wouldn't be able to use a cane anymore," said Natsuki on the way to the station.

"Same here."

"Wouldn't it be easier if she just went into a nursing home? If *you* suggested it, she might go quietly. She always listens to you." Her sister's tone was resentful.

"Maybe." Mitsuki thought a moment. "But it's too soon. Let's give her some time."

Before parting at the station, they agreed to watch how their mother fared in rehabilitation and bring up the idea of a nursing home if and when it appeared definite that she could no longer live on her own.

Mitsuki lived near a station on the Marunouchi subway line. She dragged herself home, sluggish from the day's shocks, and as soon as she walked in the door Tetsuo appeared. She felt somehow that he had just got off the telephone—with the young woman, most likely.

Unaware that she'd seen the pink tissue case, he addressed her normally. "So, what happened?"

As she slipped off her shoes, Mitsuki gave him a brief rundown. Then she washed up and set on the dining room table the ready-made meal she'd picked up at a convenience store on the way home: hot rice topped with seasoned ground chicken.

"You didn't eat yet?" he said. "Shall I pour you something? A glass of light beer?"

"Thanks, would you?"

Tetsuo raised the thermostat a bit for her benefit, then went into the kitchen and took a can of beer from the refrigerator. For himself he chose a bottle of aged sake. Every evening they shared a nightcap.

Normally she would have proceeded to tell him all about her mother's condition, but with the tissue case haunting her thoughts she felt leaden, unable to bring herself to speak. If it weren't for her mother, she might have gathered her courage and confronted him, sword aloft, but she wasn't up to it. She sat at the table and picked up her chopsticks in defiant silence. Twice before she'd found him out, and each time he'd been seeing a woman older than him; now that she herself was getting on in years, it was painful to think that he was probably seeing some-one considerably younger than she was.

Oblivious to her train of thought, Tetsuo stood in the white, compact, tidy kitchen pouring amber liquid into a fragile-looking wineglass, one of a set they'd bought at an antiques fair. He wore an apron slung low around his hips, like a café waiter. He did have style, she had to admit. Compared with thirty years ago when they'd first met in Paris, he had more money now, and he dressed better. He'd grown up in the dowdy town of Toride, where his father had been the accountant for the sub-subcontractor of a home appliance plant run by his brother, Tetsuo's uncle; but originally his parents came from farmers' stock, way out in the country.

When he first took her to the old homestead where his father was born, the floors covered end to end with frayed tatami mats of woven rushes, she'd felt as if she'd wandered into a Japanese folktale. The polish he'd managed to acquire despite those humble origins was a sign he had brains, never mind the nonsense he churned out for magazines and academic journals. He had physical stamina, too, which kept him from looking worn-out the way she did. It was only natural that some young woman would see him as a catch. All the more so since he'd be entirely open to being caught.

Still, he'd be no one's sugar daddy, she mused, eating her food and covertly keeping an eye on him as he got out a little something to go with the drinks. As he himself knew quite well, he wasn't some cipher who could only attract women with money. And he wanted to move to a condominium in the center of the city, so he regularly saved money and purchased stocks even while continuing to indulge in pleasures like dining out, dressing well, and occasionally traveling overseas. Since they were paying off their mortgage with a low-interest loan, he hoped to use their savings for a down payment in the event that a suitable property came along. Mitsuki was glad to have cash on hand for reasons of her own: she wanted to be able to lend her mother money if it was needed. She had no complaints about her husband's handling of their finances.

"What a wonderful husband!" her friends all raved. "He even cooks!"

To assume on the basis of a single tissue case that he was having an affair with a younger woman might be a stretch, yet she was strangely sure of it. There was his past record, to begin with. And even granting that he was making a name for himself in the media, for the last six months he'd been away frequently and was often late getting home.

When he joined her at the table, she said, "The words 'portable toilet' came as a pretty big shock to her."

"I bet they did, for someone as stylish as Noriko."

Her mother had always been known as a beauty. Now that she was a bent-backed, white-haired old lady, people had stopped calling her "beautiful" as they had done in the past and instead more often described her as "stylish." It was true; her mother had gone on being stylish, extravagantly so for a woman of her means, and that she did so was symbolic of a lifetime spent chasing nameless dreams.

"Hard to imagine a portable toilet beside that bed of hers," he added pensively.

Her mother's bed was always done up with fancy linens—a definite extravagance.

Her mother's last trip to Isetan Department Store had been to buy new bed linens. Mitsuki had offered to pick out something herself, but her mother had insisted on coming along. She had always loved expeditions that gave her an occasion to dress up, a long scarf elegantly wound around her neck; and apart from the occasional restaurant meal, department store shopping was one of her last remaining pleasures. With that too on the verge of slipping away, she had asserted her maternal authority and demanded that she be allowed to select the sheets she herself was going to buy and use. Natsuki had tagged along partly for the chance to enjoy a sisterly chat, despite knowing what a trial it was to accompany their cane-tapping mother on a shopping expedition and be weighted down with purchases.

Letting her cane dangle from her wrist by a leather strap, their mother had again taken advantage of one of the walkers provided for elderly patrons, leaning on it as she walked past dazzling displays of goods, her eyes gleaming with excitement. Isetan had always been her department store of choice.

A few years back, when she first discovered a row of walkers at the store entrance, she had all but wept at such thoughtfulness: "Oh, would you look at that!"

"There are lots of rich old people in Japan, Mother," Mitsuki had pointed out drily.

Mitsuki used her mother's card to pay thirty thousand yen for a set of floral sheets and pillowcases. While certainly not cheap, for her mother this was by no means extravagant, either. She rejoined the others with a sense of relief, and they were all heading for the elevator when her mother came to an abrupt stop.

Displayed before them was another set of floral bed linens. The design was completely different — more delicate, in hues of greater subtlety and sophistication — and the material had a satiny luster. Mitsuki herself could hardly tear her eyes away. But these cost well over twice as much as the others — nearly half her mother's monthly pension.

Faced with their objections, her mother had tightened her lips. "My bed is becoming the center of my life now, after all. Where's the harm if I do pamper myself a little?"

In the end Mitsuki had had to return the just-bought sheets and pay for the new set instead. Even though the clerk was looking on, she'd been unable to refrain from scolding in a voice that she knew sounded shrill and hysterical: "Mother, you're not rich! You can't go around spending this kind of money on yourself!"

"Yes, yes."

Her mother owned many sets of fine bed linens. She had them professionally laundered and replaced them when they grew faded.

Alongside bed linens splashed with flowers like an homage to spring, a portable toilet would lay bare the ugliness and sadness of old age.

Tetsuo was slowly sipping the amber-colored sake, radiating the pleasure of a man who likes his drink. Mitsuki looked away and informed him that this year she wouldn't be able to spend New Year's at his parents' house.

This was perfectly true. Her mother was helpless, thrown into a new environment with precious little to celebrate. For the time being, Mitsuki would need to visit her every day. She also wanted to dispose quickly of the errands her mother had enumerated, delegating some to her sister. Besides, the shadow of that young woman loomed over her. Having to play the role of a happy little wife in front of Tetsuo's family was the last thing she wanted to do.

After a short silence, Tetsuo replied that in that case he would change his plans and leave a day early, on December 30. "That way you won't have to worry about my meals and all. It'll be easier on you."

The shadow of the slender young woman loomed larger.

At some point they had begun sleeping in separate rooms, saying it was because they each had their work to do. That night as she lay in the dark with her head on her pillow, Mitsuki was haunted by an image. Rather surprisingly, it was the image not of a slender young woman but of her mother in a wheelchair.

Old people in wheelchairs...

On the way to and from the station she always passed through Silkworm Forest Park, built on the site of a former sericulture laboratory. In the park there was a statue of a silkworm moth with its wings outspread, but the only remnants of the days when silk had been the mainstay of Japan's fledgling export industry were a pair of impressive brick gate pillars, a curving wrought-iron gate, and towering trees. In the daytime, on the path encircling the park she often saw old people in wheelchairs being pushed by a spouse, a daughter or daughter-in-law, or a home helper—the latter readily distinguishable by their gentle expressions and tones of voice.

What she found shocking was the hollow, blank look on the faces of the wheelchair occupants. No, not blank—sullen. Though sunlight poured down and flowers bloomed year round, it seemed they lacked the energy to enjoy life's bountiful blessings and felt only frustration as a result.

Would it now be her turn to wheel her sullen-faced mother through a park?

# 5

## FINALLY SELLING THE LAND

Twenty-four hours earlier, her mother had been able to get around with the aid of a cane or a walker, and Mitsuki had been unaware of the existence of a pink tissue case. Half dazed by how completely life could change in a day, she set off for the hospital. Tetsuo offered to go along, but she said it would be enough if he stopped by the next day on his way to Toride. She headed for the station, her mind busily reviewing what needed to be done.

She went first to the hospital store. The day before, at the nurses' station she had been handed a list of items her mother would need for her surgery and hospital stay. Disposable underwear. A mug with a built-in spout. Towels large and small—those she could bring from home; underpants and pajamas she intended to buy new. The ones her mother was now using had come from Isetan; if sent to the laundry along with her towels, they would have to be marked with a felt pen, which would be a shame—a desecration, almost.

The hospital was large and so was the store, overflowing with such a variety of daily necessities that a person forced to shop only there for life could probably manage just fine. Just inside the entrance was the food corner, offering soy sauce, seasoned seaweed, pickled plums, instant miso soup, cookies and crackers, followed by toothbrushes, toothpaste, and cups. In the back were the more specialized items appropriate to a hospital store.

Mitsuki looked at several sets of women's pajamas before finally making up her mind to buy four. With that many on hand, even if a couple of them became soiled her mother would still have enough to get by. At more than three thousand yen apiece they weren't exactly cheap, yet they were the sort of thing her mother never wore, sturdy flannel pajamas for solid citizens that fairly shouted, "Hello, pajamas here, at your service!" They came in aqua, pink, yellow, and lilac, each with a slightly different floral pattern, and were cheerful in their way. They were also light, soft, and warm, and the texture on the inside was pleasant to the touch. Satisfied, Mitsuki headed next to the female undergarments section.

A man was standing there, clad in a dark suit. Not a young man. Something about his back, the angle of the shoulders perhaps, seemed fraught with sorrow. The very air seemed to congeal around him.

She hesitantly moved forward and he edged away to one side, apparently not wishing to interfere with her shopping. An echo of sadness hung in the air. She sensed that he wasn't standing there in front of women's undergarments at a loss, uncertain what to get, but rather had chanced on a place where he could come face-to-face with his sadness in grateful solitude.

Regretting the intrusion, Mitsuki ran her eyes over a pile of undergarments in front of her, picked out six undershirts and six pairs of underpants in her mother's size, and tossed them in her shopping basket. These too were solid white cotton things that fairly shouted, "Hello, underwear here, at your service!" She left, amused and sorry at the thought of her mother having to put on anything so prosaic.

The man lingered in her thoughts. Some visitors, like him, were full of sadness—this fact, perfectly natural in a hospital setting, somehow chastened her. She took a deep breath before heading for the register.

"You're late!" her mother burst out the moment Mitsuki appeared.

"Well, I had a lot to do before I could get here. People to contact, things to buy."

Her mother stared at her, her dark eyes flashing. When she got that look in her eyes, no good could come of it. Pretending not to notice, Mitsuki set down her purchases and began to sort through the various forms she'd been given at the nurses' station on the way in.

"Hospital Policy on Protection of Patients' Privacy." That needed only to be read, but the forms marked "Surgery Consent" and "Blood Transfusion Consent" would have to be signed and stamped with her seal. She couldn't possibly write out her mother's full medical history, so on that form she merely wrote "cardiac hypertrophy," "autonomic dysfunction," and "osteoporosis," noted past fractures, and listed the medicines she and Natsuki had brought in the previous day.

After she handed in the forms and returned to the room, her mother again stared at her. "Mitsuki," she said, "I'll go into a nursing home."

She must have been contemplating this all night, ever since hearing the words "portable commode."

"Really?"

The patient in the next bed might have pricked up her ears too.

"The truth is, I won't be able to go out anymore, will I?"

This was so.

"I'd rather be dead than end up this way, but since I failed to die, I suppose I have to be realistic. I can't live alone anymore. If I can't, I can't."

Mitsuki was impressed that now, when something so critical was at stake, her mother's brain could function as clearly as in the old days. She was grateful, too. But then an anxious thought struck her. Was a person so used to having her own way even capable of communal living?

"Everything won't be to your liking in a nursing home."

"I know that."

"Even if you have a private room, the time you get up in the morning and your mealtimes and bath times are all set. You'll have to put up with a lot."

"I know that," she repeated, looking up at the ceiling. "The thing is, I failed to die." Then, eyes still on the ceiling, she began to sob like a little child. When Mitsuki was young, her proud mother had never wept in front of her, but in old age that had changed. Now, unable to wipe her eyes, her right hand immobile and her left arm hooked up to an IV, she went on sobbing helplessly, flat on her back.

Mitsuki went over and touched her arm softly. She did this to compensate for not being able to say the words "I'm glad you're alive, Mother."

Her mother said, sniffling, "You and your sister come see me often, will you?"

"Of course."

"Promise?"

"Promise." Then Mitsuki said, "Remember that place we went to see before? Is that one all right? It's a little far from Chitose Funabashi."

Two years before, after a friend of Natsuki's had searched for a nursing home for her mother, Natsuki had inherited a pile of information and given it to Mitsuki, who, after some checking on the computer, found a place almost exactly midway between their two homes: Golden Years. The deposit and monthly fees were high, but once they sold the land in Chitose Funabashi, with that money and her pension their mother could live there till past one hundred without going bankrupt. One day they had invited her to go take a look at the place; she hung back, protesting that she was still perfectly capable of living by herself, but they dragged her there anyway. She'd remained unconvinced, although pleased by the homey front hall with its rosebud wallpaper.

"It was nice," she answered now. "It'll do. Once I'm there, I won't be going anywhere anyhow, so how far it is won't make any difference to me. As long as it's easy for you and Natsuki to get to, that's all that matters."

"If you lived there, we could come see you all the time." But not every day, she added as a precaution.

"Come as often as you can. Seeing you two girls is the only pleasure I have left now." Once again there were tears in her voice. They were probably sincere, but then again, knowing her, they could be a ploy to gain sympathy.

Realizing that her mother's decision was genuine, Mitsuki let out a sigh of relief. At last they could sell the land in Chitose Funabashi. The new house meant little to her, and the old house where her grandmother had lived was long gone. She felt only a sense of liberation. They hadn't been able to sell the land for her father. They'd had to hang on to it in order to provide for their mother's old age, after she'd all but abandoned him. Now, at long last, they could let it go.

"The land in Chitose Funabashi"—how many times had they said it together, her mother, her sister, and herself, like some sort of magic incantation?

Their father had gone from job to job before starting an import-export business and had become a regular corporate employee only after that venture failed, when he was around forty. The survivor's pension their mother received therefore didn't amount to much. For years she had worked part time selling woolen *chabaori*, kimono half-coats designed by a friend from her choir-singing days who was known to the family as "Auntie." (How tall and stunning their mother had looked in a kimono!) The extra income had helped, but that sort of work offered no pension. Her current income, including her national pension, came to around 160,000 yen per month. Enough for a frugal widow but nowhere near enough for their self-indulgent mother.

Auntie had not only a superb sense of style but also a good head for business and was a skilled investor. Knowing their mother's improvident ways, she had encouraged her from the first to put some money in an investment trust. This precaution, plus their father's retirement bonus and life insurance, had yielded a nice little nest egg.

Lately, however, her savings balance had been declining at an alarming rate. Every time Mitsuki looked at her mother's passbook, she quelled her uneasiness with thoughts of the sixty-eight *tsubo* of land in Chitose Funabashi, Setagaya Ward. The house there was no longer worth anything, but the patch of land it stood on was quite valuable. Her parents had bought the place shortly after she was born without thinking too much about it, but as more and more Japanese gave up farming and moved to the city, real estate prices had soared in Tokyo, especially in Setagaya. That land was the family's sole asset, and a precious one.

The value of that asset would have been much less if the Long-Term Care Insurance system had been enacted earlier. Mitsuki would then have talked her mother into selling half of the land—the backyard—so her father could live out the rest of his days in a decent place rather than that extended-care hospital. But before the insurance system came along, affordable private nursing homes were nonexistent, leaving only two other options: a public nursing home with an impossibly long waiting list or a private nursing home so expensive that a family like theirs could only sigh. Selling the entire plot of land might have been enough, but that would have left nothing for her mother's old age. So almost by default, the land in Chitose Funabashi remained untouched.

Her mother had her own ideas of making do. When her savings ran out, she would borrow from Natsuki's husband, Yuji, she said, using the land as collateral. "After all, I invested a lot in that girl." She didn't know that Mitsuki was thinking of dipping into Tetsuo's and her savings to prevent poor Natsuki from feeling any smaller around her wealthy in-laws than she already did.

Just then Natsuki burst onto the scene.

"I've been running all over!" she declared as she came in. "I took cookies to the neighbors and the lady at the laundry shop, and then I went back to Mom's house to find those things you use to thread—"

Mitsuki cut short the flow of words. "She's going into a nursing home," she said. "She brought it up herself."

Natsuki's face registered her astonishment.

# 6

## FRONTAL LOBE MELTDOWN BEGINS

"Is it true?" Natsuki went over to her mother's bedside.

"You come see me as often as you can, now."

Her initial surprise having subsided, Natsuki seemed about to make some ironic quip, but out of respect for her mother's decision she only said, "I will."

That day Natsuki and Mitsuki sat by their mother and wore reading glasses as they worked, expanding the elastic waistbands in the new pajamas and underwear and writing KATSURA with a magic marker on all her things. Once their mother passed the age of seventy, compression fractures had caused her spine to curve, and as her height decreased her waist had expanded, making the stomach oddly protrude. In the last few years this had become especially pronounced, to the point where she couldn't wear anything without first letting out the waistband.

"Never had to do this in home ec class, did we?" said Mitsuki, struggling with the bodkin her sister had brought.

Natsuki, despite her weaker eyesight, was managing slightly better. "That's for sure. Even when my kids were little, I never needed to do anything like this."

When they wrote KATSURA, they tried to make the lettering as small and inconspicuous as possible. Mitsuki would never forget the way her father's name had been emblazoned on his pajama pocket. Though by and large the hospital saw to his needs, families had been expected to do the laundry. She used to make the round-trip on train and bus loaded down with clean, folded laundry on the way there and a bagful of dirty clothes on the way back. Then professional launderers appeared, offering their services.

Her mother, on one of her rare visits to the hospital, had managed to be the first to pick up that information. She'd called with excitement in her voice: "Guess what! From now on we don't have to do his laundry anymore!" Quick as always to take action, she'd gone straight to the hospital store, bought a magic marker, and written his surname on all his few belongings that very day. The next time Mitsuki visited her father, there he was, sitting in pajamas with his surname written large on the breast pocket, for all the world like a jailbird. The memory of her mother's insensitivity wrenched her heart.

As she and Natsuki toiled, their mother suddenly said, "When the money comes in from the land in Chitose Funabashi, leave me what I need, and you two go ahead and split the rest. It's better to have money when you're young."

Despite her callous treatment of her husband, she had always been generous with them, willing to share whatever money she had.

"But you could live to be a hundred for all you know."

"Oh, no. Heaven forbid."

For the first time since her fall, she was in a fairly good mood. Soon sorrow that her life was over would send her spiraling into despair, beginning a rapid slide into dementia; this was one of the last times when she would be herself.

Back home, when Mitsuki told Tetsuo the news, a funny look came over his face.

"I see," he said, after a pause. "Then you'll be selling the property in Chitose Funabashi. So that's that." Doubtless he had hoped her mother would pop off one day soon so that half the proceeds would be theirs. Mitsuki felt a stab of pleasure.

The following day was December 30, the day Tetsuo was leaving—supposedly for his parents' house. His decision to leave a day earlier than usual nagged at her as she got ready to visit her mother in the morning. He said he would stop by the hospital that afternoon on his way. She couldn't think of a way to dissuade him.

Before setting out, she handed him the customary New Year's gifts for him to take to Toride: four decorated envelopes containing money—a substantial sum for his parents and progressively smaller amounts for his sister-in-law, niece, and nephew. At eighty-one and seventy-six, his father and mother were still going strong. The younger son had taken over the father's job and lived with them, as did his wife and children. Tetsuo's brother, like his parents, was a good person, and so was his wife; thanks to her, the burden of actual caregiving, which traditionally fell to the wife of the firstborn son, would never land on Mitsuki's shoulders. Even if Mitsuki and Tetsuo were called on to provide financial support down the road, this arrangement was a boon for which she was infinitely grateful. Back when Tetsuo proposed, he had promised her she wouldn't have to look after his parents, and that promise, at least, he had kept. But perhaps because he was a man and so little affected by such matters, he himself didn't seem particularly grateful to his brother and sister-in-law.

As he took the money envelopes, Tetsuo imitated his father's voice and turn of speech: "A fine daughter-in-law if ever there was one."

Her sister-in-law's round-cheeked face came to mind.

Once she left the apartment, she found herself walking with surprisingly light steps. She decided not to think about Tetsuo.

With all that needed to be done to empty out the house in Chitose Funabashi in preparation for her mother's move to Golden, she worried whether her strength would hold up, but now at least the end was in sight. The way leading to her mother's death was clear. After years of vexation, at long last she saw the possibility—no, the assurance—of relief.

She had already contacted Golden first thing that morning. There was likely to be an opening soon, they said, but should her mother be discharged from the hospital first, they could accommodate her in a sister institution until a room did open up. The idea that there was "likely to be an opening soon" was faintly disturbing; yet this was far better than hearing there was no chance of an opening in the near future. It was good news.

The station was lively with cries of people selling New Year's decorations and the usual year-end bustle. This too lifted her spirits. She had no way of knowing that this momentary grace would be followed by endless days more trying than anything she could have imagined.

"You're late!"

As her mother lay fastened to her bed, eyes glaring, the first words she spoke to Mitsuki were the same as the day before. What came next, however, was different. She suddenly extended her left hand, the only one she could use now, and wailed, "Oh, Mitsuki."

Mitsuki wondered what was wrong as she went over to her mother, who clutched her fingertips with surprising strength before launching into a feverish appeal.

"Last night they came and took away *all* my medications. Isn't that terrible? I beg and I beg, but they *won't* give them back. Without my medications right here where I can reach them, I don't know what to do. *Please* go talk to the nurse and tell her she's *got* to give them back."

Over the past few years Mitsuki had often heard her mother's tearful pleas, but never had she seen her look this miserable. With her brows knit and the corners of her mouth drooping, her face conveyed a kind of animal sorrow. The nervous strain of having worried over this all night made her forehead, which seemed to have shrunk noticeably of late, look even narrower.

"They wouldn't even give you your Halcion?" This was her mother's nightly sleeping medication.

"No! Or my Depas, or my Takeda."

Depas was an antidepressant. Soon after Mitsuki became hypersensitive to air-conditioning and started to see a specialist for treatment, her mother claimed to suffer from the same condition and tagged along to receive the same prescription from the same doctor. At first she'd taken half a Depas several times a day, but lately she'd been having her home helpers use a kitchen knife and a carving board to chop the pills into quarters so that she could medicate herself at more frequent intervals. As her anxiety increased, she clung to the small, thumb-sized plastic vial of Depas as if it were a talisman. She would take a Halcion before bed, and if she woke up during the night she'd take out the vial of Depas from under her pillow, swallow a small white quarter of a pill, and go back to sleep. During the day she took one roughly every two hours. Because Mitsuki herself relied on Depas, her mother, who relied on Mitsuki, was all the more prone to addiction.

The Takeda was for constipation.

"I can't sleep and I can't move my bowels, so I'm uncomfortable, and without my Depas I'm at my wits' end. I'm so nervous I don't know what to do. You've *got* to get them back for me."

At the nurses' station, Mitsuki learned that at bedtime her mother had been given her usual dosages of Halcion, Depas, and Takeda. When she explained that her mother had always managed her medications herself and was ill at ease without having them nearby, the pills were returned with disconcerting alacrity. Evidently her mother had been so shrilly insistent that the exasperated nurse had consulted with the doctor and received permission to return them if the family approved.

After being duly warned about the danger of an overdose, Mitsuki apologized for all the trouble before returning to her mother's room.

What was going on? Had the decision to enter a nursing home somehow made her mother let go of herself? Had it set off a meltdown of her frontal lobe, the seat of memory, judgment, and rational thought? Her mother's sole memory of the night before was the terror of having her medications taken away.

"Oh, Mitsuki!" her mother cried out in relief when Mitsuki came back into the room holding up the medications like war trophies. She went over to the bed, and her mother proceeded to grab her hand, nuzzling it and planting kisses on it with exaggerated delight. She had never seen her mother put on such a physical display of emotion, in such an un-Japanese way (though, come to think of it, who knew what she may have done in private with That Man?). Perhaps in her sorrow she had lost all restraint and metamorphosed into one of those Westerners on the silver screen whom she had idolized since schoolgirl days.

Thank God for the curtain separating the two beds in the room.

Her mother swallowed a piece of Depas, and that seemed to relax her a little. "I wish I were dead," she kept moaning, but Mitsuki didn't take the bait, instead sitting where her mother could see her and telling about her phone call to Golden while marking KATSURA on various personal articles. There were still a good many items left to label: her mother's false teeth container, her toothbrush and toothpaste, a tissue box, a glasses case. Her mother had always liked seeing her daughters wait on her, and Mitsuki knew that watching her carry out this small task would have a soothing effect.

Then in came Tetsuo. He was wearing a camel hair coat he'd bought on sale in February and carrying a deceptively simple arrangement of flowers in a basket, chosen with his usual good taste. The tapered petals of some large, dark-purple flower whose name she didn't know stood out against the deep green of the leaves; the effect was somehow too chic for a hospital sickroom.

Mitsuki had put off mentioning that Tetsuo would be coming. Her mother looked startled when he showed up, but her face, etched with sad vertical lines, quickly brightened as she widened her eyes, donned a company smile, and exclaimed, "Tetsuo dear!" When he thrust the basket at her, the smile became her trademark coquettish simper. "Oh, aren't they lovely! Flowers like this just light up the room!"

Seated just beside her mother, Mitsuki sensed the effort it took for her to accommodate someone from the outside world.

"So how are you, Noriko?"

"Oh, this is the end of the line for Noriko."

# 7

## "O-MIYA'S BLOOD"

Tetsuo and her mother exchanged flirtatious banter as always.

"You look lovely as ever, broken bones and all."

"Listen to the man. I don't have my teeth in—I'm a sight."

"You, Noriko? Never."

The frivolity of these exchanges didn't usually bother Mitsuki, but today it grated on her nerves—and not only because of the tissue case. The basket of flowers he had brought was wrong somehow, and she couldn't help feeling that Tetsuo himself didn't quite fit in.

Hospitals, however clean they are kept and however well disinfected, are filled with the faint smell of death, emanating from the sick and elderly. Neither sunlight streaming through windows nor the brisk efficiency of doctors and nurses can conceal the adversities of sickness and old age that arrive suddenly and without warning or stealthily, little by little. Tetsuo popping in with his basket of flowers seemed to represent less the vigor of good health than rank insensitivity to life's unavoidable tragedies. This wasn't his fault. Life was at full tide in him, so that he emanated blithe unconcern, that was all; still, he seemed like a thoughtless intruder.

Mitsuki couldn't help suspecting that her mother rather shared this impression.

What she normally thought of Tetsuo was hard to say. Around the time Mitsuki had begun to feel vaguely uncomfortable around him, her mother had seemed to feel the same way. And yet, while at some point she had taken to speaking ill of Natsuki's husband Yuji with complete abandon, she never came out and said a word against Tetsuo.

He stayed less than ten minutes. Mitsuki walked him to the elevator, and as he pushed the button, he mentioned casually that she needn't call his parents' house until New Year's Day. To her ears this sounded like an order. He was well dressed, better than usual for a trip home. Her conviction deepened; but this was not the time to bring anything up. When she returned, she was taken aback to find her mother staring fiercely at the wall, all trace of her former affability gone, looking almost savage. As soon as she spotted Mitsuki, she started in, her tone vicious: "Ooh, I just can't stand it."

"What's the matter?"

"What's the matter with *him*, you mean! Those *flowers*! And me flat on my back. I'm sorry, but they'll only be in the way, so you've got to take them home." She pointed with her chin at the offending arrangement on the tray table.

Mitsuki rose to her husband's defense. "How will Tetsuo feel?"

"He's gone off to Toride, hasn't he? He won't be back."

"Still, if he knew he'd feel bad."

"They're in the way. I don't want them here in front of me."

"I'll put them up on the shelf where they'll be out of your way."

"I don't want them anywhere I can lay eyes on them."

"I have to go shopping on the way home. I can't take something that big with me."

"Then throw them out! Who needs them?" She added spitefully, "Besides, there's something funny going on if you ask me. Him all dolled up like that."

Mitsuki was speechless. She'd known her mother could feign sociability, but never before had she been witness to a transformation so complete and so stunning. Discovering her mother capable of such duplicity was painful. And there was something else equally painful: despite failing faculties, her mother had somehow discerned the truth. Perhaps as her frontal lobe degenerated and she began to lose control, some sort of sixth sense came into play.

Inflamed by her own words, her mother seemed to feel the misery of her situation more keenly.

"Kill me! There's no point in going on living this way, so just kill me!" Unable to sit up, she twisted her body as she shrieked.

Mitsuki raised her voice. "I have no intention of killing you and ruining my life by becoming a murderer!"

The poor woman in the other bed—what must she be thinking?

Her mother began weeping soundlessly. Mitsuki regarded her steadily. She felt less pity than irritation. She too wanted her mother to die—had long yearned for her death with an intensity far greater than her mother's. At the same time she had done what she could to make her happy, perhaps shortening her own life a little in the process. And she would have to go right on doing exactly the same thing.

In a slightly calmer voice, she said, "Look, Mother, you just have to accept your situation and get through it the best way you can."

Finding words that can provide true solace to those facing the rigors of old age is never easy. Without great love, the task is difficult indeed. Her mother seemed to sense the difficulty she was having and said no more.

After that, Mitsuki finished labeling the few remaining items. Her mother asked constantly for Depas. Every third time, she would give her a quarter of a pill and a sip of water. She helped her eat supper and get ready for bed, seeing to it that she rinsed her mouth and wiped her face before leaving with a reminder that Natsuki would be in the next day.

Her mother was still overwrought.

Mitsuki was exhausted and thirsty. Lugging the basket of flowers, she searched for a juice-vending machine. She was wandering blindly down a corridor when she spotted a middle-aged man in a dark suit coming toward her. She realized it was the same man she had seen the day before in the hospital store. Today too his expression was desolate, the air around him congealed with sadness.

After he went into a patient's room, she paused to read the nameplate by the door: WAKAKO MATSUBARA. A pleasantly old-fashioned name. Must be his wife. A man his age was unlikely to grieve for his mother with such abandon. Looking around, she saw an unfamiliar nurses' station and watched as a female patient past middle age, wearing a knit cap, was wheeled into a different room. She looked thin and haggard. This must be the oncology section, and Wakako Matsubara too must be a cancer patient, just as she had imagined.

Night came on early in the winter; outside it was already dark.

Leaving the subway station, she walked home through the lamplit park. As she trudged along, she saw a couple of homeless people; felt the presence of the huge trees around her; looked up at the chilly winter sky. She sighed. Everything was as usual, but she felt acrimony churning within her. The sheer venom of her mother's rejection of the flowers was one thing; the coquettish simper rising like a mask on that face where misery had etched so many lines was quite another—it had been sickening, almost unreal.

Mitsuki remembered her mother's mother as a very old woman who had doted on her. But people who knew her grandmother's history—she'd been a geisha—referred to her in private as "O-Miya." And they used to say of Mitsuki's mother, "She's got O-Miya's blood in her veins." Could that simper have something to do with "O-Miya's blood"?

One thing was certain: her mother must have often simpered that way for That Man.

The following day, Mitsuki stayed home all day. Her sister would be visiting the hospital with her family, including her son, Ken, a graduate student home from the States for the holidays. She tried to make some headway on a patent translation due first thing in January but soon gave up, unable to stop thinking about what had to be done before her mother went into the nursing home. That had to come before all else. She started making a to-do list in her notebook, only to flop down on the bed. Exhaustion from the past three days flooded over her and settled in her bones.

That evening when her sister called, Mitsuki asked, "Was she still going on with her 'Kill me!'?"

"I wasn't there alone, so she behaved herself. She was pretty sociable, actually. But it was weird. And there was a lot of 'Do this, do that,' so I got worn out."

After she hung up, the telephone instantly rang again. It was Tetsuo, who had instructed her not to phone until New Year's Day, tomorrow. Perhaps feeling guilty, he asked after her mother.

"She's the same," Mitsuki replied, thinking of the discarded basket of flowers. "What about you?"

"Same here too."

"Are your parents well?"

"They're fine. You know us, we're a tough bunch."

She hung up without offering anything more. What Tetsuo might make of his usually talkative wife becoming so taciturn, she didn't know.

Later, as she got ready for bed, she heard a distant sound. It was the tolling of a temple bell, resonating through the winter night air. After a pause it sounded again, a low, lingering tone. That would be the bell at Myohoji temple, being struck 108 times—once for each sin of mankind—to purify human souls for the coming year. A new year was beginning, she realized and stretched out under the covers.

She felt cold. Since she'd gotten sick, her body turned to ice when she was tired, especially the lower half. She laid a hand on her belly and felt an eerie chill through her palm, as if she were carrying a dead child.

## LIVING GHOSTS

As she lay awake with her eyes closed, the sound of the New Year bell resonating through the darkness brought memories that fortunately came less frequently now, memories of the hospital where her father had been confined.

The hospital had been far away, necessitating a transfer from train to train and then to a bus. Back then, crumbling hospitals were being rebuilt across the country, but extended-care facilities were given last priority and her father's hospital remained shabby and dreary to the end of his stay. The inpatients too looked shabby and dreary as a result. Her diabetic father's weak eyesight had been a saving grace.

His floor had had a wide corridor with a nurses' station and restrooms midway. Patients requiring more care were assigned wards closer to the station; those requiring relatively little care, wards farther away. Her father, one of those requiring little care, had been at the far end. Many of his ward mates were stroke victims, paralyzed on one side but mostly able to shuffle around by themselves or, if walking was impossible, to propel their own wheelchairs. They could be seen around the cafeteria and washrooms, and would even drop by the other wards for a friendly chat. In short, if they'd only had family members willing to take them in, most of them needn't have been in the hospital at all. Like her father.

He'd been given three square meals a day; he'd been kept cool in summer and warm in winter; he had benefited from modern medical treatment. His situation could have been far worse. Certainly there was no comparison to the plight of Mother Teresa's unfortunates. Yet not long after her father's death, Mitsuki had been struck by an obituary of the saintly nun describing her "Home for the Dying" in India as a place offering shelter to "all those people who feel unwanted, unloved, uncared for throughout society, people that have become a burden to the society and are shunned by everyone." The words shook her. Every time she'd gone to see her father she'd felt consumed by guilt at having abandoned him, undoubtedly because the entire hospital building was indeed very like a "Home for the Dying."

When he was first admitted, he used to walk to and from the restroom with his back straight. "Walk tall," he had always told her when she was a little girl. Walking that way, like someone with things to do, might have represented the last vestige of his self-respect. He'd been born to an old family of physicians, and a trove of sepia photographs from his childhood showed how devotedly he had been raised and with what high hopes. Even after his father's sudden death plunged the family into impoverishment and ruin, all his life he had maintained the air of a man of fine breeding, a member of the prewar middle class. He lived in a world so different from his ward mates that she never saw him talking to them. None of them struck up a conversation with him, nor he with them. In fact relatively well-off families like theirs hardly ever placed their aging members in such wards; they usually had a spare room as well as one or two nonworking women who could stay home and provide care.

The hospital head was a devout Christian and a man of character, and perhaps for that reason nearly everyone on staff from the head nurse to the cleaning ladies had always been kind. Even so, her father's plight had been pitiful.

Severely ill patients could not move around. Those who wandered on foot in the corridor tended to have the typical bandy-legged walk of people wearing diapers. Some had a long white cloth wound around their middle so that if they tottered or fell, a nearby staff member could quickly scoop them up. Dressed in pajamas much alike, males and females indistinguishable, they wove their way around the wheelchairs, drifting up and down the corridor like living ghosts.

The concentrated smell of sickness, old age, and death was so dreadful that unless she took a deep breath outside in the sunshine before going in, she used to feel swallowed up by that darkness.

The last space on earth allotted to her father was the second bed from the window in an eight-man ward: a space measuring, with the curtains drawn, just two meters square—smaller than a prison cell. There was no chair. In the beginning he used to sit on the bed, time heavy on his hands. Mitsuki would open the narrow locker containing his few belongings, help him into his Burberry coat, put leather shoes on his feet and a soft felt hat on his head, and take his arm to go out for a stroll. He had always loved going for walks. Outdoors, as in the Chitose Funabashi area of her childhood, there were houses, bamboo groves, even a stream. If she shut her eyes to the detergents polluting the stream, it was as if time had turned back. She could almost hear his voice admonishing her: "Walk tall."

He was by then half blind. At first he could perch on his bed and listen to the radio or cassette tapes, almost as at home. It was perhaps a little over a year later that she found out he was getting cheated at the hospital store. She went along and saw him take a pack of the cookies he always bought to the register, hand over a thousand-yen note, and start to leave. The exchange between him and the cashier was smooth and practiced; clearly the same thing happened every time.

"What about your change?" Mitsuki reminded him, from a little distance.

The woman looked up with a start before saying, "Oh, yeah," and then calmly counted out a handful of coins. She might be hard up for all Mitsuki knew, but did that give her the right to take advantage of a half-blind old man?

"Dad, always make sure you get your change, okay?" She said this purposefully loud enough for the woman to hear, feeling sad for the human race, herself included.

He sat on his bed so much that the mattress soon developed a sag in that spot. Mitsuki wanted to ask for a bed by the window for him but didn't quite have the nerve, and in the meantime he began spending more and more time stretched out on the bed.

Three or four years after he went to live in the hospital, after Mitsuki and Tetsuo had moved into their little condominium, she made up her mind to have him stay with her at least for the short length of time that Tetsuo was to be in Africa. By then her father's eyesight was even worse and his brain foggy; he seemed unable to understand why she had brought him there even though it wasn't New Year's. After spending the night, he'd announced, "Mitsuki, I'm going home." Realizing that the hospital had become his "home" brought some relief, but at the same time it filled her with pain.

Around then their arm-in-arm walks were confined to the hospital rooftop. Later they would merely walk up and down the hospital corridor. Since that wasn't enough exercise, she would seat him on a bench in the corridor and have him move his arms up and down or sideways. He obediently followed her instructions. It was completely meaningless. What must he have thought?

"Okay, Dad, I'll be off then," she would say before leaving, taking his hand in hers, and he would lift his head from the bed and say, "You be careful on your way home, now." He never once forgot to say it, till the last. He also thanked her without fail.

Once he came down with pneumonia and was moved to a ward by the nurses' station, but managed to recover and live another year despite his weakened condition. Oh, how she had wished for his death, for his sake.

Mitsuki and Tetsuo lived near the Horinouchi crematorium. In the past, ashes from cremated human remains used to drift down from the crematorium smokestack. People said that accounted for the low real estate prices. Naturally there was also a funeral hall. Often there would be a man in a black suit and armband standing at the station, holding a sign with a family name edged in black to point the way. Every time she came across such a scene on her way to visit her father, she would feel a hot rush of envy. Some people went ahead and died the way they were supposed to. Her father stayed stubbornly alive.

Though her mother's side of the family was long-lived, her father's mother had died young and his father had not lived to see fifty, so everyone assumed her father wouldn't live long, either. Yet on and on he had lasted, to her distress and Natsuki's too. His death came in his seventh year in the "Home for the Dying."

Her mother, the one who had consigned him there in the first place, used to go reluctantly to see him in the beginning, but her visits quickly diminished in frequency, coming at longer and longer intervals. Mitsuki stopped saying anything. In her father's last year, after That Man ceased to be a part of her mother's life, perhaps out of sheer defiance her mother had ended her visits altogether. Mitsuki and her sister each went often in the beginning, but their visits dwindled from twice a week to once a week, and then they took turns. By the time he became bedridden, one or the other of them would go every couple of weeks.

Mitsuki was the only one present at his death.

It had been her sister's turn to go see him, but she kept putting it off, lengthening her stay in her summerhouse on the coast. Mitsuki was feeling a bit miffed, and just as she was thinking she would have to go herself, the hospital called to report a sudden change in his condition. He was dying. It was early September, before the start of the fall semester, and by sheer luck she'd been home to take the call. She phoned the summerhouse but no one answered; she had no choice but to leave a message on the answering machine. Next she called her mother.

When she said she would be going over alone, her mother—instead of grabbing her cane, hailing a taxi, and rushing to his side—had coolly responded, "Thanks. Would you?" Clearly she had no intention of making a show of penitence. Mitsuki herself didn't want to see her mother go waltzing up to her father's deathbed, but she wondered whether staying away demonstrated shallowness or the spirit of a rebel. A dozen years on, she still didn't know.

Tetsuo had been at the university on some errand or other, and so she'd had to content herself with contacting his secretary. Her sister had been out for the day with her family, unreachable till late at night. Mitsuki had watched over her father all alone as cyanosis turned his legs purple from the toes up.

It was a quiet death.

"There's no precise cause of death," the doctor had told her, seemingly at a loss. "It's as if he lost the will to live, that's all I can say."

After a while Tetsuo came and put an arm around her shoulders, staying with her while she consulted with the mortician. This was after she'd found out about his first fling and he had ended it, leaving them closer than before. Her father had repeatedly declared his disdain for monks, and Mitsuki had no intention of giving him a traditional and expensive Buddhist funeral with incense and chanting. The mortician looked disappointed on learning this.

Natsuki, having failed to be present at her father's passing, wept incessantly at the crematorium. He had gone to his death after a lapse of more than two weeks when she hadn't bothered to go see him; would that knowledge torment her the rest of her days? He had always been partial to her, whether because she was his first-born or because she looked more like their mother. He had given her a father's straightforward, perfectly ordinary love, a love all the more precious for that.

He had loved Mitsuki too in his way.

The temple bell tolled on, counting and forgiving human sins, while Mitsuki took her medicines: an anti-anxiety drug, an antide-pressant, a hypnotic, and a sleeping pill. How could she, her sister, and her mother ever be forgiven for what they had done to her father? The bell's slow, solemn reverberations conveyed the eternal sinfulness of the human condition: parent and child, child and parent, no one ever exempt.

# 9

## MOTHER SITTING IN A WITHERED MOOR

The whirlwind of busy days continued into the new year.

One day Mitsuki went back home, and as she started to take off her coat, she looked down and saw that the large buttons were buttoned wrong. She was less embarrassed at the spectacle she must have made than struck by how busy and exhausted she'd been lately. Her mother would never be any happier no matter how much she tried to do for her, and this realization produced in her a sense of futility that added to her exhaustion.

Mitsuki thought of the women who materialized in Silkworm Park at night out of nowhere. Not prostitutes, but mature women who walked swiftly and stone-faced along the perimeter of the park in the lamplight, swinging arms bent at the elbow with the fists clenched, focused on building their physical fitness. Back when she first set up house with Tetsuo, she used to turn cold eyes on them as only a young woman could. Why did they knock themselves out to walk like that, she wondered, showing disgracefully shapeless bodies with no waist whatever? They could already walk in good health; why try to do more?

But along the way her viewpoint had changed. Women like that might well be caregivers for elderly charges, keeping themselves in shape so as not to succumb to discouragement. For all she knew, some of them might be looking after an old crone demented enough to eat her own feces—in which case they probably had no desire that someone like herself, who had never so much as changed her mother's diaper, should feel a sense of solidarity with them. But she did.

The operation took place January 5. Beforehand, her mother reminded her, "Did you tell the doctor I'm a member of the Society for Dying with Dignity?"

"I did, I did."

"No heroic lifesaving measures."

"They won't be called for anyway, not in surgery to fix broken bones."

Her mother of course survived the surgery just fine, although it turned out to be more complicated than expected, lasting five hours. Mitsuki was thankful that she lived in a country where her mother, as a "latter-stage elderly" patient, was able to have major surgery virtually free, and she felt indebted to the doctors and nurses who, though fatigued, had surely done their best for her. At the same time, she was perhaps not as modern in her outlook as she might have been, since she found it hard to believe that her mother was entitled to have all these people devoting themselves to her care. The thought of Japan's rising deficit made her somehow—absurdly—apologetic.

Regardless of how she felt about it, the hospital staff religiously followed procedures to promote her mother's healing. The day after the operation, the catheter came out, and they sat her on a bedpan. Remarkably, the very next day they wheeled her to rehabilitation.

Little by little, her mother recovered physically. The damage to her psyche, however, only deepened. The humiliation and inconvenience of not being able to relieve herself unassisted was stressful, exacerbating her tendency not only to constipation but also to frequent urination, as dread of having to ask for help made her think constantly about her bladder. She was too distraught to eat much of anything and, although for some reason her stomach remained bloated, the wrists lying on top of her covers became as thin as chicken bones.

She wanted her daughters with her in the evening from mealtime till bedtime, so reluctantly they took turns sitting with her at dinner. They would sit beside her bed and scold her when she tried to use her good left hand, urging her to make the effort to use the right hand for rehabilitation. At the same time, they would pick up dishes that were hard for her to reach and place them directly in front of her, trying to get her to eat even a little. When she broke her other hip a dozen years ago, she'd kept them busy bringing her gourmet items from the food court in Isetan's basement: tangy pickled plums from Wakayama Prefecture; sweet and salty simmered beef from a famous old Tokyo shop; flaked salmon fillet from Niigata Prefecture. This time she picked at the foods she was offered, showing little enjoyment. She exhibited no sign of wanting to recover—or of wanting to live, for that matter. Nor of course did she exert herself in rehabilitation.

After a few days, classes resumed at the college where Mitsuki taught. She also continued to accept a few patent translation assignments. If she turned down too many, offers would stop coming in, but knowing she would have less time now, she cut back. Just as she had feared, her mother's demands slowly increased, a resurgence not of her will to live but of sheer habit.

First, she said she wanted a little hand mirror.

Mitsuki had taken her a comb, facial cream, and other items she used frequently, but had purposely not taken a mirror. At home her mother never tired of looking at herself in her vanity-table mirror, so it was hardly surprising if she should want to see her face now; but what was the point of looking at her mottled complexion without benefit of foundation or lipstick, without even her teeth in place? The hand mirror of lacquered wood that she normally used would take up too much space and was too heavy for her chicken-bone wrists anyway. Mitsuki had done nothing about getting her a new one, out of equal parts pity and laziness.

Not feeling quite up to a trek to a Muji shop, where everything sold was simple and of good design, on the way home she stopped at a place specializing in items for girls. Half dazed by the plethora of glittery, fluffy goods that greeted her eyes, she snatched up a mirror with a light purple frame topped with little glass diamonds in the shape of a tiara. It just fit in her palm.

The next time she went to the hospital she handed the mirror to her mother, who took one look at her reflection, said a toneless thank-you, and handed the tacky thing back.

Even on days when she never set foot out of the house, her mother had always carefully applied her makeup. Doubtless it had been one of the few small pleasures left to her in old age. Now even that had slipped away.

"Mitsuki, can't I watch DVDs here?" she asked peevishly one day—knowing full well that it was impossible. She showed no interest in the television in her room. Even at home she used to mock television, saying things like "NHK is trashier than ever." Apart from the evening news, the only programmed TV shows she ever looked at were ballet, opera, or orchestral performances on satellite TV, events she would never attend live again. The TV screen at home was primarily for movies—foreign movies, naturally, on DVDs that Mitsuki ordered for her from an online rental service that sent them through the mail.

If she couldn't watch movies, then she craved music. Mitsuki brought her a portable CD player, but on top of her other diminished faculties, her right arm was useless; even the simple operation of opening the lid was beyond her. Nor could she press the buttons of a portable radio.

"This is no fun!" She spoke accusingly, as if her plight were Mitsuki's fault. She kept asking for all sorts of things—every request either impossible to fill or absurd. When she asked for a large-print paperback, Mitsuki brought her one, but she lacked the energy even to put on her glasses, and complained again, "It's just no fun."

Finally Mitsuki spoke up, on the verge of tears: "Mother, have you got any idea what you're doing to us? My health isn't great either, but I manage to come visit you, so could you *please* try to bear up a little? I have my work to do, too. This isn't fun for me either!"

Her mother was momentarily chastened. "Mitsuki, you're angry!" Then, "If you get angry, what shall I do?"

The two women stared at each other.

Her mother repeated, "I only have you, Mitsuki, so if you get angry, what shall I *do*?" There were tears in her voice. She sounded theatrical, yet her words had the ring of truth. In fact, by giving up on Natsuki (and frequently reminding her of it), she had put herself in the position of having no one to truly rely on but Mitsuki.

Ever conscious of the ears in the neighboring bed, Mitsuki said loudly, "That's what I mean—just try to bear up a little, would you please?"

Her nerves were so jangled that she left the room on the pretext of going to the restroom and wandered down a series of corridors till she came to the library and sat down on a sofa. She had poked her head into the library before, realized that nobody ever used it, and kept it in mind as a place where she might get some work done. The moment she sat down, tears came. She was always on her guard around her mother and so could never cry in front of her, but now everything she had been holding back came pouring out.

As she was holding a handkerchief to her eyes and quietly crying to herself, someone came in. It was the dark-suited, middle-aged man she had first seen in the hospital store. Startled at the sight of her, his face reflected his discomfort as he turned on his heel and fled. Tears that Mitsuki had kept hidden even from her husband, this man had now seen — yet for some reason she felt consoled.

Senility is virtually indistinguishable from madness. As her hospital stay lengthened, Mitsuki's mother grew more senile; she also slipped further into madness. Approximately a month after the operation, she was moved to a rehabilitation hospital where every morning she was helped out of her pajamas and into normal clothes for the day and where she took her meals in the dining room, surrounded by other old people. This new environment was more like the outside world, requiring a certain amount of sociability. The brand-new hospital had a sunny dining room with all the spaciousness and cheerfulness of a children's play area. The sight of a stream of old-timers hobbling in there was disconcerting, but none of them had the fierce look in their eyes that her mother did.

Dining room meals were accompanied by a buzz of conversation and laughter. While some patients ate silently and alone, the air was filled with tension only in her mother's vicinity, as if being out in public laid bare her self-pity. Her sorrow was palpable.

She inevitably attracted notice. She would sit and stare into space with a stony expression. Other people saw her but she did not see them. It was as if she sat alone in a withered moor, a cold wind soundlessly scattering dry leaves around her. Why was it so hard for her to accept her fate?

Mitsuki's exhaustion and irritation increased.

## (10)

## REMNANTS OF FRAGRANT DREAMS

The land in Chitose Funabashi was sold with unexpected speed to a developer who said that the plot, hardly large to begin with, would be split into two even smaller parcels. The developer wanted the land vacant, and in return for their bearing the cost of demolition, granted them a little longer to clear out the house. When Tetsuo heard the selling price, he suggested they negotiate, but to Mitsuki the main thing was making sure they could pay the deposit at Golden without having to go into debt.

Their mother had once mentioned in passing that Natsuki and Mitsuki could split any extra money—but this Mitsuki had no intention of telling Tetsuo. Her sister, with the easygoing attitude of the rich, never brought it up. And as there was no way of knowing how many more years their mother might live, the money was impossible to divide anyway.

She and Natsuki took turns visiting their mother in the hospital, and together they traveled to Chitose Funabashi to pack up the house. Until now the house had belonged to their mother, even though they knew that one day it would be sold. Now that it was actually sold and scheduled for demolition, going there felt strange, as if they were visiting a ghost house already vanished from the earth. But this was no time for sentimentality. They worked like beavers.

At this stage of life, friends and acquaintances began to share all kinds of stories about their mothers. Reports of hoarding were typical. They heard about one woman's mother who used the second floor as a storehouse she didn't open for decades; then the first floor too began to overflow with hoarded articles, until her bed was piled so high with layers of coats and scarves that she had no place to sleep and ended up spending her nights curled in an armchair. This mother never allowed her daughter to throw anything away. There was no place to walk but a narrow pathway like an animal trail formed between stacks of possessions against the walls on either side; she used this only to go from her bedroom to the mouse-infested kitchen and back.

Fortunately Mitsuki's mother remained fastidious in her habits. No matter when Mitsuki went to see her, she always found her seated primly in an orderly space with her face made up. And even in old age, she had no qualms about discarding things.

"Is it okay if I throw this away?" Whenever Mitsuki asked this, pointing at some item not in use, most often the answer would be "Sure."

They didn't expect cleaning up to be very much work. And yet, once they began emptying drawers and clearing shelves, an amazing amount of stuff turned up, even in that tidy house. She and Natsuki were stunned. Their mother's possessions spoke eloquently about her old age and the sort of person she was, all the more so because parting with things generally came so easily to her.

They were moved to pity and at the same time rather amused.

What first struck them was the amount of medicine she had stockpiled. The prescription drugs included Chinese medicines, sleeping pills, anti-anxiety drugs, tranquilizers, expectorant, rash salve, medicine to control finger tremors, eyedrops, tonic, hypertension medication, and something for osteoporosis. Showing her usual organization, she had labeled each drug in her large round handwriting with its use and the date, but some were a decade old. There were also a goodly number of over-the-counter drugs. The never-ending stream of medications they uncovered revealed what poor health she had been in these past few years.

Mitsuki used to call her every night at eight, and she would complain, "I'm just so tired. I don't want to go on living." Mitsuki would make some perfunctory reply without even trying to sound sympathetic. Her mother's acupuncturist said that her mother had a particularly good constitution with strong powers of recovery. Sure enough, even if she caught cold and ran a fever, she recovered faster than either of her daughters ever did; so quite apart from the way she'd treated their father, Mitsuki had never felt much sympathy for her—especially given her own precarious health. Now for the first time, faced with her mother's medicine hoard, she felt a twinge of regret.

Her mother must have harbored the illusion, as so many old people do, that one day she would get well again. Besides medications, all manner of other things that had become increasingly superfluous were carefully stored away in drawers. She kept a well-stocked sewing box even after her fingers were no longer able to do her bidding and would never hold a needle again. Her collection of fine stationery, envelopes, and cards must have seemed equally indispensable, although for some time Mitsuki had been handling all her correspondence. The same went for her slips with elaborate lace trim at the neck and hemline. Over the past few years, since becoming sensitive to cold she'd taken to wearing trousers even on dressy occasions, but she must have clung to the hope of being able to wear a nice dress again someday.

And the stockings! She would have nothing to do with panty-hose and always wore the old-fashioned kind that fastened at the thigh—but when had she accumulated so many? Back when she was still able to go shopping at Isetan by herself, no doubt. With so many unopened packages of hosiery—finest quality, no less—they could have gone into business as street vendors. Trying to find anyone old-fashioned enough to wear such stockings would be a chore, so with many a sigh they ripped open one package after another, sorting the packaging and contents into burnable and unburnable trash.

The pantyhose Mitsuki bought simply didn't come in such thin, gossamer silk.

The closet too was full of useless items their mother couldn't part with: costly shoes the wrong size for either of them, along with several floor-length gowns custom-made for chanson recitals. The cream of the collection was a mink coat whose very existence they had forgotten, bought back when the family was relatively flush. At first she had looked stiff when she wore it—less with excitement than with lingering shock at the price tag. This was of course long before animal rights activists took to raising their voices on behalf of the poor creatures made into coats. But in no time she started slipping it on at the least oppor-tunity and would set off as proudly as a young girl in her first high heels. Faced with the heap of dark fur that emerged from a large wrapping cloth, Mitsuki and Natsuki were at a loss. The smell of mothballs stung their nostrils.

Lying around the house were other indulgences purchased right up to her mother's hospitalization. Once she could no longer go shopping by herself, she would ask one of them to pick up var-ious items for her. There was a ton of cosmetics. For Natsuki, the musician, to buy opera and ballet DVDs made sense; but she was also the one asked to buy cosmetics.

"Mom's worse than I am," she used to say. "The foundation alone costs over twenty thousand yen, and she uses it up three times faster than I do!"

Their mother must have known that Mitsuki would refuse to buy anything so extravagant.

There was of course a mountain of scarves—a crucial part of her wardrobe. As her body began to take on a deformed shape, the styles she could wear grew fewer, but a scarf could set off any outfit. And knowing Mitsuki's fondness for fabrics, she would take advantage of any occasion, including trips abroad, to request one. The scarves filled a shelf to overflowing—everything from featherlight watered silk to heavy cashmere with colorful embroidery.

The remnants of their mother's penchant for luxury, a penchant she could ill afford, spilled from all corners of the house, plastered and rebuilt in the seventies, casting a peculiar aura of romance through the dull, humdrum space. Hues of all shades appealed to the eye, while, wafting through the pungent odor of mothballs, the scents of silk and perfume appealed to the nose. Humdrum or not, the space was filled with poetry, the remnants of her dreams.

"I don't go in for jewelry, so where's the harm?" When indulging a lavish taste, she would declare this out loud as if reasoning with herself. The clear implication was that she was unlike her own diamond-bedazzled mother; but whether their grandmother had actually been dazzled by a diamond was by no means certain, so this was also a little family joke. Seen from the perspective of anyone rich, the luxuries their mother allowed herself were—could only be—small. And anyway, she was of a generation uninterested in designer brands. Her dream was one shared by other girls of her day: a yearning to look like the illustrations of dewy-eyed maidens in the magazine *Girls' Friend* or the female stars of the silver screen. But why had she spent her whole life so obsessively consumed by such dreams?

Long before becoming unhinged in old age, she had already been fairly balmy. How much of it was owing to the personality she was born with, how much to upbringing?

One day, hearing Natsuki call her name, Mitsuki stepped out into the hallway and found her sister, still wearing her coat, sitting on a cushion surrounded by a flood of items from the back of the storeroom. They had never cleaned out the storeroom after their father died; it was the one room in the house that had been kept closed off. Now, along with color slides of his frequent trips to the United States, out came childish drawings, compositions, and report cards from their elementary school days; musty, clothbound photo albums from their parents' youth; notebooks their father had filled with letters from his best friend, who died in the war, carefully preserved; and bundles of glossy stills of movie stars that their mother had collected as a girl. As expected, there were several of Greta Garbo, Marlene Dietrich, and Gary Cooper. There was even one of the French actress Arletty. As if peeling back layers of family history, they became absorbed in examining each find.

In the very back was a wooden storage box lined with tin. Mitsuki opened it to find brown-stained rice paper tied with twisted strings. When she undid them, all at once the lid of memory was lifted. Here it was: the *Golden Demon* kimono.

Natsuki remembered it too, quickly exclaiming, "It's still here!"

When their grandmother had walked out on her first husband, she'd sold everything she could, except for the kimono she'd been wearing as a young wife when she happened to run into her first love, "Kan'ichi," again: whether true or not, the story was part of family lore.

Mitsuki was in high school when she first read the old novel *The Golden Demon* and came across this passage portraying O-Miya on that crucial day:

69

Her lacquerlike hair, arranged in a chignon so perfect that one might have mistaken it for a wig, was adorned with an ornamental hairpin trimmed with tiny beads of coral, and the white collar of her under-kimono, visible at the neck, was of a cool beauty beyond description. She wore an unlined five-crested kimono in heavy crimped silk of deep violet-gray, with an embroidered olive-gray obi.

The heirloom kimono in her family was supposed to be this "unlined five-crested kimono in heavy crimped silk of deep violet-gray." Its heavy silk was indeed crimped, but it was lined, not unlined. Their mother had apparently inquired about this discrepancy long ago, and Grandma had answered without batting an eye: since she could only wear the unlined kimono during summer, she'd had it lined so that it could be worn most of the year.

The violet-gray silk exuded the fragrance of aloeswood, and the sisters, after dipping in and out of the Showa era, found themselves abruptly transported back over a hundred years to the time of Meiji.

## GMAIL EXCHANGES WITH THE WOMAN

The whole time she was in the rehabilitation hospital, their mother retained the look of someone trapped, hunched, and alone in a wind-whipped wasteland. She still wanted them to visit her around supper-time. No other patient was so constantly attended by family; keeping it up would have been impossible if either Mitsuki or her sister had regular jobs. They tried visiting with less frequency but she pestered them to come, and then when they did, she looked desolate and forlorn.

Why couldn't she be like other people?

It was as if she could no longer endure the misery of having ceased to be her former self. For better or worse, her nerves had been desensitized during her long hospital stay, and she accepted without protest the portable toilet they placed by her bed every night before she went to sleep. But in a more abstract way she continued to be horrifically miserable, her misery a source of pain not just for her but for them too.

One day Natsuki reported, "She's gobbling Depas."

"What do you mean?"

"Her supply keeps magically dwindling. I'll bet *that's* why she's groggy all day."

She must reach for the Depas without thinking, to numb her sorrow. They agreed that the hospital should now take charge of her medications, but the next day when they broke this to her she turned pale and went into a frenzy. Finally they consulted a psychiatrist who prescribed a stronger tranquilizer that the hospital would administer once a day.

Her physical therapy wasn't progressing well, either. A dozen years ago at this point she had gritted her teeth, endured the pain, and made an effort to walk again, but now she was letting life slip through her fingers. She did recover to the point where she could stand up from her wheelchair by herself and use the railing to ease herself onto the toilet. She was at risk of falling, however, so someone had to be there just in case. Unable to achieve her goal of relieving herself in private and annoyed as ever by the hassle of constantly asking for help, she suffered even more from constipation and an overactive bladder.

In the midst of all this came word from Golden that there was now an opening: a resident was moving to an associated nursing home in Kobe, where her son had been transferred. Did they make up stories like this because people were reluctant to take a room where someone had died? Anyone put off by news of death had no business entering a nursing home in the first place.

Mitsuki paid the initial deposit immediately, glad that she would have time to prepare her mother's final living space. One thing she liked about Golden was that they let you redecorate as you pleased. Supposing that her mother would live many more years, she set out to make the small room elegant and comfortable. She selected faux plaster wallpaper and distressed hardwood flooring, above the standards of nursing homes. So her mother wouldn't have to look down on the parking lot, she hung embroidered lace curtains made in France, having ordered them, naturally, from Isetan. To display antique bric-a-brac her mother cherished—a porcelain basket weave bowl, a little perfume bottle of Venetian glass, a silver box inlaid with pearls and lapis lazuli—she added a shelf to one wall. She also brought in a tall vase of dark-red faceted glass, a gift from Grandpa Yokohama that her mother prized, and filled it to overflowing with a sumptuous arrangement of artificial flowers, again from Isetan.

Tetsuo's eyes popped. "God, you're spending a lot of money."

"Well," she defended herself, "she did come into a lot all of a sudden." *And it's her money,* she wanted to add, but refrained.

Mitsuki used to worry more about her mother's budget than her own. With inward apologies to Tetsuo she had occasionally helped her out: "Here, Mom, let me pay for this." It felt good now to spend her mother's money with abandon. She wanted her to end her days swathed in small luxuries—though given the way her mother had warehoused her father, why this should be important to her she couldn't have explained. But it was somehow *because* her father had died without even a chair to call his own that she wanted her mother's remaining years to lack nothing in comfort.

Following the doctor's recommendation, she chose a sturdy yet stylish German wheelchair. She replaced her mother's flat-screen TV with a larger model. She invested in a pricey new wardrobe of polyester clothes that could be tossed in the washing machine and dryer. Wool vests and cardigans would have to go to the cleaner's, and these too she bought all new, choosing items that would be easy for others to help her mother in and out of.

After a little more than two months, the hospital said there was no point in continuing intensive physical therapy.

Right around then, Tetsuo left for Vietnam.

In the past, Mitsuki had gone with her husband on his sabbaticals, first to California, then Okinawa, but this time she'd all but given up on the idea of accompanying him, even before her mother's latest accident. It had gotten so that if she was away from Tokyo for even a few days, her mother grew so anxious that her blood pressure shot up; she would then send for Natsuki and be whisked to the hospital. Now she'd actually been in the hospital since December. Leaving was not an option.

On top of all else, there was the dratted tissue case. Ever since finding it, Mitsuki had been glad of the chance to live apart from her husband for a while.

On the day Tetsuo paid her mother a last visit, he said to Mitsuki, "When she gets settled in at the nursing home, come to Vietnam for a week or two."

"Okay."

He would be going with the younger woman; of this she was now certain. While he busied himself with travel arrangements, she'd been at her mother's beck and call, the distance between them yawning wider all the time. By now he lived in a different universe. Once she had her mother squared away, she would sit down and think what to do about her marriage — so she told herself, trying to block from her mind the vision of that tissue case, so sweet-looking and so sinister.

"Sorry I won't be here to help with the move."

He sounded genuinely regretful. In fact, simply coping with all the cardboard boxes would be a huge task for her and her sister. She hated to impose on Natsuki's husband, Yuji. Tetsuo was a good worker and would pitch in if he were around, but she no longer wanted his help anyway.

On the day of his flight he caught a cab to Shinjuku, where he would take the Narita Express to the airport. She waved him off, and then he was gone.

Assumption soon turned to fact. Just before her mother went into Golden, Tetsuo called to say he had safely arrived. Shortly afterward he emailed her that he had moved into the apartment as planned, but the place only had a dial-up line, and email would be difficult unless he went to a four-star hotel as he was doing now. She wrote back a line or two, switched off the computer, and got up. Then a thought struck her. She sat down and switched the computer back on.

She went to the opening screen for Gmail and typed in not her email address, but his. Years before, he had given her his password. Long before switching to Gmail, he used to fly off to remote spots around the world on what he called his "research," and he'd given her the password so she could check his email for him while he was away. Chances were slim that he was still using the same password, but she typed it in on the off chance that it might work—and, miraculously, it did. Once in, she couldn't help seeing a long chain of exchanges with some woman, and once she saw that, she couldn't help starting to read, with no time for compunction.

She was up all night going through the correspondence he had carried on with the young woman over the past two years. Their relationship evidently went back even further, but Gmail covered only those two years. Midway through, she got up and went to the freezer, took out ice cubes and wrapped them in gauze to cool her eyes as she read, since she was afraid of going to the hospital the next day with eyes puffy from weeping. When the ice melted, she went and got more after wringing out the gauze at the sink. Soon her fingertips felt frozen, and the chill spread throughout her body.

Yielding to pressure from the young woman, Tetsuo had sent her Mitsuki's photograph in an attachment. She'd written back smugly, "Pathetic. I have to say, I feel bad for her."

Humiliation stung Mitsuki, and for a while she could read no more.

The woman was young and therefore cruel. Clever, too. Though Mitsuki had planned to think about her marriage later, the woman had very kindly worked it all out for her, looking far ahead. Tetsuo's going to Vietnam with her had a purpose. The idea was to establish that he and Mitsuki had lived apart for a whole year; if Mitsuki suggested joining him, he was to dissuade her in a lazy, offhand way. Then just before returning to Japan he would send her a letter announcing he wanted a divorce and never again set foot in their Tokyo home. At least, that was what she had made him promise.

While wringing out the gauze, Mitsuki looked in the mirror. The face reflected there was pathetic indeed. Just how alluring could the other woman be? Knowing Tetsuo, she must be at least as attractive as Mitsuki had been in her younger days.

Toward dawn, she took a long hot bath, but she couldn't get warm.

The next day there was a rainstorm, of all things. On her way to the hospital, Mitsuki was pelted by rain as the wind blew it sideways. She walked along wiping her face, unsure if she was brushing away raindrops or tears. Rain soaked into her shoes, wetting her toes.

When she walked into her mother's room, her mother greeted her with "This morning I moved my bowels, and I feel good!" Her gaze used to be so sharp that it was tiresome to be around her, but now she didn't notice Mitsuki's swollen eyes.

"That's nice," Mitsuki said.

# (12)

## THE TIME OF CHERRIES

There is a chanson called "Le temps des cerises" that was written in the nineteenth century but continues to be sung even now.

> *Quand nous chanterons le temps des cerises*
> *Et gai rossignol, et merle moqueur*
> *Seront tous en fête!*
> *Les belles auront la folie en tête*
> *Et les amoureux du soleil au cœur!*
> *Quand nous chanterons le temps des cerises*
> *Sifflera bien mieux le merle moqueur!*

> When we sing in the time of cherries
> The merry nightingale and the mocking thrush
> Will all join in the fun!
> Beauties' heads will fill with folly,
> And lovers' hearts with sun!
> When we sing in the time of cherries
> The mocking thrush will be second to none!

Cherries that slowly plump up and turn red symbolize youth, its freshness, its beauty, and its excess. Hanging from trees they are like pendant earrings; they ripen by the blood's wild surging; fallen on the ground, they are drops of blood.

Mitsuki had always liked the original French lyrics—especially the line *Les belles auront la folie en tête*, where the melody rose on the words *la folie*, lingering so that for a brief moment the singer's voice hung lightly in the sky. "Beauties' heads will fill with folly." French, the language of romance, sums up with gallantry all girls who long to be beautiful and to be loved: *les belles*. But the word actually means something more like "pretty young things." Every young girl loses her head, but not over any one young man in particular; before that, before all else, she realizes that she is indeed a pretty young thing, the object of men's admiration, and the knowledge goes straight to her head.

Chanson lyrics are a treasure-house of wisdom. Where today's popular songs mindlessly extol the world of youth, the chansons of a generation ago, which the entire world embraced, take a step back to convey what youth is and to remind listeners that it soon vanishes, that time's march is unstoppable. They extol not youth but life, declaring that the very pathos of youth's brevity makes life wondrous. Chansons are for people who have already lived their lives.

Or so it seemed to Mitsuki. The longer she lived, the deeper her conviction grew: the heads of "pretty young things" fill with folly.

Mitsuki too had been one of those "pretty young things" before she met Tetsuo.

She was no beauty. The story was that at birth, she'd been so queer-looking that her parents exchanged looks and wordless sighs. Her mother had kept the story alive by retelling it over and over. They had already settled on the name "Mitsuki" if the new baby was a girl, she said, but then hesitated because the character for *mi* meant "beautiful."

Mitsuki grew up unhurt by these jabs. Her grandmother told her she was pretty and so did her sister. Other people assured her she looked pretty as well. In an impoverished Japan just recovering from the war, a little girl in matching outfits with her sister, sometimes even wearing white gloves and clutching a little purse her father had brought back from America, couldn't have helped being adorable.

Besides, her mother had never singled Natsuki out for praise on account of her looks, even though she resembled her and was much the prettier of the two. If Natsuki wasn't belittled like Mitsuki, neither was she considered particularly beautiful—a source of some pain to her.

Natsuki got hurt easily anyway.

In their mother Noriko's astonishingly unshakable view, the word "beauty" applied only to a goddess of the silver screen, whether of the East or the West—the sort she had swooned over as a schoolgirl. In the real world, the word referred to someone like herself with finely sculpted features of a vaguely Western cast. Others had regarded "O-Miya" as a beauty, in her prime, but Noriko had only ever known her mother as a doddering old woman and seemed to give the idea short shrift. Her assessment of her daughters was no less critical.

As an adult, Mitsuki came to understand that mothers have a streak of sadism in their treatment of their daughters. Her mother, whose standards for beauty were so stringent, had seemed to take pleasure in looking down on her and her sister.

In private, they had voiced their dissatisfaction: "If she wanted us to be beautiful, what on earth did she marry *him* for?" Their father was never known for his looks. "You can say that again." "I mean really!" They had chattered on in this vein, forgetting that if their mother hadn't married their father, neither of them would ever have been born.

Their mother not only belittled Mitsuki for her looks, or rather her lack of them; she pitied her. Even in height, Mitsuki lagged behind the others. And alas, she resembled their father.

"Still, you *have* gotten better-looking." As she grew up, their mother would offer such scant comfort—comfort that was as presumptuous as it was unnecessary. By the time she was old enough to be conscious of men's glances, plenty of them were heading her way. Soon men started to flutter around her. So in the end Mitsuki too joined the ranks of *les belles*—the pretty young things.

Even now, when she was out walking, taking the train, or entering a restaurant, she would look around at young girls and marvel. Whether from heredity or upbringing or the mix of hormones that had bathed them in the womb, girls' consciousness of their femininity varied. Some of them seemed so oblivious that she could picture them as they must have been yesterday, covered with mud on the soccer field. Others exuded awareness from head to toe, some giving off a soft fragrance and others a deadly perfume. It had less to do with their clothing and more to do with subtle mannerisms—a way of sitting or moving the head.

Natsuki's and Mitsuki's mother was decidedly feminine, and their grandmother, having been a geisha in youth, must have been so in her day as well. The sisters also were definitely more conscious of their femininity than most girls, if less so than their mother. In this day and age, that wasn't such a good thing. Very feminine girls did not, for the most part, devote themselves to their studies. As a result, they couldn't hope to enter a top university and get a top job. "That's why I make it a point never to go on about a woman's appearance in front of Jun," Natsuki often said. The mother of a girl and a boy, she had given her daughter the breezy, androgynous name "Jun" and was careful not to raise her the way she herself had been brought up.

But being aware of one's femininity wasn't altogether a bad thing either. Fortunately for Natsuki and Mitsuki, they had grown up at a time when girls like them were only expected to find a husband. "Pretty young things" could, in the season of ripening cherries, give themselves over headlong to the folly of youth.

Looking back, she thought that must be why she had been so involved in the drama club in college while studying French literature with other "pretty young things." That must be why after graduation she'd poured all her earnings from tutoring English into voice lessons and rejoiced on receiving bit parts at a theater through connections to former members of the drama club. Eventually a girl she met at the theater had taken her to a *chansonnier* on the Ginza and arranged for her to sing there on slow nights, which she had done with great satisfaction, all for the same reason.

Young girls fresh out of college were made much of everywhere.

Mitsuki was all the more valued at the *chansonnier* since not only did she take after her mother and sing a little, but she also had her father's gift for languages and could, with the aid of a dictionary, translate the back covers and lyrics of albums imported directly from France. What if she had gone on working and singing there, she sometimes wondered. What would have happened? For one thing, she would never have met Tetsuo. At the time she had assumed people were supposed to get married, so she probably would have married someone, but who?

Their mother had always been preoccupied with Natsuki, a tendency that grew even stronger just as Mitsuki was making her debut as a "pretty young thing": first, she'd sent Natsuki to Freiburg to study, and then she'd had to send their father to bring her back home—and before that hubbub had time to die down, the undreamed-of marriage proposal had come out of the blue. Their mother, still working then for Auntie, had no attention to spare for what her younger daughter might be doing after college.

Only when everything quieted down and she finally caught her breath did she realize that Mitsuki was dabbling in activities that were vaguely improper. Daughters, even if they found jobs, were expected to retire happily upon marrying. Natsuki hadn't looked for employment after graduating from a music conservatory. Before going to Freiburg, she had taught piano to neighborhood children while continuing her own lessons in preparation for her studies abroad. But unlike Natsuki, Mitsuki had no clear objective in life. What's more, the *chansonnier* where she worked served liquor, and on evenings when she was asked to sing, she also entertained drunken customers, returning home late at night.

Mitsuki's mother couldn't very well force her to find a job. But one day, she found an opportunity to ask Mitsuki what she intended to do with her life. She'd been out of college for some two years. It was a balmy spring afternoon, and the two of them, her mother then still in her fifties, were folding laundry.

"Mitsuki, what do you want to do with yourself?"

## (13)

## STONE BROKE

"You know," her mother said, reaching for a towel, "a proper young lady shouldn't spend time in a place like that."

By "a place like that" she meant the *chansonnier*.

"Everyone there takes their work seriously," said Mitsuki, folding her father's white underwear. The faces of the other singing staff rose in her mind. France still epitomized Western civilization, and the chanson was the fragrant, last fleeting flower of the country's golden age. Many of those engaged in transplanting that flower here in this Far Eastern archipelago were dedicated students of the art. "And I only sing now and then."

"I know. If I were only younger, I'd like to do something like that myself."

The topic was a delicate one; Mitsuki sensed that her mother was attempting to placate her.

"Anyway, I know you're too smart to take up drinking and smoking just because you frequent a place like that."

This was a subtle dig at Natsuki, who had fallen into such unladylike habits in Freiburg.

"But you can't go on this way forever, you know. You need to settle down."

Mitsuki sensed that her mother meant "You need to find a husband before it's too late," but was refraining from saying so out loud. Women were supposed to marry before the age of twenty-five. Mitsuki did plan to marry someday, but after being left to her own devices for so long, she found it annoying to have the topic brought up. Without thinking, she countered, "Just pretend I'm studying abroad in Paris. At a bargain price."

After a moment, her mother quietly asked, "Mitsuki, do you want to study in Paris?" Her hands had left off folding towels.

Picking her father's socks out of the laundry pile, which smelled of spring sunshine, Mitsuki said, "It doesn't matter if I do or not, does it? We're stone broke."

As she said the words "stone broke," her voice might have revealed a trace of rancor. She knew the family coffers must be nearly empty. She went on laying out her father's socks in a pool of sunshine on the table while images of her family's profligacy over the past few years unfolded in her head like scenes from a movie. In every case, her mother had loosened the purse strings for Natsuki.

First came Natsuki's two years in Freiburg. The exchange rate, after over two decades at 360 yen to the dollar, had risen, but even so, the expense had been considerable.

Then there was the rebuilding of the house in Chitose Funabashi, undertaken during Natsuki's absence so it wouldn't interfere with her practicing. The rest of them could live in an apartment while the new house was being built. Their practical mother had planned this long before Natsuki ever left. For one thing, the old house, built after the war, was showing its age, but beyond that, she had in mind her daughters' coming marriages—particularly that of Natsuki. Eventually both girls would find husbands, she reasoned, and when talk of marriage arose it would look better if they were living in a nicer house. Since rebuilding was inevitable anyway, they might as well do it when they had the chance. An architect acquaintance of hers oversaw the construction of a house designed to her taste, not large, but vaguely Western in style. Grandma was by then long gone, so the new house had no tatami rooms.

They'd taken out a loan to pay part of the construction cost, but the rental apartment and moving expenses had not been cheap. They'd also bought some new furniture, including the large dining room table where Mitsuki and her mother were now sorting laundry.

Shortly after they'd finally moved into the new house, a thick airmail envelope edged in red and blue—not the usual aerogram—arrived from Natsuki. She wrote that she wanted to stay on in Germany another year and continue her studies. Instantly her mother sensed that this was not the whole story. She placed an overseas call and grilled Natsuki, who finally grudgingly admitted she was having an affair with a German professor of piano, a married man with a family.

"I *knew* there was something fishy about that child volunteering to stay on and continue with her piano." Her mother had spoken with barely repressed anger.

Natsuki had set off from Japan forlorn and on the edge of tears, and after arriving in Germany she had sent letter after letter with a litany of complaints—the food in the dormitory was awful, nothing but potatoes and cabbage; her room was cold; Germans weren't nice—and expressing her longing to go home.

After a year or so, the letters tapered off. Once the affair came out into the open, her mother had ordered her to return home immediately, but Natsuki dug in her heels and refused. On opposite sides of the earth, mother and daughter shouted at one another over the phone day after day, at a time when the cost of international calls was prohibitively high. Finally her father had been forced to fly to Germany and bring her back, at even greater expense.

Once home, Natsuki had done nothing but sulk, yet in less than a year she'd received a marriage offer beyond anybody's dreams. When she flew off from Haneda Airport, she had been a typical Japanese young lady; she came back an Asian woman of indeterminate nationality. The daughter who had listened obediently to her mother was gone. She let her wiry, slightly frizzy hair hang loose down her back, hippie style, and wore tight jeans and high heels. No matter what her parents said, she obstinately resisted changing her behavior.

"Why did we ever let her go?" muttered her father, to which her mother replied, "Who ever thought she could be this stubborn?"

Only in visiting the home of her mother's relatives, always referred to as "Yokohama," did Natsuki show resignation, or better yet, philosophical acceptance. She would even put on a skirt at her mother's urging and kept mum about her indiscretion in Germany. Knowing her mother's fixation on "Yokohama," she must not have had the nerve to rebel.

Philosophical acceptance led eventually to marriage to Yuji, another frequent visitor at "Yokohama," and still more outlandish expenses for the family.

While Mitsuki gathered up her father's socks, her thoughts turned to the elaborate wedding for Natsuki and Yuji in the Imperial Hotel, so vivid in her memory that it might have been the day before. The glitter of chandeliers in the wedding hall ceiling rose in her mind's eye (why did wedding hall chandeliers always look so garish?). She could see her mother greeting guests, more flushed with excitement than the bride as she floated gracefully through the sea of men in black morning coats and women in black crested kimono. She was reminded once again of the strength of her mother's lifelong attachment to "Yokohama," and familiar feelings assailed her, the *basso ostinato* of her life. Deliberately avoiding looking her mother in the eye, she began laying out pairs of her father's socks on the table.

"Mitsuki, do you want to study in Paris?" Her mother stopped folding laundry and repeated the question.

"It doesn't really matter if I do or not, does it?" Looking down, Mitsuki repeated her answer.

The swirl of emotions inside her darkened further. Her mother's sudden question struck her with awareness of something she normally gave little thought to: the unequal treatment of her and her sister. "Yokohama," the hilltop house named after the nearby port, had lodged in her mother's heart since girlhood with the particular shine of things forbidden—and so, for as long as she could remember, Mitsuki and her sister had been treated unequally. The inequality was as regular and predictable as the sun's rising in the east.

## LESSONS AT "YOKOHAMA"

One day back when Mitsuki was in the fifth grade or so, the three of them—her mother, her sister, and herself—had got off the train near Yokohama and climbed the twisting road that led to the house on the hilltop. Along the way, they passed the wintry park on the right. The uphill path was long for Mitsuki's small legs, all the more so because she had to fight the north wind sweeping down from the crest of the hill.

It was getting on toward evening, the hour when the day's melancholy hangs heavy in the air.

"Mitsuki," her mother said, turning to her, "take your sister's bag." In response to Mitsuki's wondering look, she explained, "If her fingers get frozen, she won't be able to play well at her lesson."

Natsuki's music bag wasn't heavy, but Mitsuki was shocked by her mother's command. This happened at a time of great disparity in the sisters' physiques. Natsuki, already in middle school, was bursting with health. She had begun menstruating and was tall and well filled out. Mitsuki, whose growth was slower, had a sticklike body balanced on a pair of childish legs that looked as if they might snap in two.

Her mother had issued the command with the two of them right before her eyes.

Natsuki may not have felt comfortable handing over her bag to her little sister, but their mother's command was absolute.

Mitsuki's soul slipped out of her small body and looked down from on high at the three of them climbing the slope. Leading the way was her mother, wearing more makeup than usual and wrapped in a woolen coat, her heart a mix of eight parts excitement and two parts anxiety. She was nervous about whether Natsuki would be able to demonstrate the fruits of her practicing. Behind her came the two sisters, a pair of ducklings, one large and one small, trailing up the hill after the mother duck.

Natsuki, the larger duckling, definitely wasn't thinking about anything. Mitsuki, the smaller duckling, had likewise thought of nothing until she was handed the music bag, merely moving her childish legs automatically and getting out of breath. With this sudden imposition, she felt not bitterness but something more like righteous indignation stirring in her immature heart.

Mothers were supposed to be fair.

All the unfairness she had suffered until then was encapsulated in that moment. Forever after, whenever she encountered an instance of the ongoing unfairness, this indelible scene from her childhood rose unbidden in her heart.

It wasn't as if she had never been given the opportunity to play the piano. At the time, piano lessons were de rigueur for every family that could afford them. Back in the Edo period, unmarried girls used to write poetry, study calligraphy, play the koto, and learn traditional dancing, but as the country modernized, the contents of such lessons gradually shifted, becoming more and more Westernized until one kind of lesson came to symbolize the enlightenment brought about by the West: piano lessons. That pianos were available only to daughters of the well-to-do gave the lessons even more cachet. The image of a graceful woman seated in a Western parlor before a darkly gleaming piano, slim fingers dancing over the keys, was implanted in girls' hearts; and after the war, as Japan became increasingly wealthy, families who could manage it vied to buy pianos (usually the modest upright kind) so their young daughters could learn to play "Für Elise" and "Turkish March."

Her own family was no different. But individual dreams intertwine with the flow of history in myriad ways. Her mother's unfulfilled dream had borne a touch of pathos. And so Natsuki, the elder daughter, had been fated to study piano with Uncle Yokohama even before she was born. To make matters easier, she had inherited more of their mother's looks than Mitsuki and temperamentally was much more suited to the piano. In the way of all mothers, their mother had sought to relive her life through Natsuki, but with a determination made all the more intense by her passionate nature.

At first the sisters had studied with the same teacher. Every Saturday, after school they would have a quick lunch, change into good clothes, and set off again, music bags in hand. Uncle Yokohama did not teach children; about this he was adamant. And so for the first few years they had learned the basics together from a most charming student of his, his favorite. After a while, Natsuki alone moved on to Uncle Yokohama. Mitsuki, still small, didn't really understand what this meant, and as she wasn't crazy about practicing anyway, she often felt that she might be the lucky one.

Uncle Yokohama was their mother's cousin. An important man, people said. He'd been instrumental in the founding of the music department of the first women's college in Yokohama—the first in Japan, for that matter, dating back to 1875—where he was a professor. Later, he became the college president. Natsuki was his youngest pupil.

Naturally, his other pupils were invariably from distinguished families. Although their mother had in all probability nudged him to lower the cost of the lessons, they must still have been a burden. Besides, she was planning even then to send Natsuki to study someday in Freiburg, where he had studied; making a pianist of Mitsuki too would have been an impossible strain on the family resources. There was also the plausible excuse that having both daughters follow the same path was hardly interesting.

Their mother was not entirely unmindful of the resulting unfairness and tried in her way to make amends. Having herself once longed to be an accomplished young lady, she'd arranged for both of them to take ballet lessons as well, but when Natsuki began going to "Yokohama" for piano, she stopped having her take ballet. And while she had Mitsuki stay on with the charming piano teacher, she took the trouble of switching her ballet lessons from a local studio to one that was more professional.

To all appearances, there was no cause for complaint. But in fact, the sisters' treatment was anything but equal. The difference lay in not only the money but above all the enthusiasm that their mother invested in each of them. On days when she didn't have to go to work, she would sit beside Natsuki as she practiced, wearing a look of intense concentration. And she invariably went along to the lesson, dressed up in a prettier kimono than usual. The ceremony of the two of them setting out together for "Yokohama" continued until Natsuki finished middle school.

But never once did their mother go to watch Mitsuki's ballet lesson or even attend her recitals. Before going onstage Mitsuki would change her clothes, folding the discarded garments herself while watching out of the corner of her eye as the other children's mothers folded theirs. Sometimes as she reached behind her back in her struggle to fasten the hooks on her costume, one of the other mothers would take pity on her and lend a hand. Even on recital days, it never occurred to her mother to give her money for anything but the round-trip train fare, so while the other children were treated to strawberry milk after the performance, she had to go without. She would be thirsty, too, which made it all the harder to bear. She felt like an orphan.

And at home, she was always the one who had to help with the chores. After the death of Grandma, whom their mother had taken advantage of, they had a young live-in maid for a while, but when she and her sister were older and needed less care, the maid left. That's when Mitsuki was put to work. Granted, Natsuki was by nature dilatory—"Really, just asking that child to do anything wears me out!"—but this unequal treatment was always justified in the name of her piano practicing.

"Mitsukiii!" their mother would cry in a ringing voice. An energetic woman, she was not at all averse to working outside the home and kept herself busy with domestic tasks as well, not just cooking, cleaning, and laundry, but sewing and gardening too. Her work schedule was irregular, and so sometimes she would be home on weekdays. When that happened, Mitsuki had to give up her favorite pastime of lying lazily on the sofa reading novels. Through the sound of Natsuki's practicing would come their mother's ringing voice, summoning her: "Mitsukiii! Mitsukiii!"

But perhaps because the inequality was routine, Mitsuki had never found it particularly galling—at least, not usually. Nor was she jealous of her sister, who had to sit at the piano day after day after day. She told herself that she was better off helping her mother and being praised for being "such a good girl."

When she was little, she would be sent out on errands. The people next door had a farm, already a rarity in Chitose Funabashi, and Mitsuki would set out with a round bamboo basket, picking her way through the fields to buy eggplants or cucumbers. Some days she would carry a pan with handles to the tofu vendor to buy a block of tofu; on other days, she would take a plastic shopping basket (then considered modern and smart) to the supermarket (likewise considered modern and smart) to buy meat and vegetables. When she got older, she would stand beside her mother in the kitchen and help get dinner ready, chopping with a knife or stirring with chopsticks while Natsuki's piano played on in the background.

"The little housewife," her father called her proudly.

When the piano lesson fell on a Sunday, Mitsuki could go with her mother and sister to "Yokohama," a treat she looked forward to. She wore a felt beret and leather shoes. The train ride was long, with two transfers, but from the moment they arrived at "Yokohama," they were in a different dimension, one where the air and the very flow of time were nonpareil. Their mother's elation was infectious. When they stepped into the spacious entrance, smelling of well-polished wood, she led the way to the sitting room, her back with the obi tied in a simple bow exuding her pride as an insider. She would slide open the door, kneel gracefully, and say hello to Grandpa Yokohama, the piano teacher's father. By then retired, he would be sitting on the veranda in a rattan chair, wearing a padded kimono and smoking a pipe in style. A maid brought in drinks and sweets on a tray. The previous pupil's lesson would still be going on. Their mother's voice was bright and charming and Grandpa Yokohama was all smiles, in a good mood. He had taken to their mother from the first, back when his wife, her blood kin, was still alive, and his affection for her never wavered even after the subsequent fiasco.

When the previous pupil's lesson ended, Mother and Natsuki would be shown into the parlor, a large room with two grand pianos side by side. Mitsuki would sit alone next door in the combination living-dining room, engrossed in a novel. The maid would bring her a fresh cup of tea.

Sometimes Grandpa would come out to ask the maid for a cup of coffee or some such thing, and speak fondly to "Noriko's little girl."

"You like books, don't you, Natsuki?" he would say. He never knew which of the sisters was which, but his voice was unfailingly gentle.

The teacher's wife, known in the Katsura family as "Madama Butterfly," sometimes came in too. One of Japan's leading sopranos at the time, she used to walk around the house in high-heeled sandals like a foreigner. She would give the maid a hasty order of some kind before disappearing back into the room detached from the main house, where she practiced her singing.

When she saw Mitsuki she would say, "Well, I see Noriko is here again with her girls!" But unlike Grandpa's voice, hers held no gentleness, and the way she said "Noriko" sounded vaguely contemptuous.

Little Mitsuki sensed the condescension in her voice. Then the inequality between her sister and herself no longer mattered in the least. She felt sorry for her mother. It was as if her mother, after a lifetime spent yearning for all that "Yokohama" represented, was being put firmly in her place.

# ⑮

## THE HOUSE ON THE HILL

"Yokohama" had been engraved deeply in her mother Noriko's mind since childhood. The "Yokohama" house at the top of the hill was always drenched in bright sunshine. Her family lived in a little rental house below that was always in the shadows. Even as a child, she must have dimly sensed that the steep terrain represented the difference in social status between the two families. Looking up from below the steep rise, "Yokohama" was in plain sight, but to get there you had to take a winding detour.

Very like Noriko's own life.

After years of moving from place to place across Japan, her father was transferred to Tokyo before she started elementary school. The family settled in a house near his older sister, who had married into "Yokohama."

As a little girl with bobbed hair looking up at the house on the hill, Noriko hadn't known anything — not even that her mother wasn't allowed to cross the "Yokohama" threshold. Or that her parents weren't properly married. Or that because her parents weren't properly married, she herself was illegitimate — a disreputable love child. All she knew was that the sunny house on the hill held everything shiny and bright, everything that was lacking in her house and that formed the object of her yearning and envy.

All the rooms in the house where her family lived had straw tatami mats. "Yokohama" had a Western-style parlor redolent of fine polished wood, with a shiny grand piano played by the cousin seven years her elder—the future Uncle Yokohama. She had never heard the sound of piano playing or seen such a parlor before. The walls were lined with elegantly bound books—Western books too, naturally—and there were unfamiliar Western-style pieces of furniture too, a "sofa" and "armchairs." Next to the parlor was the dining room, with a table as high off the floor as her small head was. There was the aroma of roasted coffee beans in the air, and tropical fruit brought back by her cousin's father, the future Grandpa Yokohama, who was captain of an oceangoing merchant ship. It was because of him that the family lived near Yokohama, Japan's gateway to the West, but little Noriko knew nothing of this. On his days off he smoked a pipe in his study. The yard was planted with grass instead of moss, and the garden, marked off by a circle of bricks, bloomed with roses, dahlias, tulips, and other Western flowers. A Scottish terrier, a breed then rare in Japan, had the run of the place. To top it all off, living next door was a French woman married to a Japanese. On Sundays Noriko went to church with her cousins and discovered the pleasure of singing, something she did well.

As she warbled in church with all the strength her small body could muster, Noriko had surely believed that she would always be able to come and go at "Yokohama" as she pleased. But the adult world is prone to sudden, violent shifts without regard for the feelings of small girls. Eventually her father found work in Osaka through family connections, and Noriko had to move there with her parents, both of whom were originally from the western part of Japan.

What a different world it was! The sound of the multiplication table being recited in the unfamiliar rhythm of Osaka dialect was dumbfounding, the sniffling and shouting in church—a church in name only, to her—astonishing. She felt as if she'd been sent to civilization's remotest outpost.

As she grew up and it became increasingly clear that people looked down on her and pitied her, memories of "Yokohama" grew all the more resplendent in her mind. As she pored over the illustrations of stylishly dressed Japanese girls and Western girls in the pages of *Girls' Friend*, and later as she began going to see foreign movies, the world depicted there overlapped in her mind with those memories. But "Yokohama" was far away. One time she persuaded her father to have a new dress made for her, a rare treat, and to let her go back by herself during summer vacation—but the two weeks flew by, serving only to deepen her longing and envy. She returned chastened to Osaka.

When her cousin, now a rising concert pianist, came by on tour, he was surrounded by fellow musicians. She could only look on from the sidelines. Feeling out of place, she was dazzled by their aura—the aura of what she later recognized as "high culture."

The desperate longing that most Japanese used to have for the West became inseparably entangled in Noriko's mind with her veneration of "Yokohama." At the same time, that veneration served as the sort of guidepost people have when they seek to better themselves even a little through art or learning. The more impoverished her status, the more intense her hunger for the world of the house on the hill.

After graduating from a girls' higher school—as private high schools for girls used to be called—Noriko made the greatest decision of her lifetime, prompted by a proposal of marriage from the son of a local barber. By then her father had already set up house with another woman, and she and her mother were living alone in a row house in the back streets of Osaka. Downstairs consisted of a concrete entryway with a tiny anteroom, a kitchen, and a three-mat room; above was a six-mat room with a clothes-drying platform at one end. It was closer to downtown than the place they had lived in previously, and so older, dirtier, and more run-down. Their neighbors were a colorful mix: a young woman who recited ballad-dramas of the puppet theater for a living; an old woman who taught girls the art of kimono making; the mistress of a geisha house; a concubine; and assorted cooks, carpenters, and dancers.

Even if she refused the marriage proposal, Noriko understood that unless she could escape her present circumstances, she would have no choice but to go on living a small life in this back alley far removed from her dreams. Fear verging on desperation prompted her to come up with a scheme: she would get her maternal relatives to look after her mother while she invited herself to stay with her paternal relatives—at "Yokohama"—ostensibly to polish her household skills and her manners. With the determination of a seventeen-year-old, she pushed to have her way, and the adults in her life yielded to her determination.

Noriko's mother felt a lingering regret over the failed proposal from the barber's son: "He said he'd take me in along with you." The need to marry someone who would take in her mother as well as herself was a burden Noriko had to bear, as an illegitimate child.

"Him? Nothing doing."

"You're always hankering for the moon."

"I don't care. Nothing doing."

"Just what kind of fellow would suit your fancy, I'd like to know?"

Someone like her cousin, was the obvious answer. No point in saying so to someone as woefully uneducated, as innocent of high culture, as her mother.

And so off Noriko had gone to "Yokohama," with such determination that almost overnight she switched to the refined speech of uptown Tokyo. From her aunt she learned housekeeping—cleaning, laundry, cooking—but with formidable spirit made it clear that she hadn't the slightest intention of settling for the status of domestic helper. To differentiate herself from the maids, she affected a long-sleeved kimono even when helping around the house. Her aunt and uncle had only two children, the concert pianist and another son, younger than she was. Her aunt may have felt a little uneasy about Noriko's presence, but the strong family resemblance helped, and soon she began treating her almost like a daughter. Her uncle, with male nonchalance, welcomed their unexpected guest wholeheartedly.

In no time, Noriko spread her young wings almost as if she'd been born into "Yokohama" from the first.

Her mother Noriko's two years in "Yokohama" must have been sweet, thought Mitsuki, and at the same time bitter. She found several old photographs of Uncle Yokohama carefully mounted in an album. He had a noble air; the photographs might have been stills of a movie star.

Noriko's cousin graduated from the Tokyo School of Music (later Tokyo School of Fine Arts) and then enjoyed a brief career as a concert pianist. Photos taken after performances showed him dressed in a black tuxedo and snow-white shirt, surrounded by bouquets of roses. The bouquets, suggestive of their donors, made it seem as if he were surrounded by a dozen lovely young ladies, his students and admirers.

Noriko he had of course consistently ignored. In time he became engaged to marry. His fiancée had everything Noriko lacked. She was not only the daughter of a renowned university professor with a raft of prominent relatives but also a gifted soprano seen as having a brilliant future. She in fact went on to great success: when the Fujiwara Opera, Japan's first professional opera company, gave its first overseas performance in New York City, she sang the lead in *Madama Butterfly*. Noriko too could sing, but her parents had never given her proper lessons, and she lived on the consolation of having sung a solo at her graduation from girls' higher school. The contrast with her cousin's fiancée was stark.

Thinking over her mother's life, Mitsuki surmised that the marriage of the much-admired cousin must have brought her mother a degree of sadness, but probably no very deep wound. He had never paid her much attention and had always seemed to exist on a higher plane; she was probably content just to be allowed to polish and repolish his grand piano in his absence. When he married his Madama Butterfly in a splendid wedding and reception at the Hotel New Grand in Yokohama, young Noriko, though no doubt envious, had evidently been more entranced by the figure she herself cut in an exquisitely embroidered kimono, worn at the peak of her youthful beauty. The story went that afterward, when she heard that one of the guests had inquired if she were perhaps a princess of some sort, she had jumped for joy.

In any case, once she joined the "Yokohama" household she acquired kimono made especially for her, new ones for every change of season. She took classes in tea ceremony and flower arranging. She joined a church choir and so met the woman her daughters would know as "Auntie," becoming such friends with her that people mistook them for sisters. She even received a generous allowance to use with her friends. She never knew its source, but it was easy to imagine that her aunt must have contributed some, and probably her father also.

The Noriko who lived in a back alley of Osaka on frayed tatami mats had seemingly vanished from the earth like smoke. But reality was not that obliging.

Seeing how entranced Noriko was with her own transformation, her aunt must have had mixed feelings. Taking in a girl of marriageable age was tantamount to agreeing to find her a husband—but Noriko's illegitimate birth was a barrier. Finding someone willing to take on her mother, persona non grata at "Yokohama," made the task all the harder.

Yet Noriko seemed born to the role of charming young lady. She attracted attention. One thing led to another, and soon she had the effrontery to fall in love with a tenor who was a frequent guest at "Yokohama."

"*Si, mi chiamano Mimi.*" Yes, they call me Mimi. When Mitsuki was little, her mother's soprano voice used to soar through the house thanks to the arias taught her by that tenor, whose family pedigree was every bit as illustrious as that of "Madama Butterfly."

Though she carried her head high in that world, Noriko understood that she and her tenor could not meet openly. For a while they used her tea ceremony and flower arranging lessons as pretexts to take long walks together. He promised to win over his parents and marry her—but he was studying voice with their support and was moreover about to leave for Germany to continue his studies there, again with their support. No sooner did he inform them of Noriko's existence than he was sent packing on the first ship out of Yokohama.

Accused of lax supervision, "Yokohama" could only apologize.

Pity gave way to disapproval: instead of "poor Noriko," people said, "Noriko, that little upstart."

# 16

## THE FAMILY REGISTER

There was nothing for it but to marry "that little upstart" off without delay. Having made up her mind to it, Noriko's aunt plunged into the task with characteristic vigor—a vigor that Noriko herself was heir to. Armed with a suitable photograph of her niece, she moved resolutely beyond the pool of "Yokohama" regulars to ensure that the picture circulated among any and all families that might come up with a prospective groom. Noriko's looks spoke for her. In person, her intelligence and quick wit were no less captivating. Just like that, a suitor appeared, one whom it was hard to fault.

He wasn't wealthy, but like her father he was of samurai stock and a college graduate. Seven years her elder, he earned a fair salary, and he was good-looking besides. Moreover, as the second son he wasn't obliged to live with his parents. Best of all, he was willing to take in her mother. Anyone could see he was really too good a match for someone of Noriko's background.

Noriko's aunt was satisfied with the fruits of her labors. Her father was grateful. Her mother, after the humiliation of being shunted off to relatives, could now look forward to living with her daughter again. Grandpa Yokohama, the one to whom Noriko felt the closest, had no doubt that this suitor was all she could want in a husband. At age nineteen, Noriko, "the little upstart," felt the full weight of the pressure to marry, and with it a measure of relief.

Wedding plans were set.

Noriko's father was determined to provide his daughter with a handsome dowry and so, in a departure unimaginable from the modest lifestyle he had always followed, he loosened his purse strings to buy her a pair of solid paulownia kimono chests from Kawagoe, a carved dressing table with cherry-blossom motif from Kamakura, and a set of bridal quilts of figured satin from Kyoto. This prodigality was a form of atonement for burdening his daughter with her mother. How could he have known that a few years down the road she would run off with another man—Natsuki and Mitsuki's father?

"If it weren't for the war, I could never have married your father—the Katsura family was of good lineage. They would never have heard of it."

As children, Mitsuki and her sister had often heard their mother say this, without understanding what she meant. Puzzled by the absence of wedding pictures, they once asked her why there weren't any. "Well, it was just after the war," she said. Wartime suggested chaos and so, still without really understanding, they let it go.

The truth came out after Mitsuki started college. One day for some reason their mother went to the ward office in Itabashi, where the old Katsura Clinic had been, to get a copy of the family register. Their father was away. After the three of them had eaten supper and cleared away the dishes, she sat at the table holding a manila envelope. "Natsuki and Mitsuki, come here." There was tension in her voice. Mitsuki and her sister exchanged glances before joining her.

"I took a good look at this copy of the family register," she informed them. They stared at her blankly. After a pause she added, "I was married once before, but there's no record of it here."

They were grown by then and took the revelation fairly calmly. It was their mother who seemed worked up. She explained that she hadn't wanted to disturb them so she'd said nothing before, but in fact this was her second marriage. She had vaguely known that after World War II the family register system had undergone drastic change and was now focused on nuclear families, so the record of her illegitimacy was bound to disappear; but for years she had believed the current register must certainly contain a record of her divorce, which she had worried would hurt her daughters' chances for marriage.

At the time divorce had been considered beyond the pale.

She spread out the bluish paper happily. "There isn't even any record of your father's divorce!"

"Wait, you mean he was married before, too?" asked Mitsuki.

"Well, yes."

This revelation was a bit more shocking. That someone like their mother might divorce and remarry they could well imagine, but the idea that their bookish father would do anything so bold came as a surprise.

"How did that happen?" Natsuki asked.

"His first wife was overly serious, not at all interesting. Not much to look at, either." The answer was clear, concise, and resounding with superiority.

Years later, they heard their father's first wife had actually been a sweet, attractive woman; their mother had pushed her way into her house and made off with her husband by force, prying him from her grasp as the poor thing clung to him, weeping. This version of events came from relatives on their father's side with no fondness for their mother, leaving its accuracy in doubt; yet knowing their mother, it was strangely credible. The first marriage hadn't been long and was childless, so his first wife had gone home to her parents and eventually remarried.

Mitsuki became a bit anxious. "Did *you* have a child?"

"One, a girl." She added with some hesitation, "But she died."

Left behind by her mother when she was five years old, the girl had been raised by a stepmother, and she'd had a younger half brother too, but at the age of twelve she drowned in a lake. The sisters listened speechless to this tale.

Their mother topped it off by saying a bit proudly, "She was a stunning little thing."

Imagining the twelve-year-old's small coffin, Mitsuki and Natsuki were overcome with pity for the elder sister they never knew.

As to why she herself got divorced, their mother said little, whether out of consideration for the husband she had left or shame, after all, at her selfish ways. "Your father was an intellectual," she said, as if that were explanation enough.

They later learned that their grandfather had flown into a rage and disowned their mother when he heard the talk of divorce. After all the expense he had gone to, this was understandable. But perhaps because she was his only child, he must have soon relented, for by the time they were old enough to remember, he'd become a familiar figure, their Kyoto grandfather. Fortunately—if such a thing could be said—their great-aunt suffered a stroke and died without ever knowing her efforts had come to nothing. Their great-uncle, Grandpa Yokohama, though not a blood relative, was tolerant and allowed their mother to keep coming to the house to visit, although he would have been within his rights to forbid it.

"Anyway, I wonder—why aren't the divorces mentioned here?" she murmured aloud, carefully inserting the bluish paper back into its manila envelope. The question had no answer.

It was after Natsuki was fetched home from Germany and sent to "Yokohama" that their mother again produced the family register copy.

Mitsuki knew that while their mother could be as calculating as anyone, she wasn't so by nature. When she sent Natsuki to accompany Madama Butterfly's pupils at their voice lessons and thereby give her access to that coveted "Yokohama" circle—the circle from which she herself had ultimately been shut out—she probably did so more from ingrained habit than anything else. It was unlikely that she had a definite motive of marrying Natsuki to someone from those rare heights. She could scarcely have imagined that just such a proposal would come her daughter's way.

At the time, Madama Butterfly had a female pupil whose family was old money with government connections; after graduating from the Yokohama music school, she'd married a doctor and kept up with her singing while raising a family. She'd been treated with due respect at "Yokohama." Her younger brother was a cellist named Yuji Shimazaki.

It all started when Yuji drove to Chinatown for dinner with some friends one day and stopped in on the way back to pick up his sister. He ran into Natsuki and was instantly smitten. The next time she was there, and the next, he found an excuse to be present. It wasn't long before he asked her out on a date.

As soon as their mother heard this, she'd set out for "Yokohama" with the copy of the family register tucked in her purse. In case the Shimazakis started poking around, asking questions, she wanted nothing said about the divorces unless absolutely necessary.

"Yokohama" must have been dumbfounded to see Noriko wave around a copy of the Katsura family register. She had grown up during a time when the family register—the bastion of Japan's prewar social structure—played a crucial role in people's lives, recording everything from ancestral social class under the bygone system (nobility, samurai, commoner, untouchable) to illnesses, marriages, births, and deaths. The constant mortification she had endured before marrying was beyond most people's ken: she had been listed as an illegitimate child, albeit one recognized by her father; her mother and grandmother, both former geisha, were also illegitimate and, what was worse, unrecognized by their fathers. In her mind, it meant a great deal that her daughter Natsuki was untarnished and would be the first woman in at least four generations to marry with her head held high. Yet the stigma of divorce remained a threat. Going to "Yokohama" was an act of pure maternal love, motivated by determination to show that the record was clear: nothing on paper could stand in the way of her daughter's marriage.

Yuji, three years older than Natsuki, was just back from New York City with a master's degree from Juilliard, paid for by his parents. He met Natsuki precisely at the moment when he was searching for an orchestra position and a wife. That she was a little different from the prim girls he knew may have intrigued him. Her relative lack of interest in him may have added further to her charm. When he took her home to meet his parents, his father kept exclaiming, "What a lovely lady! Wherever did you find her?" She was at her comeliest just then.

From the Shimazakis' perspective, her father's status as a mere corporate employee must have posed a problem, but Yuji and his father (who had married into the Shimazaki family, taking his wife's surname) evidently went to bat for him. Yuji's father had vastly increased the family holdings, which gave him a strong voice in family affairs. Natsuki's having studied abroad spoke well for her family. And in a betrothal, fortunately it was the paternal lineage that came under greatest scrutiny. "Yokohama" stayed quiet about the rest.

The Katsuras had known dimly that the Shimazakis were richer than they were. On learning that Natsuki was marrying into a family of old money, at first they were elated, then slightly uneasy.

What must have gone through Natsuki's mind? No doubt Yuji's ardent wooing gradually won her over. No woman pursued that ardently would be displeased. And she must have been unconsciously driven by the knowledge of how furious her mother would be if she turned him down.

"Yokohama," serving as matchmakers, were triumphant. Who would have thought such an offer would come to the daughter of "poor Noriko"—or "that little upstart"? It must have set them back on their heels a little to realize Natsuki would now be richer than they were, but then again they had no daughter of their own (as in the previous generation, there were only two sons). All was well.

Seeing the air of triumph on "Yokohama" faces, their mother Noriko perhaps remembered the look of distress her late aunt wore long ago when the affair with the tenor came to light. Bittersweet emotion must have swept over her at the thought that she was actually marrying her daughter into that elite circle.

## 17

## A WORD OF THANKS

Marrying into a moneyed family proved to involve a great deal of rigmarole. To begin with, before the ceremony the families met over a formal dinner in the Hotel New Grand, accompanied by "Yokohama" as matchmakers. Naturally Mitsuki was invited too. Among the distinguished attendees, the father of the groom stood out, energetic and manly and anything but stuffy. Their mother, even while conscious of people's eyes, couldn't help instantly hitting it off with him. The rest of the Shimazakis spent their time name-dropping, leaving the Katsuras with little to do but shrink into their seats.

Then it caused a commotion when they found out that Natsuki's future in-laws were planning to come to Chitose Funabashi bearing traditional symbolic betrothal gifts known as *yuino*. "Yokohama" begged off, judging this bit of ceremony unnecessary, and Yuji himself was all for skipping it, but his mother, in whose veins flowed the blood of hidebound traditionalists, overruled him. The formalities must be observed. Yuji had already been to the Katsura house, and everyone had more or less assumed that one day his parents would come over too, but the pomp of the occasion took them aback—all the more so as the two families had already met over dinner. To the Katsuras, the ancient Japanese tradition seemed out of keeping with a wedding between two devotees of Western music. Their sense of incongruity marked the first of many jolts they would receive during the course of their association with the Shimazakis.

At least the house in Chitose Funabashi had been rebuilt—that much was a relief. Natsuki had visited the Shimazaki home in an upscale residential district near Shibuya several times. Having spent two years in Germany, she was disdainful of Japanese living space in general and did not hesitate to make her feelings known. "That house of theirs is nothing grand!" This declaration did not, however, make their own house any grander.

The Shimazaki home was full of antiques. It stood on three hundred *tsubo* of land, not sixty-eight like the Chitose Funabashi house, and the classically landscaped garden boasted a reconstructed teahouse that had once belonged to a feudal lord famous for his appreciation of the tea ceremony. The three women tried looking at their newly rebuilt house as it might appear to the Shimazakis and lost heart. What to do? Replacing the still-new dining room table and sofa for the sake of this onetime visit would be ridiculous. They decided finally that the most effective way to improve the decor would be to replace the curtains with heavy drapes. Having neither the time nor the money to get them custom-made, they decided to sew them themselves and also make some throw cushions trimmed with the same material to scatter on the sofa.

They worked night and day to get ready. One day, their mother looked up from her sewing machine and said, "You know what? If the neighbors spread fertilizer that day, it'll be a disaster."

The family next door still had fields to tend and occasionally spread fertilizer on them. When that happened, the odor was intense even with the windows shut. They had long since switched over from night soil to chemical fertilizer, but all the same, the smell was pungent and persistent. Since Mitsuki was always the one sent over to buy their vegetables, she knew them well, and so it fell to her to call on them, explain the situation, and ask them politely not to spread fertilizer on the big day.

"Natsuki's gettin' hitched, is she?"

Mitsuki nodded. When she was a little girl, this man used to come over with his manure buckets and scoop up excrement from their household to take home. Come to think of it, that smell they all used to wrinkle their noses at had been partly of their own making.

"Who's the lucky guy?"

"He's a musician, and a whole lot richer than we are."

The neighbor in a straw hat with a towel wrapped around his neck owned various plots of farmland in Chitose Funabashi. He must have been pretty rich himself.

"Well, how about that," he said. "That's great. Congratulations. We'll sure miss her piano playing." When Natsuki practiced piano as a little girl, his three daughters sometimes used to stick their heads out of the window overlooking the field and listen.

When the day came, they laid out new slippers for the guests and served special tea with salted cherry blossoms. Besides a decorated envelope containing a wad of betrothal money, among the *yuino* gifts was a bizarre assortment of objects that ancient Japanese had apparently thought auspicious, including clam shells, dried kelp, and hemp thread. The array of objects laid on stands of unvarnished wood, symbolizing purity in Shintoism, made the family feel strange—almost as if they themselves were now connected to the unbroken line of Japanese emperors. Even Natsuki's father, who normally derided such ancient customs as nonsense, accepted the gifts with a show of solemnity.

Soon came the day of the wedding. Although Yuji was the second son, Natsuki still was marrying a Shimazaki. The ceremony and reception at the Imperial Hotel were not the only extravagance. His parents built the newlyweds a house in Kamiyama-cho, not far from the family home in Shibuya. To install Natsuki's battered old upright Yamaha in such a house was unthinkable, so her parents included a grand piano in her dowry. Also, despite their growing suspicion that kimono might soon become mere relics of bygone days, they outfitted her with one for every occasion: a formal black *tomesode*, worn only by married women; several semiformal *homongi*, worn on visits; and two mourning kimono, one in heavy *habutae* silk and one in summery silk gauze, since death knows no season. For each kimono there was a matching obi. In keeping with the grandeur of the occasion, Natsuki appeared in her wedding dress at the reception and then changed twice into long-sleeved *furisode*, one of which, resplendent with silver and gold embroidery, was borrowed from Auntie. Shimazaki guests outnumbered Katsura guests two to one, even though to keep up appearances and spare the Shimazakis the embarrassment of taking a bride from a family with no connections, Natsuki's father had swallowed his pride and prevailed upon some of his relatives, who generally held themselves a little aloof, to attend.

Money should be spent on oneself and not on social obligations: this was an article of faith in the Katsura family, yet Natsuki's wedding violated all their rules. After she was married and gone, nobody could say how much was left in the investment fund that Auntie had given strict orders never to touch.

Standing in a pool of balmy spring sunshine folding laundry with her mother, Mitsuki repeated, "We're stone broke."

There was a short silence during which she kept her eyes down, matching socks by color—brown, dark blue, gray—before her mother's voice rang out firmly from across the table: "I'll borrow the money from Auntie. Overseas travel doesn't cost a fortune anymore, the way it used to. We can pay it back in no time."

She must have been doing mental calculations. After Father's business failed, his fluent English had helped him land a job at a well-established corporation where he earned a good salary even though he was starting his career over. She herself still worked for Auntie, however much she grumbled that as fewer people wore kimono anymore, the business had no future. The family income remained decent. Mitsuki looked up.

"Only for a year," her mother said. "You need to settle down."

Mitsuki was used to unequal treatment. She couldn't believe she was going to be allowed to study abroad. As she stood there not knowing what to say, her mother continued, "And no singing lessons. I hate to be the one to say it, but with your voice, they won't lead to anything. As long as you're going to study abroad, learn French."

"Can I really go?" she finally asked. She herself did not think her singing would ever lead to anything. She sensed that she sang merely because she was carried away with the pleasure of being a "pretty young thing." Her mother's voice was far richer.

Her mother nodded. "If you know French, you can earn money translating. Articles from fashion magazines, say." Sensing Mitsuki's lack of enthusiasm, she added, "Or novels."

"Maybe someday." Mitsuki forced a smile and looked down. Having sorted all her father's socks into pairs, she began to roll them into balls. Her heart flooded with gratitude toward her mother for making such a generous promise without so much as consulting her father. The words "thank you" rose in her throat, but she quickly swallowed them. Despite her genuine gratitude, lingering resentment surfaced once again. She knew without being told that Natsuki, after all she had cost their parents, had never said a word of thanks. She, Mitsuki, was no poor stepchild; it struck her as odd that she alone should express appreciation. She continued working, face down.

"You generally do as you please," her mother said. "And you hardly ever complain."

She said nothing.

"That's why I've let you take a backseat to your sister, without really meaning to."

This attempt at an excuse only inflamed her resentment. The door to her memories opened wide. Scene after scene rose in her mind's eye, starting from early childhood. Though she had intended to say thank you, the words that slipped out were petulant: "Never mind. I'm used to it by now." The sound of her own words hardened her heart still more. She kept moving her hands busily without looking up.

Her mother said softly, "I'm sorry, Mitsuki."

Perhaps then, for the first time, her mother decided to do something to make up for all the previous unfairness. Just a month or so ago, while Natsuki was off being fitted for her wedding dress in a high-end bridal shop in Aoyama, she, Mitsuki, had been seated at a sewing machine, spreading out cloth she had picked up at a bargain sale at a craft store in Shinjuku, clumsily sewing a gown to wear at the *chansonnier*. To her sister's gala wedding she had worn a hand-me-down kimono.

Having always been left to her own devices, she had at some point learned to fit into the adult world, a world where as a young girl she had value. She was by no means dissatisfied with her life. Her father had been a literary young man, though circumstances had forced him to enter the corporate world; he had no use for the constraints of corporate life and believed that art was best for his girls. Growing up in such a home had afforded her considerable freedom. She was grateful, and well aware that in the eyes of others she had had a privileged upbringing. Yet now for the first time it was clear to her that in fact, the difference in treatment between her sister and her had always rankled more than she had ever let on even to herself.

She did not know then that her festering resentment would pave the way for her marriage to Tetsuo, whom she was to meet in Paris. She kept looking down, making no attempt to hide her intransigence from her mother.

"What else could I do? You know how Natsuki is." Her mother conveniently shut her eyes to the role her own driving passion had played in making Natsuki the way she was.

Probably her mother's mind had opened to the possibility of her, Mitsuki, going to Paris because Natsuki's time in Germany had not proven a total waste after all. Her father had been somewhat concerned about what Mitsuki was doing with her life and quickly added his approval. Rather than have her live in a dormitory or a single apartment, they arranged for her to stay with a proper French family, to guard against the same sort of indiscretion happening again. Her father consulted an American he had befriended while in the import-export business, a man who then, whether as a skilled negotiator or merely someone prone to exaggeration, let on to his French acquaintances that Mr. Katsura was highborn and had founded an impressive enterprise (the failed export business). As in a game of telephone, details were blown out of proportion. In short order, a French family offered to take in Mitsuki, with the proviso that "we're not sure we're qualified to look after such a fine young lady." They had one daughter who was shy, they said, and a bookworm. They declined payment, but the Katsuras insisted on covering at least the cost of Mitsuki's meals. Her hosts lived in a house in Saint-Cloud, on the western outskirts of Paris, beyond the Seine. Only after Mitsuki arrived did she realize that this was a highly sought-after residential area.

"I'm so jealous," said Natsuki, watching her pack. "If I'd had the choice, I'd have gone to Paris too."

Hearing this, Mitsuki felt strangely content, as if she had come out ahead.

Behind Natsuki's back, her mother said, "If you must have a romance, make sure it's with someone you can marry, will you please? And he's got to be Japanese. I can't speak any other language."

Apparently, as far as her mother was concerned, Westerners should stay in the world of the silver screen where they belonged. Mitsuki shrugged off her mother's words. The notion that they might be prophetic never crossed her mind.

And so one day under an autumn sky, Mitsuki set off for Paris.

# 18

## UNDER A NEW SKY

Paris took Mitsuki by surprise, and not just because the finely articulated cityscape lined with sandstone seemed so beautiful after Tokyo's busy clutter. She was surprised to see so many Japanese people. Early modern Japanese literature made it seem as if only scions of wealthy families—people who in the old days would have had a title—might be found wandering the streets of Paris. But times had apparently changed.

Of East Asians then living in Paris, the preponderance were Vietnamese from the former French colony; the next largest contingent consisted of some of the world's Chinese. Most of these immigrants worked in Vietnamese or Chinese restaurants. The only Asians who traveled halfway around the globe just to visit Paris were Japanese, and few of them had much of a family pedigree. Many came just to shop. The avenue de l'Opéra, on the Right Bank of the Seine, was inundated with so many shopping-mad tourists that it was known as *l'avenue des Japonais*. Others came to study. The Latin Quarter on the Left Bank was roamed by Japanese students, most of whom were from families less well off than Mitsuki's—the children of local government employees, schoolteachers, and small shop owners.

The reasons for this shift were many. Airfare had become more affordable, and Japan was the first East Asian country to enjoy relative prosperity. Besides, going overseas for language study wasn't nearly as daunting as going to study music. The latter required years of formal training starting in early childhood, but no such barrier existed for language study. And so, even if it meant scrimping to send one's offspring an allowance, Japan had embarked on an era when studying in France was open even to those of modest means.

The days when France was "so very far away," as one Japanese poet wistfully wrote, were themselves now very far away.

"*Ojosan.*" Young lady. Someone addressed her this way in Japanese as soon as class was over on the first day she set foot in the Alliance Française. "I reckon you just got here," he went on, speaking in Osaka dialect, which to Tokyo ears always sounds a bit comical.

While feeling with some embarrassment that at nearly twenty-five she was hardly young enough to be called *ojosan* anymore, Mitsuki found his manner sufficiently winning that she accompanied him to the school coffee shop, where other students from Japan sat in a circle. The air, thick with smoke from cheap Gauloise cigarettes, stung her eyes and nose. There was none of the earnestness she used to feel at the *chansonnier*; this was more like a gathering of idlers who had more time than they knew what to do with. Most of them were male—whether because few families could afford to send a daughter overseas or because doing so was too worrisome, she wasn't sure. In this easygoing crowd, she alone felt tense.

"Say hi to Mitsuki Katsura," the boy who had invited her said by way of introduction, and another boy commented that it was a nice name. He spoke standard Japanese.

"Where ya from?" asked the boy who had invited her.

"Tokyo."

"Yeah? Whereabouts?"

"Chitose Funabashi."

"Funabashi? Hold on, that's in Chiba, isn't it?"

He had mixed up the name of her hometown with that of a similar-sounding city in a nearby, decidedly unposh, prefecture. She smiled. "No, it's in Setagaya Ward."

A flurry arose.

"Wow, didja hear that? Setagaya!"

"Yeah, where all the bigwigs hang out. Politicians and entertainers and such."

"Wow!"

After graduating from elementary school, Mitsuki, like Natsuki before her, had gone on to a private girls' school in the same ward. Even after that, most of her girlfriends in the private college that she'd attended had grown up in a similar environment. But no one talked about "Setagaya Ward"; instead they spoke of particular towns within the ward—Kaminoge, Fukazawa, Kyodo—and everyone knew that Chitose Funabashi didn't sound nearly as nice as the others. At the *chansonnier* too, even people who were not from Tokyo had been familiar with the city and its neighborhoods. There in the Alliance Française in the middle of Paris, she felt less that she had left Japan behind than that she had stepped out of Tokyo.

From that day on she'd been marked as a girl of privilege, when on the other side of the earth she had been caught up in her family's desperate attempt to keep up appearances before the Shimazakis. Now, under the Parisian sky, she was transformed. Her staying with a French family in the premier residential district of Saint-Cloud only reinforced that impression in everyone's mind.

Her host family was not particularly wealthy, and their house was one of the smaller ones in town, yet to Mitsuki it seemed impossibly luxurious. Their bay window was spacious and deep, unlike the poor excuse for one in her house back in Japan. She felt like a fairytale princess. While her compatriots lived in tiny garrets with communal showers that had no hot water to speak of, she enjoyed a comfortable room with a spacious private bathroom where she could soak her skinny self in a hot tub, playing with clouds of foam like a glamorous movie star. As night came on and the others gravitated to the student cafeteria, shoulders hunched in the evening chill, or returned to their dark roosts to cook a solitary meal, Mitsuki sat at a dining room table lit by a chandelier with a cloth napkin on her lap, tucking into a meal served in courses, beginning with hors d'oeuvres and ending with dessert—a nightly routine that, to her astonishment, never varied.

The difference between her lifestyle and that of the others was only too plain. At dinnertime she would leave the students, still clustered together, to return to her home in the suburbs like a sheltered girl with a curfew. The occasional weekend she spent with her host family at their Breton country house overlooking the English Channel, traveling to and fro by car, seemed the ultimate in grand living. No matter how she explained to the others that her family was paying only the cost of her meals, the message didn't sink in. They preferred to go on seeing her through the lens of class prejudice.

Then Natsuki and Yuji came for a visit. Anyone could see they were rich.

To top it all, when asked what she had done after college, she answered with well-founded hesitation, and somehow the word spread that she had been a stage actress or a singer. The absence of rumors that she'd been a film actress showed, to her rueful amusement, that rumors have their limits after all. Film actresses had to be beautiful.

But though she was no beauty and, at nearly twenty-five, past her prime by the standards of the day, circumstances had conspired to allow her to be here in Paris, the world's fairest city, for her life's season of ripening cherries—and with an unexpected aura of glamour. Japanese boys clustered around her as if they considered falling in love a sine qua non of their sojourn in the City of Light. They vied with each other to see her off to her train station.

Take that, Mom.

If only her mother, who had offered such condescending commiseration on her looks, could see the puppy-love expressions on those young men's faces!

A young woman who is entranced with herself casts a spell on men of every nationality and race. She attracts glances. By the time Mitsuki had shed the fish-out-of-water look of a traveler, she would walk down the street and young men would call out to her. Coolly hiding her pleasure, she passed them swiftly by. All Paris seemed to whisper in her ear, *Time for love!* and she felt as if she were waltzing on clouds. It wasn't long before all the attention became bothersome and made her reluctant to linger long in a café.

When cherries ripen, the heads of "pretty young things" fill with folly. Mitsuki's own youth and femininity went straight to her head. And yet, as her twenty-fifth birthday drew near, she was, strictly speaking, no longer a "pretty young thing."

One day, lying on her side in bed, she casually laid her right hand on her belly and found her navel was no longer in the center. Though overall she was as skinny as ever, her middle had expanded slightly and her navel, faithfully following the law of gravity, had shifted somewhat in the direction of the floor. She turned over experimentally on her other side, and the same thing happened again. The expression "out of shape" took on vivid clarity in her mind.

At the same time, this vexing discovery meant that her head was no longer filled with the frothy visions of a "pretty young thing" but had matured to a certain extent. She remained entranced with herself, but that was far from all. She was now able to observe the outside world. The city of Paris came to her as a revelation, as it had to countless Japanese visitors since the country's awakening to the West a century ago. During solitary rides on the train, bus, or Métro, while sitting in a café or strolling down an avenue, her thoughts were of Paris. She took to wondering how she might possibly extend her stay in the beautiful city. Only then did it sink in that she was not self-supporting.

Fall ended and winter set in. She was sitting one day in a café talking to a Japanese youth who had become her frequent companion—Tetsuo. "Some girls become prostitutes on the sly," he was saying, "just to keep from going back to Japan."

Her eyes widened. "Seriously?"

"Yep."

"Compared to that, surely it would be better to go back to Japan!"

"The trouble is, they don't want to. And anyone who would do such a thing is guaranteed to have a hard time supporting herself if she does go back."

Mitsuki had been trying to work out how someone like her might possibly stay on in Paris and be financially independent. In front of her was a pot of herb tea called *vervaine*—lemon verbena—the very tea which she had often come across in French novels and wondered how it tasted. She ordered it in cafés just for the fun of saying "*vervaine*." In front of Tetsuo was a cup of espresso, the cheapest drink on the menu.

"Anyway, at least Japanese people have a country to go home to. Some people don't even have that." He added with finality, "The trouble with you, Mitsuki, is you don't know what's going on in the world. You've got so much to learn." He was smoking a Gauloise.

Winter days in Paris were short. Mornings were still dark at eight, when she left the house, and by a little after three in the afternoon, darkness again set in. Day after day, the sky hung like a thick gray curtain, barely penetrated by the sun's faint rays. The air was bitingly cold.

# 19

## CITY OF MIRACLES

"You've got a lot to learn." Every time Tetsuo saw Mitsuki, he told her this, and, with a meekness that in retrospect seemed ludicrous, she would feel ashamed of her ignorance.

Before winter set in with determination, Mitsuki had transferred from the language school to the Sorbonne, where she enrolled in a course on French civilization for foreign students. She became friends with a short-haired, boyish-looking girl named Masako, who was studying on a Rotary scholarship, and would often sit in a café with her and chat. Mitsuki was hardly ever alone with any of the male Japanese students. Japanese girls being scarce, they flocked around as she sat with Masako, and she preferred it that way. It was only sometime after New Year's that she often found herself talking alone with Tetsuo.

Two years her senior, Tetsuo was a *boursier*—a student on a fellowship from the French government—just entering his third year in Paris.

Japanese students in France generally were of two kinds: those paying their own way, and, far fewer in number, the elite *boursiers*. The two groups had little to do with one another. The former included students lacking even basic conversational French. The *boursiers*, who after passing a demanding examination had come to France with high expectations, held themselves apart from the rank and file. They were the university professors of tomorrow.

Tetsuo was something of a maverick in that crowd. Despite being in Paris, the city of miracles, most of the others merely trudged from library to garret and back again. Young though they were, they were as fusty as their books, and although they lived in Paris they might as well have been anywhere else. Tetsuo was different. He was definitely in Paris.

Paris had many faces.

For the Gypsy woman wearing a headscarf with a baby on her hip and a cup in her outstretched hand, begging for coins, it was surely not a welcoming face. Nor was the city kind to immigrant workers returning to their cocoons on the eastern outskirts, pressing their exhausted, swarthy faces against the windows of crowded buses. And with the French language still riding high, neither was Paris tolerant of travelers unable to *parler français*.

Parisians and Parisiennes scurried to and fro looking irritable. The Métro was dark and dirty, and the labyrinthine cavern one had to pass through to change trains reeked of ammonia, the smell of concentrated urine. Only a short way from the city center stood modernist square buildings, bleak, deteriorating, and devoid of charm.

Urban blight was everywhere.

And yet for Mitsuki, living the life of a fairytale princess, Paris let its most beautiful face shine. Everyone in her host family was extraordinarily kind. Her plump host father was silently kind. Her plump host mother called her "*ma petite japonaise*" and was chattily kind. Their book-loving daughter helped her memorize French poems. "*Sous le pont Mirabeau coule la Seine*" began one by Apollinaire, and indeed the bank of the Seine as it meandered west of Paris was only a short walk away. Far in the distance she could see the Eiffel Tower.

What she loved the most was the way the family's daily life bespoke a living, unbroken continuity with the past. The house was new, built after the war, but many details of its design reflected traditional French architecture: the graceful curves on the newel post at the foot of the stairs in the entrance hall; the arched doorway of the drawing room; the vintage fireplace in a corner, topped by a large gilt-edged mirror. Items throughout the house were redolent of history. The carved wooden furniture in her bedroom—a bed, desk, and wardrobe brought from their country house in Brittany—was over a century old. And the family's life maintained ties to the lives of past generations. For an evening meal with company they lit candelabra on the dining room table, and after a glass or two of wine, Mitsuki was hard-pressed to tell whether this was the twentieth century or the nineteenth—or even earlier. The daughter had modern tastes, so there was a scattering of contemporary bric-a-brac that blended into the traditional decor to oddly pleasing effect.

Mitsuki's wonderment at the family's way of living was inseparable from her wonderment at the city.

The Paris that she discovered hardly resembled the Paris that chansons had led her to envision. As evening came on, the streetlamps on Alexandre III Bridge would light up, magically transforming the bridge into a shimmering palace in midair; Notre Dame Cathedral was majestic from a distance, delicate close up; and seen from Montmartre at night, the incomparable capital appeared strewn with thousands of stars fallen all at once from the sky. Yet behind that romantic exterior lay a Paris that was prosaic to the core. More than prosaic, it was solid and dependable, like the sandstone buildings that lined its streets.

The world of chansons teemed with lovers, embracing *la vie en rose* or killing themselves one "gloomy Sunday"; nameless poets and winsome seamstresses; harbor prostitutes, scoundrels, and beggars who slept under bridges. The actual Paris afforded fewer glimpses of such romantic figures than it did of stern-faced bureaucrats and city planners with outspread blueprints, putting their grown-up heads together to pool their wisdom. Parisians were said to have lamented the loss of the twisting, medieval byways that once branched out in all directions, yet the concerted efforts of many had resulted in a city where the past was not unthinkingly destroyed, but what deserved to be saved was saved—and what needed to be made new was made new. People had combined their wits to make the most of changes wrought in years past, sometimes through repeated bloodshed, and create a city of miracles. Terms such as "history," "civilization," and "accumulated knowledge" that had hitherto seemed mere abstractions took on concrete significance in ways she could see, touch, and smell.

Mitsuki mulled Paris's good fortune in not being a city of the Far East, and France's good fortune in never having experienced the kind of cultural shock and disjunction that countries on the other side of the world had to face upon encountering the West. How many Japanese, following their country's opening in the Meiji period, had come to Paris and returned to their remote archipelago with bittersweet memories?

Students from Japan, whether self-sponsored or *boursier*, inevitably included some who took it upon themselves to rebel against Paris and disparage it. "It's a stone prison," they would say, or "It's cold, like the people," or "It's artificial and stifling. You can't smell the earth."

Tetsuo was different. He liked Paris. And just by virtue of being there, he seemed to have undergone a physical transformation, turning into someone visibly in tune with the city. His clothes were tasteful, and like the French students he would casually wrap a narrow scarf around his neck and carry a slim leather briefcase. Moreover, he had the height and the features to carry off the look. That he himself was aware of all this in no way detracted from the effect, but made it all the more agreeable.

When did it start? Before she knew it, he was always around. At first he would sit in some unobtrusive spot when they all went to a café together. After a while he took to sitting near her, then in the seat beside her. Unlike most *boursiers*, he was not too proud to mingle with the other students, and he seemed to have endless free time. Looking back, it was evident that this was because he spent little time in the library, but at the time this elementary deduction escaped her.

Soon he would invite her on walks. They strolled almost every day through the quaint little streets north of boulevard Saint-Germain, a route she never tired of. Rue Jacob. Rue Fürstenberg. Rue Bonaparte. Surprisingly, there were hardly any tourists.

Like a receding tide, the other male students melted away, leaving, besides Tetsuo, only the boyish Masako. From time to time, Mitsuki told her host family she wouldn't be home for dinner. Tetsuo cooked for her himself in his garret, wearing a dishcloth slung low around his hips for an apron. Such attic spaces, with a skylight in the slanting ceiling, had once housed servants before being rented out to the poor, including artists and students. With the Latin Quarter often beyond their means, many Japanese students in those days lived like Tetsuo, occupying a shabby garret a little removed from the heart of the city.

Naturally, as Mitsuki and Tetsuo spent more time together in the garret, they exchanged more than mere words and looks. He was not Mitsuki's first lover, but he had apparently had a number of older women as lovers in the past from whom he had learned a great deal; his manner was skilled. When Mitsuki reacted with some surprise, he said with a straight face, "As I've been saying, you have a lot to learn." She doubled over in laughter on the narrow bed.

For someone who was always trying to enlighten her, he was no saint. Even this discovery increased her regard for him.

She loved best climbing the stairs to his dingy garret. There were six flights, dim even in the daytime, leading to the top. French people were so thrifty that even if you switched on the stair light, it turned off automatically every time you went up a flight of stairs, so you had to switch it on again at each level. As she mounted the stone steps, surrounded above and below by darkness, her high heels clattering, she would feel a welling excitement. The higher the floor that residents lived on, the more impoverished they were—and the closer to the stars. The closer to the stars they lived, the bigger their dreams must be.

That's how it seemed to her.

*Si, mi chiamano Mimi.* Yes, they call me Mimi. Sometimes she would imitate her mother and softly sing the old aria. To any onlooker she was just another flat-faced girl from the Far East, but in her own mind, she felt like the little Parisian seamstress of a century ago.

"I feel like Mimi." When she first set foot in Tetsuo's attic room and told him this, for once she became the teacher, enlightening him about Puccini's opera *La bohème*, how it was set in the Latin Quarter where poverty-stricken artists, musicians, and philosophers lived; how even though the characters could hardly pay their rent, they were constantly building castles in the air. Mimi's lover Rodolfo, a penniless poet, lived in carefree poverty with the soul of a millionaire.

As she explained the key role a candle played in the lovers' meeting, they decided to celebrate her birthday with a candlelit dinner.

Mitsuki's twenty-fifth birthday came with the advent of spring.

## (20)

## THE PROPOSAL IN THE GARRET

She didn't let on to her host family that it was her birthday. They were so good-hearted that she felt conscience-stricken just telling them she wouldn't be home for dinner and couldn't bring herself to say she would be celebrating her birthday out. She left the house not knowing that Tetsuo had chosen that day to propose.

Young though she still was, climbing six flights of stairs in high-heeled boots hadn't been easy, but as she visualized the lighted candle on the table above, she felt as thrilled as if she truly were mounting to the stars.

She knocked, and a moment later the door opened. She caught her breath. She had pictured a single taper on the small table, but candles were everywhere—the floor, the windowsill, the bookshelf—their tiny flames swaying and dancing. The sight was magical; she felt faint.

Throughout the meal she was in a trance. At the end when he served her a steaming cup of lemon verbena tea, she little imagined that the coming revelations would mark a turning point in her life.

It began when Tetsuo's face stiffened. "There's a job waiting for me in Japan," he said. His eyes held hers as he leaned toward a candle flame, an unlit Gauloise between his lips. "In Tokyo."

Only then did it strike her that he had been quieter than usual during the meal.

"Starting when?"

"This fall."

She was relieved. If it could wait till the fall, then that would be around the time she too went back to Japan—assuming she went back.

"What are you going to do?"

"I thought I'd take it." He kept his eyes fixed on her face.

She was a little distressed. The idea of marrying him had occurred to her. She had imagined, however, that it would mean staying on in Paris a while longer. She would move into his garret, and they would sleep together in the narrow bed close to the stars and eat baguettes and cheese, scrimping so they could get by if her parents helped—which they would hardly refuse to do if she married a Japanese scholar in the making. But if he had a job lined up in Tokyo, then marrying him would mean leaving Paris. She felt torn. She didn't want to be separated from him, yet part of her wanted to stay on where she was. Seeing her distress, he began to explain.

A special delivery letter had come from a professor he knew well, someone whose name Mitsuki was familiar with as it appeared rather often in the media. The professor would be leaving his post at a national university at the end of March to create a new faculty of international studies at a private university. His first order of business was to assemble a team of teachers. Though details were not yet clear, Tetsuo would probably be asked to teach French—the language, not the literature—among other subjects. If that condition was acceptable to him, he was welcome to join the team. He would start as an assistant lecturer, but would soon be promoted and receive tenure.

Thinking it over later, Mitsuki realized that that professor had known Tetsuo much better than she did. Tetsuo wasn't a born scholar and had no particular urge to pursue a single discipline, whether French literature or something else. On the other hand, his willingness and ability to adapt to whatever was required of him would be a great asset in starting up a new faculty.

She thought a moment and then inquired innocently, "Shouldn't you go ahead and finish your doctorate?" In the back of her mind was the face of her father, who surely would have become a scholar if his family had not suffered financial ruin.

"No," said Tetsuo with finality. "I'm in my third year, and the thesis is going nowhere."

She had always assumed that the reason he didn't talk about his thesis was that he thought it would be over her head. She hadn't known he was stuck. No wonder he had so much time to spend with her.

"Besides," he said, "a doctorate is no guarantee of finding a job in Tokyo." He lowered his eyes, rubbed out his cigarette, and added in a low voice, "If I couldn't get a job in Tokyo, you wouldn't marry me, would you?"

This was the first time he had ever said the word "marry." Her pulse quickened; flustered, she didn't know what to say. The silence between them lengthened. The glowing candles made shadows on the walls, marking the silent passage of time.

Eventually Tetsuo looked up. "I'm not from a good family." His dark tone took her by surprise. His face looked grim in the candlelight.

"My family is nothing to brag about either," she responded, her tone purposefully light.

More than once she had explained to Masako and him too that her family was by no means wealthy, that her current situation and her sister's marrying into money had both come about purely by chance. She didn't want the two people closest to her to misunderstand. But to what extent they did understand, she had no way of knowing.

"It's worse than that." He sounded gruff.

"What do you mean?" she said. "You told me your father was a businessman."

"I exaggerated." He laughed and added in a self-mocking tone, "I didn't want you to turn against me."

"So he's not?"

Tetsuo's father was the third son of poor farmers. Though currently an accountant in his brother's plant, he was a businessman only in the broadest sense of the term. Neither he nor his brother had a head for making money, and although Japan was experiencing rapid economic growth they lagged far behind, enmeshed in poverty.

"My mother was always too thin." She would join them at the supper table, he said, but at her place there would be only chopsticks and a half-full rice bowl, as she urged his father, his younger brother, and him to eat everything. She strove to keep the family presentable and sewed his father's old underwear into underthings for herself. Tetsuo earned top grades and on his teacher's recommendation applied for and got into a selective high school, but then more of his friends were of good family: sometimes, having nothing fit to wear to Parents' Day and realizing how embarrassed he would be, she would go off by herself and cry.

Tetsuo continued speaking in a detached tone of voice. Her people were poor farmers too, and at one point she'd been obliged to take in her much younger brothers. The room he and his brother shared with their uncles got so crowded that he'd had to move his desk out into the hallway to do his homework.

By the end of his high school years, his uncle's plant had finally started to ride the tide of Japan's high economic growth. From then on things went smoothly. The family even had a little money to spare. His mother gained weight, and the house was rebuilt. But apart from Tetsuo, no one in the family had ever been to college.

When he went back home, the scenery changed year by year but the topics of conversation never varied: ups and downs of the high school baseball team, marriages and deaths, who knew and who didn't know their proper places at Buddhist memorial services. He felt stifled and wanted nothing more than to leave that world far behind.

His father never went beyond elementary school under the old system. His mother graduated from senior elementary school and was somewhat more of a reader than his father. She'd wanted Tetsuo to go to university, but his father's reaction had been less than enthusiastic. And so when a low math score kept him from getting into the University of Tokyo, rather than taking a year off to bone up for the examination he had gone to a national university that specialized in languages (one of a handful of institutions a rank below the most prestigious schools) for fear that otherwise his father would balk at his attending college at all. When he said he wanted to go to graduate school, there'd been more trouble, his younger brother having already finished vocational school and gone to work for their uncle. Their normally placid father was incredulous and irate: "You're telling me a college graduate hasn't had enough of being a student?" His mother's tearful pleas on his behalf carried enough weight that he was able to enter graduate school, but he resolved at the time to make a drastic leap, fearing that otherwise he would never escape.

"So after I got into grad school, I studied like a maniac to be a *boursier.*"

His efforts paid off. In his second year, just as he was getting his master's degree, he passed the competitive test and set off in the fall for Paris.

Mitsuki kept her eyes fastened on him as he talked. This Tetsuo was different from the one she knew so well. Normally he acted vaguely condescending toward her, but now his face was pale and stiff as he talked on. She saw his cheek twitch.

In a voice barely audible, he swore to her that if she married him, she would never want for anything. He was the elder son, but she would never have to look after his parents in their old age. If his tradition-bound relatives criticized her, he would defend her. He must have sensed that his constant reminders about how much she needed to learn had spurred her to think about graduate school; he promised that if she decided to go, he would give her unstinting emotional and financial support.

On that day, Tetsuo had been earnestly in love with her. Until then she had never thought he loved her that much. Seeing him that day, she herself fell gloriously in love. And promised to marry him.

Still pale, Tetsuo pressed the point: "You're sure somebody like me is good enough?"

Her cheeks might have flushed pink when she answered: "I'm sure. Somebody like you will do just fine."

She felt as if all the candles in the room had burst into song, serenading them with "L'hymne à l'amour."

# 21

## THE SISTERS' CONTRASTING FATES

That night, ignoring the risk of missing the last train back, Tetsuo escorted her home as far as the front gate. Her host mother, having quickly spotted her flushed cheeks, soon let out a joyful "*Oh la la!*" and in no time the entire household was in an uproar. Her host father brought up a bottle of champagne from the basement, chilled it rapidly in ice water, and together they drank a toast.

Things happened fast after that.

Mitsuki had inherited her mother's ability to get things done. She sat down and wrote a long letter to her parents explaining everything, including Tetsuo's family background—careful to emphasize that his married younger brother worked in the family company and lived at home with his parents in the old-fashioned way, so she wouldn't have to look after her in-laws in their old age.

"If it's all right with both of you, I think we'll just register the marriage at the Japanese embassy here." Writing the words, she felt so proud she could have danced on tiptoe. The hoopla surrounding her sister's wedding was still fresh in her mind. Above all she remembered the peculiar closeness that had developed between her mother and sister. Natsuki's sulks on coming back from Freiburg had all but been forgotten as, clearly on the best of terms, mother and daughter went on jaunts to shop for her trousseau. Mitsuki, who was sometimes pressed into service to help carry things, had been excited at her sister's Cinderella marriage. Yet seeing her mother eagerly examine the luster of gold thread in a purse held out reverently by a uniformed clerk, glance at the price tag, and ponder the cost, her younger daughter's existence totally forgotten, she'd felt her load of shopping bags grow heavier. The old hurt came flooding back, along with something close to a resolution that when she married, it would all be different. She'd felt alienated from her sister, perhaps even a bit contemptuous of her for living her life under the perennial sway of their mother's passions. The letter she penned to her parents doubtless overflowed with pride in her having chosen her own path in life, unlike her sister.

Her mother quickly wrote back: "You're a smart girl. Your father and I trust your judgment."

That June, after registering their marriage at the embassy with Masako as witness, she and Tetsuo traveled through Europe on the cheap with money her parents sent them as a wedding gift. Then they went back to Japan, and she presented him to her family. What he may have thought on discovering that just as she had said, her family wasn't wealthy, she had no idea.

Her parents were well content with her Paris souvenir. "He's handsome, and he's got quite a way with him, doesn't he?" Neither of them was concerned about his family background. Her father was a progressive who disapproved of worrying about a person's antecedents, and her mother had probably had more than enough of extravagant in-laws, both financially and emotionally. Anyway, they doubtless took Tetsuo's having studied in Paris as a sign that his family, even if not "good," was good enough. His table manners passed muster: he ate his soup without slurping and wound his spaghetti neatly around his fork.

When they finally met Tetsuo's family, she and her parents were somewhat dismayed. The phrase *"He's the one that matters"* began to pop up in their conversations. The families had little opportunity to get together after that, but what gatherings there were sparked guarded murmurs on the Katsura side: "Not exactly sophisticates, are they?" And after the arrival of a gift, someone would moan, "What on earth do we *do* with it?" But not even her mother ever breathed a criticism of Tetsuo.

The following spring, Mitsuki did enroll in graduate school. She chose the French department of a fine private university once famous for the freewheeling ways of its literature students—a far cry from the genteel, urbane college she had attended before. She had no intention of ever pursuing a scholarly career. But having done little more than amuse herself by singing in the *chansonnier* and reading every novel within reach, she was determined to raise herself at least to Tetsuo's level. She also thought that mastering French might one day help their budget. She could easily afford the tuition using money she earned as an English tutor for high school students, and with hand-me-downs from her mother and sister for the taking, she wouldn't need to buy any new clothes.

When Natsuki saw French books lining the shelves in the cheap rental apartment where the newlyweds lived, she said enviously, "You're so lucky."

"Lucky? We're as poor as church mice."

Mitsuki had felt jubilant. And on that happy note, her life's season of ripening cherries drew to a close. If only time could have stopped there...

Family troubles soon intruded on her idyllic life. To begin with, Natsuki spun out of control.

She seemed happy Mitsuki was back, but signs of her growing dissatisfaction with married life showed on her face, which always all too transparently betrayed her emotions. It wasn't that her marriage was a disaster. Far from it. Yuji played in Japan's top-rated orchestra. Jun, their first child, had come along in short order. The young couple and their baby lived near his parents, not with them, so there were no in-laws on hand to grumble if Natsuki chose to forgo cooking and instead visit the food court in the basement of a Shibuya department store every night to pick up ready-made dishes from famous Kyoto restaurants. She took on a few pupils as well, so she enjoyed the status of being a piano teacher. She led a life of seeming elegance and ease. And yet she was unhappy.

She felt isolated in the Shimazaki family. It wasn't only that they set great store by ceremonial social functions such as twice-yearly seasonal gift giving and visits to the family grave at the proper times. That much she could have borne. Nor was their love of golf a problem in itself, or the way on New Year's Eve they sat around the television watching the tedious year-end songfest from beginning to end. The trouble was that the world of high culture that so enthralled her mother—and that had dominated her own life—had little place in their lives. Not only high culture but anything remotely cultural seemed to leave them cold. They didn't watch current films, let alone old ones. The television was always on, never music. They read magazines but not books. Yuji's sister majored in voice at music school only because she'd taken it up in high school after lazily neglecting to practice the piano.

The family happened to produce a cellist thanks to Yuji's maternal grandfather, a lover of Western music who managed to turn Yuji (as the second son, he could pursue a career of his choice) into a classical musician. The grandfather had been a man of taste with wide interests; the collection of antiques on display in the house—including various bowls for the tea ceremony, from rustic Raku and Hagi wares to colorful Kutani—were testimony to his artistic bent, which no one else in the family seemed to share.

Not even Yuji was an exception. For the life of her, Natsuki couldn't see how the Yuji who guffawed at stupid comedy shows on television could be the same as the Yuji who set off conscientiously for rehearsals bearing his antique, Italian-made cello. She could only think that he was two different people.

She began driving to her parents' house with Jun to complain about the Shimazakis. Her mother quickly joined in, making fun of them. Having previously felt intimidated, she seemed to take glee in ridiculing their banality.

But Natsuki, possibly encouraged by her mother's attitude, didn't stop there. In no time she fell in love with a lanky architect whose hair swept diagonally across his forehead. Their romance began one spring afternoon when she had taken Jun in her stroller to Yoyogi Park to enjoy the cherry blossoms. As she was sitting on a bench in tight jeans smoking a cigarette, he had struck up a conversation with this opener: "It's better here in the daytime. At night when the rabble come out to eat and drink and carouse, it's positively sickening, don't you think?"

Before their eyes, people were securing seats for the night revelries to come. With his forelock falling at an angle, this self-styled nihilist seemed always to look askance at the world. The ridiculous thing was that one day out of the blue, Natsuki brought him home to meet her mother and broached the topic of divorce.

Natsuki's astonished mother had not been impressed with her beau. "He didn't look healthy," she told Mitsuki later. "His color was bad."

The architect had looked on with a thin smile while Natsuki, in their mother's words, "blabbered on." He worked for a small architectural firm and planned to open his own office one day. He was living with his parents temporarily because his salary was low, but he did have a steady job, and once they were married they could rent a cheap apartment somewhere. His people were in business

**140**

and fairly well off, but he didn't get along with his stepmother and didn't want to take their money. Natsuki could help out by teaching piano, but not in a cheap apartment; she wanted permission to give lessons there in the house in Chitose Funabashi.

"I'll have custody of Jun. He's okay with that," she added, proudly indicating the man with the sweeping diagonal hair whom she believed to be a genius, destined to be a world-class architect.

All her life, Natsuki had been indulged by their mother. Anything she wanted was hers—the sole exception being the fiasco in Germany. She must have dragged the architect along because she had a premonition that for once her mother would not give in easily. But she was so used to wheedling that she had no idea when she had crossed a line.

Their mother later told Mitsuki that listening to this folderol, she'd felt "so dizzy I almost fell off my chair." Since the architect was there, she'd refrained from giving vent to her shock and fury, but over the next few months, she and Natsuki had been at daggers drawn. Baby Jun was mercifully too tiny to understand any of the drama going on around her.

Their mother's greatest fear had been that Natsuki would confront Yuji directly about a divorce. But Natsuki exercised admirable restraint, knowing that if she did do such a thing she ran the risk of being cut off by her parents.

They talked in circles.

"Mother, you did the very same thing!"

"Not the same at all."

"You left the husband that 'Yokohama' found for you."

"I married him because I had no other choice."

"Well, what choice did I really have when I married Yuji? None."

"How can you look me in the face and say such a thing?"

"Because it's true!"

Then came shrieking and tears. Eventually the architect had enough and took off. The peculiar intimacy between Natsuki and her mother may have contributed to his disenchantment.

Natsuki's suicide attempt took place soon after.

Knowing when her mother would be out and when she would return, she had driven over to Chitose Funabashi with Jun and swallowed a large quantity of sleeping pills. On coming home and finding her unconscious, her mother had called an ambulance. Natsuki had taken a huge overdose, but she was found so quickly that she was able to have her stomach pumped and be released after a night in the hospital. Her mother telephoned Yuji and lied: "Natsuki's come down with a sudden high fever, probably the flu, so I'll keep her and Jun with me for a few days."

When Mitsuki was summoned to the hospital, the moment she walked in the room her mother exclaimed: "How could she do this! It's like a page from a trashy novel!"

What had Natsuki been thinking? Had years of living her life in harness to her mother's passions caused a buildup of anger that suddenly boiled over? Or was it just a way of getting back at her mother for failing to give in to her demands?

## (22)

## THE KATSURA FAMILY DISINTEGRATES

The damage to Natsuki's relationship with their mother was irreparable. Their mother took to regarding her with a cold eye, as if freed of something that had possessed her. Natsuki, the daughter she had brought up in her own image, was incapable of understanding her and all she had been through: the stigma she had borne because of her own parents, who flew in the face of propriety; her efforts to remake herself; the hope and determination she had invested in Natsuki. She as good as cut herself off emotionally from her—and yet the two of them had been so closely bound that the tie between them could never be truly severed. Their mother seemed to take a certain pleasure in overt snubs while Mitsuki, caught in the middle, had to listen to her sister's grousing.

Natsuki idealized Mitsuki's marriage, in part because she had always envied her sister's greater self-reliance.

"You can have intellectual conversations with Tetsuo, can't you?"

"More or less."

"Must be nice."

But Natsuki made no more missteps. She soon gave birth to a son, Ken. With her impulsiveness and good looks, she must have had other admirers, but there were no more upheavals. Her life stayed on an even keel as she managed to play the role of a contented housewife.

Perhaps to assuage her sense of isolation, she acquired two kittens, a brother and sister. She also became increasingly dependent on Mitsuki.

Starting from that time, their mother too had drawn closer to Mitsuki, markedly changing the dynamic among the three of them. Even so, if the Katsuras had led tranquil lives after that, Mitsuki suspected her marriage might have turned out differently.

Marrying Tetsuo may have been in part a reaction against slights, real and imagined, she had endured while growing up, but no woman's marriage is ever entirely free of family baggage. What matters is how the family situation evolves.

If only she hadn't had to put up with her mother's folly! If only that long messiness hadn't ensued — that long, vexing messiness that sapped her strength and wrapped her in meshes of woe.

Later she realized that That Man had made his appearance in her mother's life shortly after her mother became disenchanted with Natsuki.

Around then "Yokohama" too had lost its former traction with her. The fascination for all things Western that had long held the population captive had eased as Japan became rich and modernized. Her mother's yearnings for "Yokohama" had eased too. Besides, "Yokohama" was no longer what it had been. Grandpa Yokohama, who used to pet her, was gone; the much-admired Uncle Yokohama, now retired, had lost his princely good looks and even developed a paunch; Madama Butterfly, no longer Japan's top diva, had lost her flair too.

And yet the old nameless stirrings that had always driven their mother were unassuaged. She still needed some outlet for her unceasing quest for exhilaration. This was all the more apparent after she stopped working for Auntie and had more free time on her hands. Her marriage of nearly thirty years had long since cooled off.

And so in her late fifties she took up chanson lessons—and immediately started paying even more attention to her appearance. Having stopped working for Auntie, she gave up wearing kimono entirely. She seemed a notch lower in quality, somehow. At a recital she had insisted they attend, Mitsuki and her sister found that the other singers were not only younger than she, they were exactly the sort of people she would once have dismissed as "loud and flashy ladies." The event had not a speck of artistry. It seemed merely a way for rudderless women of a certain age to kill time.

That Man was the last straw.

He stood backstage dressed in a white suit, a man in his mid-forties with a habit of tossing back his long hair—the picture of affectation. Women of all ages surrounded him, fussing over him. Among them was their elegantly tall mother, even more conspicuous in a floor-length gown.

"Don't tell me that's the teacher," murmured Natsuki.

"Who else could it be?"

"Ye gods."

He was not only affected but vaguely seedy-looking, the sort of person who years ago might have been a strolling guitarist in the back alleys of Shinjuku. But troubadours have a distinct aura of knowing life to its depths, something that he lacked. He had neither their fierceness nor their warmth. For Mitsuki of all people to say so would have sounded presumptuous, but he struck her as someone who knew little of life's harshness.

"Yuji must never see this." Natsuki spoke seriously.

After the recital, Mitsuki had called her mother. "If you're going to take singing lessons, why not study with a proper voice trainer?" Long ago her mother had been a soprano able to hit a high A.

"Oh, at my age I don't have the voice for that anymore. I never got the training I should have had when I was young. Chansons are about all I'm good for."

This answer made perfect sense, but Mitsuki still was put out. It was as if, having washed her hands of Natsuki, her mother was now going out of her way to let it be known by taking up chansons that she had switched allegiance. When she asked the meaning of French lyrics, Mitsuki wouldn't explain, saying only, "Lots of them are better in Japanese translation." In fact, she thought *sakurambo*, "cherry," was far more charmingly suggestive of a girl's sweet, round flesh than *cerise*.

If her mother could study under a seedy man like that without thinking twice, her old nameless yearnings had definitely lost luster. Not only that, the place was a chanson studio in name only, and, going along with the demands of the time, also taught American show tunes and even Japanese popular songs. Called C'est Si Bon, the studio was located one station from Chitose Funabashi, heading toward Shinjuku, and the instructor lived with his wife and children seven stations down the line the other way.

Shortly after the recital, her mother had started doing secretarial work at the studio several days a week. She was fond of going out and now had somewhere to go, besides which she would be paid for her trouble. What was wrong with that? At first Mitsuki had thought nothing of it. But when she dropped in for visits to her parents' home, she soon began to sense that things were somehow off kilter. She eventually came to see that her mother was infatuated with the chanson instructor. For a woman of her years to become infatuated with any kind of a teacher happened all the time, and, given that their family had seen more than its share of elopements and divorces, plus one attempted suicide, there seemed little to be gained by expressing disapproval.

Years went by before Mitsuki saw just how deeply involved her mother was with That Man. One night, sometime after eight, a colleague of her father's had called her at home with alarming news: her diabetic father had collapsed and been rushed to the hospital by ambulance. He'd been dehydrated but was now conscious and stable. After he collapsed, they'd kept dialing his home telephone number, but nobody answered. Finally the caller had looked through his address notebook and come across the name "Mitsuki Hirayama," which he remembered was the name of one of his daughters.

Mitsuki hurried to the hospital in the city center. She first notified Natsuki, but since Natsuki had two small children to look after and their father's condition was stable, they agreed that she needn't come along. Riding in the subway, swaying as she gripped the overhead strap, Mitsuki felt a premonition that her life hereafter would consist of the endless repetition of such scenes. Once a semi-neglected daughter, now she would bear the full weight of the Katsura family's various burdens.

It could not be mere coincidence that the man had stumbled on her telephone number and not her sister's.

When she got there, her father was alert. He did not say, "Where's your mother?" Looking back, she could see that pride had kept him from asking, but also by then he must have been used to the late hour of his wife's return home. Mitsuki continued calling home with no luck, until it occurred to her that her mother might still be at the studio. That was when it dawned on her that a tasteless drama was being played out.

There was a row of telephone directories in the hospital, and in the Yellow Pages she soon found the listing for C'est Si Bon. A man's voice came on the line.

"This is the daughter of Noriko Katsura speaking," she said in a clipped and formal manner. "Is my mother still there by any chance?" She heard the man call, "Noriko, it's your daughter." After a pause she heard the receiver being handed over to her mother.

"Mitsuki, what on earth do you want?" Her mother's voice was defiant and shameless.

The hour was by then past ten o'clock. Mitsuki had avoided calling on days when her mother worked at C'est Si Bon, not knowing exactly when she would be back. She had never imagined that her mother would stay out so late.

# 23

## A MAN SOMEHOW LACKING

The mother who went off to "Yokohama" with a singing heart never truly aggravated her, nor did the mother who forgot her existence before Natsuki's wedding. She'd still felt close to her, still could turn to her when in need. But from that time on, her mother became repulsive to her. She felt as if her mother exuded venom.

Her father's diabetes worsened. After reaching retirement age he had become president of a subsidiary, but ill health forced him eventually to resign. When Mitsuki went home for a visit, she would find him sitting slumped over, hollow-eyed and abandoned in a house with cobwebs. He had eye surgery, but afterward, perhaps as a reaction to the anesthesia, his mind was fuzzy. In time he developed digestive ailments unrelated to the diabetes and was hospitalized repeatedly.

Once after he had been in the hospital nearly a month, shortly before the planned day of his release, her mother was summoned for a consultation. She asked Mitsuki and her sister to come too, so they did. From now on, the doctor said, the patient's home care would require extra effort. He needed to be on a strict diabetic diet, have insulin shots, and take medicine four times a day, after each meal and before bed. As his eyesight continued to fail he would need assistance with personal hygiene besides.

Their mother made a face.

There was a short silence before the doctor added with a slight frown, "Or of course, you could put him in an extended-care hospital somewhere." Perhaps seeing how shamelessly their mother's face lit up at this suggestion, he went on, his frown deepening, "If the family is unable to provide the care he needs, that might be his best option."

After that she would quote the doctor's words to them like holy writ: "The doctor himself said it would be better for your father this way." She turned a deaf ear to their offers to come by regularly to help out.

"You're ill, anyway," she said to Natsuki.

Though Natsuki had never fully regained her strength following the suicide attempt, her children were now at an age when they required less attention. Normally there would have been no reason why she couldn't have shared in caring for their aged father. But just about the time his eyesight faded, she developed uveitis, an incurable inflammation of the eye. Repeated examinations turned up no cause; it was as if she were keeping their father company in his eye troubles. The only treatment was a high dosage of steroids, with side effects causing her face, neck, and body to swell up like the proverbial "fat lady" of opera. Stopping the treatment caused a gradual return to normal, but after repeated bouts of this on-again-off-again course of treatment, she tired easily and was often laid up in bed.

"And *you* never were strong to begin with," she said to Mitsuki. "Besides, you have your work to do."

The doctor found a hospital near the city limits that would accept their father and wrote a letter of introduction. The wards there held eight.

Mitsuki was aghast. She briefly considered taking him in. But she was then still living in a small 58.8-square-meter condominium and in those days Tetsuo often worked at home; having an invalid in the apartment would have made normal life impossible. She quickly banished the thought and tried to shake off a sense of guilt. Natsuki, chronically fatigued and less and less comfortable with her in-laws, was hardly in a position to take him in either.

"Oh, if we only had a tenth of the Shimazakis' money!" Natsuki wailed.

"I know."

"I can never let Yuji find out the kind of place he'll be in." She also wanted to keep him in the dark about their mother's involvement with That Man.

And so their father never went home, but took off his pajamas and changed into a suit for the ninety-minute taxi ride to a hospital far away. Mitsuki and her mother accompanied him.

He apparently still thought that after a short stay in the new hospital he could go home. Sitting beside him in the taxi speeding away from the city center, Mitsuki patted his arm and said nothing to disabuse him of the idea.

The next day when she alone went to visit him, she brought posters of Monet's water lilies and tacked them up on the wall over his bed.

At first their mother reluctantly took turns visiting him along with her daughters, but over the years she reduced her visits, though she was always careful to check in with Mitsuki: "I wasn't planning on going this week, if it's all right with you." She must have felt some guilt. And for Natsuki, the period of their father's hospitalization corresponded to the time when her health was at its lowest ebb. As a result, Mitsuki's burdens continued to grow in middle age. To be home in time to make dinner for Tetsuo, she had to see her father on days when she didn't teach. Besides this physical burden, there was the heavier emotional burden of her unrelenting pity for him, night and day. The stress of maintaining normal relations with her mother as the "understanding daughter" steadily became more of a trial. Yet when she tried to put even a little distance between them, her mother was swift to react; to fend off the threat of abandonment, she would sound a little contrite and for a while be on her best behavior, trekking to the hospital like a dutiful wife.

"I saw him yesterday. He was fine." She would go out of her way to make these reports.

But eventually, her mother had played her final card, claiming that the chanson instructor—a man a dozen or more years her junior—had promised he would get a divorce and be with her in her declining years. Her visits to the remote hospital became even less frequent. Perhaps her husband's unexpected longevity made the prospect of seeing him face-to-face increasingly distressing—or infuriating. Mitsuki, while dubious that That Man's promise could be trusted, decided that if she didn't have to look after her mother she could perhaps go along with the deal.

Then her father contracted pneumonia.

This was just after she and Tetsuo had returned from his first sabbatical, the one in California, during which she traveled back several times to check in on her father. Grateful that classes had not yet begun, she took a room in a small nearby hotel and went to see him daily, raising him up a little when he was conscious and spoon-feeding him soup in accordance with the nurse's instructions. At night she would go back to her hotel and vacantly read a book or watch television. Natsuki, who was having another bout of eye inflammation, would call every night and ask apologetically how he was doing. Mitsuki would tell her in a slightly sulky tone. She also had long telephone conversations with Tetsuo nearly every day. She had not yet found out about his first affair, and this was part of the reason why she would vent all her anger at her mother — who had yet to put in an appearance during this crisis — holding back nothing and seeking his comfort.

When she called her mother on her first night at the hotel, her mother sounded flustered, but said in an ingratiating tone, "Your father's so lucky to have you. I'll pay your hotel bill."

The next few days went by without further contact. Then one night her mother called. "How is he?"

"Hard to say. Even the doctor says he can't tell yet."

In fact her father had passed the crisis point, but she somehow didn't feel like sharing this information.

"Oh."

Silence. Mitsuki purposely said nothing. Her mother apparently decided to ignore her aloofness.

"There's one more thing, Mitsuki." She said this with what sounded like determination, but then shifted to a honeyed, cajoling tone. "I've been thinking. When this is all over, I want us to go to Europe again. On me. By then your father's life insurance money will have come in."

Mitsuki felt the room spin.

"I want to see Paris once more before I die." Her mother's voice had a sunny lilt redolent of her younger days.

For a moment she was speechless. Then she said frostily, "Why not go again with that teacher of yours? It's your money. Suit yourself." Her fingers gripped the receiver. She had accompanied her mother to Europe twice, once in graduate school and again several years later. The first time, Tetsuo had come too. Then her mother had gone a third time with the chanson group, led by That Man.

"Actually…when I go with him, something's lacking. I don't feel like I'm getting the full experience. His French doesn't sound like French. I mean, his background is what it is. Once was enough."

Mitsuki no longer remembered how she may have responded. All she could remember was that then, for the first time, it came to her with burning clarity: she wished her mother would die.

That night, before falling asleep she had murmured into the darkness the words "Today, Mother died." From then on she waited for the day when she might say those words out loud for real.

All along she had thought her mother and That Man an unlikely pair. She now knew what she had always sensed deep down: he wasn't someone her mother wanted for his own sake; he was merely a makeshift entertainment who would allow her to keep on chasing her nameless dreams. Dyeing her hair black, suppressing her seventy-plus years, dressing up to go out to restaurants where even though she was no drinker she would tap her wineglass with his, little finger raised just so—all of it had the feel of makeshift entertainment. That Man was a mere expedient, someone to be her dance partner on life's stage as she sought to squeeze as much as she could out of her remaining time.

And yet even as a mere expedient he wasn't quite up to the job. Tickets were expensive so she didn't go often, but when she did attend the ballet or see an opera by an overseas troupe it was always Natsuki or Mitsuki she wanted with her, not him—precisely because when he did go along, the occasion lacked a certain something.

Mitsuki should have known that the only man to romance her mother, an old woman living on a pension and dwindling savings, would be no prize. Rather than indulging in such a sleazy romance, why couldn't her mother have shown more self-respect and gone on pursuing her dreams on her own? Was she that desperate to escape from her husband, who bore the twin stigmas of sickness and old age—the inevitable suffering of life? Perhaps she wanted to think that such suffering should have no place in *her* life.

# 24

## SEASONS OF LIFE

After her father recovered from pneumonia, Mitsuki went home and spent two days at her computer composing an eight-page letter to her mother. This time she was determined. If her mother wanted to keep on with That Man, fine. She and her sister would take care of their father—and sever their ties to her. She concluded with a request that her mother not telephone her, but respond in writing.

Two days later, her mother's ear-splitting voice sounded over the telephone. "What were you *thinking*, sending your mother a letter like that? I nearly had a *heart attack!*"

Later that afternoon, out walking, her mother was struck by a bicycle and knocked down, breaking her left hip. The shock of the letter might have been what kept her from watching where she was going. She had surgery, spent forty days in the hospital, and for some time afterward was barely able to stand. That Man couldn't cope, having a job and a family, so Mitsuki had no choice but to come to the rescue. Natsuki also pitched in, with bad grace. Mitsuki's letter and ultimatum were consigned to oblivion as That Man faded out of the picture.

After the accident her mother turned overnight into a wrinkled crone with bent back. From then on she stopped dyeing her hair.

Her first time out on crutches, hobbling along, she had said morosely, "I guess my chickens have come home to roost."

The words *Yes, Mother, they have* came to mind, but Mitsuki couldn't say them. *Give me a break* was what she really wanted to say. Her mother just didn't get it. Yes, from now on she would have to use a cane, but Mitsuki and her sister would be the ones who would have to take care of her. Mostly Mitsuki. Why should her mother's chickens come home to roost with *her*?

Carrying both their purses over one shoulder and clutching shopping bags in both hands, Mitsuki had said nothing. She could not bring herself to needle her mother by asking what had happened to That Man's promise to look after her—not because she felt sorry for her hobbling mother, but because she knew that needling would accomplish nothing.

That Man was never spoken of again between them.

A year or so later her father died, and by the time his life insurance came through, her mother had difficulty getting around, so talk of a trip to Europe evaporated. Mitsuki constantly dreamed the same dream, waking just as the thought hit her: *Why, Dad's in such good shape, I could easily take him in!*

Feeling sad and rueful about her dead father while resentfully looking after her steadily aging mother: that had been her life ever since. The absurdity of being forced to be her mother's caregiver turned sorrow over her father's end into a residue of resentment that festered like a sore.

Even after That Man's departure from the scene, the intensity of her mother's insatiable passions never lessened. If anything, whether because she was trying to contain lingering feelings of guilt or because she was unhinged by the physical and emotional shocks she had endured, by the time she began applying makeup with her former meticulousness Mitsuki's cane-tapping mother had grown more self-centered than ever. Mitsuki wondered about herself: was it because she was Japanese that she didn't simply walk away and be done with her? Was she swept up in a cultural climate where a woman's virtue had long been inextricable from her role as caregiver? Or was the prospect simply too exhausting? Did she sense that severing their connection would drain her of all her strength and that once her weeping and wailing were over, her voice a dry rasp, she would only take pity on her mother and so fail to extricate herself after all? Baffled, she continued to be her mother's mainstay.

Little by little her mother shed the trappings of vulgarity and returned to her former self. That was some comfort. Aiming to be able to go out walking by herself again, she had her old acupuncture therapist come to the house once a week for an entire year. Seeing how determined her patient was, the therapist exerted herself with more zeal than anyone could have hoped for. And so, despite having suffered a hip fracture in her seventies, for a time Mitsuki's mother had been able to take the train alone, aided by her cane, and get out to see the foreign films she claimed she couldn't live without.

The aging process naturally continued unabated. Her mother resisted every step of the way. When she could no longer get out to the movies by herself, she finally got Mitsuki to buy her a VCR, a purchase Mitsuki had been putting off because of her mother's hopeless inability to handle machinery. She explained over and over how the remote worked and wrote out the necessary steps in big letters, as for a kindergartner. With that piece of paper in hand, her mother was able to manage the controls. Then she kept them busy renting a continuous supply of videos for her. She also read voraciously, the way a goat eats paper, and books had to be bought. She still wanted to go to the theater, to go shopping, and to eat out, but such outings were impossible unless one or both of her daughters accompanied her. Pooling their resources made it less exhausting, so as far as possible they would both go along.

"Guess what's coming!" she would announce over the telephone, breathless with anticipation. Four out of five times Mitsuki would say no, but on the fifth time she would relent. When it came to the theater, her mother's interest was not confined to things Western; she enjoyed Kabuki plays as well. Mitsuki and her sister shared her love of the theater, so they would both go, although any pleasure they might have derived from the performance was offset by the immense logistical difficulty of taking their mother out. The greatest challenge came from her increasingly overactive bladder.

She became nervous about whether she could make it safely there and back without mishap. When they came to pick her up, she would be sitting at the table waiting for them with her makeup on, a scarf around her neck, and all the accoutrements of theatergoing, Noriko-style: two lightweight folding pillows to tuck under her bottom so she could see the stage, compression spinal fractures having shortened her sitting height; a warm lap robe so she wouldn't be cold; a plastic bottle of tea so she wouldn't be thirsty. While Mitsuki and her sister divided these items between them, slipping them into their handbags, their mother would go to the bathroom. As they were leaving, she would no sooner get her coat on than she would decide to go again, "just to be on the safe side," and remove her coat with the slow, fumbling fingers of old age so frustrating to those waiting. As soon as the taxi deposited them at the theater, she went again, and if time allowed she would go once more before the performance began. At intermission she headed straight for the ladies' room. Her movements were so slow that this took time; she would barely make it back before the curtain went up, apologizing to the others in her row as she squeezed past them to reach her seat. And of course the moment the curtain fell, she had to go again...

One night when they arrived home after a performance of *La bohème*, she made an announcement: "I won't try to go to the theater or the opera anymore."

She could be decisive in this way. Yet she was fundamentally incapable of giving up with good grace. She would lower her sights a smidgen, but keep them always just above what she was capable of doing on her own. As a result, the burden on Mitsuki and her sister never lessened.

To avoid a scene, Mitsuki made a point of never mentioning her mother's treatment of her father. One day, however, exasperated with her mother's stream of demands, she said with tight-lipped anger, "You left Father in that horrible place all those years. You know very well you shouldn't be this demanding now."

"How can you bring up what happened so long ago!" her mother exclaimed. So although her faculties were beginning to slip, she clearly remembered what she had done and knew moreover that Mitsuki had not forgiven her. Mitsuki took comfort in this knowledge.

Life has its seasons. During the springtime and early summer of her life, the intensity of Noriko's quest had given her—and her daughters—a future. But in the autumn of her life, that quest had become increasingly frustrating and vacuous. Now in frozen midwinter there was something eerie about her as she continued to struggle—not only eerie but tragicomical, as life's tragedies so often are.

One morning Mitsuki received a phone call from her mother. This was after, moved by a certain pity as year by year her mother's life slipped away, she had begun calling her every evening at eight. Natsuki too had grudgingly taken to calling her once every few days. For her mother to call without waiting for their nightly chat was usually a sign of trouble. When she heard her mother's voice come on the line that morning, Mitsuki braced herself.

"Guess what I did last night after talking to you?" Excitement hovered in her mother's voice.

The previous night had been stormy as a typhoon approached. At the end of their conversation, Mitsuki had said, "You be careful now," and her mother had replied, "I will. I'll get out a candle just in case." A flashlight would be better, Mitsuki had thought, but rather amused at her mother's old-fashioned ways, she had let it go.

"Come on, guess!"

"I give up. What did you do?"

Her mother tittered, the way well-bred ladies used to do. "I put out all the lights in the house, lit a candle, and sang my heart out. Sang every aria I could think of. Nobody could hear me in the middle of that storm."

Mitsuki was speechless. She pictured the scene to herself: in the dark of night, as rain lashed and a typhoon raged, a white-haired crone singing operatically at the top of her lungs. With the entire neighborhood engulfed in darkness, on and on she sang in the glow of a single candle.

"But I can't sing the way I used to, and besides that I've lost my sense of pitch. I can tell."

"Oh?"

"It's the end of the line for Noriko."

Word came of the passing of Mitsuki's host mother in Paris, a woman younger than her mother.

With the time of ripening cherries far behind them both, Mitsuki and her sister had continued piling on years, each with her own thoughts. Even Mitsuki's memory of Tetsuo's first affair grew dim and remote. At the time she had been overcome. That earnest youth among the flickering candles in the garret in Paris, so stiff and nervous that his cheek twitched—that pale youth who had cast himself at her feet—how could he betray her? Her shock had been so great that the second time, she'd felt almost nothing. A corner of her mind had shut down. In life, did getting older inevitably mean getting inured to unhappiness? Part of her accepted this, but another part rebelled. Her health eventually broke down.

Then came her mother's cataclysmic fall—and, close on its heels, her discovery of Tetsuo's unforgivable emails. That had given her a shock of a completely different order. It was more than the shock of knowing he was planning on leaving her for a younger woman. It was the shock of knowing with certainty that she herself was finished as a woman—that she had taken her first step toward old age. This unpleasant truth that she had fended off by remaining busy was thrust under her nose.

But the only time she cried was the time she stayed up all night reading the emails. After that she pushed all thought of Tetsuo out of her mind, even just before bed. Above all, she needed to get her mother out of the rehabilitation hospital and settled in Golden. As she told herself this, lying in the dark with her eyes shut, the image rose in her mind of her mother sitting alone in the hospital dining room staring stonily into space. The thought that she would have to confront that figure again in the morning weighed on her.

And indeed, at the hospital her mother remained the same, sitting alone in a desolate moor swept by a cold wind, dry leaves whirling soundlessly around her.

## (25)

## A PROPER THANK-YOU

By the time her mother left the rehabilitation hospital the cherry blossom buds had come out, signaling the start of a new school year.

Mitsuki decided to limit her work to patent translations, which she could do at home, and take a year's leave of absence from teaching. Physically and mentally, she was exhausted. To fill in for her she turned to her old friend Masako. Like her, Masako had started out teaching French part time and, when universities ceased to require a second foreign language for graduation, managed to keep her job by switching to English. Always willing to lend a hand, she was divorced and strapped for cash, and luckily in excellent health. Before this, Masako had filled in for Mitsuki when she had accompanied Tetsuo on his sabbaticals. If there was a class that didn't fit her schedule, she'd obligingly found someone else.

Mitsuki explained over the telephone that this time she wouldn't be accompanying Tetsuo but rather needed to take some time off because of the state her mother was in.

"Sorry to hear that," said Masako. "My mom hasn't changed. Still hands out free advice to the neighbors. She's not just a good talker, she's a good walker too."

Heredity was a factor then, Mitsuki thought, picturing to herself the toned muscles of Masako's legs.

"Believe me," she said, "you don't know how lucky you are."

"You sound pretty down."

She had a right to be. There was Tetsuo's betrayal now, on top of all else.

Both of them were busy, so they ended the conversation without making plans to meet.

When they were in their thirties, friends who were housewives had looked older than they did; she and Masako used to agree complacently that women who didn't use their brains were at a disadvantage. Now in their fifties, they were finding that working women aged faster after all, struggling to maintain their stamina while juggling myriad demands on their time. And any working woman with an elderly parent to care for was a disaster.

The day her mother moved into Golden happened to be the day Tokyo's cherry blossoms came into full bloom. The day was memorable for another reason: for a short time, her mother had been herself again. It was as if knowing that she was entering on a new life had lit a final flame in her soul.

Loaded into a van, wheelchair and all, she took an interest in the outside world for the first time since her accident, eagerly looking out the window and commenting: "Would you look at those cherry blossoms! Spring came out of nowhere this year." For the first time in a long while, her dark eyes glistened.

Clouds of white blossoms were everywhere along the cramped, ugly streets, in places where you would least expect to find them, telling of spring and the joy of new life. Neither her mother nor she suspected that these were the last cherry blossoms her mother would ever see.

On entering the room decorated with familiar, lovely things, her mother broke into a genuine smile. She exclaimed in delight over the vase from Grandpa Yokohama, overflowing with sumptuous artificial flowers. She looked in turn at the embroidered lace curtains at the window, the bed made up with linens from home, the wall shelf displaying her beloved bric-a-brac—all of it arranged for her pleasure. Slowly she spun her wheelchair in a circle, taking it all in, before turning to Mitsuki.

"Come here, Mitsuki."

She said this in a firm voice, as if she were about to deliver a lecture. There was a glint in her eye.

"What is it?" Mitsuki asked a little impatiently, interrupting her unpacking.

"I want to say a proper thank-you, so come sit down."

When she sat down, her mother gripped the wheelchair arms, bowed rather ceremoniously in her direction and said, "Thank you for everything. I really mean it." Her voice shook slightly.

Her mother was no fool. She knew that Mitsuki did not particularly wish her to live many more years. At the same time, she understood that Mitsuki was doing all she could to ensure that she lived out her life in comfort. She was expressing appreciation for those efforts.

"Thank you so much." Tears welled in her eyes.

Touched, Mitsuki too spoke from the heart. "I know life here won't be easy, Mom. I wish things were different."

That was the last time her mother was her old self. The deterioration of her frontal lobe continued unabated.

After moving into Golden, she again kept to herself. Ninety percent of the residents were further gone than she was; the other ten percent were in good shape, yet she made no attempt to enter their circle. Her deafness made normal conversation difficult, her pride made it excruciating, and she may also have sensed the approach of senility. She held herself aloof. A few of the other residents who were from incomparably better families than she jabbered to themselves in the excessively polite language associated with society's upper echelons. Among them all she maintained a ridiculous air of haughtiness, alone in her misery.

Memories of physical sensations from long-ago schoolgirl days seemed to come flooding back. Sitting in her wheelchair, she would turn when Mitsuki came into the room and say with tears in her voice, "Last night I dreamed it again ... I was running and jumping." Her face would be stricken but her eyes would be shining.

Mrs. Kiyokawa, the head caregiver at Golden, was the sort of person who calmly let annoyances slide harmlessly right over her. She had no trouble putting up with her mother, Mitsuki noted, reassured somehow that Mrs. Kiyokawa was around her age and presumably familiar with life's vagaries. The staff were all friendly, the food decent. Her mother took to saying that she was "perfectly happy." Even so, as if in punishment for having sought too much gaiety in life, her spirit was bedeviled by misery.

She reached constantly for relief in the form of little white pieces of Depas. At Golden they finally managed to loosen her grip on her sleeping medicine and stool softener and take charge of them for her, but Depas, her tranquilizer, they could not get her to relinquish. She became even drowsier than before. Twice she tumbled out of her wheelchair and had to be taken to the hospital for X-rays. The first time it happened, they sent for Mitsuki; the second time, she couldn't come and Natsuki came instead. Naturally, Golden began to insist that they needed to control her Depas as well. But Mitsuki knew that taking away the little vial her mother clutched like a talisman would only speed her descent into madness. She came up with the idea of using a placebo.

The dispensary only stocked placebos in powder form, so she took to stopping by a pharmacy on her way home and picking up various kinds of white-pill supplements. At home, she cut them into small pieces, testing them for smell, flavor, and hardness. She finally settled on some chewable calcium pills that she herself took. About the size of a fairly large coin, they were easy to chop but felt harder on the tongue. Praying that her mother wouldn't notice, she emptied the vial and refilled it with the placebo.

"This new Depas is a little harder than the old." She handed her the vial with this caveat.

Her mother nodded, never doubting her trusted daughter's word, and popped a piece of a calcium pill into her mouth.

Her mother's growing dementia showed in a variety of ways. Now when a visitor came by, even if she understood who it was, she could no longer ask pertinent questions. When Mitsuki called at eight she would pick up the receiver and say hello in a bright tone—but then be incapable of relating the events of her day. She understood only in the vaguest way that Tetsuo wasn't in Japan. Mitsuki arranged once again for the delivery of DVDs of foreign films, but even if her mother could be reminded (with great effort) how to work the remote, she could no longer follow the story line.

"Bo-ring," she would say with a scowl, and after a few minutes change the DVD for another.

And yet she was convinced that the self that loved foreign films was her true self. Clutching an armful of DVDs to her chest, she would declare dramatically, like a maiden of a bygone era clutching a trove of love letters, "These are my very life!"

By the time it was hot enough for air-conditioning and Mitsuki's bus trips to and from Golden had become uncomfortable, her mother no longer knew whether she felt hot or cold.

"Mitsuki, am I hot now? Or am I cold?" When she telephoned with this tearful inquiry, it was Mitsuki who felt like crying. At her mother's request she had purchased long-sleeved, mid-sleeved, and short-sleeved sets of underwear—all for nothing.

Mitsuki and her sister took turns visiting daily at first, then with gaps of a day or two at most. It wasn't so much that they pitied her, but rather that the speed with which she was failing made it hard to stay away more than two days at a time. They needed to meet constantly with Mrs. Kiyokawa to plan new ways of coping.

Mitsuki's nerves got no rest.

Her mental energy exhausted, she had nothing left for thoughts about Tetsuo. Sometimes as she lay in bed in the dark just before falling asleep, the memory of those emails would come rushing back, humiliation would stop her breath, and she would cover her face with her hands. But in the bright light of day, the idea of losing her husband to a young woman seemed so tawdry that she could scarcely believe it was happening to her. She felt scornful of the whole idea.

When Tetsuo called again, she answered him abruptly.

"How's your mother?"

"She has galloping dementia."

# (26)

## FATAL SASHIMI

Their mother began showing the food obsession typical of older people with dementia.

Isolated at Golden, she still wanted Mitsuki or her sister to come at dinnertime, and when they did, she was permitted to eat in her room. Seeing how thin she was becoming, they started to bring her some of the sliced sashimi she loved, and soon she came to expect it. She had a tendency to choke on her food, and at Golden she'd been put on a minced diet, so the artistically arranged slices of fish from the supermarket had to be cut up mercilessly with kitchen shears. Even though the result looked unappetizing, she would eagerly devour it. Out of consideration for the kitchen staff, Mitsuki took leftovers home in plastic containers and threw them in the garbage. She had no intention of eating minced leftovers all by herself in her apartment.

Having acquired a taste for sashimi, their mother next asked for cake for dessert. Telling themselves that eating was now her sole pleasure in life, Mitsuki or Natsuki would pick up little cakes on their way to see her—fancy confections from a patisserie, the kind of thing they would serve to company.

After that it was afternoon snacks.

They would bring two or three cellophane-wrapped sweets and caution her, "Just one a day now!" before putting them in a drawer. At first she followed these instructions, but it wasn't long before she would wolf them all down at once. To stop her from ruining her appetite for meals, they left the snacks with the staff. Then she started pushing her call button many times a day, pleading for snacks. The staff gave in. The sisters bought smaller and smaller snacks to keep her from overindulging, but she kept pushing her call button relentlessly. They asked the staff to give in to her demands only every third time and went around to various stores buying different kinds of bite-sized cookies, which they divided up in little plastic bags.

No matter how they indulged her, she wore a constant look of demented misery. "Some people take a year to settle in," Mrs. Kiyokawa said consolingly to the ashen-faced sisters.

When they came into her room bearing sashimi, cakes, and cookies, the first thing they saw was her slight figure slumped over in the wheelchair. She had become a mass of sorrows and frustrations barely comprehensible to herself. If only she would become an empty shell, how much easier life would be for her! They began to long for her to become completely senile. Once she was completely out of her mind and no longer able to tell the two of them apart, happiness and sadness alike might fade away.

But visualizing the long road ahead and the continuing exhaustion they must endure on the way, they felt as if they were being dragged into a bottomless swamp.

Never did they imagine that her days at Golden would terminate so quickly.

At nine-thirty one midsummer night, Mrs. Kiyokawa called from inside an ambulance. The siren could be heard over the telephone line. "Your mother has a fever. The first two emergency rooms we went to were full and turned us away. We've contacted a third one, and they are willing to admit her, but I need your permission." She added apologetically, "This one has almost entirely private rooms."

"Please go ahead," Mitsuki said quickly.

There was no longer any reason to fret if her mother went into a private room. She telephoned Natsuki right away and told her the news, adding that since it was already late, she would go over alone to check on things. She looked up the hospital on the Internet, put on some lipstick, slung her purse—heavy with the items she always carried as protection from air-conditioning—over her shoulder, and went out to hail a taxi. Once settled into the back seat, she put on a hat, wrapped herself in a cardigan and scarf, and laid a lap robe across her knees.

She had rushed off like this just recently, when her mother had fallen from her wheelchair and was taken to the hospital. Here we go again, she thought. How many more times would there be? Outside her window was the meandering night scenery along Ring Road 7, which she usually looked down on from a bus window. The night scene was Asian to the core, motley buildings jumbled together. For all she could tell this might as easily be Seoul or Taipei. Before her there was only barrenness and bleakness—a scene totally without identity.

Mrs. Kiyokawa was waiting when she emerged from the elevator. Her usually youthful face looked drawn and old.

Mitsuki found her mother lying faceup in bed wearing an oxygen mask, her large-pupiled eyes wide open. It had been a while since she'd seen her lying down instead of sitting in a wheelchair. All those snacks hadn't put any meat on her bones; her frame, stretched out under a thin blanket, was now flat as a board.

The oxygen mask made her large pupils stand out even more. Her eyes stared at the ceiling, not glinting as usual but seemingly covered with a thin film. Her lips were purplish. Her breathing was labored, her mouth ajar, and for some reason her tongue was twisted to one side. Phlegm stuck somewhere in her bronchial tubes made a strange gurgling noise.

But she was conscious. When she saw Mitsuki, she held out her left hand. Mitsuki clasped it gently, and her mother returned her grip with astonishing force.

Her bony fingertips were hot to the touch.

Then the night shift doctor came in. Since he was a gastroenterologist he couldn't be sure, but he suspected aspiration pneumonia, caused by dysphagia—difficulty swallowing. Even if the antibiotics helped, she faced a long uphill battle.

"Considering her age," he concluded gravely, "the outlook isn't necessarily good. You and the other family members need to prepare yourselves."

Prepare themselves? She looked at him in surprise, but his expression was bland, as though he had said the most ordinary thing in the world. Mrs. Kiyokawa's face was still drawn but showed no surprise. Mitsuki thanked the doctor and walked Mrs. Kiyokawa to the elevator.

She was in a daze. When her father came down with pneumonia, she couldn't remember ever having been advised to prepare herself. Use of cell phones was not allowed in the hospital, so she asked at the nurses' station and found that there was a telephone room downstairs. She descended the dark stairs, still in a daze.

She reported what the doctor had said, and Natsuki replied, "This may very well be the end then." For once there was not a trace of irony in her voice. She sounded quietly moved. Her sister's calm allowed Mitsuki to slowly grasp the situation.

She went back to her mother's room. Nothing had changed. Her mother was still breathing with difficulty, eyes wide open. Mitsuki bent over her and stroked her upper arm, mere skin and bones. Speaking slowly, she explained in a voice loud enough for her mother to hear: "Mom, you've got pneumonia. Your fever is high, so until the antibiotics start to do their job and you get better, you'll have to stay here in the hospital a little while."

Her mother nodded and said "Mkay." She sounded like a child.

With a cardigan around her shoulders, Mitsuki continued to stroke her mother's arm while her mother, struggling to breathe, did nothing but open and close her eyes. Mitsuki was fighting exhaustion, yet was caught up in excitement at the same time.

Then her mother spoke. "You have things to do. Go on home."

The voice was phlegmy and hard to make out, but that was definitely what she had said. Though taken aback by this unexpected display of consideration, Mitsuki decided to follow the suggestion. "I'll come again tomorrow," she said, gripping her mother's hot hand, and stood up.

After leaving the room, she stood just outside the open door and looked back in. Still lying motionless with her eyes closed. Maybe she'd gone to sleep.

The buses had long since stopped running. She got in another taxi, slipped her arms back into the sleeves of her cardigan, put on her hat and scarf, wrapped her knees in the lap robe. Thus bundled up, she watched the night scenery run backward this time out the car window and thought about last night's sashimi.

Yesterday she had taken a different route and so had dropped by a different supermarket. A package of flounder sashimi, a favorite of her mother's, contained five slices so exquisitely thin they were translucent and cost just over a thousand yen. The package next to it contained a generous assortment of scallops, salmon, and amberjack sashimi and was only six hundred yen. She used her mother's money for such shopping, and as her mother was presently comfortably off, she should have gone ahead and bought the flounder, but she had formed the habit of being careful with her mother's money. Her instincts told her that a thousand yen for five extra-thin slices of sashimi was too much.

In her mother's room, she'd cut up the sashimi into tiny pieces as usual, using a pair of kitchen shears, but there was so much that she ended up doing it in rather slapdash style. She should have watched as her mother ate, but instead she stood diagonally behind her, sorting little cookies into plastic bags for the staff to keep and only glancing now and then at her mother's back as she hunched over the food.

Her mother ate ravenously, like a hungry ghost of Buddhist lore. Her bent back told the shameful way she was eating—so shameful it was hard to believe this could be her mother—and Mitsuki couldn't help wanting to avert her eyes. Her mother had always taken care to eat gracefully during meals, but those self-conscious manners were pitiably gone.

Around the time she finished off the sashimi, she started choking. Mitsuki had rushed to her side and found a sticky, semitransparent substance pouring from her mouth, more than she could wipe away no matter how many tissues she used. Where could it all be coming from? Ashamed, her mother regained a sense of what was happening and wiped her mouth, apologizing. After ten minutes or so the coughing fit had passed.

Today she had choked on her food again at lunchtime. Golden called and said they would keep an eye on her, but at night she'd developed a fever.

The doctor's words rang in Mitsuki's ears, but no. Her mother would never die so easily—the idea was preposterous. But just supposing she did die, then by buying the less expensive sashimi and failing to cut it up properly, would she, Mitsuki, have committed matricide?

Before she knew it, the taxi was near Myohoji temple.

When it pulled up at her building, she got out, raced indoors, slipped off her shoes, and went straight to the computer on her desk in the bedroom. She turned it on and did a search for "aspiration pneumonia," which turned out to be a common cause of death in the elderly. It did not happen out of the blue. Rather, it was related to problems in swallowing and was common in cases of dementia, occurring when improperly ingested food entered the airway and eventually the lungs. Another contributing factor was the inability to cough when lying down. "Aspiration pneumonia occurs at night," one article said.

Even if her mother now died, she, Mitsuki, wouldn't be a murderer. But she would definitely have shortened her mother's life all the same.

By the time she got into bed, she felt defiant. If she *had* shortened her mother's life, so be it. Surely her mother would have no complaint if she could die before turning into something even less like her old self. Now perhaps all of them—her mother included—would be free of her: the thought swam in her head, along with an image of her mother's face bearing the seal of death.

It was the middle of the night, too late to call, but she had no doubt Natsuki was lying awake too, gripped by a similar fever of excitement. As she stared into the darkness, Tetsuo's still unsuspecting face floated up in her mind.

# 27

## LOW-CALORIE INFUSION SOLUTION

The next day, Mitsuki met up with her sister, and they went to see their mother together. When they arrived, she was sleeping, but her oxygen mask had slipped out of place. Seeking oxygen, her open mouth was cavernous, a dark pit. Her tongue was still twisted to one side, and she was wheezing. Not only her lips were purple; in the light of day, purplish speckles covered her entire face.

Mitsuki readjusted the mask, touched her mother on the shoulder, and whispered, "Mom." Her fingers encountered mere bone—artificial bone at that, since this was her right shoulder.

She hadn't been asleep after all, it seemed, for she instantly opened her eyes wide and looked at them with recognition. "Natsuki's here too?" Her tongue couldn't move. Her voice was barely audible.

"Gorgeous me, in the flesh." Natsuki pointed at herself comically.

Their mother, despite the state she was in, smiled contemptuously and said, "You're nuts," before turning to Mitsuki. "Where am I?"

She might be able to give a flippant response, but her powers of comprehension were clearly gone. Mitsuki bent over the bed, her mouth close by her mother's pillow, and repeated the explanation she had given her the night before. Once again, her mother nodded and said, "Mkay," docilely, like a child—then added, apropos of nothing, "I'm hungry."

Lately she said this often, making it impossible to know whether she actually did feel hungry. But last night the doctor had intimated that she might soon die, and Mitsuki frankly hoped she would. Her inability to wish that her mother would get well enough to eat again gave her a pang.

Still bent over the bed, she told her mother that she couldn't eat anything now, but that the bag overhead contained nourishment that she was getting, so not to worry. In fact the bag contained a low-calorie solution that was not enough to support life for very long.

"Can't I have some candy?" she whispered, looking up at the IV bag.

"No candy."

"No fun."

Neither of them responded.

"This is no fun!" she croaked again, her tongue stiff, her voice slightly louder than before. She kept breathing with her mouth open to get oxygen, so the inside of her mouth must have been bone dry.

"You'll have to be patient, Mom," Mitsuki said in the gentlest voice she could muster. "That's just how it is."

From below the oxygen mask, her mother replied in a low, husky voice, like a man's. It didn't sound like her voice, but the words were definitely hers. "I've had it. I can't—this is for the birds."

"She was saying that before too," said Natsuki behind her in a low voice, and despite the gravity of the situation Mitsuki felt laughter bubbling up, when in came the doctor.

Thanks to her mother, Mitsuki had had occasion to meet all sorts of doctors, and while knowing it was rude, she couldn't help taking private stock: medium height and weight. Balanced features. Looked to be in his early forties. Hair shiny, expression smooth. Probably sincere but looked like a pampered son who had never known hardship.

On the outside at least, the sisters listened respectfully, like dutiful daughters, as he spoke.

"First we have to see whether the antibiotic does the job."

They nodded.

"She's not young anymore, so don't get your hopes up. You need to understand that."

This was virtually the same thing the other doctor had said the day before.

"One more thing. If she pulls out her IV at night, restraints may become necessary. Is that all right?"

They assented and saw the doctor out. No sooner was he gone than Mitsuki cried out: "Oh! We should have him take a look at that paper."

"What paper?"

"You know. That signed statement from the Society for Dying with Dignity. It's a copy, but she was always adamant about it. Insisted we show it to them if they ever came for her by ambulance."

Mitsuki ran out into the corridor and caught up with the white-coated doctor. She showed him the paper and explained politely but firmly that her mother had joined the association in her sixties and always stressed that she wanted no heroic measures.

In recent years Mitsuki had taken to carrying the statement around in her purse (along with the tag for a hard-to-find brand of underwear that her mother liked, inscribed with the product name and her size). The number of Japanese doctors antagonistic to the concept of death with dignity was decreasing, she had heard, but this doctor in his forties could be a diehard right-to-lifer for all she knew.

He glanced at the paper she held out.

She took the precaution of adding that when her mother was no longer capable of eating on her own, she didn't want a nasogastric tube or, God forbid, a gastrostomy.

A nasogastric tube was a slender feeding tube inserted through the nose and down the esophagus into the stomach; a gastrostomy was an operation to implant a feeding tube directly into the stomach. Being your elderly mother's caregiver meant learning words you'd never seen or heard of before—words you were better off never having to encounter. How sad, she thought.

When she was a little girl reading novels, many in translation, she'd picked up new terms naturally: "fir tree," "windmill," "fireplace," "carriage and four," "fairy." The illustrations were pretty, but those unfamiliar words themselves had had the magical power to take her out of the shabby little house in Chitose Funabashi and into a mist-shrouded realm that was and was not of this world. The novels she'd read in adolescence had been full of words that filled her with dreams of one day becoming a grown-up woman: "silk stockings," "black lace gloves," "velvet cloak," "rouge," "satin obi."

Back then she could hardly wait for her life to begin.

And yet at some point life had forced her to learn words utterly devoid of poetry and romance. "Femoral-neck fracture": that term for a broken hip she had learned a dozen years ago at the time of her mother's accident. "Dysphagia," "nasogastric tube," "gastrostomy": until recently she hadn't known any of these words, but now they rolled off her tongue. And now she could add "aspiration pneumonia" to the list.

The doctor handed the document back, nodding, and said, "Yes, of course. I understand."

When she returned to the room, her sister asked, "How'd it go?"

"He said he understands."

"Really?"

She sounded relieved yet vaguely doubtful.

They took turns going to see her and always kept fresh flowers in her room. Before, whether at the hospital or at Golden, they had avoided bringing her flowers so as not to cause the staff extra work. Now they sensed that this stay might end up differently from all the rest, which meant that one or the other of them would be going to see her every day, so they could tend to the flowers themselves.

The antibiotic did not take effect.

It was uncomfortable having to frequent the hospital in mid-summer, with air-conditioning at its peak, yet Mitsuki found these visits more peaceful than before; since her mother mostly slept and didn't speak, there was no need to interact with her.

Administered only the low-calorie solution, her open mouth a dark cave, she grew even more emaciated. As instructed in the "Patient Guide," they had brought along a toothbrush and tooth-paste, but brushing her teeth was out of the question since any water going down the wrong way could be fatal. A nurse wearing plastic gloves would moisten the inside of her mouth with damp gauze, carefully remove clumps of dried black sputum, and clean her tongue. Two front teeth were so loose she was in danger of swallowing them, so they were pulled, first one and then, two days later, the other, leaving her mouth even darker than before. When she was awake, a nurse would perform suction, inserting a narrow tube down her nose to remove phlegm. This was apparently very uncomfortable, and she would try to

**180**

brush the tube away with both hands. Mitsuki assisted the nurse by holding down her mother's hands. It was distressing to see her writhe and struggle, but after suction her breathing came a bit more easily.

Another two days passed peaceably by, then three, then four. Mitsuki and her sister visited their mother on alternate days and kept in touch by telephone, discarding the withered flowers in her room and replacing them with fresh ones. Mitsuki took her laptop with her and worked on translations while she was there. Once in a while she would look up and check on the bag of milky fluid hanging over her mother's head.

"I want some candy."

When her mother was conscious, she would say this. She no longer remembered her stay in Golden, but she was able to tell Mitsuki and her sister apart. When she opened her eyes and saw Mitsuki, she would say her name and stretch out her hand.

After a week, the sisters began to allow themselves to think openly that their mother was really dying. They had never truthfully expected that day to come — had purposely avoided the thought — so it felt almost unreal. Though reluctant to have others see her as she was now, the following day they divided up a short list of people whom they thought she should see once more before she died, and contacted them.

The next morning, the doctor requested a family conference. He wanted to confirm that proceeding only with low-calorie IVs was acceptable if the antibiotics continued to fail to take effect. They reassured him that it was fine with them, hoping after the words were out of their mouths that their feelings hadn't come across too baldly. Continuing low-calorie sustenance meant their mother would be dead in a matter of weeks.

Soon now, the day would finally come.

Eating a late lunch together, they could not hold back their excitement.

"Unbelievable."

"Mind-boggling."

Little did they imagine that the doctor would have more news for them the following morning.

# 28

## THE END POSTPONED

"Anyway, she's gradually beating the pneumonia on her own," the doctor told Mitsuki over the telephone just after the test results came in. "It looks like her final call won't come this time."

This sounded sarcastic to her.

He said he had something he needed to discuss with the family, but it was still early in the morning so she decided to get in touch with Natsuki later, after she had found out the details. She took off for the hospital alone. The smooth-faced doctor was sitting at a computer in the nurses' station. When she said good morning, he looked up and told her that he wanted to switch her mother's IV to a high-calorie solution.

"That will increase her chances of recovery. Once she recovers, we can begin therapy for her dysphagia so she can eat again."

He went on to explain that her mother was now receiving "peripheral hyperalimentation," scant nutrition inserted through a vein in the arm or leg. If she was switched to high-calorie intake, she would have "central venous hyperalimentation" with nutrition going directly into a main artery, allowing her to absorb a far richer glucose solution.

More new words Mitsuki would rather not have to learn.

"At her present weight, about seven hundred calories a day should be sufficient."

The number itself meant little to her. The doctor's voice receded. Her mind went blank. He went on for another minute or two but the interval seemed interminable, a deviation from the laws of physics.

"Very well, please go ahead."

The voice scarcely seemed her own. A new world had been on the verge of opening, a world where she could finally breathe freely and bask in sunlight, and now she was shut again in blackness.

How would her sister deal with the shock of this turnabout? Mitsuki went slowly downstairs to the telephone room. *She won't do us all a favor and die*: before she knew it she was mouthing the words. The stairway was blurred by what she realized were her tears. Fortunately she met no one on the way, and the telephone room was empty.

"Nooo!" Natsuki wailed and then was silent.

Over the line she could sense her sister too plunging from sunlight into darkness.

"She's not going to let us be free, is she?" Natsuki's voice was low and faint. She slowly began to make the convulsive noises that signaled tears. After a bit she said brokenly, "I mean really, when will we *ever* be free of her? At this rate, we'll die before she does! No joke. I might die, for real."

"Don't be silly," Mitsuki retorted. "If anyone keels over, it'll be me."

Her voice had an edge. After all the time and money that had been lavished on her, Natsuki had never truly been involved as a caregiver until their mother's fateful fall. Once she lost favor with their mother, her chronic ailments had provided an easy way out, and in the end she had gone through but a portion of Mitsuki's travail.

"Maybe you've been through a lot more than I have," Natsuki allowed. "But I suffered more actual damage. I wasn't allowed to live my own life!"

Mitsuki had indeed lived her own life. But her life was a mess. She pictured Tetsuo standing in the kitchen with that young woman. He held his liquor well and liked to sip wine while cooking, the way Westerners did. Long ago in the kitchen of a garret in Paris he had prepared a meal for her, and she, swooning in the glow of myriad flickering candles, had said, "I'm sure. Somebody like you will do just fine." That had been the start of the mess, but this Natsuki did not know.

She changed the subject. "Anyway, it's a good thing we have money. Just imagine, we're keeping her room at Golden while paying for a private room here at the hospital! Last time, she was in a double room, and I was on pins and needles, remember?"

"I remember." Then Natsuki said again, in a low, faint voice, "She's not going to let us be free after all, is she?"

After hanging up, Mitsuki went out for lunch and then returned to the hospital. She had brought some translation work, but all she could do was stare in stunned silence at her sleeping mother. The gurgling sounds in her chest were unchanged.

When her mother opened her eyes, she said into her ear, "Your pneumonia is getting better."

Wearing an oxygen mask, her mother widened her eyes as if to ask, *Really?* She seemed to understand that there was something to be glad about, and her toothless mouth curved in a smile; but her smile bore a trace of the artificial simper her daughters disliked so much.

Feeling blackness deepen inside her, Mitsuki said, "I know you're uncomfortable, but don't worry. You're getting better and better."

Her mother nodded.

They went on taking turns visiting her. Unlike before, these visits were dreary. Yet as the dreary visits stretched on, to her surprise Mitsuki found herself wishing now that her mother would go ahead and make a full recovery. A few months ago the sight of her in her wheelchair had seemed unbearably pitiful, but if her mother's life was to be spared, she wanted her to regain enough strength to sit up in that same wheelchair and resume her former life in Golden.

And yet to all outward appearances, her condition remained the same as ever. Dark, cavernous mouth, hollow eyes turned to the ceiling: how could a patient recovering from pneumonia look like this? Even if she were cured, it was hard to believe she would ever be able to swallow again, let alone sit up. One day Mitsuki asked the nurse in private and was told that even if the pneumonia responded to treatment, regaining the ability to swallow was rare at her mother's age. Did this mean that the only effect of the high-calorie solution would be to drag out the process of her wasting away?

In time the doctor suggested a blood transfusion. Her hemoglobin level was dangerously low, and there was blood in her stool, a sign of internal bleeding, though he could not pinpoint the source. After talking it over with her sister, Mitsuki hardened her heart and said no. If the unexplained bleeding went on and their mother died of pneumonia, that was her fate, they concluded. So be it. But once again she defied expectations. The bleeding stopped of its own accord, and her hemoglobin level rose.

The second time the topic came up, Mitsuki gave in and said yes. The bleeding had returned. Her pneumonia was almost entirely cleared up, and he was more eager to administer blood. The sisters consented, but they remained skeptical. Even if her pneumonia continued to improve, as long as she had unexplained hemorrhaging, the goal of returning to Golden could only recede further into the distance.

That day, Mitsuki arrived at the hospital just as the plasma for her mother's blood transfusion came in. A minivan marked JAPAN RED CROSS pulled up in the emergency parking space, and two men in work uniforms got out and went inside, carrying a shiny silver cooling box between them. She remembered the Red Cross staff in front of Isetan always urging passersby to donate blood. They would stand with a placard indicating in red letters how many more liters of which blood types were needed in one hand and a megaphone in the other, shouting till they were hoarse: "We need more blood! Please donate today!" This was that precious, hard-won blood.

A blood transfusion would put their mother back in the pink, the doctor said, but it did no such thing. She just lay in her bed, breathing with difficulty, as before. Mitsuki went on clasping her mother's hand when she reached for hers and stroking her arm to comfort her. Now and then her mother would murmur, "I'm so tired."

*So am I*, Mitsuki felt like saying, but didn't.

If her mother didn't hold out her hand, Mitsuki would sit by the bed and work on a translation. Sometimes a memory would come to her of the grieving man in a dark suit whom she had encountered more than half a year ago at that first hospital. What might have become of his Wakako Matsubara?

She looked at her mother, sleeping with mouth open.

There must have been a time when her death would have been a terrible blow. If she had died before Mitsuki grew up, Mitsuki would have yearned for her the rest of her life, despite everything. Had her half-sister, the one who was left behind and drowned in a lake, spent her short life longing for a mother known only in dim memory?

Was there ever a right time for one's mother to disappear from the face of the earth?

Eventually the dysphagia therapy got under way with great fanfare, carried out by a team of three: her doctor, a therapist, and a nurse. The nurse would raise her up in bed and, after the therapist carefully massaged her throat muscles, feed her a tiny spoonful of thickened liquid. Then the doctor would check with his stethoscope to see if she had been able to get the liquid down. She never could.

In time antibiotic-resistant bacteria began to show up in her lungs, a common complication of chronic pneumonia. They were instructed to wear a special mask when entering her room, and always wash and disinfect their hands when leaving. The appearance of resistant bacteria made the goal of returning their mother to Golden recede ever further into the distance.

Summer seemed to go on forever.

Mitsuki didn't think about anything, but just dragged her weary body back and forth between the hospital and her apartment under burning skies. Her sister went by taxi. Mitsuki mostly took the bus, but on days when she was particularly beat she took a taxi. Her sister urged her to pay for taxis out of their mother's money, but she was reluctant to do so every time she went to see her mother in the hospital.

The bus air-conditioning was at its midsummer peak.

She wore winter underwear as a precaution, but by the time she walked to the bus stop she would be dripping with perspiration; the frigid air on the bus couldn't have felt more unpleasant. She tried slipping handkerchiefs beneath her underwear, one in front and one in back, and removing them when she boarded the bus. Even then her underwear was soaked with sweat. She took to carrying an extra set to change into in the ladies' room at the hospital — yet another item for her to lug back and forth.

After she entered her mother's room and put on a mask, the first thing she did was turn off the air-conditioning. The nurses, technicians, and aides were young, and moving around besides, so chilly air didn't bother them. Her mother, who had come down with air-conditioning syndrome shortly after Mitsuki did, showed no sign of being cold, whether because the IV fluids kept her warm or because she was barely conscious. She only lay with her mouth open.

# 29

## BONES UNDER GRAVESTONES

The people they had contacted back when they thought their mother would soon die now began stopping by her room.

First to come was Masako. Divorced, she had struggled on her own to raise a daughter who'd recently developed an eating disorder and had no fixed job. She donned a hospital mask and leaned solicitously over the bed, murmuring, "I owe her so much." She often used to visit them at the house in Chitose Funabashi, and during the fuss surrounding her divorce, she had taken shelter there with her daughter instead of returning to her stuffy, disapproving parents. Mitsuki's mother had welcomed her gladly during her troubles.

Someone from their father's side of the family came too. Orphaned at a young age, he had been kindly taken in by the impoverished Katsura family and grew up close to their father, calling him "Big Brother," though they were not related by blood. He had no great love for their mother but came to see her anyway out of a sense of duty. He offered words of comfort to Mitsuki and her sister: "Whenever I used to go see your father, he would tell me how good you both were to him."

Uncle Yokohama's much younger brother and his wife also put in an appearance. Time had taken its relentless toll; both Uncle

Yokohama and Madama Butterfly had passed on. Cousin Noriko was a precious link to the family's bygone glory days.

Next came Auntie's daughter, Satsuki, with whom the sisters felt a special bond on account of their names, which were patterned after hers. After her visit, the three of them went into a coffee shop to catch up and commiserate. Auntie had entered a nursing home around the same time as their mother and was now confined to a wheelchair. Satsuki's naturally curly hair, once so adorable, was streaked with gray; she didn't dye it as the sisters did theirs.

One day a sixtyish woman whom their mother had become friends with at the chanson studio dropped in. They had hesitated about whether to contact her, since the acquaintance was not of very long standing, but when their mother parted from That Man and quickly aged, this woman had taken pity on her and shown her kindness, not just calling her on the telephone but occasionally going to the house in Chitose Funabashi and fixing her a hot meal.

She knew what had become of That Man. "It's a good thing he had his wife's pension from teaching junior high school. They live quietly on that now. He has grandkids. He's just your typical granddad."

The last to appear was a relative from their mother's side. The connection was complicated, but their mother had treated her simply as a niece, and in fact she, Mitsuki, and Natsuki all shared the same grandmother—the one known as "O-Miya." This niece, though pretty, was a no-nonsense person seemingly free of "O-Miya's blood." Standing at the foot of the bed, she looked at the sleeping figure and declared, "She lived her life the way she wanted. What more could you ask?"

Everyone looked at her lying in bed and politely said the same thing—"Still as beautiful as ever." When someone came, Mitsuki or Natsuki would rouse her and say the visitor's name loudly in her ear.

Their mother would open her eyes and be surprisingly capable of a normal response, clasping the visitor's hand and saying in an affected tone, with tears in her eyes, "How *lovely* to see you!" They must have all gone away never realizing how advanced her dementia was.

Their mother did not get better.

Phlegm that she could neither swallow nor spit out gurgled constantly in the back of her throat.

Before anyone noticed, autumn breezes began to blow, and the summer heat thankfully receded; but for Mitsuki, caring for a mother who was hovering between life and death, there was no rest.

One late afternoon, she took a walk to the nearby Myohoji temple for the first time in a long while to give herself a little lift. Founded some three hundred years ago in the Edo period, the temple was believed to have the power to ward off evil spirits and promised help in everything from getting married and giving birth to prospering in business, recovering from illness, and passing college entrance examinations. What to pray for? Mixed in with old worshippers she saw young ones too, standing with palms together and heads bowed. Past the main gate with its statues of guardian Deva kings on either side was the well-swept compound with a large founder's hall in the center and a smaller main hall in back. The area behind that was shaded by tall trees, their leaves just beginning to show a scattering of yellow, orange, and occasional scarlet in the surrounding deep green. Her feet turned of their own accord toward a small gate still deeper in the compound, the entrance to the graveyard. Normally her spirit was soothed by the quiet of rows of gravestones, small and large, each with its narrow wooden tablet for the repose of the deceased; but today the myriad whitened bones from three centuries back seemed to rattle ominously under their gravestones.

Soon her mother had another blood transfusion.

Mitsuki no longer thought it possible that her mother would ever recover the ability to swallow. Even if she did return to Golden, she would be bedridden, condemned to a life of intravenous feeding while waiting to die. How many months—years—might that go on? Could they possibly get her back on the low-calorie solution? The doctor, his expression smooth as always, did nothing but sit and stare at the computer. Mitsuki hesitated, uncertain whether to broach the topic.

Then, to her consternation, the doctor brought up the idea of a surgical feeding tube. One Friday in October he stopped Mitsuki as she passed by the nurses' station, where he was seated as usual in front of his computer. Her mother's veins were reaching their limit, he said; he wanted to implant a tube directly into her stomach.

Mitsuki couldn't believe her ears. She had shown this doctor her mother's signed statement from the SDD, had spelled out to him that neither her mother, nor she, nor her sister wanted any kind of tube feeding. He had said, "Yes, of course. I understand." Did the man have amnesia? Speechless, she stared at him hard enough to bore a hole in his face.

He then delivered another blow. "Her pneumonia isn't entirely cleared up either, and with her hemoglobin level making these sudden fluctuations, even with a surgical tube in place I'm afraid I can't authorize sending her back to the nursing home."

Mitsuki gave him a steady look and managed to ask in a normal voice, "Where, then?"

"An extended-care hospital."

That night, the shock was so great that she and Natsuki met for dinner in Shibuya.

"How could he *say* such a thing?"

"She can't sit up. And doesn't even know it. Her internal bleeding hasn't stopped, either. How in God's name can he open a hole in the stomach of someone like that?"

"Someone who never wanted it in the first place."

In their mind's eye they both saw the same scene: a deluxe suite in the extended-care hospital at the end of the Toyoko line where for nearly a year a certain figure had been lying inert with tubes down his nose: Natsuki's father-in-law, who would soon turn ninety-three. That dynamic, manly patriarch had seemed more likely to end his days with the flare of the ancient general Taira no Kiyomori, who, according to *The Tales of the Heike*, turned bright red with a fever so high that when cold water was poured on him it "burst into flames, filling the chamber with thick black smoke and whirling fire."

Yuji's father had always gotten along well with Natsuki's mother and was fond of Natsuki, and of Mitsuki by extension. Then in his mid-eighties he had developed stomach cancer and after a gastrectomy quickly grew frail. He suffered two severe strokes and was put on a liquid diet, ensconced in the two-room suite. Growing steadily more senile, he eventually contracted aspiration pneumonia and was hospitalized. He recovered but could no longer tolerate a liquid diet. As he had no stomach, he wasn't a candidate for a surgical feeding tube and so was fitted with nasogastric tubes instead.

The Shimazaki family had been summoned to the hospital and informed of the impending change. Natsuki, sitting next to Yuji, cried out despite herself, "Couldn't you just leave him be and do nothing?" Yuji's elder brother and his wife, as well as his sister, had been present too. As the wife of the second son, Natsuki had the least say of anyone in the room, yet she'd felt so strongly she couldn't keep quiet. Watching as her hollow-eyed father-in-law was propped up in bed to have fluids poured down his throat had been painful enough; now they wanted to put in feeding tubes as he lay unconscious. As soon as she spoke, Natsuki realized her faux pas and looked around at the family. They were looking expectantly at the female doctor—they'd all been thinking the same thing.

The doctor's response, however, was unsympathetic. "In that case, I'm afraid the family would have to take over his care." She added with emphasis, "But you should know that caring for an elderly terminal patient is far from easy. Often the patient ends up being returned to the hospital."

And so Yuji's father lay unconscious in the deluxe suite with his neck immobilized and a tube down each nostril.

A former classmate of Natsuki's from the Yokohama conservatory said something one day that made her gnash her teeth with rage. Apparently the classmate's own mother had suffered from Alzheimer's, and when she developed trouble swallowing, the hospital in Sapporo, near where the family lived, agreed to let her die a natural death. She was gone in a matter of weeks.

Natsuki had taken out her fury on Mitsuki over the telephone. "That high and mighty doctor, why didn't she tell us we had that choice? That other hospitals do that?" As usual, she'd been calling from the piano room, where she had taken refuge with her two cats for company.

She was venting her frustration on Mitsuki because neither Yuji nor his family shared her wrath. Unlike the Katsura family, the Shimazakis, as befitted a family of old money, were too genteel ever to question the system. Yuji's father, the sole exception, ended up lying flat on his back in bed, a vegetable—a fate he would surely never have wanted. Lately the nutrition he was receiving had begun to show its effects; he was putting on considerable flesh.

Back when their mother heard the particulars of Yuji's father's situation, she'd still been able to get around with a cane. "Oh, the poor man, what a terrible shame," she had said in tears, for she'd been growing sentimental. After blowing her nose she had declared, "I wouldn't want to go on living that way. What a waste of taxpayer money. When my time comes, tell them no thank you. And no poking holes in my stomach, either. Heaven forbid." She reached for another tissue. "The poor man doesn't even know he's alive. When it's my turn to go, I want to die on my own terms. You two are my only hope, so please do whatever it takes to keep that from happening. I'm counting on you."

Natsuki remembered the conversation, too.

The sisters said good night after agreeing that never under any circumstances would they allow a feeding tube to be put in their mother. Mitsuki felt depressed, knowing that it was up to her to think of a way to keep that from happening.

# ( 30 )

## A SLEEPLESS NIGHT

All that weekend, Mitsuki sat at her computer like one possessed and researched the topic of feeding tubes.

Outside her window, the leaves of the hydrangea bushes were just starting to turn golden in the autumn sun. Six months before, those same hydrangea bushes had just started putting out tender buds. She had sat glued to this same computer, going through Tetsuo's email correspondence with the young woman. This time she was spurred by something different, a kind of shock that went beyond the personal.

Doctors recommending feeding tubes for patients in her mother's condition, even when the patients expressly didn't want them: to what extent had this become standard practice in Japan? To what extent was it standard practice in other countries with advanced medical technology? She researched the topic in Japanese and other languages and learned that feeding tubes, invented as a way to provide temporary nourishment, had begun to stir new ethical debates among those on the frontlines of terminal care. Once upon a time, a person unable to eat would die, but today it was no longer so simple. Scandinavia and various other countries in Europe had rejected forced feeding as a means of prolonging life; in the United

States the practice was controversial, but in Japan, routine and unquestioned.

Just as she had suspected. Still, it was maddening.

On Monday she met with the doctor and pleaded that he continue just a while longer with the same approach.

"All right," he said. "A bit longer, then."

On the way home, the autumn sky was a clear blue. But the natural world seemed to have little to do with Mitsuki; indeed she was barely aware of its existence. She sighed and entered her building, then stumbled into her apartment.

She had to hurry and find a hospital where her mother could die in peace. Natsuki had left everything in her hands, but she had no idea what to do. She threw down her bags and stretched out on her bed, only to get up again a few minutes later with an idea. Why not call the SDD, the Society for Dying with Dignity, and talk to someone?

A soft-spoken woman perhaps in her sixties came on the line. Mitsuki explained the situation, and the woman promised to fax over a list of nearby facilities that would be more cooperative. She added sympathetically that "life-prolonging measures" usually referred to artificial respiration and cardiac massages. Whether tube feeding fell in that category would depend on the judgment of the primary physician.

Hearing this, Mitsuki's heart sank. Even if she spent the day calling each hospital in turn, how was she supposed to get through to a doctor who would respect her mother's wishes? Wherever she called, the voice of a harried receptionist would come on the line. How was she to explain the situation to that harried voice, how and through what channels finally reach the ear of an understanding doctor?

"Please take care not to fall ill yourself, my dear," the soft-spoken woman said before hanging up. Mitsuki was left speechless.

She stayed busy all day that day, now going over the list of recommended institutions, now stretching out in bed, now tackling the piled-up housework, now returning obsessively to the computer. She didn't feel like telephoning her sister. Having her as a companion in indignation would accomplish nothing. There was simply no time. She had to come to a quick decision and act. Determination not to let anyone do anything more to her mother inflamed her. Even with a feeding tube in place, someone in her condition couldn't last more than a few months at most. If she did by some chance last longer, was that what she would have wanted?

Her mother was no longer able to understand that she couldn't walk. Conversation with her was often painful. On her good days she would ask, "Mitsuki, why can't I walk? Lying here like this all the time wears me out. I want to get up and go somewhere. I want to go outside."

"Yes, Mother, but even before you got sick you couldn't walk. Don't you remember?"

"Really? I couldn't walk?"

"No."

"What if I used a cane?"

She had used a cane for so many years that she seemed to remember that, but all memory of her days in a wheelchair was gone.

From time to time she would say, "If there was a strong man around, he could carry me somewhere, couldn't he? It's no fun living like this." And then she would murmur, "I'm so tired."

That night as she lay in her bed, Mitsuki shed tears of pity for her mother for the first time. She held them back, so there were only a few, but they were tears of genuine pity nonetheless.

The liberation that their mother's death would bring no longer seemed to matter. In old age, Noriko Katsura had faced up to her impending death with admirable practicality. Names in her address book were marked with a red pen: a double circle indicated those who should be notified by telephone, a single circle those for whom a card would be enough. She had also decided that she would rather forgo a funeral and have her ashes scattered, like their father. In her complete reliance on her daughters in old age she may have been following tradition, but in her staunch belief in a person's right to have a say in how her life ended she was anything but traditional. Her mother's life must not end in a way that she would have scorned.

Mitsuki stared into the dark and pondered.

Then it came to her: Tetsuo was away. She could take her mother in. That would solve everything. The tiny lettering on the list of medical institutions from the SDD danced before her eyes, but she lacked the patience to scrounge around in that data for the name of a doctor who would allow her mother to die. There wasn't time anyway. She had briefly considered the hospital that let her sister's friend's mother die a natural death, but what taxi—even one for the handicapped—would carry a dying old lady all the way north to Sapporo?

Caring for her at home was at once the worst choice and the best.

Her mother probably would balk at having Mitsuki tend to her toilet needs, so they would need to hire help on a twenty-four-hour basis. Whether to continue the suctioning she didn't know, but in any case it would be better to have a trained nurse on hand. If possible it would be better to withhold all artificial nutrition and hydration and just moisten the inside of her mouth with gauze.

Whatever suffering came her mother's way, she, Mitsuki, would have to be prepared for it. Long ago, that's how people all used to die, right in their own homes.

Since her mother's fall, Mitsuki had had a number of sleepless nights, but never before had she felt such tension, as if her whole body were under compression. What lay ahead rose before her eyes: her mother lying face up in bed with a phlegm aspirator in one corner of the room, a heap of diapers in another. To what extent would she understand why she was there? How could she ever explain it to her?

At the first gray light of dawn, she was reminded of how from ages past the morning has always brought relief to those who suffered through the night. She felt ready to face what would come.

"I'm going to take Mom in."

Timing her call, she announced her decision to her sister. There was a pause. Then her sister said, sounding a little surprised, "You didn't talk it over with Mrs. Kiyokawa?"

The head caregiver at Golden still showed up at the hospital now and then with a bouquet of flowers.

"You're right."

How foolish and arrogant she had been to sit up all night in torment, convinced that she had to take on the world single-handed! Natsuki had assumed all along that she would seek help. She called Mrs. Kiyokawa then and there, and things proceeded to unroll so smoothly that her nightmare vision vanished into thin air. A clinic run by the doctor at Golden who had seen their mother once a week would take her in under the conditions they desired.

Mitsuki couldn't keep the excitement out of her voice. "No high-calorie solution?"

"That's right." Mrs. Kiyokawa herself sounded curiously upbeat. "If that's what the family wishes."

It took less than a week to transfer her to the clinic. Getting the clinic doctor's confirmation took one whole day, and the next day when Mitsuki went to the hospital her mother was just having what was to be her final therapy session. As before, it occurred under the expert guidance of the doctor, the therapist, and a nurse, and as before it ended in failure. On cue, the doctor again suggested surgery to implant a feeding tube. Mitsuki swallowed the angry words rising in her throat and informed him that Golden was on good terms with a certain clinic where, in view of their mother's condition, they planned to transfer her and then figure out the best course of action.

The doctor's face brightened; he looked as if a load had just been lifted from his shoulders. This Mitsuki had not been prepared for. She had been braced for a certain amount of resistance, but the look on his guileless face said as clear as day that he was relieved to see the last of a difficult patient. As he sat in front of the computer staring at numerical data, had his heart never once been moved by her mother's plight? Did Japan's current medical system leave him no other choice? Was he forced to give up feeling and thinking like a normal human being?

The day of the transfer was soon set.

On that day, Natsuki and Yuji came to help. The clinic had instructed that her IV be stopped before she was moved, and Mitsuki and her sister watched with emotion as the line was taken out. Never again would their mother be force-fed to postpone her death indefinitely.

As a token of their appreciation, Mitsuki offered the doctor a big box of cookies to share with the staff. After first refusing it for form's sake, he bore it off to the nurses' station. Nowadays everyone seemed to feel the need to go on a diet, but she hoped at least some of the nurses who had looked after her mother might have a sweet tooth.

The doctor and nurses all gathered in the hallway and watched ceremoniously as their mother was carried by stretcher into a specially fitted taxi, remaining out front until the family drove out of sight. Before getting into the taxi, Mitsuki and her sister kept bowing in some confusion. To the last, they never knew what was going through the doctor's mind. His smooth, unreadable face seemed to symbolize the riddles of Japan's medical system.

Rocked by the motion of the taxi, their mother was carried along toward her new destination. Her eyes were closed, but it was impossible to tell if she was asleep. She had lost so much weight since the start of her ordeal that she looked almost skeletal.

At the clinic, her attending physician was evidently taken aback on seeing her for the first time in two and a half months. After exchanging greetings, his first words were "I'm surprised to see how changed she is. She probably won't remember me."

## DON'T YOU LOVE ME?

"In any case, we hope you'll choose the path of least suffering for her," Yuji told the attending physician, who seemed unable to recover from his shock at his patient's deteriorated condition.

They had asked Yuji to come because of what had happened with her previous doctor. Mitsuki and her sister talked it over and reached the conclusion that just to be safe, a man of the family—the more conventional the better—should lay out the crucial points. Yuji, although a cellist, didn't necessarily dress like an artist. He certainly didn't affect a "literati shirt." The older she got, the more Mitsuki had come to appreciate his very conventionality.

The doctor nodded and then said these heartening words: "Families who are the most attentive generally reach the same conclusion, that the patient's own comfort should come first." He might be saying this simply to make them feel better, Mitsuki thought, but she was grateful nonetheless.

From then on, the sisters' days were spent just waiting for their mother to die.

The little clinic was new and clean. Examination rooms were on the first floor, private patients' rooms on the second and third floors, six on either side of the corridor. Half of them were empty.

In the other half, old people lay in bed, each with chin pointing up and toothless mouth wide open. The atmosphere was neither rushed, as in most hospitals, nor stagnant as in most nursing homes. Autumn sunshine poured through the windows, and time passed tranquilly. It was more like a hospice than a clinic.

As they visited their mother, her death now a looming certainty because of the decision they had made, the sisters' hearts too were tranquil. The clinic caregivers were all female, which they liked. Several times a day one would come in the room to swab the inside of her mouth, aspirate her, or change her diaper. She received two IV bags of low-calorie solution per day. She wasn't wearing an oxygen mask anymore. As ever, her dark, cavernous mouth gaped wide open. Knowing that freedom lay around the corner, Mitsuki no longer found the sight terrifying.

One day she fingered the base of her mother's jaw on either side of her head and felt hard swellings. Weeks of breathing through her mouth to gain oxygen had stiffened the jaw muscles until they'd developed tight kinks. Mitsuki sat and massaged the swellings with her fingertips for a while. After she went home, she reported her finding to her sister, and the next day Natsuki said she'd spent over an hour massaging the same spots. Perhaps in these final days she was seeking reconciliation with her mother, and with her own past. She'd always been cleverer with her fingers than Mitsuki, and now was no exception.

It was around then that Mitsuki began to sort the papers in the filing cabinet under her desk and try to work out how much money her mother would leave the two of them.

They discussed what clothes to dress her in when the time came. The first idea was one of the floor-length gowns she'd had made for her chanson recitals. The association with That Man made them flinch, but the gowns had been ridiculously expensive and Natsuki, who had plenty of storage space, had taken several of them home.

There was one in black silk that had been especially becoming on their tall mother; sending her off dressed in that, surrounded by a hundred crimson roses, would suit her perfectly.

Burial clothes fit for a star of the silver screen...or a hostess of a Ginza club. They both reached the same conclusion: "Let's not."

Instead they settled on a dress of pale-gray mohair with a longish hem, as soft and light as a wisp of cloud. Even after her back grew so bent that she couldn't wear it, she'd been unable to part with it. That one took up little space, so Mitsuki had taken it home with her. That dress and a silver-colored scarf of gauzy silk would be fitting attire for their mother's final journey.

Rather than a hundred crimson roses, they decided instead to fill her casket with simple flowers such as might grow wild in a meadow. They hoped that the angelic garment and simple flowers might have a purifying effect on their mother, who seemed almost to have been burdened her whole life long by frustrated passions from past lives. When she set off on her journey to the next world, they hoped that she might go to a place as pure and peaceful as possible, be it nirvana, heaven, or paradise. Or, if she were to be reincarnated in human form, they hoped to lessen her burden in the life to come and so reduce her suffering and the suffering of those around her.

But she wouldn't go quietly—as they should have known.

After a week or so, Mitsuki went into her mother's room expecting to find her asleep as usual, but instead her large-pupiled eyes were open. She focused them on Mitsuki and held out her hand.

It was as if the dead had returned to life.

After putting on a hospital mask, Mitsuki clasped her mother's outstretched hand and said loudly into her ear, "We moved you to a hospital in a more convenient location," repeating what she had told her on the first day.

"Oh. I'm in the hospital?"

Her voice was feeble. Mitsuki had expected her not to under-stand that she had been moved, but she seemed not to remember ever having been in the hospital in the first place.

She looked up at the ceiling and said, "This may be where I breathe my last."

At such times she had an uncanny way of coming out with statements that got straight to the point.

Mitsuki ignored this. "It's a nice room, don't you think? I'm Mi-tsuki. Do you know me?"

"Of course I do. Why wouldn't I?"

Her voice might be feeble, but she sounded almost her usual self. *Incapable of a simple yes or no*, Mitsuki was thinking wryly, when her mother said her name and held out her hand again. When she took it in hers, her mother started talking loquaciously, asking after Auntie, then others. Finally, when Mitsuki was about to leave, she said, "Give us a kiss"—words borrowed from the silver screen, words Mitsuki hadn't heard since she was a child. Fearful of resis-tant bacteria, knowing it was coldhearted of her, she leaned down and gave her mother a pretend peck through her surgical mask.

The next day her sister telephoned her. The doctor was as sur-prised as they were. Possibly their mother's body, on the edge of starvation, was marshaling its forces a last time.

That night Mitsuki dreamed that somehow, without anyone's knowing it, her mother's IV had been switched to the high-calorie solution. She awoke screaming in the middle of the night.

After three days their mother's talkativeness tapered off, but she remained communicative and agitated. She was awake more and complained of pain with a grimace. "It hurts."

"Where does it hurt? Here?" Mitsuki would ask, massaging her.

The nurse put it down to nerves, but there was no doubt she was in pain. Couldn't they give her a bit of morphine? The nurse tilted her head to one side and, with a troubled look, slowly replied: "I'm afraid…that's not a good idea."

Bit by bit she was dying. Was "It hurts" her way of expressing the eerie sensation of being dragged off to the next world? Unable to make her comfortable, Mitsuki found the incessant cries of pain hard on her nerves.

Her mother also repeated words she had said time and again over the past year: "What's the use of going on like this?"

Instead of saying, "Don't worry, Mom, it'll all be over soon," Mitsuki took her mother's hand in hers and stroked it. The skin was covered in purple splotches and crisscrossed with big blue veins. Stroking that death-marked hand, she took to dreamily remembering a lake scene.

It was a place she saw years ago with her mother from the garden of a lakeside hotel. Her mother, after being run over by that speeding bicycle and aging overnight, had wanted to be taken to that hotel, built on the same site that her own mother had visited a century before. Perhaps her sudden transformation into an old woman had given her the urge; she wheedled with her usual persistence until Mitsuki gave in. When at last she was set free, Mitsuki thought, she would go back to that hotel. She would sit and contemplate the lake and take her time thinking through what to do about Tetsuo.

Mitsuki was turning down patent translations now. She spent her time sitting next to her mother's bed reading a French novel she had come across when clearing out her library to make space for her mother's things. The novel was Flaubert's *Madame Bovary*. For a long time it had felt like a forbidden book to her, but now with her mother at death's door the taboo was somehow lifted. After every few lines she would look up at the IV bag. Two hundred calories, twice daily.

One day a nurse came to change the IV bag and said gently, "Just hang in there a little longer, Mrs. Katsura, and you'll be right as rain." Her mother, awake, put on her company smile and mouthed the words, "Yes, thank you."

As soon as the nurse bustled out of the room, her mother glowered. "Something's fishy." She turned her eyes to the IV bag. "There's something fishy going on. She's lying. Look at me. I'm not getting better."

Mitsuki could have wept. Why oh why, when she was on the point of dying, did her mother have to become so lucid?

Dealing with her newly communicative mother was an intense emotional strain. Her mother planted kisses on her hands one minute and wanted to be cradled the next. Over and over she would say, "I wish somebody would pick me up and carry me away." Pity lacerated Mitsuki's heart. But then her mother's everlasting chant would start up — "It hurts. It hurts." — and pity would turn again to a mounting irritation.

A few days later Natsuki called, hysterical. As a gesture of love, she had tried to comb their mother's hair. "You know what she did? She shook me off and said, 'Don't you touch me!' I was so upset I threw down the comb and walked out."

Mitsuki could envision the wounded look on her sister's face, the same look she remembered from when they were little — a look that had cropped up more often since Natsuki's rift with their mother, who would never say such a thing to Mitsuki. It saddened her to know that even as she lay dying, their mother could be so hostile to Natsuki. Was there to be no end to this silliness between them?

She dragged her weary bones to the clinic that evening to check on her mother. She touched her on the shoulder, and her eyes opened.

"Mother, you mustn't be mean to Natsuki. It isn't nice."

This seemed to mystify her mother. Mitsuki gave up trying to get through to her and murmured, "This is no time to be nursing grudges. She's doing the best she can."

Something in Mitsuki's voice seemed to trigger a response. Her mother spoke up.

"Mitsuki, don't you love me?"

## 32

## DREAMS WANDERING DESOLATE MOORS

*I hate you, Mother, I hate you!*

For years, ever since she saw how horrible her mother was being to her father, she had longed to yell this at her. Now she was silent. That was the kindest thing she could do at this point. To Mitsuki's surprise, her mother persisted.

"Tell me. Don't you love me?"

"How can you say that, Mother? Don't I take good care of you?"

She could not make her voice sound loving. She was angry with her mother for asking such a critical question now, at the end of her life, when she was half demented. At the same time, it was sad to think that at this stage of her life her mother should need to ask such a question. With death hovering just out of reach, something inside her mother could have been taking advantage of her dementia to ask the question that had lain between them all these years.

That turned out to be her last conversation with her mother.

Again that night, she sat up late taking care of her mother's paperwork. For the first time in a while Tetsuo sent her an email. His emails always reminded her that she had yet to tell him anything about her mother, even that she was in the hospital. His message ended, "You must be glad the season for air-conditioning is over." He always was considerate in his way.

*Mother still won't die. She still won't die. She still won't...* That was all she wanted to write, a hundred times over. She could think of nothing else. Nearly out of her mind with vexation, vaguely picturing him over there with his inamorata, she forced herself to type: "Thanks for writing. It must always be hot where you are." And then turned back to her mother's papers.

Numbers just kept whirling in front of her.

At nearly one in the morning, she gave up, went into the kitchen to open a can of light beer, and sat down to stare absently at the news on television. None of it made any sense to her. Her nerves were jangled by the slight amount of alcohol she had consumed, and one thought went round and round her mind: on four hundred calories a day, her mother would not die anytime soon. What if she went on for another month or two, asking questions like "Don't you love me?"

She wouldn't die.

Her mother just wouldn't give up and frigging die.

The house was full of dust balls, the laundry was piled up, she hadn't even had time to dye the roots of her hair. She was barely stumbling along, exhausted, but her mother wouldn't die. Her husband was off in a foreign country living with a young woman, and she needed to think about that, but her mother wouldn't die.

Mother, when are you *ever* going to die?

Whether she only screamed the words in her mind or actually screamed them out loud, she wasn't sure, but with the echo of her own voice resounding in her head, she reeled into the bedroom, changed into her nightgown, washed her face and brushed her teeth, and swallowed her various prescription pills. Do not take with alcohol, they always warned at the pharmacy, but over the past few years she had taken to downing them with beer. If tonight that led to trouble, so be it.

The next thing she knew, her face was wet with tears, like a child's. She lay down, quietly sobbing, and pulled the duvet up to her chin.

The phone rang.

It was one-thirty in the morning. The call could only be from the clinic.

It was the night-shift nurse. Her mother's blood oxygen level had dropped to 92. If it went any lower, they would be unable to put her on a respirator; was that all right? she wanted to know.

Yes, of course it was. Forcing calm into her voice, Mitsuki told the nurse that she had just taken a sleeping pill, then asked, "Is she in immediate danger?"

"No, nothing immediate... How quickly could you be here?"

In less than thirty minutes, Mitsuki replied.

"When the blood oxygen goes below eighty-five, it's touch and go, but at this rate if you came in the morning you would be in time."

Mitsuki marveled that you could calculate the time of a person's impending demise based only on their blood oxygen level. "In that case I'll get some sleep and be there in the morning," she said and hung up. Then she called her sister. She hated to wake her, knowing she was chronically fatigued from steroid side effects, but felt that she should. Natsuki had missed being with their father at the time of his death. Mitsuki doubted that she would venture out alone at this time of night, but should anything happen before morning, she didn't want to be held responsible for her missing their mother's death as well.

"You're sure she'll hang on till morning?" Natsuki still sounded a bit hurt by her mother's sharp words.

"That's what the nurse said. And they'll call right away when the numbers do drop."

"When that happens, I'll go too."

Of course. With her sister it was always "I'll go too." Though that night, it hardly seemed to matter.

In the morning, Mitsuki showered to wake herself up. She was in a hurry but, anticipating a long haul, she took a rice ball out of the freezer, heated it in the microwave, and ate it just to have something in her stomach. By the time she got to the clinic, it was going on eight o'clock.

Beside the nurses' station stood a machine she had often seen there before; its display screen now recorded the data of her mother's dwindling life. Besides a little pink heart flashing on and off in time with her pulse and making small beeps, there were wavy ECG lines and numbers indicating blood pressure and blood oxygen level.

Her mother's eyes were open, and she was taking short breaths. She didn't look much different from herself on a typical bad day, but when Mitsuki bent over her, her eyes didn't move. The surface of her eyes was cloudier than usual, like dead fish eyes. But when she softly squeezed her mother's hand, the pressure was faintly returned...or so it seemed. Thinking perhaps her mother could still hear, she put her mouth down close to her ear and said in a gentle tone, "Mom, it's me, Mitsuki. I'm right here and I'm not going anywhere. Don't worry." She may only have imagined it, but it seemed as if her mother gave a slight nod. Her open eyes remained fixed on the ceiling.

Next to the pillow, possibly for the family's reference, was a tiny machine that registered her blood oxygen level. The figure hovered in the 90s and sometimes went as high as 98.

Natsuki finally came, having waited till the supermarket was open so she could buy them each a boxed lunch, as they had agreed the night before. Since there was no telling when the inevitable would happen, Yuji and Jun had gone to work; if and when there was any change she would contact them. There was no point in sending for her son Ken, off at graduate school in the United States.

She was having her family come later not just to spare them, Mitsuki knew, but to keep vigil with her, just the two of them, for as long as possible.

From then on into the night, they waited. Sitting on hard stools all day was a form of torture. Every time they got up to use the bathroom and walked down the corridor, they would see empty beds in other rooms and yearn to go and lie down for ten minutes. They took turns sitting at the head and foot of the bed. When their mother's hands fluttered in the air as if in search of something, whoever was sitting by her head would take her hands in theirs and hold them for a while, speaking soothing words. The one sitting at the foot of the bed would lay her head on the covers and rest. They were both wearing masks, so conversation was difficult, and anyway they had already said everything there was to say.

Her hands kept fluttering, the withered, bony fingers waving in empty space as if in search of something. As the light faded from her mind, what scenes unfolded before her? Did her spirit, full of unfulfilled longing, wander desolate moors in search of a last gleam of light?

Mitsuki prayed silently that her mother might know that she and Natsuki were there beside her.

After five that evening, her oxygen level sank below 90. Natsuki contacted Yuji and Jun on her cell phone, and they arrived toward six-thirty. Once the oxygen level dropped below 85, it plummeted. The two sisters looked like just what they were, a pair of worn-out, ailing, middle-aged women, but Yuji, perhaps because he played golf, was fit and glowing with health. Jun, in her twenties now, was simply young. At some point the monitor was brought just outside the room; they could hear close at hand the electronic beeps sounding in time with the beating of her heart.

The attending nurse brought in some moist gauze, folded over. "The eyes get dry, you see," she explained, closing their mother's eyes gently with the tip of a finger and laying the gauze carefully on top of her lids. Only when she had finished did they realize gratefully that this way their mother would die with her eyes closed. The thought of those large-pupiled eyes staring sightless in her dead face was terrifying. People spoke of death as "eternal sleep," but dying and going to sleep were entirely different physiological phenomena.

Now when they went out into the corridor, they found the doors to all the other rooms shut, apparently to keep the other patients from sensing the flurry of activity that accompanied a death. Then they glimpsed her doctor, dressed in street clothes. The head nurse must have called him at home. After a bit he reappeared in a white coat. Evidently this had been his day off; they realized only then that he hadn't come by earlier.

Everything proceeded with surprising smoothness.

How many times a month someone died in the little clinic they had no way of knowing, but it was like watching a professional show with daily performances. Theoretically, Mitsuki and the rest had leading roles in the production, but they watched in a daze while events unfolded around them. The monitor was presently wheeled inside the room. The doctor waited just outside the door, in deference to the family. With their mother's every heartbeat, the little pink heart on the monitor flashed, and there was an electronic beep. The beeps grew farther apart. Her breathing seemed to stop. Even then, the beeps continued for some time. Just when it seemed over, after ten seconds or so there would be another tiny beep. This went on for two or three minutes.

Then all at once the doctor came in. "I think that's it."

The nurse switched off the monitor.

"She's gone."

Mitsuki and her sister bowed their heads. The doctor looked at his watch.

"Time of death, seven twenty-three p.m."

I think that's it: the doctor's choice of words struck Mitsuki as peculiar and lingered long in her ears.

## 33

## THE UNDERTAKER'S MENU

Day in and day out, she had been inwardly awed by and grateful for the nurses' brisk professionalism. After her mother died, they were transformed into a different set of professionals: purifiers of the dead. Their faces bore a solemn gravity almost religious in nature. The family was shooed from the room.

Yuji got the telephone number of a nearby funeral parlor from the clinic and placed a call, after which they all waited downstairs in the waiting room. Yuji picked up a magazine and read it. Jun, a young and overworked career woman, put in eyedrops and went back to her laptop. Natsuki and Mitsuki sat quietly.

In less than an hour, a nurse came for them.

Their mother had shrunk some ten centimeters in old age, but since she was lying down, the gray dress appeared to fit her perfectly. The nurse had applied powder and lipstick to her face. The sisters got out their own cosmetics pouches and lightly penciled in her eyebrows, adding a touch of gray eye shadow to match her dress and scarf. Mitsuki would have liked to outline her lips in bright red with a lip pencil, but she refrained.

"She always hated the way her front teeth stuck out a little."

"I know. She thought it was her one flaw."

"Talk about self-confidence!"

After that they put knee-high stockings on her. Both of them remembered from childhood that except when wearing a kimono, she always wore stockings. There was little purple cyanosis, but her once-slim legs were swollen beyond recognition.

Eventually a pair of undertakers wearing black suits and circumspect expressions appeared and carried the body out to a waiting minivan. The family piled into Yuji's Mercedes-Benz. The funeral parlor was modern and new inside and out, with a lobby suggestive of a decent but not grand hotel. Any hint of death had been completely eliminated. There was not even the scent of incense, in the old days a constant companion of the dead.

The moment they settled down on the sofa in the lobby, Yuji, as the man representing the family, was the one to tell the undertakers, "No funeral."

Mitsuki still remembered the disgruntled look on the undertaker's face at the time of her father's death. But times had evidently changed. The younger of the two undertakers responded with a glibness that caught them by surprise: "Certainly. In that case, we have a simple plan that should suit you nicely." With that, he produced a color flyer labeled "Serenity Plan." It resembled a restaurant menu.

| | |
|---|---|
| Mortuary (per day) | 10,500 |
| Casket (paulownia wood) | 63,000 |
| Dry ice (per day) | 8,400 |
| Pair of flower stands | 31,500 |
| Stretcher car (daytime, 10 km) | 12,600 |
| Hearse (standard vehicle) | 18,900 |
| Cremation (classic service) | 47,250 |
| Cinerary urn (porcelain) | 10,500 |
| Waterproof sheet | 5,250 |
| Administrative expenses | 52,500 |
| Total | ¥260,400 |

Other items were listed as optional: crematorium staff gratuity, cremation certificate, extra urn for partial burial of remains.

"Are more families skipping the funeral these days?" Mitsuki asked, curious.

"I would say the market is polarized," the younger undertaker answered courteously.

"I beg your pardon?"

"Some families, like yourselves, choose to forgo a funeral, and others choose a full-blown service with all the trimmings."

He sounded like a market analyst — or a caterer. Perhaps when the bereaved family was more outwardly grief-stricken, he changed his tone to match, and death acquired its proper solemnity.

When all was ready, they were ushered into, of all things, a tatami room — somehow jarring in this otherwise modern facility. To Mitsuki's further astonishment, there lying on the tatami was her mother's corpse, head pointing north and a white cloth laid over the face in the traditional manner. She had always slept in a bed; Mitsuki could not recall ever having seen her recline on tatami. It was as if in death she had been forcibly dragged back to her starting point, a life lived on fraying mats. For someone whose lifelong motivation had been the pursuit of nameless dreams, this seemed a form of ridicule — and, at the same time, of consolation.

*"Aujourd'hui, maman est morte."*

Back home, following a long telephone conversation with her sister, she got into bed and in the darkness spoke those French words for the first time in years. The taboo she had unknowingly imposed upon herself against uttering any French was gone. She tried saying the words in Japanese — those words she had wanted to speak aloud for such a very long time: "Today, Mother died."

Then, after taking her medicine as usual, she fell asleep in a world without her mother for the first time in her life.

The remains were cremated two days later.

Back when their father died, the sisters had been fiercely angry with their mother and chose for his memorial photograph a black-and-white one from his student days, taken long before he'd ever met her—before he'd met even his first wife. His face, framed by an old-fashioned stand-up collar and round spectacles, had looked heartrendingly young. What sort of future had he imagined for himself? He wore an expression not to be found in contemporary Japan, a mix of reserve and high hopes. In the crematorium, on a stand by the chamber door, the youthful photograph had seemed oddly out of place.

They did not intend to choose any ordinary photograph for their mother either, but there were so many—being photographed having been a kind of hobby of hers—that they had trouble deciding. In the end they chose one from her thirties. She was standing outdoors with the two of them; they were holding hands in a circle, as if about to start dancing. The picture was in color, a rarity at the time. She was wearing a mauve kimono embroidered around the skirt with silver and gold and topped by a white wool *chabaori* jacket, one of the many she owned from her job with Auntie. The sisters had on matching navy dresses and white cardigans decorated with a scattering of little lace flowers set with pearllike beads—presents their father had brought back from America. Their mother looked sweetly maternal, her head tilted to one side as she clasped their hands. Theatrical as could be. The love of their father, who took the picture, was all the more strongly evident for his not being in it.

They were fond of the picture, but Mitsuki wondered aloud if it wasn't rather inappropriate for the purpose at hand. It showed their mother as not only young, but at play with her children. Natsuki had no qualms. "No, it's perfect," she declared. "I mean, that's *exactly* the mother we would have wanted." Her breezy indifference to convention sometimes took Mitsuki by surprise.

What emerged from the furnace were bones so trifling they could scarcely believe their eyes. Strange to think that a woman with these measly bones could have wielded such a saucy tongue. The crematorium clerk ran a magnet over the heap, drawing out the various metal screws that had held her bones together.

Her ashes filled the urn only halfway. Mitsuki got into Yuji's car clutching the urn. Lingering heat warmed her lap.

Straight off the next day, they had to begin dealing with the aftermath of her death. Mitsuki hesitated to contact Tetsuo's parents. Their names were naturally marked with a double circle in her mother's address book, and she felt bad not informing them, but if she did she would have to make clear that Tetsuo had been kept in the dark. She decided to say nothing for the time being.

Exhausted, the sisters decided to postpone a small get-together in their mother's memory until sometime after the New Year, around her birthday. She'd been born on February 11, a day celebrated in prewar Japan as Empire Day, the supposed anniversary of Emperor Jimmu's accession to the throne back in the misty past. Her name, "Noriko," was written using a character associated with the day. She used to grumble, "Why couldn't they have named me Kaoru or Naomi or something with a little more pizzazz?" When they urged people to "come dressed to the nines" in her honor, those who knew her well laughed. Many of them must have known about her abuse of their father but all responded graciously.

It was during a lull in dealing with the aftermath of her mother's death that the urge to go to that hotel by the lake resurfaced. When she told Natsuki her plans over the telephone, her sister sounded wistful.

"How long are you going for?"

Natsuki obviously wanted to join her, but didn't quite dare say so. Mitsuki realized she needed to be away from her sister as well. She needed to be alone.

"A while. I reserved a room for ten days."

"Oh, I see."

"I might want to get some work done, so I'll take my laptop, but I want to be cut off from the world, so I'm leaving my cell phone behind."

"Oh, I see."

Mitsuki knew she wouldn't be able to escape talking on the hotel room telephone to her sister, who would be in the sound-proof piano room with her two cats.

Before leaving, Mitsuki met Masako in Yotsuya for dinner at a Portuguese restaurant. Masako taught part time five days a week in various universities; weekend nights were the only times she could spare for a leisurely dinner. She lifted her bespectacled face from the menu and said, "God, you got old."

She liked to talk like a man. She always wore pants and used no makeup. Mitsuki had begun to suspect she was a lesbian.

Over the soulful sound of a traditional fado, she added, "People age fast after menopause. Not that I'm one to talk."

They were the same age, but Masako had gone through meno-pause first. A year or two ago, on hearing that Mitsuki too had experienced the change of life, she had said over the telephone, "Life is sad. Menopause comes even to Mitsuki."

Now as they chatted, Mitsuki found herself relating how Tetsuo had gone off with a young woman. Masako's familiar face in front of her, the mournful tones of the singing and guitar, the bean soup warming her from the inside, the pleasant tipsiness from cheap red wine, all inclined her to open up.

Masako stared at her. "Are you fucking kidding me?"

Mitsuki said nothing about the two other women Tetsuo had been with during their marriage. She felt too embarrassed—perhaps less for herself than for Tetsuo's sake.

Masako knew all about Paris. "After the way he chased you around? That bastard!"

"As you said, I got old, so there you are."

"Don't be an idiot. What're you gonna do?"

"Not sure. That's one reason I'll be spending some time in Hakone, just to sort things out. The hotel looks right out on Lake Ashinoko."

"Don't do anything dumb."

"Like what?"

"Like jump in the lake."

A forgotten shadow flitted across her mind. Back in Paris, Masako had told her the story of a professor with a young girlfriend who asked his wife for a divorce only to wake up the next morning and find her dead, hanged, in a downstairs room. In her mind's eye she briefly saw the wife's body dangling from the ceiling. The professor had then taken a position at a different university and married his young woman. End of story.

"Don't be silly." Mitsuki laughed and took another sip of wine. "Though, you know, there's something nice and old-fashioned about offing oneself in a lake. 'Entering the water,' they used to call it."

"Does have a ring to it."

Mitsuki imagined the loneliness of the lake in winter, shining with a leaden hue.

# Part Two

## ROMANCE CAR

It was nearly the middle of December when Mitsuki boarded the Odakyu limited express "Romance Car" bound for Hakone Yumoto.

Relieved to have set off while it was still light out, she bought a bottle of hot green tea from the young woman pushing the cart down the aisle and after a sip or two turned to look out the window. To her surprise, below was Ring Road 8. They had already passed Chitose Funabashi Station. When she had taken the Romance Car in the past, she had caught a glimpse of the old station looking just as it had in her childhood, but now the line was an elevated four-track railway, and the station had been remodeled, making it hard to spot when they went by.

Chitose Funabashi Station was a place full of memories—including some she didn't actually remember.

When she was about two, she used to wake up at dawn and pad into the tiny room where her grandmother lay sleeping. Then her grandmother would slip on wooden clogs and carry her piggyback out to the railway crossing to watch the trains go by. She had often been told this by her mother, and the image of an old woman standing morning after morning with a small child on her back, reaching behind to pat her while pointing out the trains as they went by, was at once a bit sad—wasn't there anything else a grandmother of that era could show a two-year-old?—and heartwarming. Although she had no memory of that scene, imagining it always filled her with bittersweet nostalgia—all the more so since not only her mother but her father too had focused more attention on Natsuki.

The train continued to speed west, smoothly and noiselessly, as if there were no rails underneath.

Across the aisle sat four men with salt-and-pepper hair, facing each other. The two in window seats were playing with a miniature chess set. All four were drinking canned beer. They exuded the easygoing cheer of the newly retired. On the surface, not one of them appeared to have a care in the world. But Mitsuki's bleak state of mind cast a shadow on everything in sight, making her wonder what sort of lives these men might actually be leading. When she was little, the adults she looked up to had all inspired trust; the possibility that they might be struggling with their own dark problems had never occurred to her.

She turned her eyes back out the window.

The scene lit by the sun's lingering rays was ugly. A row of square concrete boxes resembling old-style public housing was followed by newly built, standardized houses in a minidevelopment. Every rooftop was set at the same angle, in accordance with the "right to sunlight" law. The effect was to further cheapen the landscape.

They had already passed the station near which That Man, now a "perfectly ordinary granddad," lived with his wife.

After Mitsuki began reading modern classics of Japanese fiction, she had learned that this area, once known as Musashino, used to be green with woodlands, evoking the poetry of nature; but knowing that did nothing to lend charm to the sight of tiny suburban houses packed in so tightly that there was scarcely room to breathe.

As a child, she had never even been aware that the land continued west of Chitose Funabashi, where she lived.

The Odakyu line had always been the line that took her downtown to Shinjuku. On special days when she wore a big ribbon in her hair, she would change there to the Marunouchi subway line and head to Ginza in the heart of the city with her family. Taking the Odakyu line in the opposite direction, past Chitose Funabashi and deeper into the countryside, was unthinkable. She knew vaguely that heading away from the city there were bound to be other railway stations for a while, but in her mind these gave way to an endless stretch of rural scenery where eventually the rails disappeared into grassy fields.

Her worldview shook when the Romance Car was revamped and reintroduced as the Music Box Car. As she played by the tracks, a far-off warning whistle would come gradually closer, a melodic *tootle-oo, tootle-ee, tootle-oo*. Then a streamlined shape something like an airplane nose would come into view, and red-and-gray cars would go hurtling past at lightning speed—away from Shinjuku. No train that stylish could possibly be headed for the sticks. It must be about to lift off from Earth and soar into space, an intergalactic railway bound for somewhere wonderful—the future. She and her friends loved the Music Box Car, but people living near the tracks must have complained about the noise. Before they knew it, the train sped by in silence, without its melodic whistle.

Not until she was in junior high school did she learn that the Odakyu line went to Odawara Station, a former stage on the Tokaido, the great Edo-period highway. That explained its name: "Oda" was from "Odawara" and "kyu" was from *kyuko*, or express. The railway express to Odawara.

This was the time of year when the day was shortest; dusk was already setting in. Lights began to come on in homes along the way.

Little by little, there were more houses with a small garden attached, houses that had been rebuilt in a style neither Western nor modern in particular, but all much alike. Old-fashioned houses, the kind with tiled roofs and paper doors that let light shine through with a soft glow, were scarcely to be seen. The sky was a gloomy gray that conveyed the chill of winter.

After they crossed the Tama River, she could make out evergreen trees in the dim light. Past the Tsurumi River, the green increased. Soon the elevated tracks came to an end, and they went past a series of grubby old stations that still retained a certain charm. By the Sagami River, pampas grass waved its silvery plumes. Watching as the feathery plumes were gradually swallowed in darkness, Mitsuki was again glad she had left while it was light out. The scenery rolling past her window now, coming into view only to disappear, touched her heart, despite her melancholy state, with a faint excitement.

By the time the train pulled into Hakone Yumoto, the end of the line, it was almost completely dark outside. The station, which had evidently undergone renovation, was now shiny and new, with escalators, bearing little resemblance to the run-down place she'd been to with her mother years before. This could be any station in central Tokyo, she thought. Only when she stepped outside did she encounter the lonely night scene of a hot-springs town with few people stirring.

A cold drizzle had begun to fall.

She and her mother had gone from the station to the hotel by taxi but, according to the hotel home page, if you took a bus to a place called Moto-Hakone Port, a shuttle bus would come to pick you up at a port "where a pair of colorful sightseeing cruise ships lie at anchor, decked out like Caribbean pirate ships." Looking up at the drizzle, she went to the bus stop and checked the timetable.

The next bus was due in less than five minutes. A young woman with hair dyed reddish-brown was already waiting under the roof of the bus shelter, shoulders hunched.

Five minutes went by, and still no bus appeared. Mitsuki looked up from her watch to see an elderly couple, probably from the same train she'd been on, come struggling up with bags in tow, one large and one small. They were dressed well enough, but something in their faces and figures suggested a lifetime of hardship.

The old wife looked at the timetable. "Oh no, Papa, we missed it."

The old husband replied, "Well, I warned you not to go to the bathroom at the station." He did not sound accusatory.

The mildness of his tone must have been what prompted Mitsuki to speak up. "I've been waiting several minutes. The bus simply hasn't come yet."

They looked at her in evident surprise. She was wearing a black winter beret, tilted at an angle, and a woven coat that her slightly taller sister had given her reluctantly, saying, "Somehow this looks better on a shrimp like you." She also had on high-heeled boots. Even her turn of phrase must have marked her as someone from a different world.

The old couple thanked her effusively, bowing from the waist like a pair of windup dolls.

Finally the bus arrived, and after the reddish-haired young woman got on, Mitsuki gestured to the couple to board ahead of her. They wouldn't hear of it and only went on bowing. She felt awkward preceding her elders, but rather than prolong the moment with endless exchanges of politeness, she gave up and climbed aboard.

The bus tore recklessly along the twisting mountain road. The old couple sat huddled shoulder to shoulder. Local people got on and off. Eventually the young woman got off too.

After nearly forty minutes, the electronic sign at the front of the bus read MOTO-HAKONE. Mitsuki remembered that her destination,

Moto-Hakone Port, was one stop after that. As she looked at the red lettering, thinking how confusing these place names were, the old couple hastily pushed the buzzer and got off, with many a bow in her direction. Did they go through life that way, continually bobbing up and down?

That pair from another era disappeared into the dark of night.

Mitsuki got off at the next stop, but the port was a mere blur in the rain. If the shuttle bus wasn't waiting, you were supposed to telephone, according to the home page, but there was no public telephone. Regretting that she hadn't brought her cell phone—they really had become indispensable—she looked around, and a little way ahead, across the street, saw a single bright spot: a convenience store. Outside, a pale-green public telephone gleamed in the light.

The shuttle bus soon arrived. The driver was silent. The fog deepened and the darkness grew blacker, creating the illusion in her mind that she was being borne off to another realm.

The illusion persisted even after she arrived at the hotel. She had made the reservation under her maiden name. When she announced herself at the reception desk, still with a sense of being not quite anchored to reality, the clerk behind the counter gave her a quick look, picked up the receiver, and said, "Madam Katsura is here."

Out of nowhere two men in black suits appeared, as if they had been waiting; they bowed formally, hands against the sides of their trousers, and then handed her their business cards. She glimpsed the title "Assistant Manager" on one of them before being motioned with polite gestures to a table in a corner of the lobby. She sat down feeling somehow uneasy, though she had nothing to feel uneasy about. Then to her bewilderment she was presented with a pair of menus from the hotel restaurants, one offering Japanese cuisine and the other French. With a considerable show of embarrassment, they took turns explaining that while in the past the hotel had welcomed many long-term guests such as herself, today most people stayed only a night or two, and as a result the menu selections were rather limited. The lounge and annex café served only light meals and sweets. "If you notify the reception desk the day before, we can arrange to offer other dishes of your choice."

So that's what this was all about. Even so, such fuss seemed unwarranted. And all the while they apologized profusely for the inconvenience, they continued sending little glances her way. Their persistent attention felt just short of rude.

The bellhop, a young woman wearing a uniform with a small cap, led her toward her room.

"Are there only a few long-term guests?" Mitsuki asked as they headed down the long corridor.

"Almost none anymore."

"So, only me?"

The bellhop smiled. "Actually, it so happens that several people will be staying from now till Christmas." She looked at Mitsuki, still smiling.

## THE LAKE SUNK IN DARKNESS

If even one long-term guest was unusual, then several at once seemed almost divinely ordained. "That's quite a coincidence," Mitsuki commented.

"Yes, there's no record of anything like it on the computer. The manager is surprised." The bellhop's voice conveyed youthful excitement.

Mitsuki was shown to her room and, before the young woman left, asked if any of the others had yet arrived.

"Some have, some haven't."

What sort of people are they, she wanted to ask, but the question seemed too intrusive. It might be difficult to get a straight answer. She would find out soon enough.

The door was shut, and Mitsuki surveyed the room.

The inheritance from their mother had left her and Natsuki 36.8 million yen apiece. She could hardly believe she had that much money in her bank account; she would have to use it carefully and make it last. Her room here cost fifteen thousand yen per day, breakfast included, during their "single-room, single-occupant special campaign"—the cheapest deal available. The top-floor room was designed to look like a European garret with a slightly slanting ceiling, but fortunately it was spacious, like the room she had stayed in before.

Her suitcase had arrived ahead of her, sent by courier service along with a cardboard box packed with two-liter bottles of mineral water that she'd ordered from an online store. The humidifier she had requested over the telephone was on the desk, and beside it lay a coil of white cord—the Ethernet cable that she had also requested. Before making a reservation, she had double-checked that this old-fashioned hotel had an Internet connection in the rooms so that she could reread the emails between her husband and the woman. She was told they had wi-fi as well, perhaps to keep up with the new Hyatt Regency nearby. Changing the settings on her laptop would have been too much trouble, so she planned to connect with a cable as usual. The Ethernet cable that would provide entry to the emails looked sinister, like a slender poisonous snake.

Mitsuki took off her hat and, with her coat still on, crossed over to the window and flung it open. Cold air from the winter mountains flowed into the room. The blackness outside was of a depth and intensity unknown in the city. Every room in the hotel overlooked Lake Ashinoko, but the lake was now shrouded in darkness. The only illumination came from a scattering of garden lanterns, their glow hazy in the drizzle.

Mitsuki let out a long breath.

Her desk back home was still piled high with documents relating to her mother's death. The library was jammed so full of cardboard boxes containing Mitsuki's share of her mother's clothes, dishes, old letters, and whatnot, that there was scarcely room to get around. She had set off on this trip telling herself that if she didn't go somewhere and get away from it all, she could never be truly free of her mother and think things through the way she needed to. Yet now, face to face with the quiet darkness, none of this seemed to matter anymore. Her very existence seemed to fade and disappear, swallowed in the gloom.

The lake lying silent in the dark beyond was the same lake her grandmother had seen a hundred years before. On this hill overlooking Lake Ashinoko had stood the villa of a baron, a second- or third-generation member of a zaibatsu family. He had bought an immense tract of land, hired a Western architect to design a residence modeled on a Swiss lakeside villa, and invited people over for dinner parties almost every night. Her grandmother was sometimes included on the guest list, since she was married at the time to a prosperous man who was about the same age as the baron and baroness and had some sort of business dealings with them. She must have been nervous, a former geisha among so many Westernized, upper-class people, worried that she might commit a faux pas. How had she handled the knives and forks of gleaming silver? Later on she would leave her prosperous husband and elope with a penniless youth — Mitsuki's grandfather.

Her grandmother had in her long life experienced everything from virtual slavery to luxury and pomp to gritty poverty and more, but the dinner parties at the villa seemed to have left an indelible impression. In her strong Osaka dialect, she would reminisce to her daughter, Mitsuki's mother, "That house was built way out in the mountains. It was so lonely, you'd have thought a fox might come out and play tricks. But everything was in the style of Over There." ("Over There" meant the Western world.) "I couldn't eat my food in peace. Gobs of meat, and it stunk to high heaven!" Like others born in the Meiji period, she would eat chicken or duck, but any other meat she regarded with a prejudiced eye, based on the ancient taboo on eating four-legged creatures, and avoided when possible.

Mitsuki's mother had grown up in an Osaka row house hearing such talk. Yet only late in life, after the bicycle accident that aged her overnight, did she say that she wanted to visit the Hôtel du Lac—the hotel built on the site of the baron's villa. Mitsuki, with the memory of her father's lonely death fresh in her mind, had been angry and appalled that her mother would suggest such a thing, yet in the end she had gone along on the trip, in large part, she now realized, because she herself had been curious about the place.

That visit also had been in the wintertime.

According to the pamphlet they'd been given at the reception desk, the Hôtel du Lac had been redesigned more than once during its long history. Around the time the Music Box Car made its appearance, the hotel was a chalet with a red peaked roof, a popular honeymoon destination for couples during that period of heady economic growth. When Mitsuki as a little girl listened to the Romance Car pipe *tootle-oo, tootle-ee* as it flew by, there would have been several blushing newlywed couples on board. That chalet had grown old and undergone major reconstruction, resulting in the present hotel, designed to suggest an imaginary French château.

Over thirty years had already passed since the last reconstruction.

After lingering awhile by the window, visualizing the lake as her grandmother had seen it a century before, Mitsuki closed the window gently so as not to disturb the peace of the mountain night and then went downstairs, still wearing her coat. She intended to go to the Japanese-style restaurant for dinner, as that sounded a little more casual than the other. The moment she stepped inside, a tall, square-shouldered waitress wearing a kimono came up to her with a broad smile. She looked like a college student, Mitsuki thought.

"Welcome, Madam Katsura."

Did the entire staff know who she was?

As it turned out, the restaurant offered chiefly the traditional multicourse *kaiseki* style of Japanese haute cuisine. She didn't feel like eating something so elaborate on her own, so instead she ordered an assortment of dishes she didn't usually make at home, such as simmered head of bream.

Just then she noticed the elderly pair from the bus entering the restaurant and being led to a neighboring table. They were accompanied by a couple perhaps in their late thirties. The old man and woman recognized her, widening their eyes in momentary surprise before once again bowing politely.

"We got off at the wrong stop," the husband said, scratching his bald head in embarrassment. Just as she had suspected, the similarity in names between Moto-Hakone and Moto-Hakone Port was a stumbling block for tourists.

The four of them sat down.

"Really, I don't how we could have been so careless!"

"Never mind, Mom, you're here, and that's the important thing."

Mitsuki continued to catch fragments of dinner table conversation between the old couple, their son, and his plump, amiable wife. They must have placed their order in advance, for without further ado, drinks and *sakizuke*, the first course of a *kaiseki* meal, were brought to their table.

"It's a good thing we left the children home after all," said the young wife, looking around.

"Right," said her husband. "It's not exactly a family restaurant."

His mother nodded vigorously. "You can say that again!"

Every new course—soup, sashimi, *hassun* platter, a grilled dish—produced a chorus of exclamations from the two women: "This is so fancy!" "Oh my goodness, there's *more*. Would you believe it?" From the level of excitement, Mitsuki could picture the family's everyday life, and also she sensed that each one was eager to make this a happy occasion for the others.

When she had finished her struggle with the bream head and was wiping her fingers on the small damp towel provided, the final course, rice seasoned and cooked with various ingredients, was just being served at the neighboring table in a round wooden container. Everyone protested they couldn't eat another bite.

"No problem," said the young husband. "Let's just leave it then."

"And let all this food go to waste?" His mother sounded scandalized.

*Not the sort who belongs in a hotel like this.* No sooner did the unworthy thought rise unbidden in her mind than Mitsuki swiftly suppressed it. This sort of mental correction was something she had done time and again since she was old enough to remember.

When the studentlike waitress appeared, the mother looked up and timidly asked, "Could you possibly make this into rice balls or gruel for breakfast?"

The waitress, momentarily confused, responded after a short pause. "In the morning we have a different menu, and all the food is freshly prepared, so don't worry about leaving that behind." A considerate young woman, she smiled graciously.

"Sorry for letting all this good food go to waste."

"Not at all."

The son and his wife exchanged quick, embarrassed glances, but said nothing.

Mitsuki got up and, with a nod to the traditional old couple and their gentle son and daughter-in-law, headed for the exit. Outside the restaurant, she could look down on a spacious lounge with a high ceiling. Before her a staircase led to the lounge and down a corridor to one side were the elevators to take her back to her room.

She hesitated.

If she went back to her room, the laptop computer was waiting in her suitcase, wrapped in a thick cashmere shawl. All she had to do was connect it to the white Ethernet cable, and she would be able to enter her husband's Gmail account and open the door to a world where words hurtful to her flew back and forth. Having come this far, she had no choice but to do so.

Looking down at the lounge where a tall artificial Christmas tree stood covered in silver and gold decorations, she continued to waver until she saw a blazing fire in a hearth far away. This was still her first night here. The emails could wait.

The lounge contained barely a dozen people. She settled in a sofa by the fireplace and ordered a glass of red wine, then stared absently into the fire. As she watched the ever-changing dance of the flames, she forgot the passage of time. Long ago, in her childhood, her grandmother used to go out to the backyard with a cloth wrapped around her head and burn leaves in a bonfire; even then, the kaleidoscopic flames had held a strange power and fascination for her.

How long did she remain spellbound by the flames? Returning to the present with a start, she looked around and saw an old white-haired woman sitting a ways off. She stiffened. The hair, the makeup expertly applied...no, it couldn't be! Hadn't she sealed her mother's vexatious spirit in that outsized urn, along with her ashes, before she finally left Tokyo behind? Could this be her mother's ghost, tagging along? Fantasy and reality mingled in her eyes, where the afterimage of the fire still lingered.

Next to the old woman sat a conspicuously handsome young man. Not yet thirty, she thought. She sensed intuitively that they too were here for a longish stay. What might their relationship be? Her gaze went back to the old woman—who, to her surprise, was looking intently at her.

## 36

### DUST

It was a long time since sleep had been nectar.

For the last few years, she would wake up feeling stiffer than when she went to bed. This morning was no different.

Her light sleep had been interspersed with memories of the evening before: fleeting visions of jumbled scenery glimpsed from the Romance Car window, the constantly bowing old couple, garden lanterns glowing hazily in the darkness and rain. The ever-changing flames in the fireplace were there, too—and the old lady who'd been staring at her, and the gorgeous young man at her side. Back when she was well, scenes and figures she encountered while traveling would pleasantly stimulate her brain as she fell asleep, filling her with eager longing for the morning and new paths to the unknown. Now such scenery and figures only rattled her nerves, and waking in the morning was no longer pleasurable.

Conscious of how stiff she was, Mitsuki lay faceup in bed.

She checked her watch. Not yet seven. She laid a hand on her belly—an unconscious habit now—and felt how appallingly cold it was. She should go to the hot spring to warm herself, but the thought of getting up, combing her hair, putting on a civil face, and going downstairs seemed like too much trouble. On the other hand, staying the way she was, face up in bed in this dim room, would only fray her nerves and stiffen her back muscles all the more. She'd been grinding her teeth, too.

Morning after morning might go by in this fashion, and slowly she'd turn into a sallow, sullen-faced old bag.

She wanted to go back to sleep, but now she was wide awake. Grudgingly, she got out of bed, went over to the window, and opened the curtains. She drew a sharp breath. Darkness had blotted out the lake last night, but here it was before her now, placid and glorious. Tall cedars swayed in the breeze at the far end of the garden, and ripples on the lake sparkled silver in the rays of the newly risen sun. It was true, just as the ancient poetess had written: in winter, early morning was the best time of day. Those famous lines from the *Pillow Book* floated through her mind: "In spring it is the dawn...in summer, the night...In autumn, the evening, when the glittering sun sinks close to the edge of the hills...In winter, the early morning is beautiful indeed."

Nudged by the sunshine, Mitsuki roused herself and began to unpack methodically. Last night she had taken out only her pajamas. Now she spread the contents of her suitcase on the bed, hanging up some clothes in the closet, putting others away in drawers, and lining items up on the bathroom counter. To mark the end of a particularly difficult year of her life, she had brought with her the nicest things she had—the best of everything, not just coat, shoes, and outfits, but underwear too, along with necklaces, earrings, and scarves. Her makeup pouch bulged with extra eyeliner, eye shadow, mascara. She had packed these things intending less to enjoy them than to remind herself not to wallow in misery.

Usually when she traveled she took along several books to read, but this time she had brought only the one she'd been reading at her dying mother's bedside, along with a French-Japanese dictionary. She was here to think, not to read.

She looked around the freshly organized room.

Perhaps to lighten the travail ahead, she ought to have taken a suite. Or perhaps instead of being here looking out on the small, almost toylike Lake Ashinoko she should be reveling in the grandeur of the Pacific Ocean from aboard a luxury liner with the horizon stretching all around her for 360 degrees, as far as she could see. Her inheritance seemed to make possible almost any form of luxury she could imagine herself indulging in. But, however she might pamper herself, the fact remained that she was a woman in her fifties whose husband was leaving her for some young thing.

By the time she finished a light breakfast in the French restaurant, it was past eight. On her way back to her room, she stopped by the front desk to say that she'd be working in her room all day and wouldn't be needing maid service. She planned to order lunch from room service and eat in her room, she added, unable to get over the feeling that the entire staff was somehow intent on her every move.

"Very well." The man at the desk gave her a searching look.

Mitsuki stood in front of the elevator trying not to think of the task ahead. Nearly a year had passed since the shock of discovering the tissue case—the tiny flower garden—hidden in Tetsuo's drawer. All she knew was that she couldn't go on avoiding the reality she had so far kept at arm's length.

Back in her room, she headed straight for the desk, turned on her laptop, and entered the password to her husband's email. Characters danced before her eyes.

The row of emails in the inbox brought a deep, sickening feeling to the pit of her stomach. These messages that Tetsuo and the woman had exchanged would be preserved forever in Google archives—wherever and however vast they might be—far beyond Mitsuki's death and the deaths of the two writers. In years past, a person died, and eventually all those with memories of him or her also died, bringing about the complete erasure of that person's existence. Just as the human body returned to dust, mingling with atoms of the natural world, a person's existence would return to nothingness.

How very clean.

Now, as if in belated punishment for the invention of writing, any message once posted on the Internet was immortal. Words as numerous as the dust of the earth would linger forever in their millions and trillions and quadrillions and beyond. Here at the beginning of the twenty-first century a woman in her mid-fifties named Mitsuki Hirayama was about to be abandoned by her husband, a fact that would remain on record till the end of time.

What humiliation.

Mitsuki looked at the backs of her hands hovering over the keyboard—their light brown spots and blue veins. Hands normal for a woman her age. Hands of a housewife who stood at the sink day after day, washing dishes. Not that she'd ever been a model housewife, or even close. Tetsuo had said he didn't want children either, so she had never given birth, never raised a child. And though now her eyes were drawn irresistibly to little ones roaming the park on unsteady feet, the sight bringing an involuntary smile to her face, she hadn't been attracted to children in the least when she was young. Yet as if to chastise her for the choice she'd made, in the end much of her time and strength had been spent looking after her failing parents. That in itself might have caused her to neglect her marriage.

All the same, did that allow him to cast her aside for a younger woman? Her father had left his first wife, poor thing, but not for a younger woman. To dump your wife like this was beyond words. What greater insult could there be? Tetsuo was the lowest of the low, a scumbag, a miserable excuse for a man. What he was doing was rotten, depraved. Saying the words to herself was curiously satisfying.

When she got together with other married women her age, the conversation would inevitably drift to complaints about their husbands. Mostly the offenses were harmless enough: he didn't remember what day which kind of recyclable trash went out, he bought all sorts of little contraptions when there was nowhere to put them, his presence around the house was stifling... But if word got out that someone had left his wife for a younger woman, everyone's face would turn rigid. It was an offense of a totally different order. If Tetsuo left Mitsuki, he would tumble from the exalted rank of "wonderful husband" and be treated as a "miserable excuse for a man." She would become the target of all their pity.

Oh, the mortification.

On top of the cliché of being left for a younger woman there was this new cliché of tracing how it all came about, through the trail left on electronic devices. All over the world there must be a host of women sitting before screens large and small, staring at their artificial light, forced to confront evidence of their husband's philandering. And there would always be more such women.

Mitsuki took a deep breath, then began tapping keys on the keyboard and opening email after email. Sentences she hadn't seen since that first day rolled by. She came across the woman's remark that had so wounded her: "Pathetic. I have to say, I feel bad for her."

She opened the attachment and looked again at the snapshot. She was sitting at a table in a restaurant in Shinjuku Park Hyatt Hotel, where for the last dozen years (ever since That Man exited the scene) the five of them—Tetsuo, Yuji, Natsuki, she, and her mother—used to go every spring for a joint celebration of all their birthdays. By chance, the woman's request to see the faces of the Katsura clan had come just after that year's party, so Tetsuo had sent her a photograph taken by a waiter. He hadn't done it to be mean. He could not have known how she and Natsuki had wailed over the telephone:

"Oh God, look at us!"

"What a pair of old biddies we've become."

"Look at the neck and shoulders on us!"

"Ugh."

However harmless his intention, and even though she had seen the woman's remark once before, its cruelty—all the more devastating because it was true—hit home.

But as she went on reading, Mitsuki began making discoveries. On this second time through, she began to see the words in a different light; they painted a different reality. The first time, deep in shock, she had merely slid her eyes over the surface. Her frozen mind had missed key points. This time, as she perused the correspondence in a calmer state, things she had missed before swam into view—dimly at first, then with unmistakable clarity.

For one thing, the woman was not as young as the flowery tissue case had led her to believe. And Tetsuo...yes, he was committed to the relationship, had promised to get a divorce—their plans were based on that assumption—yet something in his tone conveyed the impression that he might yet wriggle out of it. Mitsuki sensed that the woman knew it, too.

Mitsuki faltered, realizing the picture was rather different from what she had imagined.

# 37

## ROWS OF NUMBERS

"One day soon I'm going to wake up and find I'm forty."

Somehow Mitsuki had missed the urgency of this statement before, but now she realized that the woman was in her late thirties—not exactly what people usually meant when they spoke of a "young woman."

No matter how sharp a dresser Tetsuo was, no twenty-something was likely to make a play for a man in his mid-fifties—was that the reason his "young woman" wasn't all that young? Or was he just too smart to let an ingenue lead him by the nose? The woman's hair must be fuller and shinier than Mitsuki's, her flesh more toned. Even so, a woman in her late thirties was a totally different creature from one in her twenties.

The late thirties was a tricky time of life. Clothes and accessories could make you look younger than you were. If Mitsuki accompanied Tetsuo to a nice restaurant serving fine contemporary cuisine, they would look like any ordinary middle-class, middle-aged couple fond of eating out; but beside this young-looking woman, he would appear dapper, sexy. In a few years the magic of clothes and accessories would wear off, and then she would only look like someone trying to look young.

Mitsuki looked at the other woman from the perspective of a twenty-year-old secure in the springtime of youth, saw her as "pretty old," and smiled derisively—savoring a sensation she knew to be awfully petty.

That explained why the woman was so hell-bent on settling matters—it was her age.

But even if he'd been goaded into it, Tetsuo was seriously contemplating divorce. He had promised to use the year in Vietnam to broach the topic with Mitsuki. Yet he somehow was dragging his heels—which only spurred the woman to greater determination.

She was a freelance magazine editor of some kind; an interview with Tetsuo had sparked their romance. Professionally, she was probably more used to sending email than texting or tweeting, and she wrote well—her emails were sprinkled with well-turned phrases that under other circumstances would have been amusing. She had a sharp mind and confidence in her looks. Plus, her assessment of the situation was admirably realistic.

What struck Mitsuki on this read-through was the level of detail in her discussion of finances. For the vast majority of people contemplating divorce—all but the very rich and the destitute—the process meant scraping together paltry assets and figuring out how to split them up and go on living. The woman knew Tetsuo's total worth—annual salary, savings, and stocks—as well as the balance on their mortgage and Mitsuki's approximate income, even how much she had saved in the Japan Post Bank for her own pension. And although talk of a formal separation still lay ahead, she had worked out how much of his assets Tetsuo would need to part with for a divorce by mutual consent, the easiest kind. Mitsuki looked at the rows of numbers, stupefied.

"If you'd divorced her when we first met," the woman commented, "we wouldn't have to hand over this much."

The law had been revised several years ago, entitling an ex-wife to half of her former husband's pension for the years of their marriage. For marriages that had taken place after the enactment of that law, entitlement was automatic. For marriages predating the law, she could receive an amount satisfactory to both parties, up to but not more than fifty percent of his pension. This was called "consensual division." In case consensus couldn't be reached, family court would decide on the allocation. This was called "pension splitting." The retirement bonus—a substantial sum—was subject to distribution to the ex-wife under the same terms. Those few women of Mitsuki's generation who worked after marriage by and large took part-time jobs that didn't provide any pension or retirement bonus. Mitsuki was no different. For women like her, this change in the law was a boon, but right now she felt less grateful than dizzy from the array of unfamiliar words.

Life, it seemed, required people to learn not only technical terms like "gastrostomy" and "dysphagia" but also "consensual division," "pension splitting," and "retirement bonus allocation."

Retirement age at Tetsuo's university was seventy, more than ten years in the future for him. Yet the woman had already worked out how much his retirement bonus was likely to be and how much of that Mitsuki was likely to demand. Not only that, she was urging Tetsuo to give Mitsuki the full amount ahead of time, without waiting for his retirement.

Since they had been married for almost thirty years, that would come to at least ten million yen.

Mitsuki had a fixed income of her own, which was a source of relief to the woman. If she'd had no income and was unable to be self-supporting, Tetsuo would be required to continue supporting her for some years, but thankfully that wouldn't be necessary. More worrisome was the possibility that Tetsuo might be forced to pay a hefty cash penalty to compensate for his behavior, since they were divorcing because he'd become involved with another woman.

"If this went to court, my nest egg could get scrambled too!" the woman wrote humorously, but clearly with genuine concern.

Logically, she said, the most advantageous course would be for him to seek a divorce without revealing her existence. But realistically, since he got along well with his wife, it would seem odd if he suddenly brought up divorce while in Vietnam. If he made no mention of his involvement with her to avoid a financial loss, then his wife, mystified by his sudden decision, might refuse to grant him a divorce, and he might well land in court. A better idea would be to let on that he had acquired a mistress while in Vietnam. And to make it easier to obtain a divorce by mutual consent, he should offer to split his assets down the line.

Mitsuki was overwhelmed by the woman's passion and logic. Her intention was clear: to avoid being greedy and get Tetsuo to go through with the divorce before he changed his mind. Her family background seemed a notch above his, but like him, she was the only one among all her relatives to have graduated from college. Judging from her age, she must have graduated after the Gender Equality in Employment Act was passed, but rather than take full-time employment somewhere she had alternated working for a few years with spending time abroad. Once, for whatever reason, she had gone to live in Tuscany. She had taken courses in Italian and studied to become a wine sommelier. It was a way of investing in herself—or of making the most of the freedom enjoyed by single women, who retained the final option of marriage as a form of lifelong employment.

In her thirties, she'd evidently worked furiously for several years. The kind of magazines she had worked for wasn't clear, but the pay was decent and also she'd been living with her parents, so she managed to set aside a nest egg. Yet she was tired of the need to constantly sell herself and had started to cut back; she saw the coming interlude in Vietnam as a chance to quit work entirely. "I don't want to go on this way forever."

Two years ago she'd moved into a cheap single apartment handy for trysts. "It's your fault I've been eating away at my nest egg," she wrote before concluding. "Anyway, please use the time in Vietnam to settle things once and for all."

When Mitsuki finished going through the emails, she felt empty and numb. This time, there were no tears. What hadn't changed was her sense that the woman truly loved Tetsuo. As was only natural for a woman her age, she'd had a number of lovers, some of them married, but Tetsuo, she said, was the only man she had ever wanted to settle down with. Even if she was motivated in part by fear of ending up old and alone, there was real love there.

Mitsuki sighed and guiltily exited her husband's email.

She looked at her watch. Past one already.

She ordered a ham sandwich and a pot of tea from room service, then went into the bathroom and, standing in front of the polished mirror, reapplied her lipstick. A woman who looked piteously crushed stared back at her.

The sandwich and tea arrived in twenty minutes. The uniformed steward who brought the order looked around the room, taking in the opened laptop on the desk, and gave Mitsuki's face a furtive look. Had he been ordered to spy on the solitary woman locked in her room, refusing maid service? Or was she overreacting out of a sense of guilt at having just finished reading words not meant for her eyes?

He set the tray on the small round table by the window. She sat in the armchair and looked outside, where sunlight from high overhead shone on the hotel garden and the lake beyond. The air seemed to have warmed up a little; the waves were reflecting dazzling light as before.

While eating her sandwich Mitsuki tried to focus on what was nagging at her. Tetsuo was definitely planning on divorce. If he were interested in parading around with a younger woman only to satisfy his vanity, he'd have contented himself with a fling. But why *this woman*, of all people? That array of figures spoke volumes about how she must have carved out a life for herself in constant consultation with her pocketbook. Yet Tetsuo's other love interests, beginning with his first crush in high school, then his girlfriends in college and graduate school, and his two previous mistresses, not to mention Mitsuki herself, had all been from a world of relative privilege. He himself had admitted wryly to consistency in that respect. Now he was about to divorce Mitsuki for this woman, so unlike the rest of them, even knowing that he would become poorer and would have to give up his dream of a condominium in the city. (The woman's nest egg couldn't possibly amount to much.) Tetsuo — the same Tetsuo who so appreciated the comforts and glamor that money could buy — was going to make this woman his wife.

Mitsuki marveled at this, struck by how little she seemed to mean to Tetsuo and also by the glimpse of a Tetsuo she had never known. Finding out about this unsuspected side of him was like a slap in the face.

And yet somewhere inside, he was hesitating. What could be holding him back? She considered this, and reached a theory so tawdry that she felt ashamed for both of them.

$$\left( 38 \right)$$

## A CHANCE ENCOUNTER

Such an expanse of blue sky could no longer be seen anywhere in Tokyo.

After resting awhile in bed, Mitsuki had returned to the armchair. She looked absently out the window. The sun lighting ripples on the lake was tilting west, and before long the air would be touched with the nighttime chill from the wintry mountains.

She put on her coat and hat, wrapped a shawl around herself, and pulled on warm gloves. Bundled up as if for a trip to Siberia, she set out.

The hotel garden descended gently toward the lake. Countless azalea shrubs grew along the way, their leaves now drearily fading or withered. The stone path wound down among them, near the lake, from where she could enjoy a distant view of the hotel.

"Not too great, I must say." She remembered her mother passing this tart verdict as she leaned on her cane and looked up at the hotel from the front garden. True enough, by no stretch of the imagination could anyone believe that the hotel was supposed to evoke the image of a centuries-old French château. Its sheer size gave it a kind of grandeur—but the poor imitation only increased the sense that this place was not France and the building was only a late-twentieth-century structure after all. Still, the weathered exterior contained reminders of a time when the Japanese imagination had been gripped by all things European. Viewed as representing a page from modern Japanese history, the architecture had a peculiar charm that set it apart from the kind of international hotels springing up across Japan—antiseptic places much alike, devoid of local flavor.

The spaciousness of the garden had pleased her mother and her. The place would be flocked with tourists in early summer, when the azaleas were in bloom, but their visit had been in winter, like Mitsuki's now, and even though it was a mere two-hour journey from Tokyo, the setting had felt appealingly remote—a sense reinforced by the flat expanse of the lake, set against the gray desolation of the ridge beyond. The only blemish, they had agreed, was the pair of brightly painted pirate ships that crisscrossed the water like apparitions from Disneyland.

Now, walking to the end of the garden and then crossing a road, Mitsuki came to a stone path that went along the lakeshore. Only bushes stood between her and the lake; beyond lay the smooth surface of the water. After hesitating over which way to turn on the encircling path, she chose to go left, enticed by the twists and turns ahead.

Unlike the smaller, standardized stones in the path through the hotel garden, here the path was set with large, rough stones that a big man could hardly carry. Had the baron arranged to have them brought in? She pictured men of long ago toting the heavy stones, muscles bulging, and laying them in the ground.

As she walked over the stones, inhaling the cold air, her mind felt calmer. Then she heard the sound of waves lapping the shore, a sound she hadn't heard in years. It was almost funny how perfect the sound was, as if created as a special effect.

Mitsuki paused to watch the waves roll in and asked herself why she had come so far. To decide what to do about Tetsuo was only a partial answer. She felt that she needed to go back further in time, to probe the layers of events that had led her to this point.

The waves beat against the shore with their familiar monotony, yet each time with subtle variations in shape, culminating in a burst of white froth and that sound, a sound like none other, the sound of waves.

She walked on for an indeterminate length of time, until arrested by the appearance on her right of a huge vermilion concrete torii gate. There must be a Shinto shrine nearby. The torii was built out in the lake, with a small pier leading up to it. She went out on the pier and stood watching for a while as the waves lapped at the torii rising before her and the pier underfoot; then she turned back. With the same sound of waves in her ears and her feet treading the same stone path, the hotel came into view sooner than she had expected. This time she walked up the road to the hotel entrance without going through the garden, but the thought of her laptop discouraged her from returning straight to her room. She decided to take one more stroll through the garden before dark and redirected her steps, going through the little gate beside the front entrance and on around back.

As she walked a circuitous route over the paved stones, watching the sky in the west turn shades of gold, purple, and orange, she saw in the distance a figure in a dark suit heading toward her. There was no side path she could take to step out of his way. She would have preferred not to speak with anyone, but the encounter seemed unavoidable.

When she saw his face, Mitsuki drew in a breath. The name "Wakako Matsubara" flashed in her mind. He didn't appear to recognize her, but he could tell from her reaction that she knew him. A quizzical look crossed his face.

The words came naturally to her. "Last winter, at the hospital."

"I beg your pardon?"

"I was in the library."

He thought, then let out a small "Oh!" of recollection.

"Yes, that was me," she said.

"You have a good memory." He was wide-eyed in surprise.

Mitsuki explained that she had seen him around the hospital a few times.

"I see." He swept back his slightly graying hair in a gesture of embarrassment. At the same time he looked her full in the face, a bit shyly. The rays of the setting sun, stronger now as the sun sank in the sky, would be merciless in lighting up her face, the face of a woman defeated by life. What had become of his wife? she wondered, but the words she spoke were innocuous.

"When did you get here?"

"Before noon today."

Was he here for long? Alone or with someone?

Silence ensued. This man had seen her crying in the hospital. He must have assumed she was shedding tears of grief. Perhaps he would think her face now an extension of those tears. Prompted by the thought, she said, "My mother was in the hospital then. She died, and I came here for some R & R."

He seemed to realize he had been under a false impression. "I thought it was your husband."

"Heavens no." Her own words startled her with their coldness.

"I'm very sorry for your loss," he said courteously, "but if I may say so, I'm glad you didn't lose your husband after all."

She said nothing.

A colorful pirate ship came into view, masts and all, and simultaneously they heard the tape-recorded voice of a female guide. In the distance the other pirate ship paraded across the water. As they took in the jarring sight and sound, he blurted out, "I lost my wife."

This man wasn't the type to make such an admission casually, she knew from her observations of his private sorrow in the hospital. The words must have slipped out, as if he felt awkward hearing of her loss while saying nothing of his own. She sensed that he would rather have left those words unsaid. She could not make some casual reply. After another short silence, she said quietly, "I see," and left it at that. She offered no words of sympathy, nor did she tell him she knew his late wife's name.

After a pause she said in a different tone of voice, "You'll be staying here for a while?"

"Yes."

"Me too." She paused again. "Did the assistant manager take you aside when you checked in, by any chance?"

"Yes! I couldn't imagine what was happening. And then it was just about the menus."

"I know! Wasn't that strange?"

They laughed. That cleared the air, and they walked back to the hotel side by side.

After the long walk she was chilled through.

The chance encounter had broken through her shell of loneliness. She finally decided to go for a soak in the hot spring.

It was shortly before the dinner hour, and the spa was fairly crowded. Women's pale naked bodies moved hazily in waves of steam. According to the explanation posted on the wall, there was a legend that hot springs couldn't be found within sight of Mount Fuji, but the hotel had taken on the challenge and found hot water one thousand meters down. Supposedly the waters were good for neuralgia, muscle pain, joint pain, and chills. The sound of bathers' plastic buckets slapping against the tile floor echoed through the room, evoking — with the help of the mysterious fantasy world created by the roiling steam — the sound of old-fashioned cedar buckets. She felt as if she had slipped back in time.

The hotel was built on a mountainside with the spa on the third floor. At one end was an outdoor hot spring, separated from the indoor bathing area by a glass partition, where bathers could gaze on the rocky face of the mountain up close. After first warming herself in the indoor bath, she worked up her courage and stepped outside. The cold air felt good. It was almost dark out, but she heard birds singing.

She stayed there a long time, immersed in the steaming water, eyes closed.

For dinner she went back to the French restaurant, and then, as on the night before, descended to the lounge, lured by the fire in the fireplace, and sat again on the sofa facing it. She still felt too weary and languid to think about Tetsuo. Tonight at dinner she had indulged in a glass each of white wine and red, and now as the waiter drew near she ordered a glass of calvados. Her inheritance allowed her to splurge, and besides, there'd been that chance encounter in the garden. The thought that her life might yet have a few surprises in store, like developments in a novel, pleased her and soothed her bruised spirit. She felt like drinking a toast in solitary celebration.

Holding a glass of amber liquid in her hand, she idly scanned the room. No dark suit in sight. No one paid any attention to a middle-aged woman looking around the room. Inevitably, the older a woman became, the less she attracted people's eyes; now that she could go virtually unseen, it was her turn to observe others. This was the law of a woman's life.

As the thought brought a faint smile to her lips, she saw the white-haired old lady from the night before come slowly down the lobby staircase, heading this way with the gorgeous young man again in tow. The old lady commanded attention; some women were able to ignore the laws of life. There was no facial resemblance, but perhaps because of the strong ego that showed through her makeup, or perhaps because of the elegant scarf around her neck, Mitsuki felt once again as if her mother had emerged from her urn. Once again, she stiffened.

## 39

## AN EVENING OF LONG-TERM GUESTS

She'd had enough of old ladies, thank you. The moment she thought this, the old lady came tottering straight toward her.

"May we join you?" With one hand on the back of the chair as support, she was getting ready to sit down. The gorgeous young man waited politely for Mitsuki's response. Only when she motioned for them to be seated did he smile and do so.

"I do beg your pardon. Now what is that, pray tell?" the old lady asked, pointing to the amber liquid in Mitsuki's hand. When Mitsuki told her, she whispered to the young man, "Very well, I shall have a *calva*, too." For whatever reason—perhaps some constriction of the throat?—her voice was weak, but unlike Mitsuki's mother she did not seem hard of hearing.

She returned her attention to Mitsuki. "You're here for a few days, are you?" As Mitsuki replied, she spoke over her: "So am I." Gesturing at the young man with a slight movement of her chin, she added, "And I am sick unto death of spending all my time with this uncultured boor."

At a loss for a reply, Mitsuki only gave a slight smile.

"But you, my dear, are reading *Madame Bovary*!" Her French pronunciation was impeccable.

Apparently they had been in the same restaurant and she had noticed as Mitsuki, sitting alone with time on her hands, opened her book with some compunction while waiting for the hors d'oeuvres.

"You have studied French?" There was a touch of condescension in her tone.

"A little."

"And you have been to France?"

"I spent a year in Paris."

"Did you?" Not in the least dotty, clearly the old lady was taking Mitsuki's measure. "Now, when would that have been?"

Mitsuki told her, and she nodded. "I was in Paris then, too. I went in my mid-twenties and stayed nearly thirty years."

Surprised, Mitsuki took a look at her companion, who, unperturbed by this reaction, kept one hand on the long scarf around her neck to keep it just so as she gazed around the lounge.

"After coming back to Japan, I always meant to visit this hotel, but it took years and years before I made it here … and you know, I had no idea it would be like this."

Unsure what this might mean, Mitsuki waited for the mysterious old lady to explain. She had turned back and was watching Mitsuki's reaction through gold-rimmed glasses, though when she spoke, her manner was deliberately offhand. "When I was a girl, my parents often brought me here."

Mitsuki looked at the old lady's face again in astonishment.

"You do know, don't you, my dear, that this was once a private villa?"

Her eyes still wide, Mitsuki nodded. Now it was her turn to take the measure of the other woman—the powdered face, the white silk scarf with a scattered design of large flowers, the purple cashmere dress shot with silver thread, the low-heeled black pumps. Typically for an older person, all the things she wore could have been purchased in almost any era, but the materials were high quality and the workmanship exquisite. They hadn't come from just anywhere. Her apparel bolstered her story of having hobnobbed with wealth and nobility years ago, while her tone and manner of speaking seemed to transcend the bounds of present-day Japan.

The hotel corridors displayed sepia photographs along with explanations, so the history of the hotel was evident even without a pamphlet from the front desk. Still, the past was not of universal interest. Seeing how Mitsuki perked up, the old lady appeared pleased. "The baron and baroness were kind to my parents, and so we children were invited along as well." She looked out the window into the night sky.

Mitsuki was lost in wonderment. She had no intention of confiding that her grandmother too had come here in days long past. This old lady plainly had had the proper pedigree, enabling her to come and go here in childhood. The world she came from was far removed from that of Mitsuki's grandmother, who'd been invited here as a wife, but who everyone must have known was a former concubine. Conversations took unexpected turns; if she brought up her grandmother now, she might well end up explaining the woman's silly, sad obsession—this was more than she wished or felt proper to tell someone on such brief acquaintance. Yet the startling knowledge that this old lady's parents and "O-Miya" could have attended the very same banquets made her feel a renewed bond with the past. Spirits inhabiting this land seemed to awaken and rise from the quiet of the sleeping mountains.

"My brothers used to come too," the old lady said. "I had an older brother and a younger one, and the older one was this boy's grandfather. We would go boating on the lake."

The young man bowed once more in acknowledgment.

So that was it. This attractive young man was her great-nephew. Nothing particularly interesting there, and yet the sight of a young man like him acting as companion to a woman so much older was, even if they were related, a bit unusual.

"How long will you be staying, my dear?"

"I'll be going back to Tokyo before Christmas." From Christmas Eve on, the hotel would no doubt be crowded. She had come early to avoid the Christmas rush.

"That's my plan as well. Do you know any of the other guests who'll be staying on awhile?" She let her gaze wander again around the sparsely populated lounge.

Thus prompted, Mitsuki too looked around—and there on the staircase where the old lady had been, as if conjured by Mitsuki's movement, was a familiar figure in a dark suit. All at once the room seemed warmer, friendlier somehow, as if an old acquaintance had materialized. Emboldened perhaps by the fearless old woman beside her, she lifted her hand before she quite realized what she was doing and waved slightly in his direction.

Now it was the old lady's turn to widen her eyes.

"That gentleman—he's also staying here awhile," Mitsuki explained.

The old lady slid her glasses down and gave him a frank appraisal before concluding, "Now *there's* someone worth inviting over."

Indeed, Mr. Matsubara's quiet refinement stood out all the more from a distance. He inclined his head in acknowledgment of Mitsuki's greeting as he descended the stairs.

"Oh yes, he'll do nicely," murmured the old lady, half to herself, and she too waved. "Invite him to join us. He and you would make a charming couple."

Mitsuki pretended not to hear this. As Mr. Matsubara drew near, she stood up and said hello. He looked a bit uncertain. As she hesitated, the old lady spoke up.

"I understand you too will be staying here for several days?"

"Yes, that's right."

"It might be tiresome for you, but would you care to join us at least for this evening? My great-nephew and I also plan to be guests here for a fortnight or so."

With the hand holding her brandy glass, she gestured to her companion.

"Thank you, I'd like that." He inclined his head again and sat down with unexpected good grace. After he had ordered a whiskey and water, the conventional choice among men of his generation, the next question came—"And how long do you plan on staying?"—to which he responded, "Until just before Christmas."

"What about your work?" she pressed, nosily.

"I'm taking some time off."

"And what do you do?"

Mr. Matsubara responded amiably even to this rather blunt question. "I'm a biologist in my company's research institute. I do pathogenic research."

It took a moment for the unfamiliar word to register. "Yes, I see. Pathogens, carriers of disease. Oh dear, it sounds terribly difficult, not in the least charming."

He was laughing. Even the young man wore a smile. Mitsuki couldn't help joining in, but at the same time she was musing about Mr. Matsubara's married life. Had he gone off to work every morning in a dark suit? When he was going to be late, had he telephoned his wife to let her know?

The old lady turned now to Mitsuki. "And who are you? A runaway housewife?"

"Something like that." She added almost as an afterthought, "I do teach college part time." She never felt comfortable saying this out loud, since she basically lived on her husband's income and felt no particular calling as a teacher.

"What subject? French?"

"No, originally French, but now it's English."

"Oh no!" the old lady exclaimed. "Just as I feared. English is taking over the world." She said this with some vehemence and then turned to Mr. Matsubara. "Your foreign language is English, I suppose." She made it seem as if no Japanese person anywhere could be incapable of speaking at least one Western language.

"At work, yes," he said, and then added bashfully, "But I studied French in school. And I spent some time at l'Institut Pasteur in Paris."

"*Mon Dieu!*" The old lady put into words Mitsuki's own astonishment. "Then we three represent the French contingent of long-term guests. This hotel has such an old-fashioned je ne sais quoi, we'll fit right in." She held up her glass in a toast: "*Alors, à la vôtre!*" With a jerk of her chin she indicated her grand-nephew. "I'm afraid *he* can't speak any language."

"Oh, come now," said Mr. Matsubara. "He speaks Japanese."

"Ah, but there's where you're wrong. His Japanese is atrocious."

The young man smiled resignedly, apparently accustomed to this abuse, and again held his tongue.

The old lady looked from Mr. Matsubara to Mitsuki and back again. She seemed to be considering something. Finally she leaned forward slowly, the way old people do, and said in a lowered voice, "Pardon me for asking, but has either of you come here to commit suicide?"

## 40

### *DRAMATIQUE*

Dumbfounded at the old lady's query, Mitsuki looked over at Mr. Matsubara. Then for the first time the young man spoke up.

"Anyone who came here to off himself is hardly going to admit it, Aunt Kaoru."

True enough, conceded his great-aunt. Still leaning forward, she tilted her head a bit to one side. "The bartender over there has a friend."

Mr. Matsubara and Mitsuki rotated their heads at the same time and looked in that direction. The bartender seemed to register their attention.

A week or so ago on his day off, Kaoru explained, the bartender had gone down to Atami, the nearby seacoast resort, with some friends. When he happened to mention that a number of long-term guests would be converging on the hotel, one of his friends had commented, "Sounds a bit ominous. Wouldn't be surprised if one of them dies in a murder or suicide." The one who said this was a successful painter who, though usually hard at work painting houses, had a reputation as a psychic.

"'What sort of person is this psychic friend of yours,' I asked, and he said, 'Someone perfectly ordinary, the sort who bleaches his hair blond and rides a Harley-Davidson.' Now, I ask you, is that ordinary?"

The bartender had been bothered just enough by his friend's prediction to mention it to the hotel's assistant manager as a precaution. The assistant manager thought the idea was ridiculous, but in order to avoid responsibility in case something did happen, he mentioned it to the manager. Nothing can hurt a hotel's reputation so much as guests committing murder or suicide. The manager too thought it was ridiculous, but just in case, he assembled the staff and instructed them to keep a discreet eye on the long-term guests. Small wonder that Mitsuki had felt she was being watched.

Naturally, the last thing they wanted was for the rumor to spread among the hotel clientele. But three days ago, just before closing time, Kaoru had been in the lounge having a drink near the bar and sensed the bartender watching her. Thinking it odd, she had summoned him over and demanded an explanation. She must have been relentless. The bartender was well schooled and at first wouldn't say anything, but in the end he gave up and confessed what the psychic had said, with the stipulation that she must never tell any other guests, since he'd been forbidden to breathe a word of it.

"So you mustn't let on that you know," she concluded.

"Mum's the word," said Mr. Matsubara with a smile.

Since they had all looked at the bartender before beginning this conversation, he must have suspected that the secret was out. Wiping glasses with a towel, he glanced over their way from time to time.

Kaoru leaned back and began fingering her glass with large-knuckled fingers. "So I'll tell you what I thought." She looked from Mr. Matsubara to Mitsuki and back again. "I thought to myself, ah, the psychic must mean me."

The young man made a slight face and looked away as if to say, *There she goes again.*

"I've become penniless, you see, and my number is up. That's partly why I decided to come and see this place one last time. It's my own version of *Un carnet de bal*." She mentioned the title of an old French movie that Mitsuki's mother also had been fond of, then paused a moment, apparently recalling the past. "All my memories here are happy ones," she said. "If I did die here, I'd have no regrets."

"And you think *I* would be the one to murder you," the young man said with exasperation.

"Yes, I do. I have a bad heart. I've already had one attack." She motioned to a small handbag lying on the coffee table. On her index finger was a large purple gemstone—an amethyst, perhaps. "I carry Nitorol spray, but if I ever had an attack and he took it away from me, that would be the end. I'd be history."

Firelight cast a reddish glow on her pale face. The other three looked at her, preoccupied by their own private thoughts.

Still commanding the stage, she began to tell them the story of her life, fingering her brandy glass.

Kaoru looked at least eighty, Mitsuki thought as she listened. Anyone who had been around that long had seen a good deal of life. And she had been born into wealth; she belonged to the generation that had lived through the war, and she had spent thirty years abroad. Her story was bound to be more colorful than that of most Japanese.

Her family lost a fortune in the war, Kaoru said, but when her brother went to study in France as a *boursier*, there had still been enough money for her to go along, ostensibly to study painting. Eventually she'd moved in with an elderly White Russian, a painter who'd barely managed to escape to Paris by way of Japan. Even after he died, she'd wanted to remain in Paris and dabble in painting, so she persuaded her parents to continue sending her an allowance while she eked out a living with various part-time jobs. Besides doing interpreting and translating, she'd taught flower arrangement and tea ceremony to wealthy expatriate American housewives. Through one of them she came to know a fashion designer and took a set of photographs at a show of his that brought her some acclaim. By the time her parents passed away, she was able to support herself as a photographer.

"But living abroad is extremely exhausting."

That, on top of the stress of her freelance work, had caused her to fall ill in her mid-fifties, and at long last she'd made up her mind to return to Japan, where she used her French to earn pocket money while slowly going through her small inheritance. Just when her reserves were running low, the stock market had plummeted. She wasn't enrolled in the national pension plan, having lived so long abroad. All she had to her name was a condominium bought with her share of her parents' estate, located near their old home by the Imperial Palace.

"I'm living there now, but it's old and run-down. Still, the location is good, so if I ever did sell it, I could afford to go into assisted living. I won't be around much longer in any case."

She made a sardonic face and gestured at the young man. "But you see, to keep me from selling, Takeru here is after me to adopt him. Says he'll take care of me himself." If she were to drop dead of a heart attack tomorrow, her estate would be divided among her nieces and nephews, with very likely nothing left for him. "That's why he follows me around like a shadow. Carries adoption papers and a copy of the family register, and I don't know what else. If I send it all off to the Chiyoda Ward office, that will be that."

"But you're afraid that the minute you do, I'll murder you," the great-nephew—Takeru—said matter-of-factly.

"Yes," she said with equanimity. "Which is why the moment I heard what the psychic said, I thought, 'Ah, he means me!'"

"A dramatic idea in keeping with the dramatic life you've lived." Mr. Matsubara said this without a trace of irony.

"Oh, but my life has not been the least bit *dramatique*," she replied, giving the word a French flavor. "I had every opportunity, but all I did was rush around. After years of living there, even Paris becomes simply a place to live. I've had my share of unhappiness, but then who hasn't?"

Kaoru paused for breath before adding, "Not a living soul has any need of me. I might as well be killed off."

No one said anything. Mitsuki listened with detachment, thinking of her mother and reflecting that nobody lives longer than those old people who constantly talk about dying or being killed. No one seemed to take Kaoru's statement seriously, nor did she seem to expect them to.

Takeru took out a pack of cigarettes and, after silently requesting permission, lit one.

"But Aunt Kaoru," he said, turning his head to blow the smoke away from the circle. "Killing someone isn't all that easy. Committing the perfect crime is hard."

Her reaction was swift. "If there was one thing you *were* any good at, that would be it, wouldn't it?"

He pursed his lips to one side, not denying it.

"Oh, I've had enough!" she exclaimed. "At my age, keeping oneself alive is altogether too much trouble. I'd rather sell off the condo, use up whatever money is left, and then just drop dead in the street." She reflected. "Then again, some people make a handsome donation to charity before they die. That might be nice, to do something decent for once in my life before making my exit."

Mr. Matsubara, who had been leaning back in his chair, a glass of whiskey and water in hand, now leaned forward with enthusiasm. "Now, there's an idea. Charity is very good."

Everyone looked at him. He added a bit self-consciously, "As a matter of fact, there's a JICA training institute near here. That's a fine organization, I think."

270

"What's JICA again?" asked Kaoru.

"Japan International Cooperation Agency. An organization that offers aid to developing countries. They welcome private contributions." Looking even more self-conscious, he added, "But then, who am I to tell you what to do? I myself haven't taken any steps yet."

"Oh, but you're young," Kaoru protested. "Why would you?"

He seemed at a loss for words. A shadow crossed his face. Mitsuki felt tense and, perhaps sensing her tension, even Kaoru lost her usual playful expression.

Mr. Matsubara quickly recovered his cheerful demeanor. "Not that I have any money to speak of. But leaving it where it might do some good is worth thinking about, anyway."

Kaoru murmured another protestation about his youth.

"Ah, but you see," said Mr. Matsubara, still cheerful, "I'm a prime candidate for suicide myself."

## 41

**UNLOVED**

Had he worked up the courage for this confession to strangers, knowing that Mitsuki knew about his bereavement? Perhaps his defenses were lulled by the dreamy air the lounge acquired when the shades of night descended and the everyday receded.

Mr. Matsubara followed up his pronouncement by explaining briefly that he had lost his wife to cancer in the spring, a shock made worse because a friend's wife survived the same form of the disease. After that he had forced himself to go back to work but had lost all motivation, so he had taken some time off to visit this hotel, where two springs ago he'd come with his wife to see the azaleas, just before her condition took a turn for the worse.

"She liked the lake better than the azaleas." His summation was simple and clear-cut, befitting a scientist.

There was a short silence, and then Kaoru gave voice to the thought wrenching Mitsuki's heart. "You loved her very much, didn't you?"

He demurred with the embarrassed smile the situation called for, and then, to deflect attention, looked at Mitsuki. "This lady recently lost her mother."

"Goodness!" Kaoru turned to Mitsuki and peppered her with questions, apparently curious about the death of someone her own age. How old was she? What was the cause of death? Had she been living alone?

To keep the conversation from returning to Mr. Matsubara, Mitsuki answered each question in detail and concluded by saying, "But just because my mother got old and died doesn't make me a candidate for suicide."

"I suppose not." Kaoru gave her a wan smile.

A memory flashed through Mitsuki's mind of the day when her mother was cremated. On the way home, with the urn containing her mother's still-warm ashes resting in her lap, she and Natsuki had agreed that no amount of celebration would be enough—though they were both too tired to do any actual celebrating. But out of consideration for Kaoru, another octogenarian, she kept this to herself.

"Very well then, we will remove you from the list," Kaoru announced.

"What about him?" Mitsuki turned toward the great-nephew.

"Who, Takeru?"

Takeru spoke up on his own behalf. "Oh, I've been on the list since I was in my cradle."

He was no dunce, Mitsuki thought. "What makes you say that?"

"I find living itself is depleting ... don't you?"

He said this in a tone languid enough to drain any listener of their will to live. His longish chestnut hair had a touch of curl. While spouting such world-weary lines, did he go to the sort of brightly lit glass-paneled salons Mitsuki didn't have the nerve to set foot in and have people dye and fuss over his hair?

"Never mind," Kaoru said. "Pay no attention to anything he says."

For five more minutes they talked about nothing in particular. Then Mr. Matsubara looked at his wristwatch, and the evening was over.

That night after getting into bed, Mitsuki stayed awake with her bedside light on, her book unopened. Tetsuo's emails receded, as did her surprise and pleasure at the chance encounter with Mr. Matsubara. The excitement of knowing that Kaoru too had been a frequent visitor at the villa her grandmother remembered so well slipped from her awareness, along with the psychic's premonition that someone in their little group might commit suicide or be murdered. What echoed insistently in her thoughts was Kaoru's remark, "You loved her very much, didn't you?"

Mitsuki stared at the ceiling and at length said aloud, "My husband never loved me." She said the words again, almost tenderly. "Never loved me." Then she shook her head on the pillow and rephrased it. "Never loved me the way I wanted to be loved." Perhaps for those few hours in the garret in Paris, surrounded by the flickering light of countless candles, he had. But not afterward. Knowing it was true, she had avoided articulating her awareness. Now each time the words left her mouth, set the air vibrating, and were captured as sound by her ears, the truth loomed larger, naked and unadorned.

No tears came.

How long had she known? She hated to admit it, but suspected she had dimly sensed the truth shortly after they were married.

It was on their honeymoon. She'd been standing by an inlet. They had decided to go to England and cross the Dover Strait by ferry, and on the way, they spent a night in the harbor town of Calais. The old city had been obliterated in the fires of war, but the harbor remained, and after an early supper they'd walked over to where large ferry-boats lay at anchor, silhouetted against the twilight sky.

Tetsuo had stood with his chin slightly raised, studying the view alongside her.

Mitsuki had a vivid childhood memory of standing on a dock as a big dark ship glided out into the offing, watching as dozens of blue, red, and yellow streamers connecting those on deck with well-wishers ashore tore, one by one, in a lingering farewell. Her family had gone to see off an American couple returning home. She always wondered if they were the ones who had found that good-hearted host family for her in Paris. Did they take a steamship because the airfare was prohibitively high? Or did they prefer traveling by sea? In her mind only the streamers were brightly colored; the scene overall was like a frame from an old black-and-white newsreel.

She'd been so small that everything was hazy in her mind, but that must have been Yokohama Harbor. Remembering, she looked up at Tetsuo. "Do you know the song 'The Hill Overlooking the Harbor'?"

"An oldie, isn't it?"

"Yes, from right after the war." Her mother used to sing it around the house, probably because it brought back memories of the park where she had often gone during her time at "Yokohama." As Mitsuki looked at the great ferries lying at anchor before her, something made her want to sing it out loud.

"It goes like this," she said, and started the first verse: *"The hilltop where I came with you…"* It felt good to sing out to the sea. Fortunately no one else was around. As she sang, she felt enveloped in the peculiar bliss of singing—the sense that, at least for that fleeting moment, the world is in harmony.

She was halfway through the first verse when Tetsuo quietly left her side and walked slowly off to the pier.

*"The ship's whistle sobbing, a flutter of cherry petals."* She sang on alone, watching his figure grow smaller.

Why?

That was the first "why" of her married life.

She herself was fond of hearing others sing at the *chansonnier*. Her past boyfriends had enjoyed hearing her sing. And Tetsuo was her husband—shouldn't he listen gladly? Those precise thoughts had not come to her at the time, but she had felt a voiceless cry tear through her, like an echo from the bottom of a deep well.

Something was wrong, in a way she couldn't explain even to herself.

Her mother used to hum as she did housework, and Mitsuki picked up from her several popular songs that were out of date yet curiously modern, like "Just a Cup of Coffee" and "Song of Araby." On the weekend she and her mother would spread out sheet music and sing to Natsuki's accompaniment on the piano: great old songs of early modern Japan like "The Flowers of Karatachi" and "This Road"; French chansons like "Under the Bridges of Paris" and "Mademoiselle Hortensia"; German lieder like "Gypsy Life" and "Rose on the Heath." The opening lines of "Gypsy Life"—"*In the shadows of the forest, among the beech trees*"—had always beckoned her young and excitable mind to an unknown world.

Soon after they started singing, her father would leave his second-floor study, come slowly down the stairs, and sit on the sofa patting their collie, Della, while he listened. When it was over, he would slowly get up and return to his study. The scene had been reenacted countless times during her adolescence, and she had always innocently assumed that every husband enjoyed listening to his wife sing.

Now that she thought about it, even in Paris Tetsuo had never shown any interest in hearing her sing. Yet he had to have known how much singing meant to her... Gradually she'd left off singing. In time she almost forgot she had ever liked to sing. It was as if she had put a precious memento of her childhood into a box and then lost the key.

Of course different families had different ways of doing things. There were no LP albums in the house Tetsuo grew up in, and nobody ever sang. His father, though poor, had been the family patriarch, his mother, self-effacing. How completely different from her family, where her demanding yet gay and cheerful mother had been the sun that everyone revolved around. Though she and Tetsuo were both Japanese, they might just as well have come from different cultures. And yet his behavior that evening in Calais could not, she felt, be written off as the product of a different upbringing. The disturbing scene lingered in her mind, unexplained, and as time passed it came to seem symbolic of their marriage. From then on, every time she felt something was wrong between them, she would see his figure growing smaller as he headed for the pier in the salt breeze.

He was a considerate husband. If she took to her bed with a cold, he would bring her a bowl of steaming rice gruel with a pickled plum on top. Yet over the years, there were other occasions when the question rose in her mind—why? Sometimes she even put it to him directly, but as the whys multiplied, the frequency of her asking dropped off. She didn't want to think he didn't love her, so she invented excuses for him in silence.

## THE 72.3-SQUARE-METER APARTMENT

Her mother had never bothered to conceal her egotistical ways, but not all egotists were like that. The world was full of people like Tetsuo, people who were generally considerate but selfish at bottom. What she wanted ultimately mattered less to him than what he wanted. She had sensed this fairly soon after marrying him but for a long time failed to admit it.

She hadn't wanted to think that he didn't love her.

Eventually the realization had become unavoidable, and this, of all things, through his dogged longing for a condominium in the city center.

In the fourth year of their marriage, they had moved from a small rental apartment into a two-bedroom condominium with a living-dining room, slightly larger but still a mere 58.8 square meters in area, on the top floor of a three-story building.

Mitsuki was still in graduate school, but Tetsuo had been promoted, so they'd begun to think about buying a place of their own. They only had a small amount of savings for a down payment though, and even on the new salary, monthly payments on a loan would have been a strain. Her mother, who had free rein with the family finances, stepped in with an offer of five million yen from her father's first retirement bonus, which had just come through.

"Five million? Really?"

"Really. You're paying your own way through graduate school, after all."

Her mother had by then distanced herself from Natsuki and was taking chanson lessons; for all Mitsuki knew, she might already have been in deep with That Man. But her father was newly employed, was in fact president of a subsidiary of the corporation he had retired from. The house in Chitose Funabashi remained cobweb-free. Mitsuki conveyed her heartfelt thanks to her parents. Tetsuo's parents, by then financially better off, chipped in another million yen since, they said, the wedding had cost them nothing.

Their new life started out happily enough.

On moving day, Mitsuki danced around her new home, piled high with cardboard boxes, and Tetsuo was exuberant too. Naturally, neither of them expected that to be their final residence. Between them they had tons of books, and they both worked at home, so they wanted someday to move somewhere bigger—though Tetsuo's salary made the prospect unlikely anytime soon.

Then the following year, after Mitsuki got her master's degree, to their surprise and delight she was offered a job teaching French part time at a private university. The invitation came from a professor who died a few years ago, a brilliant literary translator with a forehead so pronounced you'd have thought his cranium was swollen from overtaxing his brains. Mitsuki had never been much of a scholar, but in graduate school she'd fit easily into the top echelon thanks to her year with a French family; her deep love of novels had also served her well, winning the professor's approval. And so, despite having never aspired even to teaching elementary school, she became a college teacher.

Her parents too were surprised and delighted.

She taught three courses per term, sometimes at a campus downtown, sometimes out toward the end of the Chuo line. Twice a week she taught two classes in the morning, one in the afternoon. She didn't have to attend faculty meetings or help with entrance examinations. Vacations were generous. The extra income averaged out to a tidy 150,000 yen a month. In the summer there were special intensive classes that also paid well. The uplifting sensation of standing at the lectern to teach a college class vanished the moment she took in the reality of rows of faces that looked vacant if not brain dead, but she kept at it because they needed the money.

The pressure to save mounted as the Japanese economy entered its bubble years and real estate values soared. Even when the requirement of a second foreign language was dropped from the curriculum, forcing her to switch from teaching French to English, she didn't really mind, happy just to be employed. She even took on patent translation work that a friend began passing along. Anything related to biology or computers was beyond her; design and trademark patents became her specialty. Though hardly interesting, the work paid well. The sound of documents coming in over the fax machine late at night gave her a sinking feeling, but she did her best.

Around that time, her family began to collapse.

The damage started slowly and imperceptibly, then picked up speed until by the time anyone noticed, it was too late. Her feud with her mother—sometimes open, more often silent—began and went on all the while she taught college, translated patent documents at home, and went to see her father in the hospital. She was still young then, in her thirties, but slowly the layers of sediment were building up inside her.

Then the financial bubble burst, bringing real estate prices back down to a reasonable level. Finally they were able to move into a larger apartment in the same building, one with three bedrooms plus a living-dining room—a jump from 58.8 square meters to 72.3, standard size for a family of four. The master bedroom with double bed served also as Mitsuki's study, and another room as Tetsuo's study, leaving them a whole extra room for books and other overflow.

Though small, the library, as they called it, made a huge difference in their lives. The daily battle with a stream of detritus (mostly books and papers) was suddenly over. They lined the walls with floor-to-ceiling bookshelves for extra books, and as they added shelves in the middle to hold supplies of printer paper, tissue, toilet paper, and even laundry detergent, everything seemed to march into place like toy soldiers. Mitsuki's mother also gave her a paulownia chest—one of a pair from the dowry of her first marriage—where she could keep kimono, kimono accessories, wool sweaters, and the like. The living room, made to look even more spacious by the addition of a large wall mirror, was now always tidy.

Being on the first floor, they enjoyed the luxury of a small garden. A rose of Sharon bush planted there was still blossoming in September, after they'd finished moving in. The pale purple flowers seemed to sing of the joy of gracious living—or uncluttered living, anyway. Mitsuki breathed a sigh of relief. Her family might have fallen apart, but she at least was settled in for good.

At about the same time, Yuji and Natsuki sold their house in Kamiyama-cho, Shibuya, and moved into a 150-square-meter condominium in a low-rise building nearby. An enormous sofa by the Italian maker Cassina was the centerpiece of their great twenty-two-mat living room. When they had large parties, her sister flattered her into helping out: "You're so much better at it than I am." Mitsuki would put on an apron and work in the kitchen until guests arrived, then mingle among them offering food and drinks.

Mostly they were well-to-do people who made music their occupation, people she marveled at since they never read books, never even seemed to feel they ought to. Late at night she would return to the jumbled neighborhood where she lived in a place less than half the size of Natsuki's, yet a place where books made their presence felt. And she would feel almost as if she had returned to the abode of a spiritual aristocracy.

In bed she would report humorously on the evening and then lean her head on Tetsuo's shoulder and murmur, "Home is the best."

"You're not jealous?"

"No. We have plenty."

She did have one small dream—to quit teaching someday, if there was any money left for her to inherit after her parents were gone.

When Tetsuo became an associate professor, his salary went up. Mitsuki hoped eventually to cut back on her hours of teaching as his salary increased. So many people had to work daily that she was in no position to complain, and yet teaching wore her out, the fatigue lasting all the next day. Besides, her heart simply wasn't in a career, hardly surprising given the times in which she'd grown up.

Her mother had worked for Auntie until her late fifties, true, but then she had always liked to be out and about. Besides, she hadn't worked in the usual sense of the word. Whenever Mitsuki stayed home from elementary school with a cold, she was allowed as a special treat to lie down on her parents' double bed, where she could watch as her mother made leisurely preparations for work. She would sit in front of a vanity mirror, her expression intent as she carefully powdered her face with a big puff, applied rouge and lipstick, then swiftly dressed in a long under-kimono, kimono, and obi tied in back. She would twist around and give the bow a smart pat before putting on earrings, the final touch. She never looked as if she were going off to work. Watching, rather than feel inspired to grow up to be a working woman, Mitsuki used to long for the day when she too could wear makeup and pretty kimono. She never felt particularly grateful for her mother's working outside the home, although her mother, perhaps sensing this ingratitude, kept saying, "I work hard so that you girls can have nice things."

Sometime after they moved into the new apartment, the professor who had found her a part-time teaching job invited her to translate a children's picture book published in France. Translation had never particularly interested her, but once she got started she found herself sitting at the computer till late at night. She translated two more picture books, followed by a slim modern novel. The work had to be finished within a certain period of time, so she turned down patent translations to make sure she would make her deadline.

The pay was negligible.

"That's all you get?" Tetsuo had said incredulously.

"We don't really need the money anymore, so what's the difference?"

At the time he had let it drop, out of consideration for her feelings. But the 72.3-square-meter apartment that she proudly thought of as the abode of a spiritual aristocracy wasn't good enough for him—as she would soon realize.

## (43)

### A RATHER NICE OFFER

"If we lived in the city center I could just take a taxi home."

This was true. Tetsuo had begun to make a slight name for himself in the media; he often got home later now, and she did feel sorry for him, rattling around in those crowded trains while tipsy. But beneath his talk of taxis was a layer of vanity. After the umpteenth time he brought it up, she said teasingly, "The real problem is you want a fancier place with snob appeal—admit it!"

The building where they lived was already starting to look old, and no matter how the management repainted the outer walls or redid the communal floors, it was essentially a concrete box and nothing more, a leftover from Japan's pre-bubble era. Neither was the neighborhood itself anything to brag about.

Tetsuo was briefly speechless. Then, "All right, so I'm a snob. Being a snob has made me what I am."

His defiance left her in turn momentarily at a loss for words. "But we don't have that kind of money."

"With both of us working, we could swing it."

She let slip the chance to tell him that she wanted to cut back her hours.

Even then, she made excuses for him, justifying his desire: he couldn't help it; he was scarred by his childhood.

The story of Tetsuo's impoverished childhood was so redolent of Japan's postwar Showa years that it sounded almost like a fable—one filled with pathos.

The fields where he and his schoolmates romped had been covered with shepherd's purse, trembling in the breeze; they would pluck these wildflowers and bend down the stiff leaves so they dangled and made rattling sounds like little drums. In the evening the aroma of grilled fish rose up from houses everywhere. Before dinner, he and his brother rubbed shoulders on their way to the public bath, each carrying a battered washbasin tucked under his arm. When they got back, the frosted-glass overhead light would be on, hanging over the little round table and illuminating the cheap tableware and simple fare awaiting them.

One story in particular made an impression on her.

After Tetsuo started commuting to the select high school that had admitted him, he became good friends with the son of a treasury bureaucrat who lived in the upscale residential district of Mejiro. The difference in their circumstances was so great it verged on the ludicrous, but they vied with each other to read authors like Soseki and Tanizaki, or Dostoevsky and Tolstoy—the authors that bright students of their generation invariably read. His friend's house had a Western-style living room with bookshelves containing a crimson clothbound edition of Soseki's complete works. Tetsuo once gingerly took a volume in hand and found it was a first edition, probably from the grandfather's generation. He did not of course invite his friend to his house. He used the pittance his mother was able to squeeze out for his spending money to buy cheap paperback editions of the classics that he and his friend discussed, fancying themselves critics.

Then one day while running to catch the train he slipped and fell on the station stairs, breaking his ankle. After that he had to stay home from school with a cast on his leg. A few days later his friend dropped by, having looked up the location of Tetsuo's house on a map.

"How do you do, ma'am," he greeted Tetsuo's mother, removing his school cap. "I am Shoji."

Seeing the polite young man standing before her in his school uniform, Tetsuo's mother let out a small cry. She had heard all about her son's friend. She had even spoken to his mother at Parents' Day, having made special efforts to look presentable for that big event. She was proud to think a son of hers was friends with such a fine young man from such a fine home. The idea that his friend might someday turn up in the tiny entryway of her tiny three-room house never crossed her mind. As she led him into the room where Tetsuo lay in a thin futon on old, faded mats, she imagined how humiliated her son was going to be. Once out in the narrow hallway, she went into the adjacent room where his little brother was watching the Ultraman show, turned off the television, and warned him to be quiet. Then she went back to the kitchen and got out their cheap tableware to serve cheap sweets and tea.

Shoji politely demurred. "Really, ma'am, you needn't put yourself out for me. I don't want to be any trouble." His grace and poise would have done any adult proud. After she recovered from this speech, she sat with her younger boy in the room next door, breath bated.

Tetsuo bravely carried on his usual style of conversation with his friend, but once Shoji had left, he lay staring morosely at the ceiling. His mother, aware of how he must be feeling, returned wordlessly to the kitchen sink. The younger brother, failing to grasp the implications of the situation, switched the television back on with a puzzled look.

As Tetsuo told the story, Mitsuki could almost hear the sound of tap water striking the tin sink in the kitchen and the irksome sound of the television through paper sliding doors. She could see the knotty boards in the ceiling over his futon. The wish to live in a house where he wouldn't be ashamed to have anyone come over must have been implanted in Tetsuo's heart that day.

And his house had been practically in the middle of nowhere. The closest station was Shin-Toride, three stations from Toride. To get to school he'd had to take the train to Toride, transfer to the Joban line, and then transfer again at Nippori or Ueno. Riding the jam-packed train and staring at the impassive faces of the adults being jostled to and fro, Tetsuo must have vowed to himself that when he grew up he would never end up like them. After they married he had chosen the location of their apartment, convenient to Shinjuku and Ginza; but gradually he began to desire more.

Nor was his desire unrealistic.

As the years went by, magazines began displaying glossy photos of posh-looking condominiums. Unlike those inhabited by old-money families like the Shimazakis or by upstart IT specialists, or worse yet by highly paid expatriates (who in their heart of hearts regarded the Japanese as mere "natives"), these were not spacious—some were hardly larger than their 72.3 square meters—nor were they priced beyond the reach of a college teacher. Even so, there would be an expansive entry hall tastefully decorated with marble. Residents might include a pair of architects, man and wife, he with a goatee and she with a short bob and light, glowing makeup, raising herbs on their terrace and living stylish lives—people like that. Magazines gave the impression that with-it people were all moving into such places, and anyone who didn't must be out of it.

Perhaps Tetsuo's desire to relocate wasn't all that strange...

Mitsuki tried telling herself this.

287

With the matter still unresolved, it was soon time for Tetsuo's first sabbatical, and as he wanted to live in California, they went to the University of California, Berkeley, for a year.

For Mitsuki it wasn't much of a vacation. Now that their mother had basically left their father's care in her and her sister's hands, Natsuki looked resentful and begged her to come back now and then. There was always more paperwork to do, and leaving that and all the visits to the hospital up to her sister not only made her feel a bit guilty but a bit uneasy as well, so with the understanding that her mother and sister would help with the travel expenses, she promised to come back to Tokyo once every couple of months. When she did, she would find that her mother had seldom visited her father, although she made excuses to see Mitsuki and tried to be ingratiating.

After the sabbatical, all thought of purchasing a condominium in the center of the city was driven from Mitsuki's mind. To begin with, her father came down with pneumonia almost as if he had been waiting for her to come back, and she had to take a room in a business hotel near the hospital. Then came that infuriating telephone call from her mother prompting her to write a letter threatening to cut off all ties—and the day the letter arrived, her mother was struck by a bicycle.

It was just after her mother's hospitalization that a "rather nice offer" came Mitsuki's way. The timing could not have been worse. The same professor who had found part-time teaching jobs for her had telephoned: "Listen to this, Mitsuki." There'd been a lilt in his voice. He always looked cheerful, but from the sound of his voice he had to be looking more cheerful than ever. "I have a rather nice offer for you."

There was talk of putting out a new Japanese translation of *Madame Bovary* in paperback. He himself was getting on in years and had other projects he needed to finish, so rather than do it himself he wanted to recommend Mitsuki for the job and limit his participation to writing an afterword. The publisher, who couldn't very well reject his recommendation, had agreed on condition that she first submit a sample translation of chapter one. Also, since they wanted to keep the project secret from other publishing houses, she would have only two years to complete the translation.

In mingled joy and consternation, Mitsuki had requested a day to think it over.

That night when Tetsuo came back and she told him excitedly about the offer, he was frustratingly casual. "You should do whatever you want." That was all he had to say. He shared neither her excitement nor her pride—after all, the professor had handpicked her for this opportunity. It was as if Tetsuo saw, or chose to see, no significance whatever in his wife's being specially singled out.

A half-forgotten picture rose in Mitsuki's mind: the spacious entry hall in a luxury condominium building smack in the center of the city.

**44**

## TETSUO'S FIRST FLING

That night Mitsuki had lain awake beside Tetsuo, her spirits low.

She lacked the confidence to take on a large translation project with a firm time limit while continuing to teach. Her mother would soon be out of the hospital and needing extra care. Her father had only just recovered from his bout with pneumonia. Her sister, with her convenient chronic illness, pitiable as it might be, could not be relied on. Mitsuki had just returned from a yearlong absence and was hardly in a position to ask for another year off. The only way for her to accept the translation job would be to quit teaching altogether. But if she said she wanted to quit teaching, how would Tetsuo react? He probably wouldn't openly object, but he certainly wouldn't like it. If she took on the translation while continuing to teach and then couldn't finish it in the allotted time, the professor would lose face.

Tetsuo lay asleep next to her, his breathing slow and deep. To her ears it sounded like the heavy breathing of an utter stranger. She lay for a long time, listening.

The following day, Mitsuki called the professor. Unable to keep the sadness out of her voice, she explained the situation and expressed her regret.

"I see." He conveyed the disappointment that she had feared.

Ever since, she had turned her back on the French language. At the time, she had laid the blame for her decision not on Tetsuo but on her demanding mother. That same day she had gone to see her mother in the hospital, and the moment she stepped into the room her mother had said, "You look a sight."

Mitsuki ignored this, turned her back, and was stocking the small refrigerator in the room with delicacies when her mother added, "You know, you could put on a little makeup."

She spun around. "Who's got time for makeup!"

Her mother swiftly backtracked. "Poor Mitsuki, you're worn out. I'm so sorry all this had to happen."

*You're sorry? Look at you, having to use the potty and still giving me orders, wanting morsels from the food counters at Isetan. How about laying off if you're sorry?* Right there in front of Mitsuki, her monster mother lay in bed. Her mother, who had always done exactly as she pleased in life so that now Mitsuki, her daughter, couldn't live the life she wanted.

When that night Tetsuo heard about how she had turned down the professor's offer, he poured her a glass of light beer. "If it makes you feel any better," he said comfortingly, "steady part-time teaching jobs aren't all that easy to come by. Yours pays pretty well, and it's not very demanding either."

He knew what he was talking about.

Unlike Mitsuki, who taught only two days a week, Tetsuo sometimes was busy nearly every day. Besides faculty meetings, there was a succession of other meetings as well. During entrance exam season he would leave early in the morning, his face a mask of tension, and stay on campus until late at night. Mitsuki appreciated the difficulty of working for a living, and thought it selfish of her to want to be the one to stay at home and do as she pleased. Her guilt over allowing family troubles to sap her energy further inclined her to respect his wishes.

291

There was nothing she could do about it. Her mother was her mother and would go on sucking her energy dry. Mitsuki tried to resign herself but was still vaguely discontent. What about that night in the garret in Paris, surrounded by tiny candle flames like a million blazing stars, when Tetsuo had promised her so much? Hadn't he been promising, more than anything else, to put her wishes first if she married him? Why had all those bright candle flames ever gone out?

At this critical time, knowing Mitsuki was saddled with her aging parents, Tetsuo did not reach out a helping hand.

Why?

After Mitsuki turned down the "rather nice offer," Tetsuo's hankering for a condominium in the heart of Tokyo took on new meaning in her mind, forcing her to reluctantly ask herself: the man she'd married in such raptures—what sort of man was he? Was he just another selfish creature, the kind that grows on trees? Could such a thing be possible?

Not long after that, Tetsuo had his first extramarital fling.

Mitsuki had left for work, then run back home to get something she'd forgotten. Tetsuo, unaware of her presence, was on the phone chattering gaily to someone—a woman, no doubt. She stood stock-still, listening, then burst into the room—and when she saw him gasp, fled back outside. However fast she ran, she was afraid he might catch up with her before she reached the station, so on the way she hailed a taxi.

That night, when she came home after her classes, Tetsuo was already there. Ignoring him, she tossed her big suitcase on the double bed, purposely banging it around in the process, and packed it with clothes, underwear, nightgown, shoes, and makeup. While she did so, it occurred to her that this sort of scene often came up in Hollywood movies. Why did American women just throw everything into a suitcase, even if they were angry? Was it only in the movies, or did they really pack that haphazardly? Mitsuki was not especially methodical for a Japanese, but at least she took time to fold her clothes properly and lay them carefully on top of her nightgown and underwear. Her dirty laundry she put into a plastic bag. She packed her course materials too. She was damned if she'd go live with her mother, who was just out of the hospital and hobbling around on crutches. Instead she'd move in with Masako, who was divorced and raising her daughter in a cheap apartment.

To this day Mitsuki wasn't sure what she'd been planning to do next. Reality had felt unreal; while rushing around she'd felt as if she were watching the movements of someone else in a dream. The intensity of her shock, the depth of her rage, showed the love she still must have felt for him—and not only for him, but also for her life.

Tetsuo, too, roamed around the apartment in tears. Finally when she put on her heels and stood in the entranceway at the door, he came, knelt down, and clasped her legs tightly from behind. Through her stockings she felt his tears on her calves.

Half an hour later as Mitsuki lay stretched out on the bed, her emotions now calmer, his excuses began. "I kept telling her we had to end it." He covered her with a down quilt so she wouldn't catch cold and was reclining beside her on top of the quilt with his arms folded above his head. The pungent smell of his armpit came to her. It was a smell she had learned to love in Paris, sweet yet vaguely animalistic.

The other woman was three years his senior, the wife of a colleague in the International Studies Department. After entering an arranged marriage and bearing a couple of children, she had lived an uneventful life until she accompanied her husband on a faculty study tour of South America, thus meeting Tetsuo and, she said, falling in love for the first time. Without Tetsuo, her first and probably last love, she couldn't go on.

"Every time I said we needed to end it, she would sob hysterically, and I couldn't cut her off."

Mitsuki nodded, blowing her nose.

Such things no doubt happened. Tetsuo was tenderhearted, so it would have been hard for him to break it off. The gaiety in his voice as he'd spoken on the telephone still lingered in her ears, but she willingly accepted his excuse.

If she'd left him then, when she was considerably younger, she might have found someone else. She could have taken a full-time teaching position and made her own way. But at the time, the thought of divorce never crossed her mind. The two of them had a good cry together and ended up closer than before. After that had come her father's death, which she alone had witnessed, and Tetsuo's tenderness then had been a comfort.

And yet, after her discovery of his first fling, something was irrevocably altered.

From that time on, little by little she began to feel awkward around him, and without being aware of it she stopped making mental excuses for him. She even took a perverse pleasure in that awkwardness he aroused in her, and she began allowing herself to look at him from a certain distance. It was as if poisonous shoots from the tree of knowledge had begun to spring up in the soil.

His other fling came several years later. She eventually learned that it began during his second sabbatical on the Okinawan island of Ishigaki. She went with him, but by then her mother had become a concern. Approaching eighty, she was heavily dependent on Mitsuki, and to leave her in Natsuki's hands for a whole year seemed cruel to both her mother and her sister. In addition to calling her mother every night, she had returned alone to Tokyo for a month during summer vacation when the Shimazaki clan went to the coast and again during the winter holidays when her mother wanted to be with family.

Just after Tetsuo's sabbatical, one night past midnight as they lay curled in bed, reading, the phone rang. Fearing that something might have happened to her mother, Mitsuki picked up the telephone. She froze on hearing a woman's voice say, "May I please speak to Tetsuo?"

He took the phone with a calm expression.

She had locked herself in her room, the woman said, and was about to slash her wrists. Her parents were asleep. Once she hung up, she was going to pull the phone out of the wall so he couldn't call her back. Tetsuo sent for an ambulance and with his usual presence of mind — a presence of mind that never failed to amaze Mitsuki — asked that the driver pull up to the woman's house without sounding his siren and alerting the neighborhood. Then he grabbed a taxi and rushed to her house.

Flustered, Mitsuki had helped him get on his way with all possible speed.

This woman was a year older than Tetsuo. Her parents, tired of seeing her loll around the house, overcome with ennui, had sent her off to Okinawa to visit her married brother, a mangrove researcher at Ryukyu University. She and Tetsuo met that summer while Mitsuki was in Tokyo, and although he supposedly made it clear that he had no intention of ever leaving his wife, she'd pursued him even after coming back to Tokyo. Her parents, rather than storming irately into his apartment as they might have done, instead apologized to Tetsuo. Was this because — as he must have known — their daughter was no impressionable young thing but a pitiable creature with a long history of wrist slashing?

Mitsuki took one more downward step on the staircase of life.

# 45

## TELEVISION AND THE EYE OF GOD

A "ladies' man" was a man who was fond of and attentive to women. Tetsuo was a ladies' man in that sense, and yet somehow the phrase didn't seem an accurate description of him. A ladies' man might easily become a "skirt chaser," someone who made aggressive advances to women and craved their flesh. But Tetsuo wasn't like that. He had, after all, been a literary youth—one who had successfully transformed himself into someone who looked as if he belonged on the streets of Paris. He was a romantic. He liked romance, though not in the sense that he fell head over heels in love with women; what he liked was for them to fall head over heels in love with him.

The two women Tetsuo had had flings with seemed to have little in common. The first one was the wife of a colleague of his, so Mitsuki and she had once met. She'd been statuesque, dressed in a vivid suit. The second woman, as far as she could tell from Tetsuo's description, was shy and retiring and dressed inconspicuously, wearing low-heeled black pumps with every outfit—mousy as could be. They were different even in physique, one a little plump, the other thin. Yet they did have one thing in common: both of them had been madly in love with Tetsuo.

And of course, like all his girlfriends from high school on, they had been older than him. He may have sensed that being younger than a woman somehow gave him an edge.

She remembered a conversation they'd had back when her mother was infatuated with That Man. Once, as Mitsuki was venting as only a daughter can, freely enumerating her mother's faults and throwing in those of That Man for good measure, her vehemence had caused Tetsuo to let down his guard.

"Instead of a guy like that," he said, "if only it'd been me who took her out—just think what a thrill she'd have had."

Mitsuki bristled. "What's that supposed to mean?"

He caught himself and said nothing.

"What a perfectly awful thing to say!"

"Sorry. I take it back."

"Talk about narcissism!"

"I said I was sorry. Come on."

Seeing the ferocity of her response, he realized he had misspoken, but probably he never understood what had made her so angry. It wasn't only the indecency of the suggestion. What galled her was his smug assumption that any older woman he lavished his charms on would shed tears of joy. His conceit left her aghast.

The memory of that conversation had lingered for a while, leaving a bad aftertaste, but with the passage of time it had sunk deep into the recesses of her mind.

After finding out about Tetsuo's second fling, she began to wonder if there hadn't been other women as well. There were times when she appraised him with eyes so cold that she herself was surprised. She discovered that while she felt deep respect for the professor who had recommended her as a translator, she had long since lost respect for her husband. She also discovered that the world of what her mother called "high culture" was essentially alien to him. It was alien to Natsuki's husband, Yuji, too, but Yuji at least knew it was and had the grace to be embarrassed, while Tetsuo went around acting as if he appreciated that world when he did not and never would. Perhaps Mitsuki did not so much discover this as permit herself to acknowledge it.

Her mother's reverential references to "high culture" often made Mitsuki herself cringe at the sheer silliness of it all. Her mother lapsed into sentimentality when it suited her—often when watching a movie, listening to an opera, or reading a novel—and the rest of the time put her own desires first while cavalierly dismissing those of people weaker than herself. And yet her rapture was genuine; there was at the core of her being an aching need for something sublime, a wild yearning as for stars above. And so, although her mother's talk of "high culture" often evoked in her an inward sneer or outright revulsion, deep down Mitsuki herself, like many other women—like her mother—had no wish to live a life cut off from such stirrings. Nor did she wish to spend her life with a man to whom they were alien.

The Tetsuo she had known in Paris had seemed so suave, with the air of a connoisseur—so different from the other *boursiers*. Yet simply by virtue of being a *boursier*, he had also seemed an authentic seeker of knowledge. All the more so since he had awakened Mitsuki to her own ignorance.

That Tetsuo was not one to reach for the stars failed to strike Mitsuki for a long time. After a number of years she sensed dimly that he had lost interest in literature per se. Then she saw that he lacked even the scholar's ambition to understand the world through books. He would sit at his desk and write abstruse articles. He would even read abstruse books. But he taught in the International Studies Department, where he could freely choose the subject of his research; in the course of examining colonial and immigrant literature he had drifted away from books and begun flying around the world like a cultural anthropologist, becoming a spokesman for disappearing cultures and oppressed minorities—a laudable gesture, she should have thought, but somehow couldn't. The more he distanced himself from actual books, the better he was served by his inclination to be on the move.

Still, he retained a modicum of academic ambition. Using his former training, he wrote short articles that Mitsuki found baffling, based on French literary, philosophical, and sociological theories, and published them in journals no one read. None of them attracted attention, but he plugged away and in time had enough for one book, then two. Then he began to follow media currents in eastern and southeastern Asia. His third book dealt with the Asian reception of Japanese contemporary pop culture. That book sold rather well, and he began appearing more often in the media.

In Mitsuki's eyes, Tetsuo didn't seem to be acting out of any deep-felt commitment. She could only think that his efforts were aimed at hanging on to the little space he had finally carved out for himself in the media. But until his second fling came to light, she avoided taking such a jaundiced view, partly for her own sake.

Was it fate or mere coincidence?

It happened just after his second fling. It was also just after her mother, walking with a cane and prone to falling, had broken her left shoulder. Mitsuki had been standing in the kitchen in the house at Chitose Funabashi, wearing an apron and slicing pickled radish, a favorite of her mother's. Her mother lay on the sofa wearing a cast and calling out orders: "Don't cut them in slices, now. My teeth are so bad you've got to cut them up in fine little strips." The television was on, Tetsuo due to appear on-screen any minute. His first television appearance.

"There he is, there he is!" Her mother sounded as excited as if some rare animal had come into view.

Mitsuki rushed over, wiping her hands, and then stopped in her tracks. Tetsuo looked momentarily like a stranger. The medium of television, as if it were the all-seeing eye of God, laid bare the banality of his aspirations. That man wearing the "literati shirt" and prattling about something or other with a complacent look on his face—was that her husband?

"He does look handsome on camera." That was all her mother said.

Since he was naturally photogenic and the camera made him look younger than he was, he appeared on the tube fairly often after that. But Mitsuki no longer bothered to watch.

The Tetsuo who had sat amid the flickering candlelight in the garret in Paris, looking grave—how many different heroes she had happily projected onto him! It wasn't only Rodolfo from *La bohème*. There were Julian Sorel from *Le rouge et le noir* and Heathcliff from *Wuthering Heights*, not to mention Kan'ichi from *The Golden Demon*. Young men who were penniless but reaching for the stars, longing to rise above life's vulgarity, and passionately in love with one woman. Men who appeared in the novels she had read over and over in childhood while lying stretched out on a sofa or bed, face up or on her side, munching rice crackers as she devoured the pages. How naively, how rapturously she had projected those characters onto Tetsuo! And fallen gloriously in love.

When she first brought him back to Japan, her mother and sister had projected the same images onto him as she had done, but her father, as one man to another, had not. He hadn't taken a dislike to him, but she realized now that to her father the word *boursier* must have suggested someone with more of the scholar in him. When he met Tetsuo he had seemed rather surprised.

Once she became used to measuring her husband with a cold and objective eye, doing so often amused her.

There was the time they all went to the opera. Unaware that this would be their mother's last such excursion, she, Natsuki, and their mother had taken a taxi from Chitose Funabashi as usual. Tetsuo had taken the subway straight from home, meeting them at Tokyo Bunka Kaikan, the concert hall in Ueno Park. On such occasions, they didn't invite Yuji along, ostensibly because he was too busy but actually because he didn't really fit in. Tetsuo blended into the family and made himself useful, carrying their mother's coat and bags, making restaurant reservations and finding a taxi on the way home, so when he was available they often did ask him to join them.

Their mother's last live opera, *La bohème*, opened.

"*Che gelida manina…*" What a cold little hand, Rodolfo began, taking Mimi's hand in his and singing the celebrated aria. "Who am I? I'm a poet. What do I do? I write. How do I live? I live! I am a poor man…But in hopes and dreams and castles in the air, I have the soul of a millionaire!" The tenor's golden voice made them forget this wasn't La Scala or the Paris Opéra but Tokyo Bunka Kaikan, whose outdated modernist architecture oozed the sadness of a country condemned in its early modern era to a policy of "leave Asia, enter Europe." Mitsuki's mother, already in her eighties, had gazed at the stage with radiant eyes.

Next to her, Tetsuo was fast asleep. He often drifted off at the theater. After a restful Friday—he had no classes then—and Saturday, it wasn't fatigue that made him sleep through the Sunday matinee. The sight of his sleeping figure brought her not melancholy, Mitsuki noticed, but a stab of malicious pleasure.

In one email to his current inamorata, Tetsuo had written, "The family is always going artsy on me. It's hard to take." When she came across that line, Mitsuki couldn't keep back a smile; it so perfectly captured the absurdity of the Katsura household. With the other woman, Tetsuo did not pretend to be something he was not. He could be defiant—or rather, completely honest.

People sometimes were untrue to themselves.

Tetsuo had been untrue to himself during those few hours amid the flickering candlelight in the garret in Paris. That brief time had been a festival for two, a topsy-turvy world where up was down. He'd been beside himself, deeply in love for those few hours, and his sincerity had touched her, swayed her, sent her into raptures. The festival had ended when the candles burned out and he returned to his normal self. Mitsuki had simply gone for a very long time without facing this fact.

An explanation for the sad little episode back in Calais still eluded her. Had he been repelled by a woman childish enough to suppose that her singing would bring a man pleasure? Had he been alienated by the very act of singing, an act completely ordinary in her family? Had he felt, even though she was singing an old popular song, as if she was foisting the arts on him? Whatever the reason, he had definitely felt uncomfortable in her presence.

# ⑯

## HUSBAND-AND-WIFE RICE BOWLS

They were already sleeping in separate rooms by then. He had always kept a single bed in his study to use when he worked late, so the change occurred naturally, before either of them quite realized it. They went on sharing the closet space in the master bedroom, where Mitsuki's desk was, but the double bed became hers alone. Many a sleepless night she had lain there thinking about her poor late father and her outrageous mother, with scarcely a thought about herself and Tetsuo, presumably asleep on the other side of the wall.

That lapse was catching up with her now.

Here in the night stillness at Hakone, her thoughts roamed back through time, dwelling incessantly on Tetsuo and various incidents that came to mind. It was past two in the morning by the time she stopped staring at the ceiling, took her usual assortment of pills, and fell into an artificial sleep.

Even in sleep, memories continued to disturb her.

Despite the clear air, she had only a bit of murky sleep and again woke up feeling tired. She pulled open the curtains, seeking the solace of morning. The lake was the same as the day before, but she

**303**

could tell from the light shining on the ridge above the far shore that the sun was higher in the sky. As she stood watching, she felt as if she could see the sun rising higher with each passing moment. In the morning light, the previous evening's gathering in the lounge seemed unreal, a mere chimera.

She went downstairs to breakfast in the Japanese-style restaurant.

As she was being shown to her seat, she looked around unobtrusively for a figure in a dark suit, intending to just nod in greeting to Mr. Matsubara if he was eating too. He had come to this place to face his grief in solitude; last night, Kaoru's high-handed approach had surely led him to reveal more than he intended. Today he should be left to himself.

Instead of Mr. Matsubara, she spotted a young Asian-looking couple. She could only describe them as "Asian-looking," for as she passed by she heard them speaking American English and couldn't guess their ancestry. Chinese? Korean? Perhaps they were even of Japanese extraction. But unlike Japanese young people nowadays, who seemed likely to shatter with one soft karate chop, they were solidly built. American travelers with no money stayed at cheap inns or business hotels, those with money at luxury international hotels. Odd that these two should be staying at this in-between hotel where the azaleas weren't even in bloom. But they were young, life was just getting under way for them, and the air around them was charged with youthfulness, something Mitsuki had never been aware of when she herself was young.

Though the American divorce rate was around fifty percent, among Asian-American couples it was low, she had heard. Perhaps the old-fashioned ways of their grandparents and parents, who never invested marriage with futile dreams, had some influence on them. What lives would this couple lead on a continent far removed from the land of their forebears?

Farther on she saw the elderly couple who had ridden here on the bus with her. She was surprised to see they were still at the hotel, before reflecting that only two nights had passed. Recognizing her, they set down their teacups and greeted her with smiles and nods. Their son and daughter-in-law were nowhere in sight; they must have stayed only the one night.

Morning light coming through the window shone on their mild faces. They seemed to have settled in at the hotel, and no longer appeared out of their element. They shared a common quietude of mind. As they wordlessly sipped their after-breakfast tea, they had the air, unique to couples who have grown old together, of a well-aged pair of matched rice bowls for husband and wife.

Grandma and Grandpa. An old man and an old woman.

*Once upon a time, there lived an old man and an old woman...*

The elderly couple, who seemed to have stepped out of a folktale, were still tied to the Japan of old. They may well have had an old-fashioned arranged marriage. There were still plenty of such couples, amicably growing old together. Tetsuo's parents were like that. They were quietly on good terms, having married after meeting only a single time. As custom dictated, she had served him tea and cakes on a tray, and when he helped himself that settled the matter, without a word being spoken. The episode may have taken place deep in the countryside beyond Toride, but not in the Edo or Meiji eras. It had happened in the recent Showa era, in the postwar world, after that watershed of modern times, the dropping of the atom bomb. Once their younger son had children, they took to calling each other Grandpa and Grandma. Why were Japanese people no longer satisfied with that sort of marriage?

As she sat down, her eyes fell on the book lying on her table.

*Madame Bovary.* Gustave Flaubert. First serialized in *La Revue de Paris*, 1856. The story of a French country girl who read too many romance novels. Emma, a sentimental, dreamy girl, was the daughter of a farmer with a small fortune. She received an education above her station in a convent, where she came secretly to devour popular novels that talked about nothing but "*amours, amants, amantes,*" instilling in her a yearning for excitement and romance. The man she married, however, was a common country doctor, gentle but dull. Emma imagined her friends from the convent "living in the city…enjoying the buzz of the theater and the bright lights of ballrooms, their hearts buoyed, their senses aroused." To fill the emptiness inside her she took a lover, then another, ordered frocks in the latest Paris fashions, and ran up enormous debts, only to take arsenic and die an agonizing death.

All across France, many a woman reader suspected the novel was about her. Ever since, the word *bovarism* has denoted women who read too many novels and have unrealistic fantasies about love and life.

Western novels made much of love and lovers, an influence that came to Japan after the country opened its doors to the West. Although the eponymous hero of the classic *Tale of Genji* was known for his amorous adventures, in Japanese literature romantic love had always been merely one theme among many—certainly less central than the change of seasons. The Western novels that had reached Japan in the last century and a half were almost all romance novels, transforming Japanese readers—especially women—into romantics. Women became more particular. They grew discontented with the husbands chosen for them by parents, relatives, or neighbors, longing like Emma for someone to whisper thrilling words of love. Their dissatisfaction with reality increased until, like Noriko, they rejected barbers' sons and fled, each to her "Yokohama." Not all of them went so far as to commit suicide like Emma, of course, but they led small, discontented lives and then died.

Novels are heartless.

One eye on the pretty face of the bonneted young woman on the cover, Mitsuki sipped her miso soup, chopsticks in hand. The old couple stood up and paused by her table in friendly greeting. Mitsuki set down her soup bowl and said hello. "Another lovely day for a walk."

"Yes it is," agreed the old husband. "We already took ours today."

"You were out early then."

"It's our habit."

They smiled at her, their smiles much alike, and disappeared.

Mitsuki too retired to her room, but she was weary of thinking. She opened and closed *Madame Bovary* several times. Sometime before noon, she dressed against the cold and went out into the bright hotel garden.

If she followed the stone path to the right through the garden, past withered azalea shrubs, she would come to a cheap-looking chapel with a cross on top. It was made of plastered concrete, painted white, and on either side of the double doors were alcoves fitted for some reason with twin statues of Mary. Lately, as marriages founded on romantic love spread, more and more couples who had never opened a Bible in their lives were pledging eternal love at altars, under a cross, and hotels that profited from wedding receptions were vying to construct chapels in the building or on the grounds. The Hôtel du Lac must have erected that bizarre-looking structure in an effort to keep up with the times. In front of it was a vaguely Romanesque plaza with a fountain in the center that looked like a studio set, and surrounding the plaza was a fake stone cloister.

When she first stumbled on the scene, she'd been so put off that from then on, she went out of her way to avoid it, retracing her steps when she came to an old granite monument honoring the hotel founder. The meaning of the elegant inscription in classical

Chinese escaped her, even though she could read each individual character. Every time she went by, she marveled anew that in a mere hundred years Japanese people had lost the ability to read such texts, while putting up fake stone chapels all around the country.

Today she again turned around at the monument and then came back to the center of the garden, where she encountered a group of men in caps. Gardeners. They were looking at the azaleas and variously making notes in notebooks, taking photographs, and attaching number tags. Some of the shrubs had retained their leaves, others had shed them; some were small, others so big it was hard to believe they could be azaleas. As in a botanical garden, the various shrubs were tagged with their Japanese name and its scientific equivalent: "Hanaguruma; *Rhododendron macrosepalum* Maxim." Flower names rendered in picturesque Chinese characters leaped out at her: Okinawan Silk, Young Egret, River Asuka, White Man'yo, Damask Princess. The mental picture each name created seemed to open a world more aesthetically pleasing than the coming array of spring blooms. The magic of ideograms — fortunately that tradition had survived.

The group of men stood murmuring in front of a leafless shrub.
"What's this?"
"Dodan."
"You sure?"
"Dodan. Trust me."
Farther on she came to a sign explaining the cultivation and care of azaleas. On display were names and headshots of the main gardeners, who were identified grandly as "garden conductors." The rugged, honest faces made the odd, quasi-English job title seem even odder. She studied the board for a while before going down to the lake, this time turning right along the stone path. After a while the stone paving became irregular, the trees encroached on the way, and walking was more difficult. She went as far as she

could before turning back, arriving at the hotel just in time for a late lunch.

She decided on a light meal and headed for the lounge, taking a table by the window. Most of the customers were female, possibly because it was midday. Some pairs were mother and daughter, others sisters or friends. All seemed to be unburdening themselves earnestly and intimately to each other. Then a stout middle-aged man in a sweater came by, paused at a window near Mitsuki's table, and turned to call with oblivious male heartiness to someone farther back in the room: "Look here, you can see Mount Fuji!"

"What if you can?" A middle-aged male voice boomed back.

"Come on, see for yourself." He gestured with one hand. "They're gonna make it a World Heritage site, you know."

The other man sauntered up to the window, grumbling. "That? That's gonna be a World Heritage?" He too was stout and wore a sweater. The two men stood regarding Mount Fuji like a pair of carefree bears. Then there was a series of muffled loud noises, sounding like a small volcanic eruption.

"What the heck was that?"

"Cannon, I'll bet. Supposed to be a Self-Defense Force training ground somewhere at the foot of Mount Fuji."

"Hmm."

They noisily exited.

After her meal, she stood at the same window and looked out at the lake. Two gaudy pirate ships. One low, flat, glass-bottomed excursion boat. The three vessels plowed busily back and forth across the surface of the tiny lake.

Compared to the world of novels—of the imagination—the real world was a letdown.

## GAZING INTO THE FLAMES

At the end of the day, drawn by the fireplace in the lounge, Mitsuki again descended the staircase and, not quite aware of what she was doing, looked around for a figure in a dark suit. Her gaze landed instead on Kaoru, who was sitting alone next to a lamp, looking down so that her white hair stood out. Of Takeru there was no sign. Mitsuki didn't feel she could ignore Kaoru's presence, so she went over to say a quick hello.

Kaoru, a scarf again draped elegantly around her neck, was knitting. To Mitsuki's surprise, on her lap next to a ball of lavender yarn was a silver iPod. When she saw Mitsuki she fumbled to switch off the device, then removed her earphones and laid down her knitting needles. Looking up, she spoke huskily.

"I found out who else is staying on. The bartender told me. A mother and daughter and a husband and wife."

Mitsuki looked around.

"They're not here. Not likely to come down at night. The husband and wife must be in their seventies."

Mitsuki remembered the old couple she'd seen again at breakfast.

"Funny," Kaoru continued, "they didn't strike me as the type to stay in a hotel for more than a night or two." She added in a self-mocking tone, "Listen to me! What a busybody I've become. An old lady with nothing better to do than stick her nose into other people's affairs."

"Would the daughter be plump and the mother thin, by any chance?" Mitsuki had in mind a mother and daughter she'd seen in the hot spring before dinner.

"Yes! They just checked in today. I spoke a few words to them. The daughter's going to be married next month, and they came here to relax before the wedding."

The pair she had seen in the hot spring had seemed on such good terms, it made sense that they would want to enjoy a little mother-and-daughter time. In this day and age most women kept their jobs after marrying, at least until the first baby arrived; had the daughter taken time off work to come or was she that rare traditionalist, a woman who quit work on marrying?

Kaoru had a lonely air as she looked up.

"Where is Takeru, if you don't mind my asking?" Mitsuki said.

"Bed. He went for a drive before dinner, and when he came back he said he was tired so he was turning in early."

As Mitsuki nodded and started to leave, Kaoru pointed to her iPod with a knitting needle. "What do you think I'm listening to? Guess."

Mitsuki tilted her head to one side, considering. "Opera?"

Kaoru tittered the way women used to do, sounding much like Mitsuki's mother. "No, my dear, it's an old recording of *Miyamoto Musashi*. Takeru bought the tapes on Yahoo! Auctions and transferred them here for me. When I was a girl, it was a weekly radio series. I never used to listen then, but now I find the language mesmerizing."

The idea of this refined old lady listening to the epic about the legendary swordsman was so unexpected that Mitsuki laughed too. She said goodbye, still smiling, and headed for the fireplace.

She too settled in by a nook's lamplight, ordered a glass of red wine, and opened her book after putting on her glasses, but her eyes slid unseeing over the page. Added to the thoughts she had been entertaining since the night before, new faces and scenes she had encountered came and went in an incoherent jumble. Soon she was seeing again in her mind's eye the figures of mother and daughter bathing together in the hotel hot spring.

She'd gone down for a soak after sunset. A man would no doubt beg to differ, but to her naked women seemed much the same, like animals, with less disparity in age than when they were clothed. Children and the elderly were exceptions, but everyone else was simply one more naked woman like the rest. Young girls who stepped out wearing pink sandals and fluttery skirts shed their excess youth in the bath along with their clothes. Clouds of steam also made it harder to tell if two women were sisters or mother and daughter.

Yet with that mother and daughter, the difference was plain to see. They'd sat at the edge of the communal tub, soaking their feet and letting their backsides show. One had a young, round bottom and the other, roughly Mitsuki's age, a thin bottom that looked older than the rest of her. The two had seemed on amazingly good terms, sticking close together and chatting. After their pale figures left the bathing area, Mitsuki had lingered awhile before going to join them in the dressing room. They were wearing cotton *yukata* robes provided by the hotel, sitting side by side in massage chairs and enjoying the rhythmical kneading of their back muscles. They would probably sleep in twin beds and turn out the light at the same time to go to sleep. When Mitsuki came here with her mother, it had never occurred to her to sleep in the same room with her. She had reserved separate rooms for them without hesitation, and when she reported this, her mother had only said, "All right."

What sort of man might the daughter be about to marry? She had a rather vacant look, so maybe she would get along without worrying too much about whether she was loved... or unloved.

*Unloved*... The moment this word came to Mitsuki's mind, a painful wave of realization once again swept over her. She stared blankly at the red flames.

Reaching for the stars wasn't so important after all, as long as there was something lofty in a man. No, even if there wasn't anything lofty in him, just to have been loved—not adored, but cherished—would have made her happy. Choosing the wrong man might be forgiven in a girl of eighteen, but she'd been twenty-five. Life was a onetime gift, a true miracle, and at a crucial point she had stumbled. Knowing this, she had not faced up to her error but had continued to stumble along, until this very moment. That was the truly irrevocable part of it. The night before, she'd leveled heaps of slanderous charges at Tetsuo, but she herself was hardly guiltless, for hadn't she stopped caring for him long ago?

When she read his email correspondence with the woman, hadn't she been riven not with sadness but with humiliation? She should have left him long before this. Or she should have at the very least lived her life not nursing her wounds but squarely confronting the fact: her marriage had been a mistake.

She sighed, still looking blankly into the flames. Her book lay shut. Her glass of red wine, warmed by the fire, bore dark red streaks of lipstick that looked unclean.

How on earth had she come to this point?

Natsuki, who idealized her marriage to Tetsuo, often said enviously, "You're so lucky!" Every time she heard those words, Mitsuki had felt a sense of triumph. In her mind's eye she would see her small self toiling up the hill toward "Yokohama" behind her mother and sister, carrying Natsuki's music bag. Pride had surely prevented her from seeing her marriage as the failure it was. Knowing she would have to tell Natsuki the truth was painful.

But pride alone could not explain her stubborn blindness.

She took her eyes off the flames and looked around the lounge, seeking Kaoru's white head and perhaps, on some level, her mother. Absorbed in *Miyamoto Musashi*, Kaoru was sitting with back bent, assiduously plying her knitting needles, forgetting herself for a change. She looked old.

Mitsuki resumed gazing at the flames and let out another sigh.

Her mother had played no small role in all this, after all... As a grown woman, she had no desire to blame her mistakes on her mother; she even admitted that she owed her a great deal. But any woman leading an ordinary life—untouched by natural disaster, poverty, or incurable illness—was likely to be living that ordinary life in thrall to her mother, much more so than any man could possibly imagine. This was especially true in today's aging society where daughters were forced to go on keeping company with their mothers indefinitely. The problem was who Mitsuki's mother had been—someone so unlike other mothers.

By the time Tetsuo's first infidelity came to light, her feud with her venomous mother had been well under way. Sticky filaments were already wrapping around her, preventing her from forming any inclination to face up to the mess her marriage was. Being able to physically leave her mother, go home, and be with Tetsuo, who was no blood relation, had actually been a relief. Her life with him had seemed off-limits to her mother. The more indignant she became with her mother, the more she wanted her life with Tetsuo to be an inviolable sanctum. Facing up to the mess of her marriage had been the very last thing she wanted to do. And after That Man finally disappeared, the days had gone by in a welter of emotion as continuing indignation over her mother became entangled with exasperation and pity for what her mother had become.

What had made Noriko Katsura the woman she was?

What made any person the way they were? Who could say? No scientific advance, no new discovery about the firing of nerve cells in the brain, would ever provide an answer. And yet as Mitsuki grew older she had continually wondered about it, as had Natsuki. They had often commiserated over the telephone.

"She's so outrageous. Who'd believe it if we told them?"

"I know. Impossible to even try."

"No one would ever understand."

"But you never know, there could be lots of daughters stuck with a mother like that."

"I suppose so, but are three percent of all mothers like her or is it more like thirty-three percent? There's no way to tell."

"If a third of all mothers were like her, society would simply collapse, and you know it. Besides, Japanese people are supposed to have a gift for resigning themselves to what life dishes out."

"Right. Especially women of her generation. They were taught not to want much."

"We need someone to do a survey!"

"Absolutely. How on earth does a person get to *be* that way?"

"Maybe she was a mutant. Or wait a minute, think how old Grandma was when she was born."

"So her eggs would have been old too."

"Right!"

"But would that be enough to make someone turn out so damn self-centered?"

They always came to the same conclusion: "Her background has to be part of it too."

Temperament was innate. No matter what circumstances their mother had been born into, she would have caused a considerable stir. But the peculiarity of her background undoubtedly had much to do with shaping her into the woman she became...

Mitsuki's mind went in circles, coming to the same conclusion she had reached again and again before. Yes, it had all started with her grandmother, "O-Miya." If she had not seen herself as O-Miya in the novel, she would not have eloped with her "Kan'ichi." If she had not eloped with "Kan'ichi," then Noriko Katsura would never have been born. If she had never read that serial novel in the first place, then not only their mother but she and her sister, too, would never have been born. If there had been no serial novels in Japan, then she, Mitsuki, would not be here in a mountain hotel staring into the flames and telling herself she was unloved...

She herself was the offspring of a serial novel.

# (48)

## *THE GOLDEN DEMON*

More than a century ago, in 1897, Ozaki Koyo's novel *The Golden Demon* began to appear in the newspapers.

Seldom did a novel change a human life in so tragicomical a fashion—and yet so treacherous are the connections between fiction and life that who could truly say it had never happened to anyone else? No sooner did serialization of the novel begin than women all over Japan were reduced to tears, thrown into a crucible of emotion. *The Golden Demon* derailed her grandmother's life—and for all Mitsuki knew could have inspired similar tragicomedies up and down the archipelago. The very term "serial novel" still invoked *The Golden Demon*. That melodramatic work—a work that continued to run in the newspapers off and on for five years and remained unfinished at the author's death—earned an undying name in Japanese literary history because of the enormous impact it had on women of the day, who hardly had access to novels except those in the newspaper.

*Golden Demon*'s influence lingered on into the age of cinema, when, astoundingly, nearly two dozen versions were filmed. In the postwar era it was even filmed in Taiwan, a former colony of the empire of Japan. When television came along, there were made-for-TV versions. A popular song based on the story might no longer be familiar to the younger generation, but when Mitsuki was small everyone knew it. There was even a statue on the shore at Atami to commemorate a famous scene in the novel.

To be loved by someone like Kan'ichi Hazama: this was the heart's desire of myriad women who might well be said to have succumbed to the Japanese equivalent of bovarism. Few characters in modern Japanese literature have Kan'ichi's romantic appeal. Though poor, he is of samurai blood and a lover of learning. Orphaned in adolescence, he is taken in by a family indebted to his father. He and the daughter of the family, O-Miya, grow up together and in time exchange promises to wed. Then at a New Year's card party, O-Miya meets a wealthy man sporting a diamond ring of breathtaking size and ends up marrying him — a self-important man with a mustache — instead.

Indignant at his beloved's perfidy, Kan'ichi runs away from home and sells his soul, becoming a cruel moneylender. Though bitter and heartbroken, he clings to his love to the end. A young, lovely member of his profession sends amorous glances his way, but he addresses her stiffly and with evident annoyance. He clings to his love tenaciously, determinedly, stoically, as if adhering to a principle. Though O-Miya repents and comes to him to apologize, ready to die if need be, he is unforgiving and clings only to the O-Miya she used to be, prior to her change of heart. His love is an obsession.

Mitsuki's grandmother had a far more pitiable childhood than her mother — or than the fictional O-Miya, for that matter.

Born to a geisha, she was taken from her mother at an early age, adopted into a geisha house, and raised to become a geisha herself, not in Tokyo but in Kobe, adjacent to Osaka. When she was nineteen by the old way of counting (seventeen or eighteen by the modern count), a wealthy man paid off her adoptive parents and made her his concubine. As if on cue, the man's wife, who had been suffering from tuberculosis, conveniently died, enabling her to gain the coveted status of wife. When the novel first came out, Mitsuki's grandmother was legally married and mistress of several servant girls.

Having no education beyond elementary school, she had never acquired the habit of reading books, but after seeing her husband off in the morning she must have enjoyed spreading out the newspaper. To educate the public, newspapers in those days put glosses by all Chinese characters to indicate the pronunciation, which no doubt helped. Perhaps she read with a frown on her face, muttering the words under her breath in the manner of people unaccustomed to reading.

She probably had no eyes for articles on politics and the economy. First she would have scanned the articles on robberies, fires, and family murder-suicides, saving the day's installment of the serial novel till last. Given her upbringing, she may have taken an interest in the theater—Kabuki and *gidayu* ballad-dramas and such—but very likely her first encounter with the joy that literature can bring came through the serial novel.

In Mitsuki's memory, her grandmother was a bleary-eyed old woman in a washed-out smock over a faded kimono, always either busy in the kitchen or hunched over her sewing. But when she imagined her grandmother reading *The Golden Demon*, she inevitably saw her as a woman of allure, someone who had stepped out of a woodblock print. The rich man's house must have had Western-style rooms, but probably she was never truly comfortable except on straw tatami mats. Low dining tables called *chabudai* had become popular in the mid-Meiji era, and their house undoubtedly had one. Mitsuki pictured her sitting on the tatami mats with her feet tucked under her, reading the newspaper spread out on such a table as she rested her young chin on one hand. Sometimes she saw her bent over the newspaper on the floor, her lithe figure folded at the waist. Proud of being a respectable wife, had she worn her hair in the traditional chignon of a married woman, perhaps tied with a band of red silk? Or had she daringly chosen a modern pompadour? Then again, she might have preferred the older and jauntier *ichogaeshi* style.

After her husband left, the sunlight must have streamed through the paper shoji doors with particular softness.

Her girlhood had been full of hardship; during music lessons she had endured beatings with the ivory plectrum of the shamisen, and at mealtimes she often was served only leftovers. Then all changed, and she needed to please only her husband. What luxury! She may have felt a pang of guilt, but she had never been in a position to decide her own fate.

On January 1, 1897, the first New Year's Day since her marriage, serialization of *The Golden Demon* began. As she read on, episode by episode, she could scarcely believe her eyes. Could the story be about her? Once she began to wonder this, her suspicion grew. She fidgeted, hardly able to wait until her husband left the house so she could spread out the newspaper. Mindful of the servants' eyes, she would read and reread the day's installment, pressing the sleeve of her under-kimono to her eyes to wipe her tears. When she had finished, she would cut it out of the newspaper with a pair of shears and put the clipping away in a bureau drawer where she could take it out from time to time to read again.

Of course, the setting was rather different from her situation. She herself was certainly not from a decent background like O-Miya. But in the geisha house, she too had grown up with a young man with no blood relation to her. Like Kan'ichi, he had been orphaned in adolescence and, again like Kan'ichi, was taken in by foster parents because of a great debt they owed to his late father. He too was of samurai lineage and a lover of learning. Like O-Miya, she had whispered with him of a life together and, again like O-Miya, she had abandoned him in the end and married a rich man with a mustache. The young man, like Kan'ichi, had run away in disappointment.

Needless to say, her adoptive parents had had a great hand in her betrayal. Seeing how the young man excelled at his studies, they'd marveled at this evidence of his samurai blood. At the same time, they grew more calculating. Although originally they'd taken him in mainly out of a sense of obligation, they soon saw that if he graduated from the university they could rely on him in old age; a young man of his gifts might well become a high government official. As their hopes swelled, they began to treat him better. They knew he was in love with the geisha's daughter they were training but didn't want him tied to anyone so low. The family business (which was nothing to be proud of anyway) they could leave to the husband's younger brother and his wife. They would find their young man a proper bride and enjoy a comfortable retirement, making the most of their role as his guardians.

Mitsuki's grandmother, little better than a slave, would certainly have had no right to choose her own husband and probably couldn't have gone against her adoptive parents' wishes. She ended the relationship because she had no other choice. It was the sort of misfortune that befell women of those days—women of her background, especially—all too often.

When she became the rich man's concubine, her adoptive parents must have been overjoyed. For one thing, they were well rewarded. For another, the young man in their charge had escaped being tied to a geisha. How could they have known that after she vanished, he would run away, brokenhearted?

Even as she proceeded to become the rich man's lawful wife, Mitsuki's grandmother kept the memory of her first love enshrined

in her heart. Then along came *The Golden Demon*, a new installment every morning. On top of that, the rumor reached her that
her former lover had run away. She remembered then the black
look he had given her one day when their paths had happened to
cross. She grew more and more convinced that the serial novel
was written about her, and over time, reality and fiction blended
indistinguishably in her untrained mind. She came to think she
truly had left him for a diamond. Though blameless, the more
she read, the more she blamed herself. The choice between love
and money that often forms the basis of the modern novel—a
choice unavailable to Japanese women of her time and particularly unavailable to geisha—this choice, she came to think, had
been hers to make.

The accusatory lines Kan'ichi speaks on the shore at Atami
must have seemed leveled directly at her—and not only the most
famous: "Wait and see, O-Miya. Today is the seventeenth of January. On this night one year from now, I will make the moon cloud
over with my tears." He continues: "You'll rise in the world and
you'll lead a high life, and that's all very fine for you, but think how
I feel, given up in exchange for money. Shall I say I am in despair,
mortified? O-Miya, if I could I'd like to stab you—no, don't be
surprised!—stab you and take my own life."

*Ah!* At that point Mitsuki's grandmother would have cried out
in an access of emotion and, like O-Miya, collapsed in a disheveled
heap to cry her eyes out. Possibly.

When Kan'ichi becomes a moneylender and the lovely woman
in the same profession tries to steal his love, Mitsuki's grandmother
became jealous. Kan'ichi is so devastatingly handsome that the
woman can "scarce control her feelings of attraction." No matter
how she throws herself at him, he remains adamant, but even so
Mitsuki's grandmother fretted.

During gaps in the serialization, she would read and reread her clippings, morning and night. As she handled them, gradually the paper tore at the fold and the print smudged. Unbeknownst to her husband, she tried to track down the young man. To keep her adoptive parents from continually relying on her for money, her present husband had had them formally renounce any relationship with her, but timidly she went back and called on them. They raged at her—"Thanks to you, he disappeared!"—and she left in despair.

After the author, Ozaki Koyo, died leaving *The Golden Demon* unfinished, Mitsuki's grandmother made a last attempt to find the young man. Nearly seven years had gone by since the novel began serialization, and after years of childlessness, she had given birth to two sons in quick succession. She managed to find someone who'd gone to school with him and tearfully persuaded him to help her search, only to learn that her erstwhile lover had caught typhus in Taipei and died a year before, while sailing home. She lay in her futon for six months and for a while thereafter seemed half demented. Her husband finally had enough and again took a concubine. She felt relieved then and in her relief was able to resume her duties as mistress of the house and mother. It was during that interim that the invitations had come to visit the baron's villa.

Time passed. When the two boys were at an age to prepare for college entrance examinations, a live-in tutor was hired—a student who turned out to be the very image of her lost love. He too was of samurai lineage; he too was a lover of learning.

"I was thunderstruck," she would later say. "I thought it was him reincarnated."

Or could it be the son of her vanished young man? No, for both the tutor's parents were living. It was no more than a chance resemblance between strangers. Even so, her feelings for him grew daily stronger. She even felt somewhat justified in falling in love, as her husband had taken a woman on the side. The tutor gradually came to return her affection, for she was still beautiful. They became lovers, and in the end she left her husband and her two sons to run off with him—the man who became Mitsuki and Natsuki's grandfather.

In speaking of her first, long-lost love, she always referred to him as "Kan'ichi." That was perhaps only natural as, until meeting their grandfather, she had yearned less for him than for a fictional character in a novel.

The following year she gave birth to a daughter, Noriko, who after growing up asked one day what the real name of "Kan'ichi" had been.

"That's neither here nor there."

"Anyway, *Golden Demon* is set in Tokyo, Mother, and you always lived in Osaka."

"Who'd ever read a novel in Osaka dialect? Believe you me, if Kan'ichi had said those lines of his like an Osaka native—if he'd so much as called her 'O-Miya-han' instead of 'O-Miya-san'—it'd never have worked. Ridiculous."

## DAMN FOOL

As she grew older, little by little Noriko had groped through the fog of secrecy to learn the truth of her birth. She never believed her mother's story about being the real "O-Miya-san," but neither did she have any proof to the contrary. Her ignorant mother's gullibility was appalling yet pitiable. She let it lie. There was nothing she could do anyway to change the fact that she owed her very existence to her mother's overactive imagination.

The watchword of the militaristic age had been "give birth and multiply." That helped explain why the tutor "O-Miya" eloped with — Noriko's father — had had eight siblings. The most successful of the eight was the eldest girl, Noriko's aunt, who married into the Yokohama family.

The marriage wasn't a big social leap for her. True, her father was an impoverished military man burdened with a large family, but the family had been feudal retainers of Tsuwano Domain before the Meiji Restoration and afterward converted to Christianity, like many in the learned class. The "Yokohama" were descended from a physician of Western medicine in the same Tsuwano Domain and had also converted to Christianity. The aunt's good looks working to her advantage, the marriage came about naturally. Her husband, the later Grandpa Yokohama, became captain of an oceangoing merchant ship, and year by year the gap widened between her lifestyle and that of her siblings.

If the eldest girl was the family's pride, the second son, Noriko's father, was their disgrace. He graduated from Kobe Higher Commercial School, the forerunner of Kobe University, where as an honor student he had received a tuition exemption. By rights he should have gone on to lead a prosperous, respectable life, but before that could happen he was trapped by "O-Miya" and lost his way. It was one thing that she'd formerly been a geisha, quite another that she was another man's wife. Worst of all, she was fully twenty-four years his senior, easily old enough to be his mother. She wasn't even pregnant; that at least would have made it easier to understand. No, she conceived Noriko after the elopement—all unnecessarily, you might say, depending on your point of view.

"Damn fool." So said one of her more outspoken relatives.

Noriko's father never went so far as to formalize the marriage, and although he doted on Noriko he merely acknowledged paternity without erasing the stigma of her being a love child. "O-Miya" knew her place and never asked for more; she took comfort in his at least having recognized the child as his own. That she took comfort in such a half measure underscored the unsavoriness of her background and the fragility of her position.

The three of them moved from place to place until they settled for a few years in Yokohama. Then they moved to Osaka, where at school Noriko was dumbfounded by the sound of the multiplication table being recited in dialect. They settled in a row house in a dusty neighborhood on the city outskirts, facing a noisy main street, where her mother hoped to open a sundries shop on the first floor. And so Noriko, the daughter of a white-collar worker, was thrown in among rice merchants, hardware store owners, short-order cooks, grocers, hairdressers. Not that they needed the extra money. Her father was beginning to earn a fair income. Even so, her mother, in addition to opening a shop—which soon enough failed—also contented herself with poor clothes and poor fare, as if she were no more than a maid, probably hoping to lessen the burden on Noriko's father and thereby keep him longer by her side. She must have known from the outset that at some point, in some fashion, he would leave.

As Natsuki and Mitsuki grew older, their mother must have decided there was no longer any harm in speaking ill of her own mother in front of them, and her carping only increased. She remembered their grandmother "O-Miya" as uneducated, unrefined in words and deeds, warped and ignorant from her peculiar upbringing. Perennially shabby attire had only accentuated the ugliness of a woman long past her prime, an ugliness that as a girl she had found galling. "O-Miya" claimed that when she eloped she took along her jewelry and pawned it piece by piece to make ends meet: tortoiseshell combs, carved coral netsuke, jade obi ornaments, sapphire rings. (No diamond? Mitsuki used to wonder.) But their mother seemed incapable of mentally connecting her hideously old parent with sparkling gems. Nor could she believe that she had ever been beautiful. "I was so disgusted by how old and ugly she was. I used to think, I'll never let myself go to seed like that."

But even supposing "O-Miya" had tried to keep her looks, Mitsuki doubted it would have made any difference: she couldn't have possibly held on to a lover twenty-four years her junior who never made her his legal wife.

And indeed after Noriko went to a girls' higher school, her father did leave her mother for another woman. With his disreputable past, he could not hope to marry well; his sleazy wife was a former waitress in the run-down *oden* shop where he used to go to cheer himself up with a cheap hot meal. Noriko despised her. But her father kept on providing conscientiously for her and her mother. And bizarrely, he lived with his new wife on the same street as them in order to watch over Noriko until she finished school. That arrangement, painfully awkward for all concerned, lasted until Noriko graduated; only then did both parties move elsewhere. It was another six months before Noriko, scared by the talk of her marrying the barber's son, made up her mind to move in with "Yokohama."

When Noriko's father wed the waitress, "O-Miya" had wept into her dirty apron, but quickly resigned herself to the inevitable.

Mitsuki, listening to the story, reflected that their grandmother had been blessed with an innate cheerfulness, which fortunately their mother had inherited, and an unassuming disposition, which unfortunately their mother had *not* inherited. The sadness of the story was offset in her mind by warm memories of her grand-mother bustling around the house, taking care of all the cleaning, laundry, and cooking. Apparently while they were on their own in the row house, "O-Miya" always used to say she was "just the maid," and their mother had found such lack of dignity off-putting. But at the house in Chitose Funabashi she had been exactly like a maid, and there hadn't been anything the least undignified in that image.

Their mother had a fierce streak, and if "O-Miya" had been frail in her old age, she might well have found herself abandoned on a mountain somewhere like old people of long ago, as legend had it. Luckily, though small, she'd had a strong constitution, and far from being abandoned, exuded the contentment of one who has finally found her place in life. Their father had been kind to her. When Mitsuki leaned against her as she sat sewing, she'd sensed in her rounded back the relief of someone who knew, after a long and tur-bulent life, that when the end came she could safely breathe her last here on the tatami mats, without a care.

By the time she had pieced together the story of her grandparents, Mitsuki felt sorrier for her grandfather.

Thrust at a young age into the role of Kan'ichi, he'd gone from being an exemplary student with a bright future to being an outcast laden with a heavy burden. A lesser man would certainly have ditched her mother and grandmother along the way, but not only was he from a Christian family, underneath it all he was imbued with old-fashioned Confucian values as well, a man bound by his sense of duty to an almost painful degree. With the thoughtless exuberance of youth he had cast aside ambition, spoiled his life, and ended up spending the prime of his manhood embracing shame, regret, and guilt. The mistake he had made in his youth was wholly out of character to begin with, and it was perhaps only natural that he wouldn't marry a woman twice his age. A dutiful son and brother at heart, he had managed to maintain ties with his frostily disapproving parents and siblings and thus also with "Yokohama," the family his sister married into that was to have such a formative influence on Mitsuki's mother, Noriko.

After Noriko grew up, a relative had enlightened her.

"You mustn't resent your father, Noriko. He could have just as easily abandoned you and your mother to live under a bridge and be beggars."

Noriko's grandfather, after all, had been happy enough to leave her mother, the child of his mistress, in a geisha house. In contrast, her father had never abandoned his responsibilities, even if he did eventually move out. He'd seen that she graduated from a girls' higher school, regularly sent her an allowance even afterward, and to cap it off provided her with a fine dowry.

The relative's comment wounded her, but for the first time she saw those words as one way of looking at the situation. The fact that it had never occurred to her before hinted at the pains her father took to see that she had as normal a childhood as possible.

In talking to her daughters, she unfailingly bemoaned the hardship she had experienced growing up: "You just don't know how I suffered, knowing people called me names behind my back." This was true. Neither Mitsuki nor Natsuki could imagine such a thing; it scarcely seemed real. Times had changed, and while logically they understood that the terms *geisha-agari* (ex-geisha) and *shoshi* (illegitimate child) had borne some humiliating stigma, such slurs seemed ancient history. And their mother being who she was, neither of them was inclined to be very sympathetic anyway.

As Mitsuki grew older, moreover, she realized how her mother, treated like a princess by her self-abasing mother and doted on by her softhearted father, had grown up basking in her parents' love, a love that was all the more intense because the three of them were cut off from society. Precisely because she was a child of sin, she'd been pampered and made even more headstrong.

Nor was that all. After her father moved out, her mother had clung to her as the one remaining tie with him and indulged her more than ever. Her father, meanwhile, full of guilt, could not on either sentimental or ethical grounds be stern with the daughter he had so unhesitatingly spoiled, and took pains to accommodate her wishes without offending his wife. And so, no matter how much trouble she caused by insisting on having her own way, Noriko often succeeded in the end. This pattern of behavior must have become ingrained in her.

Under the circumstances, who wouldn't try to have their own way?

## 50

### GRANDPA'S TEARS

There was one anecdote that wrung Mitsuki's heart.

It happened when Noriko was still in elementary school, living with her father, who had begun to be concerned about her future. All her life she would have to bear the ignominy of being a *shoshi*, an illegitimate child, and be burdened with her mother besides. A good marriage was probably not in the cards for her. But fortunately she was bright: even though she spent all her time playing with the neighborhood kids, her grades were excellent. Her father therefore conceived the plan of one day sending her to a normal school so that she might become a teacher at a girls' higher school. Perhaps her lifelong taste for the finer things in life had not yet evinced itself, or perhaps her father, a man of simple tastes (not just frugal but "a cheapskate," Mitsuki had always been told), either never noticed or purposely closed his eyes to what kind of woman she was turning into. She was hardly suited to be a teacher, but at a time when working women were regarded askance, teaching was the most respectable occupation for a woman, and especially teaching at a girls' higher school. If she taught at such a school, she would be able to support herself and her mother.

He tried to get Noriko into a competitive girls' higher school far beyond the reach of most girls from such a remote section of Osaka. With pride, he wrote on the form the name of the school he dreamed she might one day attend: "Nara Women's Higher Normal School." The only other such school in the country was in Tokyo. Though reluctant, he would have had to write down on the same form the word *shoshi*—a word whose meaning she did not yet know.

Well pleased that her father was pinning his hopes on her, Noriko took extra classes and devoted herself to preparing for the entrance examination. Her grades became even better, and for the first time she enjoyed studying. On the day of the examination she unfortunately caught a cold and developed a fever, but she was satisfied with her score, as she reported to him. And yet when she went to see if she had been accepted, her number was not among those posted. Her father came home from work in high anticipation, but on learning that she had failed, without changing as usual into a kimono he sat erect in a corner of the room with his back turned and quietly began to cry. As Noriko and her mother looked on anxiously, his back began to shake and he sobbed, wiping away his tears on one arm.

That was the one and only time in her life she ever saw him cry, their mother used to say.

He must have guessed that she'd been rejected because he wrote "*shoshi*" on the application. Seeing him cry, she was devastated that she had let him down. He surely knew how she felt and wanted to comfort her, but to do so he would have had to explain the meaning of that offending word. As he wept with his back turned to her, in his heart he must have begged her forgiveness. "O-Miya" must have felt wretched at the sight of them. The thought of the family of three, social outcasts, each embracing a private sadness in that moment, was pitiable indeed.

After that painful mistake, he'd made it his new life's goal to marry her to someone who would take responsibility for both her and her mother, and chose for her a Christian girls' higher school where the sole expectations for the students were marriage and motherhood.

Even though her father had doted on her when she was small and tried his best to fulfill his parental obligations after moving out, all her life Noriko had resented him. And not because he left. That was unavoidable, she could see. She resented him because despite having made it his goal to marry her off, once she came of age he did nothing personally to achieve that goal. He just sat and prayed for someone to come along—someone good enough to take in her aging mother along with her. Only then would he be free from the error of his youth. Free not only financially but psychologically. No doubt he preferred a simple life anyway, but both before and after marrying the waitress he lived frugally, putting aside what he could for the wedding his daughter would surely one day have. And yet he did nothing to make it happen.

After Noriko graduated, and she and her mother moved elsewhere in Osaka, once a month he stopped by to deliver her living expenses.

"My rotten father..." She called him that in large part because he had distanced himself at that crucial time in her life.

But as Mitsuki grew to see these things with the eyes of an adult, she felt she understood how her grandfather must have felt. Had he sought a husband for her among his circle of business acquaintances, the past that he had been at such pains to conceal would have been exposed—an unbearable outcome for someone who was a walking textbook of deportment, without a dissolute bone in his body. But since he had an unusually strong sense of responsibility, perhaps eventually he would have swallowed his pride and gone to some likely acquaintance with hat in hand, asking if he knew some family with a marriageable son.

Perhaps. If she'd been a more normal daughter.

But what a daughter she turned out to be! Noriko was headstrong to begin with, and circumstances conspired to develop in her the habit of constantly testing her limits. She would read people's expressions and in a honeyed tone try to see how much she could get away with.

After her father moved out, leaving her and her mother with nothing but ratty furniture, she was undaunted. Just leaving childhood behind, on the cusp of womanhood, she went after her dreams with greater singleness of purpose than ever before.

Many of her classmates were girls from wealthy families. The sight of their fine clothing used to make her blood boil with jealousy, she said later, but she was never one to take any indignity lying down. She studied the illustrations in *Girls' Friend* and saved her allowance to buy cloth, which she industriously sewed into dresses in the modern style of Jun'ichi Nakahara, the illustrator idolized by millions. She knit herself sweaters, too. Her mother never made her precious girl do any housework, so after she came home from school, her time was her own. When she grew fond of watching foreign films, she even sewed low-necked, long evening gowns like those worn by the beautiful creatures on the silver screen. Alas, she made them from old cotton *yukata*, ripping out the seams, and used leftover material to attach abundant frills to the neckline and hem. Naturally she couldn't go outside in such garb; all she could do was wear it to bed. When night came on, she would lay out her thin mattress next to her mother's on the frayed tatami and drift off to sleep amid the ratty furniture, clad in a homemade ball gown. Lying next to her snoring mother, what dreams did she see?

However resourceful she was, there was no way she could fulfill her dreams on the pittance she received for an allowance. Naturally, she would wheedle her father into giving her things. He dealt as best he could with her interminable, unreasonable demands, consulting his wallet and taking care not to upset his wife. When she wanted a bed soft enough for the Real Princess in the story "The Princess and the Pea," he gave her an iron-frame bed such as a soldier might sleep on with a straw pallet. When she longed for a shiny black piano, he gave her a weedy-sounding organ. Each time she would be disappointed, but quickly rebound and coax him into giving her something else. Distraught at her never-ending demands, he must have been gradually beaten down, the task of finding someone for her ever more daunting. What chance was there of finding a prospective groom to satisfy her? And if he did manage to marry her off, in the end she would either be sent packing or run off of her own accord — perhaps with that fear in mind, Mitsuki speculated, he never made much effort.

And in fact, her mother did run away from her first husband.

Once when she was sorting through her aged mother's correspondence, Mitsuki came upon an envelope of old, handmade *washi* paper on which the writing, done with a fountain pen in blue ink, stood out with strange vividness. The hand was familiar. She turned it over and saw her grandfather's name. He had moved to Kyoto at some point, and the letter had been mailed from there.

"A letter from Grandpa?" she asked.

"Yes. It burned me up, and I kept it to remember. Go ahead and read it if you like."

Mitsuki's mother and father had managed to buy the land in Chitose Funabashi but couldn't come up with the cost of building the new house, so her mother had asked Grandpa for a loan.

He had written back in his neat hand, using old-fashioned, pre-war orthography: "Do you not know the meaning of the expression 'do without'? Since your self-centered actions have caused everyone such suffering and trouble, you have no business trying to build a house. Just do without for once." The letter continued in that tone, half admonishing, half querulous.

As she scanned the blue ink, Mitsuki thought of the time in her mother's life when the letter had been written. Six years after "Yokohama" had found her a dream marriage partner and Grandpa had provided her with a proper dowry, she had run off with another man, Mitsuki's father, leaving a small daughter behind. Grandpa had disowned her, Mitsuki knew. How her mother reinstated herself in his good graces she didn't know, but apparently she'd lost no time coming to him begging for a loan. Mitsuki couldn't help sympathizing with her grandfather. He must have been horribly upset. No sooner did he suppress his anger and restore their relationship than she turned right around and made this brazen request. There was no telling what further demands she might make.

After receiving the letter, her mother had resorted to cutting up the property and selling nearly half of it to raise the money. "That used to be *our* land." Mitsuki could well remember her saying this with some resentment as she pointed to new houses squeezed onto patches of land on either side of the property in Chitose Funabashi.

After their grandmother died, Natsuki and Mitsuki had gone to visit Grandpa in Kyoto, where he lived in a tasteful home in traditional style with a pine tree gracefully spreading its branches at the front gate.

"Now what will you two young ladies be doing today?" he'd asked them, sitting formally with his legs folded under him, using honorific forms even to his small granddaughters. In his elegance of speech he'd been very much like Kan'ichi, Mitsuki thought now.

She and Natsuki had been his only grandchildren. He may have wanted to treat them with affection, but he seemed constantly on guard, she remembered, not simply in deference to his childless wife but perhaps because he projected his fear of their mother's never-ending demands onto them.

After their mother became utterly dependent on her, Mitsuki learned to brace herself for some new demand whenever she heard her name coaxingly called: "Miiitsukiii!" But however she tried to maintain her guard, her mother would keep a sharp lookout, watching for a chance. Was it her mother's own fault that she was the way she was?

It was the same old conundrum. Her mother could not be blamed for the disposition she was born with—and what if her unusual upbringing had contributed to making her who she was? To what extent was she responsible for the way she turned out? Could any person's foibles be laid at their doorstep alone? There was no answer. Her mother was the way she was. That much remained an incontrovertible fact.

## 51

## SLIDE SHOW

How long had she been sitting in the hotel lounge?

She was so close to the fireplace that the dregs of her red wine at the bottom of the cloudy wineglass had clotted into something approaching jam. Would Kaoru say not "jam" but *confiture*, puckering her lips on that final vowel the way French people did? She looked around, but the white head was now gone. The only ones left were a young woman and a middle-aged man who was delivering an enthusiastic harangue, as men in the presence of a young woman so often did. Tetsuo at least had brains. Surely he wouldn't make such a fool of himself. Mitsuki stared openly at the pair, and for a bitter moment her thoughts flew to the skies of Vietnam.

High time to retire to her room. Warmed by the fire, the air felt heavy and thick, pressing on her with leaden weight. The young woman's high-pitched, ingratiating laughter bounced around the lounge, grating on her ears. Coping with her mother had drained her of vitality, Tetsuo's betrayal had been a hard blow, and now here she was, turning into a disapproving, clucking hen.

She went back to her room, still lost in her thoughts. When she inserted the card key into the wall slot, the lights came on, and at precisely the same moment, the telephone rang. It had been after midnight when she left the lounge.

"I called twice before!" Natsuki's familiar voice drew her back to reality. "The second time, they offered to look for you in the lounge, but I said not to bother. Why haven't you called? It's been three nights already."

"Hotel phones cost so much. I figured I'd wait for you to call." This was only half true. She felt guilty for coming here alone, but with Tetsuo on her mind she hadn't been in the mood to call her sister.

Then of all things Natsuki said, "You forgot about me, but I bet you've been talking to Tetsuo."

"No, just sending emails." When would she be able to tell Natsuki the truth?

"Is he managing all right? This is the first sabbatical he's taken by himself, isn't it?"

"Trust me," she said coolly, "he'll be fine."

Natsuki changed the subject. "How about you? How are you doing?"

"I like this hotel a lot."

"Getting some rest?"

She sighed. "I don't know. So many memories come back, I feel worse than ever." The sound of her sister's voice triggered a conditioned reflex, bringing back that day and the figure of their dying mother, her withered fingers floating in empty space. "I can't get Mother out of my mind."

Natsuki seemed to feel equally besieged by memories. Her response was quick. "I know. I feel worse now too. Are we *ever* going to be free?" Then, "You haven't checked your email, have you."

"No." She hadn't touched her laptop since going through Tetsuo's email correspondence with the woman.

"Go take a look."

"You mean right now?"

Natsuki said she would wait, so Mitsuki switched on her computer, went to her email, and found a message with the heading "Katsura Family Memories." She clicked on it and to her surprise found links to a number of Web albums. Natsuki had always been fond of making family albums. When they emptied the house in Chitose Funabashi, she'd taken home five cardboard boxes packed with photographs. She said she was going to sift through them; it had never occurred to Mitsuki that she might post any online. The albums bore titles like "Before Father and Mother Were Married" and "When the Sisters Were Little."

"I'm impressed that you're so technically savvy."

Mitsuki sometimes received such links from acquaintances, but she would never have expected this from Natsuki, who, like their mother and herself, was generally hopeless around the new technology.

"Jun taught me. I only picked out the good ones. She says everybody makes albums like this nowadays. The hardest part was peeling photos out of the original albums without ruining them."

Mitsuki hesitantly clicked on the slide show for the album "Before Father and Mother Were Married." Every few seconds, another sepia-toned old photograph appeared.

"Jun scolds me—says I'll ruin my health—but I work on them every night till all hours. I'm obsessed."

Natsuki too was facing up to the past, Mitsuki realized, trying in her own way to come to terms with her emotions.

The slide show began with their father, showing him as a plump, naked baby; as a five-year-old dressed up in kimono with a formal *haori* jacket and pleated *hakama* trousers, the chill of the heavy silk almost palpable; and as a youth, standing with his father in student cap and uniform to commemorate his entrance into middle school. There was a photo taken at the grand funeral his father had been given, followed by the photo they'd used at their father's memorial service, taken in his university days. Their mother had grown up in a household where photography was a luxury that the family could ill afford, so the earliest shots of her Natsuki could find were from around the time she entered girls' higher school. In every frame, she looked strikingly happy.

"She always used to complain about her childhood, but you know what? She got more than I ever did." The resentful words slipped out before Mitsuki knew it.

"Well now, wait a minute," Natsuki said. "She got more than I did too. All she ever did was shove her dreams on me. And you know how Grandma doted on you. She was such a sweetheart, nothing like Mother."

"A shame there aren't more photos of her."

When their grandmother ran off with their grandfather, she'd left all her photographs behind. The only ones they had of her were taken after Mitsuki was born, when she was already an old lady. With her kimono collar loose at the throat and her sparse white hair pulled into a bun, not even a trace of her former beauty remained. How could such a dried-up old husk have thought she was O-Miya?

As a child, Mitsuki had known nothing of her grandmother's life story. She had gone to "O-Miya" with all her loneliness—the loneliness of a little girl not getting enough attention from her mother or her father—and always received unstinting love. "Good girl. Grandma's good little girl." No matter what, she'd always been her grandmother's pet.

Could her grandmother ever have imagined that her precious granddaughter would spend her life unloved? That she would put up with a loveless marriage for nearly thirty years, never facing up to the sad truth? As she contemplated the photograph, Mitsuki felt that she had somehow betrayed her grandmother's unconditional love. At least her grandmother had died not knowing the full extent of her mother's—Noriko's—capacity for folly. People left this world, blissfully unaware of how their bovarism seeped into the lives of others.

"While I was making the albums," Natsuki said, "I wondered—what kind of person was Mother, really?"

"Good question."

"Remember the photo of her hanging laundry outdoors? She's in a casual summer dress, no stockings, wooden geta on her feet. I put that one in."

Mitsuki sighed. "I remember. I always liked that one."

The photograph showed their mother outside the house in Chitose Funabashi, wearing an apron and hanging something on the line to dry, like any other mother. Their father had snapped the picture from the side, so she didn't have the artificial smile she usually wore for the camera. She looked completely natural. The yard was flooded with light.

"All my impressions of her are from after she got old," Natsuki went on. "I can barely remember what she was like when we were little."

"Me neither."

"That picture makes me think she was more normal back then."

"I'm sure she was."

"She had to be, or you and I would have turned out a lot *more* twisted."

As Mitsuki watched, photograph after photograph came on the screen showing their mother as a young woman. Each one evoked nostalgia but seemed sadly remote from the way she'd been in old age. Mitsuki tried but failed to recall the attachment she must have felt for her mother in childhood, back when her heart was still soft and squishy with no hard corners.

"Make sure you see them all, okay?" her sister said and hung up after promising to make more albums.

For a while longer Mitsuki watched the slide show with mixed emotions. Then she exited and went back to her email. A new message from Tetsuo caught her eye. She gulped. It had just come in the last few minutes. He'd called home a number of times, he wrote, and had also been trying her cell phone with no luck.

"Did something happen to your mother?"

*She died.*

Mitsuki didn't want to write those words, but neither could she bring herself to lie and say that her mother was fine. She wrote only that she herself was so exhausted that she'd come to a hotel in Hakone to relax for a week or so.

He responded immediately—he must be in an Internet café— expressing relief and asking again about her mother. "So she's getting along okay?"

Mitsuki pondered before writing, "She's completely beyond anyone's reach now." It took a few seconds for the reply to pop up. While waiting she stared at the screen in confusion, feeling Tetsuo's presence very near.

"Sorry to hear that. Are you at the same hotel where you and she went before?"

"Yes, on Lake Ashinoko."

"That's the one with the O-Miya connection?"

"Yes. Swarming with ghosts."

"Anyway don't get worn out—you never were very strong. Take good care of yourself, okay?"

That was all. The solicitousness of his last words was like a box of Valentine chocolates, tied with a pretty bow. And all the time he had to be asking himself how to broach the matter of divorce. She couldn't help shaking her head as she closed the laptop.

## (52)

## EVERYONE IS SUSPECT

The next day was cloudy when she woke up, and soon a light rain began to fall. The monotonous gray of the sky showed no sign of brightening. Being cooped up all day by rain suited her mood, she thought, as she looked at the sky from her window. She went to the Japanese restaurant for breakfast and lunch, and twice in one day ran into the old couple who were like a pair of husband-and-wife rice bowls. The others had come by car, so they could leave the hotel to eat out. She decided just to order dinner from room service.

The rainy day spent shut in was about to end in unremitting gloom when around eight in the evening she gave in to the urge to go down to the lounge. She changed her clothes, put on some makeup, and took the elevator. While descending the stairs to the lounge she glanced around the room, and her eye landed on a figure in a dark suit. Her gloom lifted. As she hesitated, he noticed her and motioned for her to come join him.

Mitsuki sat down with unconcealed pleasure. "I didn't see you yesterday."

He swept his hair back, a habit he had. His face seemed pale and gaunt. "I stayed in my room all day. Didn't feel like going out. There was an article I needed to read anyway."

Keeping to himself all day had perhaps drawn him even further into a private realm; he had an absent air, as though loath to return to this world. A grim statistic crossed her mind: after the death of a spouse, life expectancy remains the same for widows, but for men it is shortened; many a widower dies quickly, as if impatient to follow his wife to the grave. She dropped her eyes to the whiskey and water in his hand—the same drink as the day before yesterday. Was he someone who, once he'd made a choice, stuck with it? Was that why he always dressed the same way?

"I can't help noticing you always wear a dark suit," she said, her tone slightly teasing.

"Oh, well." He swept his hair back again. "My wife used to say an ordinary man like me should dress the part. Wouldn't let me wear anything else. I'm afraid I don't even own any what you might call leisure clothes."

Mitsuki smiled. How different from Tetsuo, who was so particular about his wardrobe! Remembering the intensity in his eyes when he picked out what to wear, she felt a bit jealous of Wakako for having had a husband who willingly dressed as she wanted him to. She felt like making an irreverent observation—*This way you can wear mourning the rest of your life!*—but that would be in poor taste. She asked a question instead.

"Did your wife like to dress up?" Was she pretty, she really wanted to ask.

"Yes. Yes, she did."

"How would she dress?"

"That I couldn't tell you." At a loss, he tilted his head, trying to remember. "She always looked the same to me. Used to scold me for not noticing when she had on something new." Again that abashed smile.

To avoid talking about herself, Mitsuki kept asking questions and learned to her surprise that Wakako had studied voice at a conservatory. That Mr. Matsubara was a fairly serious classical music fan. That his favorite lunch was a bowl of noodles. That he was the father of two grown sons.

"My, look at the lovebirds!" sang out a voice.

Kaoru joined them. Only then did Mitsuki realize how much she had been looking forward to an evening alone with Mr. Matsubara. Kaoru seated herself by them with nonchalance, and Takeru joined them too, a little more reticently.

"How are you this evening?" said Kaoru. She leaned forward as Mr. Matsubara was responding, "Just fine, thank you."

"We're fine too," she said, looking back and forth at them. "Except that it's the most bizarre thing. All of us long-term guests are suspect. We could all be on a list of potential candidates for suicide!" She said this with inappropriate, unconcealed glee.

She went on to confide what she had found out about the others, beginning with the close-knit mother and daughter. As she and Takeru stood around chatting with them before lunch, it had emerged that they had never been to the nearby Fujiya Hotel. And so despite the rain they had all gone there for lunch, Takeru driving.

Mitsuki had been to the Fujiya Hotel once. It was built in 1878, just ten years after the Meiji Restoration—Japan's first Western-style hotel, well known for its eclectic architectural style with an imposing tiled roof like that of a Buddhist temple. Notables from around the world had stayed there, including Prince Albert of York, Charlie Chaplin, and Prime Minister Jawaharlal Nehru. She and Natsuki used to take their semi-invalid father on little outings, feeling sorry for him since their mother ignored him, and one time they'd stayed overnight at the Fujiya Hotel. They'd dined at The Fujiya, a French restaurant with a high, traditional coffered ceiling that greatly appealed to foreign guests.

Kaoru had had lunch at The Fujiya with the others, and over dessert, while offering congratulations on the upcoming nuptials, she'd brought up the psychic's prediction, adding with a laugh, "Of course this wouldn't apply in your case." But before her eyes, the mother's face had turned the color of ash.

"I was horrified," she said. "I thought I was going to need my Nitorol spray. It was such a shock."

Takeru spoke up. "For all we know, she may have just thought the subject was unlucky, with a wedding coming up and all. But there's definitely something strange going on." In the car on the way back, the mother's responses to his aunt had been short and vague, he said, as if her mind was elsewhere.

"What about the daughter?" Mitsuki asked.

"She's kind of ditzy," he said. "Spacey. The mother did all the talking about the wedding, too."

There was nothing they could put their finger on, but something about the two seemed not quite right. This was Kaoru and Takeru's conclusion.

Kaoru then moved on to the elderly couple.

After returning from the Fujiya Hotel, she'd rested in her room and then gone down alone to the lounge for tea. As she was looking for a table by the window, the elderly couple walked in. Deciding she might as well take advantage of the opportunity to find out their story as well, she'd waved and invited them to join her.

"Obviously I was the last person they wanted to chat with," she said, "but as I'm sure you can imagine—I don't take no for an answer!"

While the husband remained silent, the wife had gradually opened up under Kaoru's questioning and soon was pouring out their story. She even dabbed at her eyes with a handkerchief. Her husband had cosigned a loan and, as happens all too often, the other party defaulted. Now even if they gave every penny they had, it wouldn't be enough to pay off the debt. As the wife talked, the husband began to fill in details, and what had started out as a brief interlude stretched into a marathon two-and-a-half-hour tea break.

"We had pot after pot of tea."

The husband, the eldest son in a large family, had worked in a sheet-metal plant for many years. After retiring, the two of them were caretakers for a condominium building for another ten years, and just two years ago they'd moved into a house they finally built for themselves. Then a few months ago his youngest brother, who ran a business in Nagoya, suffered a severe stroke, was hospitalized, and went bankrupt. After losing his job over a dozen years ago, this brother had gone into business for himself but had no luck at anything he tried; then his wife left him, taking the children, and remarried. The years of stress had taken their toll. And the husband had been cosigner for his brother's snowballing debts.

The cosigner shares equal responsibility with the original debtor to repay the amount owed in full. If the husband declared bankruptcy, they would lose their new house and savings, but he would be free of his obligation. Still, after a lifetime of hard work, bankruptcy was a bitter pill to swallow. They were parents of a married son and an older single daughter. To escape the stream of debt collectors coming to their door, they had put their house up for sale and moved into the daughter's apartment to hide out. She was a hard worker but had a weak constitution, so they'd always planned to have her come look after them once they grew old and infirm, and in return they were going to leave her the house. (Their son had readily agreed to this, partly because he shared their concern over her future and also because after she died the house, if it was still there, would go to him or his children.) Now their plans had gone awry. They hadn't told their son anything. They were afraid to, since they knew he would insist on helping out, but he had his own family to provide for, and they didn't want him taking on debt on their behalf. But he assumed everyone would be gathering at their place for New Year's as usual, so it was all going to come out in the open very soon.

Kaoru looked at her listeners and concluded, "After the way that other woman reacted at lunch, I couldn't very well bring up the predictions of a Harley-Davidson psychic, now could I?"

Mitsuki shook her head.

"And what do you think happened?" Kaoru continued. "The husband had a smile on his face, but he said that if he died, there'd be enough insurance money to cover the whole debt. His wife's family is long-lived, he said, so he took out a hefty policy."

An alarming remark to say the least.

To keep their son from suspecting anything was wrong, they'd had a landline installed in their daughter's house with their old telephone number, but then they started getting bombarded with threatening calls from debt collectors—yakuza hired by loan sharks. That was why they'd come here, using money set aside in the wife's name for emergencies. They needed to get away and sort through their options in peace and quiet.

The words "small business failure" rose in Mitsuki's mind— words made so familiar by Japan's troubled economy that they had lost all impact until now. She had not expected the grim reality behind them to intrude on this fairyland hotel.

Mr. Matsubara, who had been listening silently, now spoke up. "It doesn't make sense to me."

Everyone looked at him.

"If he's the eldest in a big family, then there are plenty of other siblings. Even if they have no legal responsibility, surely they could share some of the burden."

"Very true," said Kaoru. "Apparently he's so used to looking after the others that it's become second nature for him to shoulder all the burden himself."

Mr. Matsubara frowned. "That's a shame."

Mitsuki reflected. What about the emotional calm she had observed in both the old husband and his wife? Was that a silent way of providing solace to each other? Human unhappiness was often banal, its banality an affront to the sufferers and to the nature of their suffering, something that could be reduced to a mere statistic. Yet knowing this didn't lessen the misery one whit. The banality of the unassuming couple's predicament didn't make it any the less pitiable.

For a while silence fell on the foursome, each of them absorbed in private thoughts.

Then Kaoru announced playfully, "What it comes down to, my dears, is this—there isn't one of us who's in our right mind!"

"What about me?" asked Mitsuki in some surprise.

"What about you? My dear, just last evening you sat here for hours, staring into the fire with a positively lethal look on your face!"

$$\left(53\right)$$

## PAPA AIME MAMAN

"No one making a face like that could possibly be in her right mind!" Once again Kaoru tittered gracefully. "I had taken you off the list, but I'm afraid you're back on it now."

Mitsuki forced a smile, but no words came.

Last night she had indeed sat here forgetful of time, her eyes on the fire while her thoughts drifted darkly from Tetsuo to the wasteland of her life to back before she was born. The look on her face must have been grim; small wonder if anyone took her for a potential suicide. She'd never thought of herself as a candidate, but coming here had brought her to the realization that she had no strong incentive to keep on going.

Indeed, why must she go on?

Even after she had parted from the others, returned to her room, and was preparing for bed, the question dogged her. Suddenly Mr. Matsubara's eager remark the other night came back to her: "Charity is very good." She had no desire for Tetsuo to end up with her inheritance, she realized — and this discovery led to the further discovery that she was unafraid of death. Yet there was nothing the slightest *dramatique*, as Kaoru might say, about any of it.

The next three days passed uneventfully.

If it didn't rain she went for walks or read *Madame Bovary*, dictionary close at hand. Sometimes she considered how a certain sentence might be rendered in Japanese. Other times she would close the book, lie back in bed, and ponder various things till her head got hot.

At night she went down to the lounge. Kaoru was always there, a different scarf draped elegantly around her neck each time, usually knitting while she listened to her iPod. Her name was written with a Chinese character meaning "fragrance," Mitsuki learned, and Takeru's with one meaning "military strength." It didn't seem to suit a young man with wavy brown hair and a delicately chiseled face like his. He never ordered anything to drink but mineral water. She sometimes looked around for Mr. Matsubara, but either he went out to eat or he used room service, for she rarely saw him. After that one time they were never alone together in the lounge again. The lack of opportunity for a tête-à-tête suggested only that he preferred to keep to himself, and vaguely disappointing as this was, she was glad in a way; she would have expected no less of him.

She did have a chance to talk directly with the elderly couple.

The day after hearing their story from Kaoru, she woke up too early for breakfast, so she was out taking a turn in the garden when she ran into them. The three of them walked together for a while before heading for the Japanese restaurant. During the meal, Mitsuki asked after their son and his wife, whom she had seen with them before. She made no reference to what Kaoru had said about their impending financial disaster. The husband himself brought up the topic.

"Seeing that you're friends with that lady," he said, "you may have heard something about our troubles."

Mitsuki nodded sympathetically. She didn't know what to say.

"Honestly," he went on, "to have to face such a calamity at my age..."

"You worked hard your whole life," his wife said consolingly.

"As did you. I feel bad to put you through this." He stroked his bald head.

He was from rural Niigata, he said, and had gone to work in Tokyo after graduating from middle school, first as a newspaper carrier for a relative who was a former prisoner of war in Siberia and kept a little newsdealer's shop with his wife. The work was hard. Roads were icy on winter mornings and steamy on summer evenings; he had to work even in heavy rain and wind; some customers tried to welsh on their bill. Fortunately his relatives treated the carriers well. Mitsuki asked where he lived in Tokyo, and he said Machida, a town way out on the Odakyu line where his wife's family used to run a laundry.

"I grew up in Chitose Funabashi," said Mitsuki, "on the same Odakyu line."

"Fancy that!" the wife exclaimed. "Were you born yet when the Romance Car used to be called the Music Box Car?"

Her question was so unexpected that, for the first time in a long while, Mitsuki laughed out loud. "Oh, ages before that!"

The couple laughed along with her.

"Work was tough," the husband said, "but you know, hearing the sound of the Music Box Car while I delivered papers helped. Gave me something to dream about."

Mitsuki nodded.

They'd talked about taking the Romance Car to Hakone on their honeymoon but couldn't afford it, and then for years they'd been short of money. When they finally saved up enough to travel, they took occasional trips to places farther away as a break from their routine. This time, about to lose everything, they had decided to come here to fulfill the dream of their youth.

"The way the Romance Car affected me—it made me feel like my job delivering papers was pretty darned important. That's how it was back then."

Indeed, back then life without newspapers would have been unthinkable.

The clang of the mailbox lid closing after you took out the paper was an essential part of the morning cacophony, along with the chink of milk bottles, the cry of the tofu seller and the sound of his horn, and the whoops of children scampering off to school.

On Sunday morning Mitsuki's father would make coffee in the aluminum percolator and read the newspaper end to end. As children, she and her sister had looked forward to the daily four-panel comic strip.

Their mother would glance through the paper, muttering when she came to the serial novel, "Utter trash." Sometimes she offered faint praise: "Not too bad, for a change." The illustrations came in for comment as well: "Awful...no imagination...disgusting." She was a harsh critic, having grown up in the golden age of girls' magazines with illustrations by Jun'ichi Nakahara and others that had a refinement forever defining for her what an illustration should be. Those artists, heirs to the aesthetic sense and techniques of the still-vibrant ukiyo-e tradition, had created sophisticated illustrations inspired by Western realism.

Their father shared his wife's low opinion of contemporary serial novels and, like many members of the intelligentsia, seldom deigned to read them. He used to marvel that the works of the great Natsume Soseki were first published serially in newspapers. "Just think! Newspapers offering their readers meaty reading like that." He was fond of pointing out that the opening pages of *Light and Dark*, Soseki's final, unfinished novel, contained ruminations on the theories of Henri Poincaré, an eminent French mathematician and contemporary of Soseki's. "Back then a name like that could appear in a serial novel without any explanation, and no one thought anything of it." Mitsuki and Natsuki, neither knowing nor caring who Poincaré was, would listen in meek silence. Only daddies needed to know such things.

If the content of serial novels was no longer as impressive as it had been, neither was the style, which had often been of a rare sophistication. After their grandmother died, their mother said one day, "You know, the idea that she could have read that novel is unbelievable to me." *The Golden Demon* was full of intricate Chinese characters and long sentences written in an ornate, archaic style. Even with the characters' phonetic readings indicated by glosses, it would have been hard going.

Over the course of a century, as newspapers increasingly became part of every household's morning ritual, subscribers were exposed not only to novels patterned after Western novels singing of *amour* and *amants* but to articles full of new words translated from the West, among them words for "democracy," "individual," and "liberty." Gradually, newspapers shaped a new language and a new breed of Japanese people.

When he was a newspaper carrier, said the husband, he used to live with his employer and attend classes at high school while he worked, but the double burden of school and work had been too much. He'd decided to see instead that his younger brothers got through school and went to work in the sheet-metal plant, putting in longer hours but getting a bigger paycheck. From then on he'd worked like a dog, and now just as he was set to enjoy his retirement, his youngest brother, always a troublemaker, had dumped this unholy mess in his lap.

"It's beyond me." The old husband repeated this, his expression calmer than that of his wife. Could he be planning to do something as radical as kill himself to pay off the debt with his insurance money? Mitsuki searched the placid face to see what might lie behind it. He was so solicitous of his wife, undoubtedly if it came to that he would choose some way to die that wouldn't appear to be suicide—go out fishing alone, say, and capsize? They were on the edge of a lake, so that scenario came naturally to mind.

Later that night she again saw the mother and daughter in the hot spring but had no chance to speak to them. It occurred to her that they might be deliberately avoiding her, knowing she was friends with Kaoru. But the mother beamed at the daughter, and the daughter responded with a smile of angelic sweetness. As far as she could tell they were a loving, close-knit pair, nothing more.

Before she went to bed, she watched the slide show again. Among the photographs was one of the original house in Chitose Funabashi. Their young mother had had a sunny disposition then. In her second marriage, which gave her more freedom because it was unconventional, she'd tried to re-create, even if on a smaller scale, the life at "Yokohama" that had meant so much to her. Behind the house, on a plot of land half the size it once was, she'd made a round flower bed edged in bricks and planted roses, dahlias, tulips, and other Western flowers. They'd also had a grassy lawn and a collie, Della. For the house she'd ordered beds, still items of luxury at the time, and manufactured by a Japanese company whose name, France Bed, gave them extra allure. She also bought a shiny black upright Yamaha piano—a grand piano was beyond their means—and in time began taking Natsuki to "Yokohama" for her piano lessons.

Perhaps to make up for bitter memories of her childhood, she not only dressed smartly herself but saw to it that the two of them always had nice things to wear. She sewed summer clothes that were simple but cute, humming as she worked the sewing machine pedal. For their winter clothes, she had a knack of finding fine-quality items at department store sales; fancier clothes with appliqué, beads, or lace she had a neighborhood seamstress sew by hand. She also gave Mitsuki and Natsuki new hats and shoes. "You two never ask for any clothes," she used to say approvingly. "What good girls you are!" But she kept them provided with such nice things—they were almost always dressed better than their classmates—that they never felt any need to ask for more.

Back then, able for the first time in her life to run things the way she wanted, their mother had glowed with satisfaction. She'd been on good terms with their father too. He and the dog Della were forever competing for possession of the sofa, so one Sunday she made an inadvertent mistake. As he lay on the sofa reading the newspaper, she set the dog's food dish on the floor by him, cooing, "Here's your dinner, Della sweetie."

He looked up from the newspaper and said, "Hey, it's me!"

The sisters, watching, had collapsed in laughter. Their mother also had laughed cheerfully and picked the dish up from the floor. "I *beg* your pardon!"

A chanson popular around then contained the chorus "*Papa aime Maman, Maman aime Papa,*" sung by a little girl (supposedly the daughter). From then on, Mitsuki sang it altering one word: "Papa loves Mama, Mama loves Della." Her father laughed—everyone laughed. If she'd only known what lay ahead for her family, she never would have sung those words.

As photo after photo came up on her laptop screen, the Hakone night and the mountains vanished, replaced by memories of a time when she'd been happy without knowing it, memories that were as far off as if seen through the wrong end of a telescope, yet vivid all the same.

They left her more desolate than before.

357

## POETRY CARDS

Watching the slide show, Mitsuki realized something: there wasn't one photograph taken on New Year's Day in her childhood.

The air always felt somehow different on that day—the most auspicious day of the year in Japan. Whether alone or surrounded by family, everyone on the archipelago always felt a little formal as they faced the New Year. That first morning, the atmosphere was charged with expectation.

As a little girl, Mitsuki had loved the way the winter morning's crystal cold enhanced that air of expectancy. And yet she had felt vaguely sad. She was proud of the way her family adopted a Western lifestyle ahead of everyone else, but on New Year's Day she wished they could be more like a regular Japanese family. She wanted them to join in celebrating the day. Instead it felt as if they were putting up a quiet rebellion.

How different from Christmas!

When December 25 drew near, tiny lights used to twinkle on a modest Christmas tree in their house, and the entire family would troop to Ginza, she and Natsuki dressed in their best. On Christmas Eve they sang "Silent Night" to Natsuki's accompaniment, and on Christmas Day the white damask tablecloth and napkins reserved for company would cover the Formica table (stylish at the time). The relative by marriage who called their father "Big Brother" would show up with his wife, and everyone would feast on Western food together, their father all smiles.

But on January 1, only two things set the morning apart: the nice smell of the *ozoni* soup her mother made, and festive chopsticks at each place, in red-and-white envelopes decorated with fancy twisted cords. Her father, as head of the family, formally wrote their names on the envelopes with a calligraphy brush: "Noriko," "Natsuki," "Mitsuki." That was all. No *kadomatsu* pine arrangement outdoors, no pile of round *kagamimochi* rice cakes indoors. No colorful array of foods in tiered lacquer boxes. In childhood she never saw the antique New Year's set with mother-of-pearl inlay, which must have been packed away somewhere. The family neither paid nor received any holiday visits. The red-and-white chopstick envelopes that were the one tangible symbol of New Year's in their house had been precious to her.

New Year's Day had always been an exceptional day in the Katsura household, in a peculiar way. What made it so was their father's mood. Three hundred sixty-four days of the year, life revolved around their sunny mother, but that one day they were ruled by his irascibility. Morning was the worst. He glowered over his *ozoni* soup as if he wanted to send Japan's ancient holiday to the devil. Rice cakes displeased him, as did all traditional New Year's dishes, including seven-spring-herbs rice gruel—a lovely name, Mitsuki used to think, although she'd never had any. You were supposed to eat it on the seventh day of the New Year, she knew, but she kept quiet lest she stir up her father's wrath.

His bad temper didn't last, though. Gradually, as the sun rose in the sky and the festiveness of the day began to wear off, his mood would lighten. Eventually day turned to evening, and they sat down to dinner. After dinner the frown finally left his face as Mitsuki and her sister brought out a traditional card game for the family to play:

the Ogura Hyakunin Isshu, a set of cards inscribed with classical waka poems, one from each of a hundred poets. That was the one New Year's tradition that their father wholeheartedly endorsed.

Before playing, they spread cushions in a circle on the wooden floor of the living-dining room and laid out the cards face up in the middle. For each round, they chose one person to read the poems aloud. As that person began reading, the others competed to be first to grab the card displaying the poem's second half.

Mostly their father was the reader. While the rest of them were fond of prose, he liked poetry, whether in Japanese or English or even Chinese. His readings of the ancient Hyakunin Isshu poems were of unmatched beauty.

> *Aki no ta no kariho no io no toma o arami*
> *Waga koromode wa tsuyu ni nuretsutsu*
> In the autumn fields, harvest huts are rough-thatched,
> And the sleeves of my robe are wet with dew.

Her mother read with the lilting cadence of a prewar schoolgirl.

> *Haru sugite natsu kini kerashi shirotae no*
> *Koromo hosu cho ama no Kaguyama*
> Spring has passed and summer comes, it seems:
> Pure white robes hang out to air on heavenly Mount Kagu.

The rules of pronunciation were different in these old poems. What looked like *tefu*, for example, was pronounced *cho*. Just knowing this made Mitsuki feel a little more grown-up.

*The Golden Demon* has a strong association with the New Year's poetry card game, which figures prominently in the opening scene. Despite this, Mitsuki couldn't remember her grandmother ever having shown any interest as they played. Instead she would put a smock over her kimono and go do the dishes, or bring everyone tea and tangerines, or sit curled on one end of the sofa, dozing. When Mitsuki grew old enough to read the novel, she tried to imagine what might have gone through her grandmother's mind as she watched the rest of them at play.

The scene takes place on the evening of January 3 in a certain year of Meiji. The large room is hot and steamy: over thirty young men and women have formed two circles and are enthralled in the poetry game. The women are dressed in New Year's finery, but some have face powder coming off, hair disheveled, and kimono in disarray. Some of the men have torn their shirtsleeves and cast aside their *haori* jackets. One young woman—O-Miya—hangs back in graceful reticence, her clear eyes wide, taking it all in. Then along comes a mustachioed gentleman wearing a gold ring with a huge diamond the like of which they have never seen. One person notices it, and a wave of admiring comments sweeps around the room.

> "A diamond!"
> "It's a diamond all right."
> "A diamond??"
> "Aha, a diamond!"
> "Gosh, a diamond."
> "That's a diamond?"
> "Look at it. A diamond."
> "My goodness, a diamond??"
> "A fine diamond."
> "A diamond sparkles something fierce, doesn't it?"

The word "diamond" is repeated so many times that the scene lingers long in the reader's memory.

When her grandmother was in her eighties, had her memory of that scene faded into oblivion, like smoke? Or had she simply grown so deaf that she felt obliged to sit on the sidelines?

Once when Mitsuki was little and tried to take her turn as reader, everyone burst out laughing, wounding her small pride. She had retreated to the sofa where her grandmother sat thinking her unknowable thoughts, or perhaps thinking nothing at all, to receive comfort at her knees.

By the time her grandmother died, Mitsuki had learned to read the poems with the same cadence as her mother. The sisters had their favorites and would surreptitiously lay those cards near where they sat. When they each realized what the other had done, they would trade taunts: "Cheater!" "You cheated first!" If they both liked the same poem, they would race to grab it. They liked the ones that even children could understand.

> *Hito wa iza kokoro mo shirazu furusato wa*
> *Hana zo mukashi no ka ni nioikeru*
> The human heart is beyond knowing, but in my birthplace
> The blossoms smell the same as in years past.

Each card bore a classical portrait of the poet in color. Those of ladies in twelve-layer robes were pretty, and so without really trying the sisters learned which poems were written by female poets. They found it strange, and a bit disappointing, that the famous beauty Ono no Komachi had exactly the same face as all the others. "Ise no Osuke" they considered a funny name for a woman, but her poem, which began "Eightfold cherry blossoms in the ancient capital of Nara," had an appealing feminine grace; the poem itself seemed to glow with beauty.

Their house had no past—or rather, no history. In a way it symbolized Japan, which after losing the war set about trying to expunge its past. Their grandmother could only live on tatami mats, but after she died and before the house was rebuilt, all trace of that old lifestyle vanished—the full-length wooden mirror, carved and lacquered; the round porcelain hibachi; the *kotatsu* heater table;

the floor cushions; and even the futon. The sole remaining pieces were their mother's pair of paulownia chests. Instead, the house filled up with small, cheap, Western-style furniture, not to mention the "three sacred treasures" of the postwar era — a refrigerator, washing machine, and television set. Yet even after the house had been wiped clean of history, and even for a while after Natsuki and Mitsuki grew up, every New Year's evening the same words that had been uttered a thousand years before would resonate quietly in their living room, connecting them to the Japan of long ago.

Another ancient poet wrote, "the nation shattered, mountains and rivers remain," but for the Katsura family it was "the nation shattered, poetry remains." Or even "words remain."

The reason for their father's irascibility on New Year's Day was largely ideological: at a time when the word "postwar" was still raw, the Shinto aura hovering over various New Year's customs revived memories of the horrific war.

But as Mitsuki grew older, she came to see that his visceral dislike of New Year's festivities was rooted also in his personal experiences. While her mother's store of rich and finely detailed memories was a bottomless spring, her father remembered little and had little wish to speak of what he did remember. Therefore he told the same stories over and over.

One story from his youth was surprisingly colorful — an account of the procession of geisha who used to come by to pay New Year's greetings, their hair done up in the *takashimada* style and their faces painted white, lifting the hems of their black kimono slightly as they walked. Yakuza bosses came too, he said. The Katsura medical clinic, located on an old highway, had flourished from the Edo period on. His father, cosigner for various loans, was also a member of the Tokyo municipal assembly. Doubtless it wasn't only geisha and yakuza who came to pay their respects on the first of the year; men dressed up in formal kimono must have streamed into the house as well. But when his father died they all scattered, leaving only debt collectors to swarm like flies. The family possessions were sold, the clinic changed hands, and his stepmother and he moved into a small property that they had formerly rented out. How very dismal their first New Year's there must have been!

Had anyone been kind or crazy enough to call on the bereft pair?

As Mitsuki sat in her hotel room in the mountains of Hakone, looking at old photographs in the hush of night, the thought of that bleak holiday, with no photographs to mark the occasion, struck her as a dream from a former life.

Her father had been fourteen when his father died, her mother fourteen when her father walked out. They each divorced someone else to be together; perhaps their two souls found mutual comfort, both of them having suffered such a blow in adolescence. By marrying they threw other lives in turmoil, endured a storm of criticism from their relations, and made social outcasts of themselves. The cheerless New Years of Mitsuki's childhood showed that not enough time had passed to soften those memories. The first three days of January, when no holiday callers came by, must have reminded her parents of how as newlyweds they'd stood together against public opinion. So those bare-bones New Year mornings with festive chopstick envelopes and little else had been happy, in their way, after all. Lingering memories of all they had endured to be together must have served to hold her mother's self-indulgence in check and bolster the marriage.

Why couldn't time have stopped then?

If time had stopped back then, her mother's life might have been the enchanting story of a starry-eyed young girl who devoted herself to her dream and proudly brought it to fruition.

As the sisters grew, their father achieved social and financial stability, and in time the marriage acquired respectability. Relatives from his side of the family started showing up during the auspicious first three days of January. The antique set of ceremonial lacquerware, including the sake decanter and cups, began to make an appearance. But at the same time, slowly and imperceptibly, the marital bond weakened.

As the holiday approached that year after her father was shunted off to the remote hospital, Mitsuki had suggested, "Shouldn't we bring him home for New Year's, anyway?"

"No." Her mother had been firm. "I don't want him in the house."

Every year from then until her father became bedridden, Mitsuki would spend the last day of the year in Toride with Tetsuo and his family, and then bring her father home to their apartment on New Year's Day. Since her mother's sordid relationship with That Man wasn't public knowledge, her father's side of the family would show up as usual. Her mother would entertain the guests, putting on a wifely smile as she calmly plied her festive chopsticks.

The box of poetry cards never did turn up when they emptied out the house in Chitose Funabashi. No telling when it had been discarded.

Natsuki's slide show was a poignant reminder of those bygone days, days that seemed to have no bearing on the present. Time had cleansed and beautified the distant past, while the recent past was wretched in every respect. Very much like the difference between her mother in youth and old age, Mitsuki thought.

## 55

## TWO POSSIBILITIES

Three days passed uneventfully.

On the third evening, Mr. Matsubara again did not appear in the lounge. Mitsuki retired to her room early for once, flopped on the bed, still dressed, and ticked off the days since her arrival in Hakone. This was the seventh night. She had come planning to stay nine nights in all, so there were only three left, including this one.

She closed her eyes and made herself face head-on the thoughts that over the past few days had risen persistently in her mind only to be quickly suppressed.

Tetsuo's attitude puzzled her. Why was he hesitating? The final line of his most recent email rose in her eyes: "Anyway don't get worn out—you never were very strong. Take good care of yourself, okay?" What lay behind those tender words?

Was he hesitating because he loved her—even if not in the way she wished? No, that wasn't possible. Absolutely not, she murmured to herself. He might still have faith in her character, but he didn't love her. He didn't yearn to be with her, to see her smile and hear her laugh. She for her part had long since fallen out of love with him. Indeed the thought of him now evoked only bitter emptiness. Yet admitting his lack of love for her was still painful.

There could be only two possible explanations. One was that he felt guilty. He was not so heartless as to cast off his wife of many years without a pang. He'd gone to live in Vietnam months ago, yet they were hardly communicating. He might sense that she had her suspicions, but surely he had no idea she knew he was over there hatching divorce plans. Broaching the topic would be difficult. And to top it all off, when he last saw her she'd been coping with a mother sinking rapidly into dementia, and her own health had been even worse than usual. In that case his hesitation—including those tender words—signified gentleness, not weakness of will.

One other possibility remained. She took a deep breath. Even to entertain the notion seemed a desecration not only of him but of herself, and yet banish the thought as she would, it kept on coming back: he might have his sights set on the inheritance from her mother. More precisely, he might be calculating the chances of her coming into an inheritance sometime soon. That might be what was making him put off talk of divorce. He didn't know her mother was gone. He could put two and two together though, and surely realized that even after the expense of installing her in a nursing home there would be plenty left over if she suddenly died.

How much did it matter to Tetsuo whether or not Mitsuki received an inheritance from her mother?

After staring up at the ceiling for a while, Mitsuki dragged herself out of bed, went over to the desk, and sat down. She lifted the lid of her laptop with both hands and switched the machine on. With a faint hum, the screen began to glow. She went to Tetsuo's email account and slowly scrolled down until she came to the message from the woman with an attachment concerning division of property. Once more, she opened the attachment. As unpleasant as it might be, she needed to grasp the figures the woman, bless her heart, had worked out in such detail.

First, the 72.3-square-meter condominium where he and she lived: by the woman's estimation, at current prices it was worth at least 30 million yen. They had been paying back the loan regularly, so only 10 million or so remained. By selling, therefore, they stood to gain some 20 million yen. Next came savings and investments, amounting to roughly 18 million yen. Since they had no children and didn't indulge in expensive pastimes like golf or cruises, the money had piled up without their having had to economize. Added together, the assets they had built up during their marriage came to 38 million yen. Even though Tetsuo earned many times more than Mitsuki, since the initial down payment on the condominium had come largely from her parents and since he wouldn't need to support her after the divorce, and above all since the cause of the divorce was his unfaithfulness, Mitsuki's compensation, in the woman's opinion, would be adequate if the assets were split fifty-fifty. In other words, 19 million yen apiece.

Also Tetsuo should promise to split his pension. The woman recommended granting Mitsuki another 10 million at the time of the divorce as an advance on his retirement bonus, for a total of 29 million. She further advised him to allow Mitsuki to keep the pension money she'd been building up at JPB, the Japan Post Bank, since the divorce would end her entitlement to a survivor's pension. How awfully considerate, to be thinking already of what might happen to Mitsuki in the event of Tetsuo's death! Of course the woman was only bending over backward to make it easy for Mitsuki to sign the divorce papers. Unless Tetsuo could obtain a divorce by mutual consent, there would have to be arbitration, or else they'd go to court. The potential cost of the divorce mattered less to the woman, Mitsuki sensed, than the need to keep Tetsuo from leaving her before it came through.

"The devil himself would agree to these terms," she wrote.

And yet Tetsuo seemed unpersuaded. "This is awfully generous."

Mitsuki thought about the calculations from his perspective. Indeed, if he gave her 29 million yen, that left him with a measly 9 million representing all the assets he had managed to accumulate while indulging himself here and there along the way. After all that studying as a child and all those years of teaching college, he would have reached his mid-fifties with less than 10 million yen to show for it. The size of the woman's nest egg wasn't clear, but she was living at home, and that would have allowed her to save up quite a bit. Yet she hadn't worked steadily. Putting it all together, Mitsuki estimated that she too had under 10 million yen—probably no more than Tetsuo did. Their combined worth would be only about 18 million yen at the outside.

But what if Mitsuki's mother were to drop dead? Then Mitsuki's inheritance would be added to the 38 million yen she and Tetsuo were presently worth. He couldn't be sure, but he could guess that she would inherit something over 30 million yen, for a grand total of 70 million or more now in their combined marital assets. With that much on hand, by stretching a bit he could finance a dream condominium worth nearly 100 million yen.

If Tetsuo left Mitsuki, he was looking at about 18 million yen in total assets for himself and the woman. If he stayed married to Mitsuki and her mother died, the Hirayama assets would come to 70 million yen or more. What a temptation! That might well be why he was dragging his heels. The woman knew all there was to know about the Hirayama finances, with one omission: he clearly hadn't told her about the plot of land in Chitose Funabashi.

If Tetsuo was stalling because he felt bad for Mitsuki, that was one thing. But if he was stalling with an eye on her mother's money, he was...what? Mean. Despicable. A total rat. She tried to work up some indignation, yet deep down she couldn't bring herself to really blame him. Sadly, aging had taught her the importance of money as well as the untrustworthiness of the human heart. What if he now found out she had come into her inheritance and did an abrupt turnaround, dumping this woman? Would he be at all shamefaced? Not likely. He'd convince himself that he had abandoned the idea of divorce out of his tender regard for his wife. That was how the human mind worked, she thought simply and without cynicism.

She left the computer, went over to the window, opened it, and let the night air cool her cheeks as she looked down at the lake, now shrouded in darkness, and then up at the crystalline sky above. As her eyes grew accustomed to the darkness, the stars above the lake grew brighter. On such a cloudless night they seemed close at hand, inching closer all the time. Before she knew it, she was leaning against the windowsill with her arms extended out toward the ever-brighter stars, as if reaching for salvation.

The stars remained indifferent in their icy beauty.

The night was not yet far along, but Lake Ashinoko was set so deep in the mountains that silence reigned and stars in their millions sparkled. It felt like the middle of the night. When she closed her eyes, the stars' bright afterimage lingered behind her lids.

The telephone rang. Startled, she drew back inside, shut the window, and went over to the desk to pick up the receiver. It was Masako.

"You sound as depressed as ever." Masako herself was as blunt as ever.

"Well, I have good reason to be."

"Cheer up, will you?"

"Uh-huh."

"Come on."

"I'm managing. I'll be okay."

After a short silence, Masako said in a lowered voice, "You know his girlfriend? She has a blog. 'Carefree Travels in Vietnam,' it's called."

"How'd you find out?"

"A hunch. I googled 'Ho Chi Minh City,' 'sabbatical,' and 'divorce.' Bingo. It's gotta be her."

"Well well."

"I don't know if I should tell you this, but she's dead serious about getting him to divorce you."

"I know." She couldn't bring herself to confess that she had read their emails.

"What're you gonna do?"

"Ask *him* for a divorce. What else?" The words popped out before she had time to think. In her heart she must have already made her decision.

"Mitsuki! Bravo!" Masako sounded happy and relieved.

She should have left him long ago; it had taken her all these years to see it. Knowing that she deserved no praise, Mitsuki simply said, "Thanks."

Masako didn't chatter on the telephone, so Mitsuki ended up speaking more concisely too.

"She doesn't seem like a bad person," said Masako before hanging up. "I mean, she even writes about air pollution over there."

# 56

## HUSBAND OR POVERTY?

Mitsuki stood still in front of the telephone.

"Ask *him* for a divorce."

She had settled on that course long ago, she now realized, but only when she spoke the words aloud to Masako did their meaning sink in. She stared at the telephone, ruminating, and slowly sat down at the desk. Sadly, she felt no sense of liberation. In fact, anxiety washed over her. How would she live?

The array of figures in the woman's email now took on greater significance.

The inheritance from her mother was a heaven-sent boon. It meant she could divorce without becoming poor. For a woman of her upbringing, a woman lacking Masako's toughness, it was a relief to think that she might be able to cling to her cozy, middle-class way of life.

She thought of friends her age stuck in loveless marriages. Friends whose parents had fallen on hard times or for whatever reasons died without leaving them an inheritance. Lacking full-time jobs and having led sheltered lives for the most part, they faced the choice between a provider-husband and independent poverty, and had been forced to choose the former. Compared to "love or money" or rather to "money or something more valuable," the choice of "husband or poverty" had a decidedly dreary ring—a dreary and unromantic ring befitting an unhappily wed, middle-aged woman about to slide into old age.

The ramifications of that choice varied. One of Mitsuki's more self-assured friends from high school had, as soon as her children were out on their own, initiated a quasi-divorce: when her husband was home she would make dinner for the two of them, but she ate in her own room as she pleased, watching television. A friend from college, a quiet type, had declared with a straight face that she was developing a "wet-tissue relationship" with her husband. That was how Mitsuki learned of the myth then circulating that a wet tissue placed over a sleeping husband's mouth and nose would cause death by suffocation. Another college friend made no complaint about her marriage, but when Mitsuki said, "You two seem to be getting along," her friend had sighed. "Don't be fooled. Ever hear of domestic violence? I've had bones broken more than once."

Apart from free spirits like her mother, most women of the previous generation couldn't bring themselves to contemplate divorce in the first place, regardless of the economic consequences. They had quietly endured unhappy marriages to the end. Mitsuki remembered a musical event at Golden at which a woman around ninety years old kept asking her sixtyish daughter, "When's your father getting home?"

Each time, the daughter patiently replied, "Mother, he's been dead for seventeen years."

Eventually Mitsuki had been moved to say, "Perhaps she might find it reassuring if you told her he'll be home soon."

The daughter had smiled wryly. "On the contrary, that's exactly what she's afraid of."

Once upon a time, divorce had been a casual matter in Japan. Then, under Western influence, it had fallen out of fashion, become taboo. Mitsuki was fortunate to be alive at a time when divorce was increasingly accepted, to have work to do, and to have her inheritance from her mother to fall back on as well. She should try, anyway, to consider herself fortunate.

Mitsuki brought the memo pad by the telephone over to the desk and wrote the figure 29, representing 29 million yen, the amount she stood to gain from Tetsuo at their divorce. Beneath it she added her inheritance from her mother: 36.8. The total came to 65.8.

People truly differed in their sense of the value of money. Natsuki's sister-in-law was worth a billion yen in movable property alone, but she was always complaining about being hard up. An old man in Mitsuki's neighborhood would come home from the public bath with a plastic basin under his arm and climb the steps into the shabby wooden apartment building where he lived, looking like he had not a care in the world. Mitsuki secretly called him "Happy Grampy." For someone like her, 65.8 million yen was an enormous sum. She wrote it out with all the zeros: ¥65,800,000. It looked like enough to buy a castle in France. And yet without bothering to do the math, she knew it wasn't anywhere near enough to live in the lap of luxury. The magic aura of the zeros lasted only a moment before fading away.

She intended to use her entire inheritance to buy a place along the lines of what she had now, if a bit smaller. Somewhere by a station not too far from the heart of the city, on a street that wouldn't overly offend her aesthetic sensibilities, in a building that didn't look too run-down, with a view that would set her heart somewhat at ease. That's what she wanted.

She also wanted some of the small luxuries that her mother had enjoyed in old age. For that, she would set aside the 29 million from Tetsuo. Once she turned sixty-five, her JPB pension would give her 50,000 yen a month, and her national pension would give her almost 70,000 yen more. But 120,000 yen per month was depressingly little to live on. Even adding in her share of Tetsuo's pension, it wouldn't be enough. And what if she lived another thirty or forty years? That possibility, till now a mere statistic, began to scare her. She remembered that Masako had purchased an annuity, using a small inheritance from her father; she could earmark 10 million of Tetsuo's 29 million for the same purpose. That would give her a little more per month anyway. The remaining 19 million she should save, and when her pensions kicked in, start using a little at a time, as her mother had done with her savings. How to manage over the next ten years or so: that was the problem. Once she had used her inheritance from her mother to buy a place to live, she would have to manage without eating into that 19 million yen. But how?

Until now, on top of her own earnings there'd been Tetsuo's annual before-tax salary of 13 million yen. From now on there would be only her combined income of under 3 million yen before taxes—a pittance. She'd taught as many classes per week as a full-time professor, but what a difference in salary!

Once again, she began to scribble figures on the memo pad.

She'd gotten a late start on the JPB pension plan, so she would need to deposit roughly 40,000 yen a month from now till she was sixty-five. For the national pension, she would need to deposit 15,000 yen per month until she was sixty-two. Besides that, adding in residence tax, national health insurance, nursing insurance, private hospitalization insurance, utilities, apartment maintenance fees, and whatnot, she would need more than 100,000 yen per month. That left her very little to live on. The more or less affluent lifestyle she had enjoyed until now must end. No more eating out. Fewer trips to the hairdresser, not to mention fewer purchases of everything from books and herbal medicines to the disposable heating pads she used to ward off the cold. Acupuncture and massage sessions would be a luxury, even once a month. Foreign travel had never seemed like a huge extravagance, but from now on she would have to plan it carefully. And however much she economized, right off there would be the substantial expense of moving. Plus she would have to replenish some of her furniture and appliances. In time her laptop would break down, and other unforeseeable expenses were bound to arise. Each time she dipped into her savings she would be robbing her old age.

There was only one thing to do: increase her workload. Fortunately, adjunct teachers could work until sixty-eight, and the demand for patent translations was rising. With her years of experience, she'd have no trouble finding extra work.

Mitsuki stared at the figure 36.8 on the memo pad, representing her inheritance. For years she'd thought that the money would mean freedom, or relative freedom, from work. Even if Tetsuo balked, she'd been determined to cut back. Now fate had decided otherwise. She would have to work harder and longer. Now that she thought about it, Tetsuo's salary, deposited in his bank account month after month—how generous it really had been! She felt almost as if she were being punished for having taken it so for granted.

She shook her head, closed her eyes, and steadied her breathing, then started afresh. She had to take a different tack, come up with a different scenario, or what was the point of living? She began by revising her thinking about the inheritance money. She would forget about using it for a condominium and use it to live, starting now.

She could get a condominium with just half the inheritance money, however small, old, far off, and ramshackle it might be. That didn't matter. She could purchase the annuity as planned but give up the idea of saving for small luxuries in old age. And why not go all the way and quit teaching? Oh, what a relief that would be! She could do more patent translating, get by till her money and health gave out, and then enter a state-run nursing home—or just die alone in her apartment. What difference did it make? The point was to give up any idea of clinging to the middle class and just live, doing what she wanted to do and making the most of however much time she might have remaining.

What if she hadn't received that inheritance? Then she'd have no choice but to accept those terms that "the devil himself would agree to." Besides moving into a cheap place somewhere, she'd have to work herself to the bone, teaching till she was sixty-eight without hope of a pension while piling on more and more translations. Did Tetsuo's woman have no qualms about inflicting such rigors on a woman nearly twenty years her senior, while becoming a professor's wife herself? Anger flared in her momentarily—but the more fitting target of her anger was not the woman, but Tetsuo. He knew better than anyone that her health, never good, had lately been worsening. And yet he had the nerve to say, "This is awfully generous."

Leaving the sheet of paper covered with numbers on the desk, Mitsuki went over to the armchair and threw herself down. With the overhead light off, the desk lamp provided the only illumination in the spacious room, emphasizing the darkness of the four corners. As she sat in the shadowy stillness, the cold anger inside her erupted for the first time into hot fury.

Tetsuo.

Tetsuo, who'd been initially attracted to her in Paris as a girl of privilege and then driven all the other boys away, making her his own. Tetsuo, who'd sworn, surrounded by the bright glow of candles, that she would never lack for anything. That same Tetsuo was now going to snatch from her the life of ease that all her life she had shamelessly accepted as her birthright. Did he figure that her sister, having married into wealth, would come to her rescue when the chips were down? Did he figure that sooner or later her mother was bound to die, so she'd be all right? Or had he simply let his mind go blank, preferring not to think about it at all?

Amid the burning silence, the telephone rang again.

As she thought, it was Natsuki, but her sister's voice was disturbed; she sounded agitated, the way she used to do after quarreling with their mother. "What's wrong?" Mitsuki asked. She was surprised at how perfectly ordinary her own voice sounded.

"I just had it out with Jun."

Imagining Natsuki's petulant face, Mitsuki realized that come what may, she could never rely on this childish elder sister of hers. The light from the desk lamp lit up the room forlornly.

"She's in her room, crying."

Natsuki herself sounded close to tears.

# 57

## THE NIGHT THE SKY RAINED STARS

Her voice breaking, her breath coming in agitated gulps, Natsuki explained.

As she spread out family photographs on the dining room table, organizing the albums, she had muttered something like "What a mother—she never had a kind word to say about her daughters' looks."

Then Jun, who was doing something with her laptop on the sofa, suddenly turned and said, "Neither did you, Mom."

"You could have knocked me over," Natsuki said bitterly. "I avoided the topic *on purpose!* I didn't want to be one of those mothers who's all focused on her daughter's looks."

"I know."

"I mean, all that talk about being beautiful or not—we had a bellyful of it growing up, didn't we?"

"Yes, we did."

"But Jun took it the wrong way. Now she hates me."

"If you explain, she'll understand."

"I tried. She says it's too late. She says I never said she was pretty, so she's never felt confident about her looks, and now it's too late to do anything about it."

"But Jun *is* pretty!" Mitsuki said, and meant it. She was a nice girl too. As an infant she had watched round-eyed from her carriage, uncomprehending, as her mother and grandmother quarreled endlessly over that architect with the hair that went diagonally across his forehead. But she had grown up normally, gone to school normally, found a job normally, like other girls of her generation.

"There's more. She's mad because when she was in fifth grade and wanted to quit piano lessons, I never tried to talk her out of it. She says it shows I thought she had no talent. All I wanted was not to bring her up the way *I* was brought up." Her voice had become shriller; she was practically screaming. "What was I supposed to *do*, for God's sake!"

At such times all Mitsuki could do was listen in silence. Perhaps daughters were condemned to resent their mothers.

"Ken is a boy so I never expected *him* to understand, but Jun is a girl! I always thought *she* understood!"

"Is Ken coming home for Christmas?" Mitsuki smoothly changed the subject, the way one does to distract a child.

"Yes."

He hadn't come home for summer vacation, partly because Natsuki had been busy looking after their mother, partly because he himself had been busy preparing for his orals.

"How's his English now?"

"Your guess is as good as mine."

Natsuki didn't pursue the topic. Calmer now, she went back to talking about their mother. "Have you noticed that after she took up with That Man she has a disgusting look on her face in all of her pictures? I'm not putting any of them online."

Particularly when she posed in a long gown in the photographs taken at the chanson recitals, the expression under their mother's heavy makeup was chilling, like that of one possessed.

"I'm still not free of her, and now Jun hates me. Life is too hard. My health isn't getting any better either."

"I know." Mitsuki repeated the words mechanically.

She went on administering comfort a while longer in this vein and hung up without having told her sister that she had decided on divorce. Her silence weighed on her. But how could she bring up the topic with her sister, who even more than Mitsuki had been sheltered from life's harsh realities? If she did tell her, how capable would Natsuki be of grasping the implications?

The clock indicated it wasn't yet ten.

In her mind's eye she saw again the shimmering night sky she had reached out to from her window, the closeness of the shining stars. Swiftly she put on her coat. On a night like this, one should look up at the stars with one's feet planted firmly on the earth. Leery of the hovering staff, she kept out of sight after taking the elevator down, slipping out the back door toward the veranda, and then hurrying over to the garden.

It was the kind of night when stars seem to rain earthward from the heavens. The air was miraculously clear. Looking up as if through magic glasses, she saw the stars, untold light-years away, grow still more radiant as she watched. She walked rapidly downhill and to the right till she came to the chapel, which she knew was hidden from the hotel. The tawdry chapel and plaza were magical at night, all light and shadow. Even the water spraying in the fountain had an uncanny beauty.

How many couples got married here every year? How many of those brides found their happy-ever-after? Just as she began to walk along the faux-stone cloister, a dark figure emerged from the shadows. She jumped. It was Mr. Matsubara.

He seemed equally startled. She hadn't seen him since yesterday noon, but his face was unshaven, and he had his usual faraway air. Even the shirt beneath his jacket was a bit rumpled.

"I come here every night," he said. "Never expected to see anyone else here."

"You come because you were married in a chapel like this?"

"No, we were married in the usual way."

With proper go-betweens and a traditional ceremony conducted by a Shinto priest, he must mean. She pictured Wakako dressed in a scarlet outer kimono and the white headdress meant to conceal horns of jealousy, sipping the ritual sake, her slender fingers gracefully aligned. Then she imagined her at the reception afterward, sitting in front of a gold screen with her gaze cast demurely down. Even in a tuxedo Mr. Matsubara would have been dressed in his usual style, she thought, all black.

"I like to come here because it's away from the eyes of the hotel staff. I started coming at night when I was in my room and couldn't take it anymore."

*Just like me.*

"The time my wife and I stayed here," he went on, as if picking up a previous train of thought, "I think she may have already given up. She'd look out the window at the lake and tick off on her fingers all the happy things she could remember. She didn't have enough fingers and toes to count them all, she said. But it only gave me more pain…"

Mitsuki didn't know what to say. For a while they were silent, standing amid the fantastic play of light and shadow and watching the cascading waters of the fountain.

Then she spoke up: "I decided to leave my husband."

He looked at her, waiting.

"He has a young woman."

Mr. Matsubara frowned slightly, as if she had said something indecent. Mitsuki herself could hardly believe that she had just uttered those words. To distance herself from them, to keep from seeming even a little pathetic, she lifted her chin and looked him in the eye. His first question went straight to the point.

"Do you still have feelings for him?"

"No."

The coldness in her voice was startling. His second question was no less pertinent.

"Can you manage financially?"

"Yes. Fortunately my mother left me a little something, so I'll be all right." Unconsciously she looked up at the stars as she replied.

"That's good." He sounded relieved.

"But I feel as if I've wasted my life."

Her admission left him wordless.

"I only wish I could give what's left of my life to your wife."

He looked down, thanked her, then raised his head and murmured, "But life is for the living."

Words he needed to take to heart even more than she did, Mitsuki thought. She smiled a little mischievously. "You seem about half alive."

That made him smile too. They turned and headed for the hotel. The stars traveled with them in perfectly orchestrated harmony. For the first time in years, she felt the urge to sing. Then she remembered that Wakako had also been a singer.

"What kind of songs did your wife like?"

"Maria Callas. More than anything, Callas. She would listen to all sorts of singers, but in the end she always came back to her."

"No, I mean what kind of songs did she herself like to sing?"

He swept back his hair. "She never sang in front of me."

Mitsuki looked at him in surprise. "But didn't you say she studied voice?"

"Yes, but she always said she wasn't good enough to sing for me. And she was a mezzo soprano, not really a soloist."

"Well, even for a mezzo...there's Handel's famous 'Ombra mai fu,' for one. It's even more famous now thanks to that whiskey commercial."

The popular aria had been featured in a television commercial for Nikka Whiskey. There were any number of arias just as easy, if not easier, for a mezzo to sing. Melody after melody came to her as they walked, songs familiar and well loved, as numerous as the stars.

"No, I never heard her sing it."

"Did you ever ask her to sing for you?"

"I did, but she wouldn't hear of it. Too shy."

Mitsuki walked on in silence. Maybe Wakako had dictated what her husband should wear, but even so, what a modest and retiring woman she must have been at heart! She felt herself redden at the contrast with herself. This very moment, if only she could, she would love nothing more than to look up at the stars, stretch out her arms, and spin in a circle as she sang, spin and spin until she spiraled up into the star-filled sky.

While they waited side by side for the elevator, he said again, to no one in particular, "Life is for the living, after all."

When she returned to her room, it was almost eleven.

Her mouth set in determination, Mitsuki took off her coat and went directly to the telephone, not bothering to remove her boots. She dialed Natsuki's number. It was a bit late to be calling, and she would probably disturb her sister's family, but she wanted to share her news before the night was out.

"Hello?" she said, perched on the edge of the bed.

"Ohmigosh, you sound just like Mother!" Her sister's voice sounded amused, unsuspecting.

# 58

## ATAMI BEACH

With Natsuki she went into greater detail than she had with Masako. She told her about Tetsuo's past two flings and said that for all she knew there might have been others.

Natsuki, after her first startled "He whaaat?" listened in shocked silence.

Feeling more wretched as she went on, Mitsuki deliberately made her voice cheery at the end, wrapping up with "And that's that!"

"I can't believe it."

Natsuki had never sounded so stricken. The younger sister familiar to her since childhood had vanished, replaced by an unknown woman on the other end of the line. She sounded as if she took this news as blasphemy against her own life. Mitsuki struggled not to be caught up in her sister's shock.

"But it's true, so there you are."

A short silence followed. Then, "Now that you mention it, you lost that happy glow you always used to have."

"Well, if I have, that's not all *his* doing." An oblique reference to their mother.

"No, I know."

Another silence, and then in the same gloomy tone Natsuki said rather hesitantly, "You know, Mother had taken to criticizing him, more and more." Even though they'd been at odds, their mother had privately said some derogatory things to her about Tetsuo, it seemed, often alluding to his shallowness.

"Did you think he was shallow?" asked Mitsuki.

Natsuki answered cautiously, choosing her words. "I don't know. Of course I always stood up for him. Sometimes little things made me wonder, but he was the man you chose so I trusted him. I never dreamed anything like this could happen."

Mitsuki imagined her sister's utterly shocked face. "Never mind. It's okay. I don't feel married to him anymore."

"Will you have enough money?" An astute question, for her.

"I have the money from Mother, so I'll be fine. I'm actually thinking I'll quit teaching."

"Really? Are you sure?" She sounded nervous.

"Oh yes. I'll be doing more translating—and if worse comes to worst I know the Shimazakis will always be there for me."

"But you have such a strong independent streak. You always wanted to do things yourself."

*And look where it got me.* Natsuki's words did not strike her as complimentary.

Compared to their mother and Mitsuki, Natsuki had less emotional resilience. Right now she still seemed dazed by the news. Mitsuki decided to call her back in a day or two, to give her time to recover. She announced she was hanging up, and her sister made a final comment in an abstracted tone, as if thinking aloud.

"What's going to happen to you from now on? I mean, you've got no children or anything."

Mitsuki was momentarily at a loss for words. Then she summoned all her bravado and said jauntily, "There are any number of people like that in this world, and guess what? They're all doing just fine."

With the remnants of bravado, she began briskly preparing for bed after hanging up. Her movements soon lost their verve, however, as Natsuki's all-too-frank words caught up with her. What kind of future *did* lie ahead for her? For the first time in her life, she would be all alone. Unlike someone who had stayed single, she'd have to make a fresh start—knowing that at her age a truly fresh start was, however necessary, impossible.

What had been a vague awareness then struck her with force: *I will die without ever having accomplished anything in my life.* This would be true even if her marriage hadn't collapsed, but now that she was forced to start over, the fact hit home. Why now all of a sudden should she be struck by the fear that she would disappear leaving no trace—except for the detritus on Google? Did she after all harbor a modern ambition to carve a place for herself in history? She hadn't fulfilled her girlish dreams. She hadn't made any real contribution to the world. And as Natsuki had pointed out, she had no children.

And yet. Burrowing under the covers, she thought it over. With the Japanese population shrinking so fast, you perhaps couldn't say so out loud, but it might be just as well to be childless. No one could age without changing for the worse. She too was doomed to become some degraded, barely recognizable version of herself. Better not to have children, who would have to watch that happen.

That night again her rest was fitful.

"Would you like to go for a drive?"

The next day after lunch as she was standing by the elevator, Takeru issued this invitation. Having spent the previous evening mired in self-pity, she was wide-eyed with surprise. Perhaps the correct response was a demurral—"You want to go out with an old lady like me?"—but she saw no reason to pander to society's norms. Nor did he seem to expect her to.

"A drive where?"

"Wherever you like. We can always add dinner into the bargain."

"What about your aunt Kaoru?"

"She's not coming." After a beat he added, "Actually, she approves."

More likely, she had issued a command after observing how Mitsuki looked these past few days.

They agreed to meet in the lobby in half an hour, and Mitsuki went back to her room, where after a moment's hesitation, not troubling to think why, she quickly showered and put on brand-new black underwear, top and bottom.

Later, fastening her seat belt in a beat-up old Toyota Corolla, she said, "Would Atami be too far?"

"Atami?"

"It's famous for the beach scene between Kan'ichi and O-Miya. The town is nothing special, though."

Before, when she came with her mother, they'd gone there by taxi after two nights in the hotel. Mitsuki remembered appallingly bleak scenery hugging the shore, but for some reason she wanted to make sure.

"Kan'ichi and O-Miya," he repeated. "I know I've heard of them…"

Mitsuki gave him a simple explanation. From her experience teaching, she was accustomed to the ignorance of the younger generation; Takeru was doing well just to have heard of the two names. After she finished talking, he drove the winding downhill road to Atami with scarcely another word. She understood that he preferred to keep to himself, and she found it pleasant not to have to make conversation.

After winding all the way down to the coast, the road finally brought them to the hilly town of Atami, which was just as drab and depressing as she remembered. Despite an astonishing and somewhat disquieting variety of buildings and signboards in every color and shape, the town wasn't particularly lively, and she couldn't help noticing a number of dirty, abandoned concrete buildings covered in mold, perhaps as a result of the humid ocean air. Even the main street seemed run-down.

They reached the shore, and Takeru parked next to "O-Miya's pine."

When she and her mother had come, they'd gotten out of the taxi and gasped on seeing the famous tree hemmed in between a wide roadway and a sprawling parking lot. Its predecessor, alas, had succumbed to exhaust fumes. The enormous stump left in commemoration seemed completely out of place, along with the small, unprepossessing second-generation pine tree waving its branches between the traffic, the parked cars, and the hordes of people. Nearby was a ridiculous statue of the fictional lovers, looking nothing whatever like the exquisite figures in the ukiyo-e-style illustrations that had accompanied the serial novel. It depicted the pivotal scene at the Atami shore—the one where Kan'ichi kicks O-Miya to the ground.

The scene is from early in the novel. O-Miya, "blinded by a diamond," agonizes over her unfaithfulness to Kan'ichi and, to escape his recriminations, leaves for Atami with her mother, ostensibly for a rest. He finds her behavior suspicious and follows her there. They stroll together along the pine-studded beach—the man who gave chase, the woman who fled and was found—and he questions her. He learns from her own lips that his suspicions were correct, and as she clings to him, begging forgiveness, he gives her a swift kick.

"Adulteress!"

The bronze statue attempted to re-create that dramatic moment: Kan'ichi with one foot raised, about to deliver the kick,

O-Miya fallen helplessly to the ground. But there was no life, no drama in the rendition. The surreal location only added to the absurdity of the effect.

Amid the din of traffic, youths took turns posing in front of the statue, fingers raised in a V sign, grinning, while someone snapped photos of them on a cell phone.

"Hey, listen," one of them said. "Somebody's singing."

Through nearby speakers came strains of "The Song of *The Golden Demon*," a once-popular sentimental ballad:

> *Strolling along Atami Beach, Kan'ichi and O-Miya*
> *Never again to walk together, never again to talk together.*

Her mother had beat time with her free hand as she sang along, flicking her wrist jauntily like a festival dancer—almost as if, overwhelmed by the tide of vulgarity, she had decided to react by doing something droll.

Though the sensational plot might cater to popular taste, *The Golden Demon* was written in a poetic, romantic style redolent of the riches of premodern Japanese literature. And a mere century on, was this what had become of the setting of that renowned work? Even granting that reality was always drab compared to the world of fantasy, this travesty was beyond the pale.

Mitsuki had grieved.

# (59)

## NOT FIT FOR A NOVEL

It had taken forever to descend from O-Miya's pine to the shore with her cane-wielding mother. The shoreline, artificially extended by sand that looked almost too white, was now far away from the pine tree, and in order to get there you first had to go up on a huge promenade that doubled as the roof of a parking lot. This was apparently designed to enable visitors to go for a stroll while looking down on the beach, but the promenade was like none other. According to the sign, it was supposed to create the atmosphere of a villa on a Mediterranean resort such as the Riviera or the Côte d'Azur. A concrete balustrade, painted white, meandered along the edge. The scale was vaster than that of the hotel chapel, the effect just that much tawdrier and cheesier.

How could anyone go for a stroll there and enjoy the experience? Even her mother, with her strong affinity for all things Western, had been dumbfounded by the white balustrade with its endless row of posts: "What the heck is this?"

The expanse of white sand below was called "Sun Beach" by day, "Moonlight Beach" by night—English names with no Mediterranean connection. It was like being suddenly whisked to California for no reason. Since it was wintertime, no one had been swimming in the sea. Instead they'd seen youngsters batting a beach ball, middle-aged men practicing their tee shots, and a couple holding the hands of a tiny tot, helping it to walk. Mitsuki hadn't felt like leaving the promenade.

"I won't ever be coming back here," her mother had pointed out, and so they'd gone walking on the sand side by side, her mother leaning on her cane. That was when her mother had blurted out, "There never was any Kan'ichi in your grandmother's life." She'd continued, "How silly, her thinking she was O-Miya!" Yet her voice quavered. Mitsuki could tell she felt not contempt but pity for such arrant foolishness, mixed with a sentimental longing for bygone days. Mitsuki said nothing and just walked along.

A year or so before they took that walk, a major newspaper had run a front-page article on the source of *The Golden Demon*: an American dime novel, as it turned out.

Her mother had called her in shock over the news, not waiting for their usual nightly chat. "They found the source, and it's a cheap novel written by some woman, an Englishwoman or an American. This is just terrible."

After hanging up, Mitsuki had checked the newspaper. The dime novel in question was *Weaker than a Woman*, written by one Bertha M. Clay. Meiji writers had not only translated Western novels extolling love and lovers but routinely reworked and adapted them, making them their own. Ozaki Koyo, the author of *The Golden Demon*, never tried to conceal that his novel was an adaptation. The news was shocking only because Japanese people had forgotten their country's literary history of a mere hundred years before, when modern Japanese literature began taking shape through translation and adaptation. They were astounded to read about it in the newspaper.

Now Mitsuki walked on that same shore alongside Takeru. In the distance was a breakwater, and inside it a row of yachts and motorboats, along with ferries and excursion and fishing boats. On the sand, a game of beach volleyball was in progress.

"Doesn't make me at all jealous to watch young people like that," said Takeru.

Mitsuki laughed. "From where I sit, you're equally young."

To thank him for the outing, she decided to take him to dinner at the Hyatt Regency Hotel near the Hôtel du Lac. He steered the car back up the winding road, taciturn again. The approach of evening brought with it dark clouds. Big drops of rain splattered against the windshield, and then with the abrupt change of weather typical of the mountains, the rain began coming down hard. By the time they reached the hotel parking lot, where there was an impressive lineup of Mercedes-Benzes, BMWs, and Audis, it was coming down in torrents.

The hotel interior was softly lit with the indirect lighting characteristic of exclusive international hotels. They passed through the soaring lobby, where the fanciful dimness enhanced the sense of luxury, and entered the restaurant. Mitsuki was surprised to see Japanese people dressed informally in hotel *yukata*, eating with gleaming knives and forks by candlelight. *Yukata* belonged to a different world—the world of traditional inns, where guests changed into cotton robes after soaking in a hot spring, had dinner in their rooms, and once their stomachs were full and they were pleasantly drunk, just collapsed on the futon laid out on the floor and went to sleep. The sight of *yukata*-clad guests sipping wine and dining on French cuisine was incongruous. So this was how international hotels were trying to bring in local flavor. Japanese-run hotels used to post reminders: "Please refrain from leaving your room dressed in hotel *yukata*." Probably many still did, Mitsuki thought, looking around with faint amusement as they were shown to their table.

After they were seated, she looked up from the menu at Takeru and asked on a whim, "Do you have Western blood in your veins?"

"You can tell?" He gave her a languid look.

"More or less."

Now that she had a good look at him straight on, she could see that the eyebrows, the bridge of the nose, and the warm brown eyes did not align quite as they did on Asian faces.

"I'm one-quarter French."

"Were you bullied for it as a child?"

"You can tell that too?" Now his eyes showed some surprise.

"Well, more or less." She returned his gaze. "A lot?"

"Not that much." He looked away.

It seemed that Kaoru's older brother, the one who went to Paris as a *boursier*, had married a Frenchwoman, Takeru's grandmother. Probably when Takeru was little his hair had been shinier and even lighter in color. Her initial automatic response to his looks now somehow embarrassed her. She sounded him out about his background.

Takeru responded with seeming reluctance. His mother had grown up in Japan and France, neither fully Japanese nor fully French. Unhappy with her in-between status, she married a Japanese national with the intention of raising their children as Japanese, but when her husband took to drink she turned against Japan, left him, and went back to France. His younger sister, still in grade school, had gone with her, but Takeru, a high school student at the time, had remained in Japan.

"I was angry at her. Not for abandoning my dad, since he was an alcoholic. But abandoning your child is different. She made me into a Japanese, and in the end she abandoned me along with Japan."

He was named after Yamato Takeru no Mikoto, the mythical hero of prodigious strength. Mitsuki smiled at this revelation.

Concerning his aunt Kaoru, Takeru was a little more loquacious. She had had a daughter by the elderly White Russian. After the daughter grew up, whether because of something in French society or in the language, she and Kaoru had quarreled — an irrevocable quarrel, normally unimaginable between Japanese mothers and daughters — and separated without another word. When Takeru's mother went back to Paris a dozen years or so ago she had searched for the daughter at Kaoru's request, without luck. Then just three months ago she had struck up a friendship with a Russian immigrant in Chinatown on the Right Bank who claimed to know descendants of a White Russian. She'd asked him to make some inquiries, and it came out that the daughter had died a quarter of a century before, alone in a tiny *appartement* on the Left Bank, cause of death unknown. It was after learning this that Kaoru had begun to talk about adopting him, Takeru.

So Kaoru, who seemed so elegantly proud, was actually an old woman just recovering from the news that her only child was long dead and doubtless had gone to her grave resenting her. She too harbored her own unspeakable grief. Small wonder that a psychic would smell death around their little group. Perhaps the heart of anyone who chose this hectic holiday time for an extended hotel stay harbored a darkness which — however commonplace its origin — forced them to hide from the world. Even that close-knit mother and daughter seemed to draw a kind of curtain around themselves.

Mitsuki learned a few other things from Takeru: that he was registered with a temporary employment agency and sometimes worked part time as a network engineer; that when he walked down the street, people would stop him and ask if he'd like to do modeling work — something that made him cringe; and that Kaoru had instructed him to get her, Mitsuki, to tell him about herself.

"My story is such a cliché I don't feel like going into it." This was the honest truth.

The newly built hotel seemed as completely cut off from the outer world as a spaceship, but glancing out the window she saw the rain was coming down harder than ever. Fat raindrops struck sideways against the window, making countless wide bands as they trickled down the pane. It was as if the hotel stood in a cataract.

While they waited for dessert, Takeru excused himself. Five minutes later he was back. "I asked at the front desk, and they said they have just one room available." He seemed to be studying Mitsuki from across the table. "Shall I take it?"

She drew a sharp breath and tried to read what was in those brown eyes. A faint embarrassment. Not what she'd taken for granted when she was a young woman face to face with a young man—a look that stirred something within her. Self-conscious, acutely aware of the brand-new underthings beneath her clothes, she forced a smile. "Would driving back be dangerous?"

"Depends on the driver."

"Then let's go back."

She looked steadily into his eyes. If something did happen between them now, it would only be a way for her to remind herself that she was still a sexual being. If that's all it was, then she might as well let it go, even if this were her last chance. She reached out and laid her hand over the back of his. He turned his hand over and wrapped it around hers. The masculine feel of his grip took her by surprise.

"You're so nice," she said. "You're bound to find someone special."

"Am I?"

Handsome too, she was on the point of saying, but stopped in time.

Outside, the rain was coming down more fiercely than she had imagined. This was less like being in a cataract than like shearing through a stormy lake. Takeru kept his eyes ahead and drove in silence. At any moment the car could veer off the road. Dying with Takeru—not so bad, she thought. Something in the way he gripped the wheel told her that while he would never go recklessly fast, if a slip of the tires should send them both plunging to their deaths, he wouldn't mind. She began to feel as if this were a loveless *michi-yuki*—the lovers' journey in classical puppet dramas, ending always in death. She too stared wordlessly at the windshield, seeing nothing but pouring rain.

Even if she died like this, her death would scarcely be noticed. In the eyes of society, a woman her age hardly existed. A woman her age wouldn't even make a good heroine in a novel. She knew it was silly of her, but she couldn't help feeling that was the worst part of it all. No one paid attention if a female character her age died—not even if she ended her own life. When Emma Bovary takes arsenic and when Anna Karenina jumps in front of an oncoming train, they are still in the flower of youth. In Kan'ichi's nightmare, O-Miya, also in the flower of youth, kills herself not once but twice, first stabbing herself and then drowning in a river. In a famous ukiyo-e-style illustration of the scene, the cloud of hair framing her pale face trailed in the water, and the delicate lines of her wrists and feet were faintly erotic. But what novelist would ever create such a scene featuring a woman like Mitsuki?

If something should happen to Mitsuki now, there would be neither poetry nor romance in her demise. And yet in this lashing rain there was every chance of a fatal accident. The rain kept increasing in intensity until it seemed a marvel that it didn't start seeping through the cracks of this beat-up Toyota. Let death come now—however unpoetic and unromantic it might be—if that was her fate. Just as she had decided to entrust her life to the raging storm, a thought pierced her: *If I die now, the inheritance from my mother will go to Tetsuo.*

Takeru's cell phone began to ring. He ignored it. The phone rang insistently, then at intervals. The mechanical sound kept ringing, ever louder, as if to urge the car on.

## THE STORM

The moment the car pulled up to the hotel, two men, one of them the assistant manager, came rushing out with umbrellas to hand them.

"What a relief you're back safely!" said the assistant manager, still looking upset. "Everyone's been worried."

They headed straight for the stairs to the lounge and hurried down them. Mr. Matsubara, sitting next to Kaoru, got to his feet. Had Takeru failed to answer his cell phone simply because he wanted to drive safely? Or did he also have a sadistic desire to worry his great-aunt, who wielded such authority over him? Mr. Matsubara at least greeted them with a smile, but Kaoru, complaining that she'd called Takeru on his phone over and over, did not.

The sight of him evidently released the tension of the past hours. Kaoru looked her age as she sat slumped back in her chair and explained the situation, her face pale. The elderly couple were fortunately safe in their room, but the mother and daughter were nowhere to be found, although their car was still in the parking lot. The hotel management feared the worst—the psychic's prediction perhaps echoing in their minds—and had formed a search party to look down by the lake. In hopes that the women would be found and a scandal avoided, they were waiting till midnight to notify the police.

"After all, it's the perfect night," Kaoru added in a hushed voice. "Don't you think? The absolute perfect night." She looked from Mitsuki to Takeru and back again. "It's my fault. I should never have passed on what that psychic said. Those two looked so happy."

With that she stood up, turned her back on them, and walked with faltering steps up the stairs. At the top she went directly to the elevator, pushed the button, and cried out over her shoulder as if in anguish, "Takeru!" Mitsuki saw the assistant manager and other employees exchange startled glances. She thought of Kaoru's daughter and her lonely death.

Mr. Matsubara said sensibly, "Since you two are back safely anyway, we should retire."

He, Takeru, and Mitsuki headed toward the elevator too.

Back in her familiar top-floor room, which unlike the Hyatt restaurant was not completely shut off from the outside world, Mitsuki could hear the rain lashing the roof and windows. It was indeed "the perfect night." She laid her hat, coat, and gloves on the bed and washed her hands, then went straight to the desk and turned on her laptop. After doing a brief search, she wrote out a few lines on hotel stationery, glancing up at the screen every so often. She used her own fountain pen.

It was still only ten-thirty. Masako would be awake.

On the telephone Mitsuki began by asking if there was a storm there too.

"Storm? It's just raining. What's up?"

She hardly knew how to continue. "I'm sorry to call so late, but I need to ask you a favor about my divorce."

Masako had quarreled bitterly with her ex-husband over distribution of property, custody, and child support. Mediation failing, they had gone to court. She had even developed alopecia areata, patchy baldness, all because her husband, determined to keep up appearances, had been unwilling to grant her a divorce. She'd done so much research that by the time the divorce came through she knew as much about the topic as any specialist. And being Masako, she had kept up with subsequent changes in the law.

Mitsuki explained the woman's proposal for distribution of assets.

"She sounds a bit desperate."

"I think so, too."

"You're super lucky, you know. All that money coming to you without your having to say a word. Going head to head over assets is an ugly business."

"I can imagine," said Mitsuki, and then confessed she was thinking of quitting teaching.

After a pause, Masako said, "Be glad you have the option. At our age, usually there're no jobs to be had. The best most women can hope for is a minimum-wage job at the local supermarket, cleaning fish."

"I know."

"You're such a bourgeoise, you have no idea what a great thing it is to have fixed employment till age sixty-eight." Don't say anything just yet to the college, she advised, and Mitsuki realized this was good advice.

Teaching meant going all the way to the end of the Chuo line, then taking a bus or a taxi, both ways; lecturing till she was hoarse; writing endless exam questions and grading answers. Ever since her health had become shaky, all of this exhausted her more than before. Beyond that, on some level she wanted to quit in sheer defiance. She knew that in order to quit teaching and live on her savings for the next ten years, she would have to double her patent translation work. So be it.

She asked Masako to handle her further dealings with Tetsuo. In the meantime she would make notes regarding distribution of assets, using the woman's calculations, and asked to have Masako's divorce lawyer, a woman, take a look at them. Masako readily agreed to both of these requests.

"Oh, and one more thing." Casually, she broached the main topic. "I just wrote my will."

"You did what?"

Mitsuki explained the fear that had come over her on the drive back through the storm. After checking online, she had verified that if anything happened to her, three-quarters of the inheritance deposited in her bank account would go straight into Tetsuo's pocket. She wanted to prevent that from happening at all costs. Her sister, though she was entitled to the remaining one-quarter, had no need of any more money. Therefore, following a form she'd found online, Mitsuki had written out a will specifying that she wished to bequeath her inheritance to JICA, the Japan International Cooperation Agency. She'd dated it and signed it, naming Masako as executor. Having left her official seal and ink pad home, she was going to set her thumbprint on the document using lipstick, then write "Will" on the envelope and seal it. "I'll put it in the mail tomorrow, so promise me that if anything happens to me, you'll be the executor."

There was silence at the end of the line.

"I know it's going to be a while until the divorce comes through," Mitsuki said. "And I just can't have that money going to him." She had begun to feel as if the inheritance from her mother were her mother's very soul.

Masako remained silent.

A dark shadow loomed in Mitsuki's mind. A thick cord hanging from the ceiling; a body dangling beneath, the neck broken. The professor's wife who hanged herself, the one Masako had told her about in Paris. At the time they both had railed at the faithless professor and pitied the abandoned wife, but found nothing particularly strange in her decision to end her life. With a lack of imagination typical of the young, they had assumed that a woman past middle age whose husband left her would naturally turn suicidal. Was Masako, still silent, also remembering that incident? Mitsuki had not the slightest intention of following that unfortunate woman's example. She wasn't that meek, nor did she have any desire to deal Tetsuo such a blow. But the dark shadow had arisen in her mind, and that was unpleasant.

After her long silence, Masako said with purposeful brevity, "Okay. Sure." Then she added, "Call me in the morning, will you? I want to make sure you're still alive. *D'accord?*"

"Okay. *D'accord.*"

When she got into bed, she felt the stiffness in her back even more than usual. Perhaps her circulation had worsened, for she felt awful, as if she were being dragged down into an abyss. Her health made her highly sensitive to barometric changes. She placed a hand on her belly. Colder than ever, as if immersed in ice water.

In this storm, where could the mother and daughter have wandered off to? Perhaps by now they lay at the bottom of the lake, tangled in seaweed. She imagined the girl's flesh, rosy from the hot spring waters, now chilling quickly in the winter lake and turning grayish white. Unless soon found, her flesh would swell and turn dark purple, then be nibbled by fish and dissolve into lake water until all that remained was white bones. Mitsuki's mother's firstborn daughter had drowned in a lake at age twelve; in what state had she been found? "A stunning little thing": the words still grated. Yet, indeed, Mitsuki's imagination could only conjure a little girl of stunning beauty, her body adrift, intact and serene. The innocence of children was a myth, she believed, yet in that mental picture she saw the undeniable beauty of true innocence.

Then, as if by conditioned response, she saw her mother as she lay dying, her eyes wide open and staring, until the nurse mercifully closed them. No trace of innocence in those eyes. Something as far removed from innocence as possible had emanated like a noxious vapor from the figure lying so flat under the sheets it had seemed scarcely human. Mitsuki had known that her mother would die before the day was over, yet the long, torturous wait had made her death seem an impossible miracle. Those hours had been filled with an air of unreality.

She'd felt the same way a dozen years before, when she'd sat alone at her father's deathbed. Then too she had waited so long that when death came, it had scarcely seemed real. Still filled with a sense of unreality, she had arranged an informal memorial service at her apartment. On the cabinet housing the television she had spread a large piece of white silk shot through with gold thread—fabric purchased in India on a short trip with Tetsuo—to make something like an altar. She had set out her father's photograph and the urn containing his ashes, flanked by candles. Then she had laid out white lilies in baskets of all sizes, some on the floor and some around the photograph. The white flowers, blooming against a background of deep green leaves, were like a requiem for her father. On the night before the service, Natsuki came over to help, and long after she went home Mitsuki had continued arranging the blooms. In time the reality of her father's death began to sink in a little. His sadness was gone from this earth, and surely someday her sadness too would ease. As she gathered up green leaves fallen on the floor, she'd prayed that the day would come soon.

Her mother hadn't gone to the hospital while he lay dying, nor had she attended his cremation, but she insisted on coming to the memorial service.

"What? You're coming, Mother?"

"Of course I am."

Her mother's stern expression and voice had brooked no argument. After all, Mitsuki thought, That Man was now out of her mother's life. Why have words with her?

The night of the memorial service, dressed in black, the ever-present cane at her side, her mother had sat in the central armchair quite as if she were the chief mourner, and graciously chatted with guests. Some of them must have known about her years-long entanglement with That Man, but if so they didn't let on. As Mitsuki served food and drinks, all she could hear was her mother's voice, then still clear and ringing. Her laughter had been especially jarring. How many more years would her mother be alive, she'd wondered then.

The noxious vapors that filled the room emanated from her mother's laughter, but the white lilies had been pristine and pure, like the lotuses of nirvana.

## 61

## LIGHTS AT THE BOTTOM OF THE SEA

Her nerves were in a state of peculiar excitement. Undoubtedly the other long-term guests were awake in their rooms, their nerves on edge as well. Kaoru would be continuing to reproach herself for ever having mentioned the psychic to that mother and daughter. Would the others also be thinking of the two women who had vanished into the storm, or would they, like Mitsuki, have been prompted to examine their own lives?

"Today, Mother died." The desire to be able to say those words for real had been part of her ever since that horrible telephone call: as her father lay in the hospital with pneumonia, her mother had blithely suggested using his life insurance money for a trip—a mother-daughter trip, of all things—to Paris. But later on after he died, as she saw to her mother's needs day by day and month by month, that fierce desire had often receded into the background—especially on days when Mitsuki was reminded that Noriko Katsura was just another old woman living alone and trying to get by.

Some days her mother would deny herself delicacies to economize. "Tonight I was a good girl; instead of flounder sashimi I had instant noodles from Seven-Eleven." When Mitsuki heard such tales her heart softened, and she was able to say gently, "You should eat what you want, Mother." At other times her mother might gaily announce during their nightly telephone conversation, "I felt good today, so I bought myself some flowers! Gerbera, a kind of daisy." Mitsuki would automatically think, *Another waste of money* — yet she was glad her mother treated herself to such small pleasures now and then. Sometimes her mother would call in the middle of the day, distraught because a man at the grocery store had been rude: "Hold your horses, Grandma." Mitsuki would feel an urge to rush over and console her, knowing how wounded her pride must be.

When she did drop in unexpectedly, her mother's wrinkled face would light up. *Natsuki and I are all she's got:* the realization always made her sad. The calendar by her mother's desk was often marked with their names: "Mitsuki," sometimes "Mitsuki, Natsuki," less often just "Natsuki." She penciled in their names not only when she knew they were coming but also on days when one or the other of them stopped by unexpectedly. Every time Mitsuki saw her name written in her mother's round hand, she would feel a pang of guilt for not coming more often.

Yet the sight of her mother being tortured even in old age by desperate desires — never giving up, watching like a hawk for any chance to feel fully alive — she found horrifying. Old age was cruel: no matter how one might wish for the mind to soar and the blood to rush, the chalice that held water from the fountain of life grew shallower year by year. Her mother's unending quest to be moved by something gave her the semblance of a lost soul condemned to eternal hunger and thirst. Or she was like someone no longer capable of sexual profligacy who sought it all the more fervently, chasing the thrill of a momentary pleasure. When Mitsuki saw this side of her mother, her blood froze.

The guilt she continued to feel over her father worked on her in ways she little understood, so that even as she wished for her mother's death she felt perversely compelled to keep her mother's old age from being bleak like his. But as satisfying her mother grew more and more difficult, her death wish for her grew stronger in a compartment of her mind separate from resentment over the past. To free her mother from frustration that could only continue to mount, and to free herself as well, she longed for her to die.

But...Mitsuki lay in bed, feeling the raging mountain storm with every fiber of her body, and stared up at the ceiling. But what if her mother hadn't been that tortured person?

Blessed is the daughter who, when her mother grows old and becomes a burden, doesn't wish for her death. Surely most daughters, no matter how admirable their mother might be, have moments when they wish she were gone. The older one's mother got to be, the more frequently such moments must occur. And Japanese women lived longer every year, lingering like specters. Little wonder if more women started wishing for the death of their mother and not just their mother-in-law, whose care in old age fell disproportionately on the wife. Mitsuki pictured women in cities and rural areas across Japan, their faces shadowed with fatigue, longing in secret for their mother's death. Such women wanted freedom not just from their mother but also from the trauma of seeing the cruelty of old age up close — the trauma of having one's own future self thrust under one's nose.

To the young, old age was a mere abstraction, but anyone caring for an aging parent could plainly see that growing old was an assault not just on body and mind but on all five senses. Was that all that awaited one at life's end?

The sound of rain beating on the roof continued.

Out of nowhere, scenes from the past arose in her mind. In her present state she could not, like Mr. Matsubara's Wakako, tick off on her fingers the times she had been happy. Memories wrapped in shining light — she had enough of those to fill several notebooks, and yet on this stormy night the scenes from the past that came to her were uniformly bleak. The shaking of the subway train she took to the hospital after the emergency call from her father's colleague. Her father sitting on the bed in the eight-man ward, bored, time on his hands. KATSURA written large on the breast pocket of his pajama top. The jarring sound of her mother's laughter at his memorial service. Her mother crying like a little child after announcing her intention to live in a nursing home. Her mother's back, further stooped from sadness and frustration she no longer even understood. Her open eyes on her deathbed. Then Mitsuki saw Tetsuo walking away from her in the ocean breeze on the pier in Calais, his figure growing smaller and smaller as she sang on alone. His heavy breathing as he lay beside her asleep in bed on the night after she received the "rather nice offer" to translate *Madame Bovary*. His telephone call with the first woman. His emails with the current woman. Numbers lined up in a row...

She crawled out of bed, threw her coat over her shoulders, and went to stand by the window.

She opened the window and heavy rain came at her. Raindrops were falling with great vigor, reflecting the light in the room, and when she stuck her head out they battered her on the forehead, the eyes, the cheeks. She forced her eyes open. Her gaze was drawn to faint glimmers below, scattered in the darkness. They came from lamps illuminating the garden, but they looked like something glowing at the bottom of the sea. Glowing and calling to her. Last night she had reached out to the stars, but tonight she was transfixed by the glimmering lights below. As she leaned out in fascination, the rain implacably soaked her hair, her neck, her coat. The farther out she leaned, the more she felt swallowed in a world of water, as if she also, like the mother and daughter, lay adrift at the bottom of the lake.

How much time might have passed, she had no idea.

Inside the room the telephone was ringing. The same sound had drawn her from the window the previous night also. Remembering, she checked her watch: midnight. Who could it be, Masako again? The sound seemed to summon her back from the bottom of the lake.

"Did I wake you?" Natsuki's voice.

"No, I was up."

"I couldn't sleep. Something's been bothering me."

"What?"

"You."

"You don't need to worry about me."

Natsuki was not a strong person, but she had Yuji as well as her children, Jun and Ken, to support her. Even if she, Mitsuki, disappeared from this earth, Natsuki would be all right. Realizing what she was thinking, Mitsuki felt a slight shock. Her face, her hair, and her coat were dripping wet. She told her sister to hold on while she finished washing up, and fetched a towel from the bathroom.

When she picked up the phone, Natsuki went on. "I was thinking. Wondering what sort of life you're going to lead now."

Mitsuki couldn't reply.

"Will you get to keep the Suginami condo?"

"Probably we'll sell it, but Tetsuo's going to give me half the money we make. There'll be other money too."

"How much?"

"Let's see . . . all in all, just under thirty million yen. Twenty-nine million, to be exact. Although it's hard to say for sure until we sell the condo and see how much that brings in."

Having just been wandering in a watery underworld, she had trouble grasping the number's reality. It might just as well be 290 million or 2.9 million. What difference did it make?

"He'll give you that much?"

"Probably. He hasn't got much choice. She's dying to get him to divorce me. I'll get a share of his pension too."

"Oh really? You can get that too?" Natsuki sounded surprised. A pause, then: "But will that plus your inheritance be enough to live on?"

Mopping her face and hair with the towel, Mitsuki summoned up the half-forgotten calculations with effort and gave a brief explanation. With half her inheritance she would buy a small condominium. With the money from Tetsuo she would buy an annuity with a future value of 10 million yen. That gave her 18 million yen left over from her mother's money and 19 million left from Tetsuo's money, for a total of 37 million. Yes, that was the figure. Whether everything would go according to plan she had no idea, but at a hundred thousand yen a month, she would use up 1.2 million yen a year. Twelve million in ten years. She'd be set for the next thirty years.

"One hundred thousand yen a month? That's how much we spend on parking and utilities! That'd never be enough for you to live on, no matter how you cut corners."

"Well, sooner or later those annuities will start to kick in. Until then I'll do more patent translations to make up for the teaching income. Actually I'm thinking of keeping up my patent translations even after that. What other work pays so well for a woman my age?"

"But you don't enjoy it."

"Work is work."

Her sister wasn't listening. "Anyway, you can't buy a decent place with half of the money from Mother. You'd be farther from us, too."

This was true. Nothing in the vicinity of Kamiyama-cho would be in her price range.

"I'll look for someplace old and small."

"You're going to move into some dump and take on extra work you don't even like? With your health the way it is?" The next moment, she cried out: "That's really pitiful!" Her voice caught. She sobbed as she repeated the word, "Pitiful! Pitiful! Pitiful! After all this time, to move into some old, cramped, run-down place and make yourself go on doing work you hate — how will you stand it? You're not young!"

Mitsuki was knocked momentarily speechless by the vehemence of her sister's reaction — vehemence of an entirely different order from the other day when she'd called after quarreling with Jun. It was as if she'd returned to childhood, with a child's divine right to dominate her surroundings.

Her sister was coming at her with all the things she had tried to avoid thinking about. She forced her foggy mind into gear and attempted to make a commonsense rebuttal. It was as if she were trying to convince herself.

"Listen, I'm unbelievably lucky for someone my age who's about to get divorced. Besides all this money I'll have coming in, I can earn my way too. All I have to do is be frugal and try not to pamper myself too much."

Natsuki protested. "That's not how Mother raised us, and you know it. She spoiled us and taught us to live and enjoy life, not pinch pennies. She said she didn't want to live like some goody-goody in a three-hanky Japanese movie. I always thought that was one thing she got right."

# 62

## CROSSING THE RUBICON

Mitsuki's head was still groggy.

Her mind, adrift at the bottom of a lake before her sister called, had trouble returning to the dry, material world. Thinking of a new life had always seemed to deepen her despondency. Perhaps an inability to imagine a satisfactory life for herself on her own was what had held her back, was what had made living seem more trouble than it was worth.

She let a few moments pass and started slowly, to gain time: "Well, depending on how you look at it, my life as a divorced woman won't be so bad—it's a life of luxury in its own way."

"What kind of luxury could there possibly be!"

What kind, indeed. The windows in a shoebox apartment in some low-cost building would look out on an ugly scene devoid of anything green. Mitsuki banished the vision from her mind. The luxuries their mother had provided them as children depended largely on their father's income, she thought. But instead she said, "Luxury depends on your state of mind, doesn't it? And what you do with what you have? I already own lots of pretty things."

Choosing her words, she began to paint a picture of her coming life—a castle in the air. If she hunted for an old one-bedroom place, she might well find a bargain somewhere not too far from her sister. She would surround herself there with the luxury of beauty. The entryway she could decorate with the dark-red faceted glass vase from Grandpa Yokohama (which she had wangled for her own when they divided their mother's belongings), and that would lend a Meiji-era ambience. In a cozy living-dining room she could put up a little display shelf like the one she'd had installed in her mother's room at Golden and set out only the choicest of items: things she had bought on her travels, the Turkish pot with silverwork or the box from Toledo with ivory inlays or the Korean folk dish; family treasures like the tiny antique sake cups and the heirloom incense burner. She would buy a little cabinet to hold her share of their mother's fine china and get rid of her ordinary dishes once and for all. Including items from their mother—all silk, linen, or cashmere—she now had enough coats, scarves, and garments to last a lifetime.

And cloths of every description. She had already collected all kinds on her travels, but now that she was free of her mother, would be free of Tetsuo, she could travel as she pleased; as soon as her health recovered she could take advantage of today's low airfares to visit far-flung places—Bhutan, say—to hunt for more choice fabrics to decorate her room.

She would be like Sara, the heroine of *A Little Princess*. After Sara becomes orphaned and is banished to the attic of her boarding school, while she is sleeping one night a gentleman across the street has the kindness to have the drab walls and ceiling hung with gorgeous cloths; Sara awakes to find herself in a chamber fit for a princess. Mitsuki had reread the book tirelessly just for the pleasure of coming to that scene. Now she could live it.

She would have different drapes for summer and winter. Her lace curtains would be French organdy, delicate as gossamer and thin as a butterfly's wing. French curtains were gauzier than those made in Japan, and they came in subtle shades of color; that was one extravagance she would definitely allow herself. She loved the way they stirred in the wind, revealing the shape of each passing breeze. On the wall she would hang an Indian sari shot through with gold thread and sewn with tiny glass bits that reflected the light like spangles. On the floor she'd lay a woven ikat carpet from Indonesia. The bed she would cover with a wondrous cloth brought back from some remote, mystical region of Bhutan and scatter on it Ming-style embroidered cushions. And her Japanese heritage she would showcase with antique kimono textiles: *jofu, chijimi, habutae, tsumugi, rinzu, sha, ro.* Plain-woven or crinkled hemp cloth, heavy silk, silk pongee, silk crepe, silk gauze. And the Okinawan textile woven from fibers of a banana tree: *bashofu.* The lovely words themselves were richly redolent of times past.

A feast of fabrics from around the world, their textures as diverse as the world's many cultures. She would create a rich harmony through the careful matching of colors and relish the challenge.

As Mitsuki went on talking, a small flame was lit in her heart and gradually grew stronger. On the other end of the line Natsuki, she could tell, was rapt, listening with bated breath, eyes shining like a little girl's. With such an audience, she was further stirred by her own words.

"And from now on, where I live will truly be my own space."

Bulky men's clothing (so symbolic of unwieldy men themselves) would vanish from the bedroom closet, men's big shoes and heavy coats from the entryway. No more men's long umbrellas. No more books that didn't belong to her. Bookshelves with nothing but her books, top to bottom! A *Little Princess* and other beloved books long packed away in cardboard boxes could now be laid out boldly, side by side with the rest. And she would be free of shopping and cooking for two; of vacuuming except when she felt like it; of washing, drying, and folding funny-shaped men's underpants. She'd relax as she pleased in a room all her own filled with all her own things.

Next to the window she would put a dainty table and a chair so delicate it might break if Tetsuo sat in it. In the evening she would sit there sipping fragrant lemon verbena tea from a pure, clear glass teacup and watch in meditative tranquillity as the sun's rays slanted slowly to the west, weaving between diaphanous purple clouds before silently disappearing.

"Now I ask you, what could be more luxurious!"

Natsuki ended the conversation by saying dreamily, "You know, you're right, that might be just about the most luxurious life imaginable."

After she hung up, Mitsuki continued for a while to live the dream she had painted in words. In her imagination, the tiny one-bedroom condominium where she would live expanded until it was a palace of cloths, big enough to hold an elephant or two. And the more her vision expanded, the more intoxicating it became. The presence of a man was not all that would disappear. What would also disappear was his spirit—a spirit that had been confining. Her spirit, boxed up ever since the episode at the harbor in Calais, would at last be free to soar.

She would rid herself of all the junk she had accumulated over the years. As if cleansing her spirit of layers of grime, she would strip her life of everything extraneous and so find out what mattered to her. She would free herself from her own past self.

The raging rainstorm forgotten, her mind feverish, Mitsuki started up her laptop and opened Tetsuo's email account. Determination to make the most of her remaining time—she didn't quite have the courage to call it her future—spread through her, putting out roots. Automatically, without thought, she began forwarding Tetsuo's and the woman's emails to herself, one by one.

Click. Click. Click.

Was this what was meant by "crossing the Rubicon"? There was no going back. The moment he opened his email—whenever that might be—he would see that his entire correspondence with the woman had been forwarded to Mitsuki. He would know that she had broken into his email account, read everything, and more—she had secured it as evidence.

As she went on clicking, Mitsuki felt an increasing sense of guilt. Tetsuo didn't think highly of his own character—in fact took a sardonic view of himself—and had always thought she was made of finer stuff than him. This humility touched her; it was an inner treasure he was unaware he had. Suddenly she felt close to him in a way she hadn't done in years. He surely never dreamed that she would stoop to this. The screen blurred; to her surprise, she was moist-eyed. When the task finally was complete, she murmured an apology, her eyes shut as if in prayer.

After a moment she came to herself. Looking again at the screen, she was struck by the ingenuity of what she had just done. It was also a bit devious. A sign, perhaps, that she was her mother's daughter after all. She gave a brief, rueful smile before starting a message to Tetsuo. "Dear Tetsuo," she wrote, and changed to the familiar form of his name: "Dear Tetchan." She wanted her farewell to be gentle. The message was so simple, it almost wrote itself.

I read your emails and then forwarded them to myself to keep as evidence. I'm sorry. So much of our marriage was pleasant. You never said a word of complaint all the time I was chasing around taking care of my parents, for which I can't thank you enough. I am truly grateful.

On November 23 my mother passed away from aspiration pneumonia. Fortunately she left enough that I'll be able to get along with the proposed distribution of assets (see the file attached to an email of September 9 last year). I'll go visit your parents in Toride, and your brother and his wife, to say goodbye. Seeing you again might only weaken my resolve, and there is no real reason for us to communicate directly anymore, so from now on please write to Masako Aoki. Her email address is below. I'll have her lawyer draw up the necessary papers and send them to you. You have nothing to apologize for. I now feel I've wronged you in many ways. I'm sorry. I hope you'll be truly happy in your new life. We may meet again someday. Until then, stay well. Goodbye.

She reread what she'd written three times and decided there was no need to sleep on it. She typed in Tetsuo's email address and added the woman's address in the cc field.

What if she sent the email only to Tetsuo? If he'd been hesitating because he felt sorry for her, her words would come as a relief. He would realize he had escaped the most painful of hurdles. But if his hesitation was due to the lure of her mother's money, what then? He might come flying back and, not realizing he was wasting his time, throw himself at her feet, clasp her by the legs, and press his face to her, weeping, as he apologized a hundred times over. For his sake and for her own as well, she had no desire to know that he was or could be capable of such groveling. If the email went also to the woman, then Tetsuo would be locked into his relationship with her. Though she might be looking out for herself in part, she seemed to sincerely love Tetsuo and look up to him. He belonged with her, not with Mitsuki. Sending the email to both of them at once would remove any possibility that he might make the wrong choice. What would he read into her doing so? Would he see it only as meanness on her part? Or would he see her true intent? She hoped the latter.

She tapped the Send button, her heart beating faster. When he might read the email she didn't know, but whether it was tomorrow or a week from now, or even later, didn't matter.

She opened Google Earth. The sight of the blue globe spinning in the center of the screen, coming closer and closer, never failed to give her a slight thrill. She zoomed in to Eurasia, then to the peninsula on the right, then to long, thin Vietnam, then Ho Chi Minh City. Somewhere in this city, Tetsuo and his woman would read the email she had just sent.

$$\left(63\right)$$

## THE NEXT MORNING

"You still alive? You were supposed to call me!"

The next day, when she was awakened by Masako's phone call, morning dazzle was pouring through the window. It was already past ten o'clock.

"I'm alive," Mitsuki said. "I was sleeping."

"Okay. As long as you're alive. Talk to you later."

A strange conversation. Thinking how like Masako it was, Mitsuki went over to the window and threw open the curtains. A wintry sky of the utmost brilliance spread before her. Last night's storm seemed a dream. But in the garden below, one of the tall cedars in the distance was broken in two, she saw, and a phalanx of gardeners—including "garden conductors," no doubt—was scurrying around assessing damage.

Last night, her eighth night here, she had slept well for the first time. Wondering what had become of the missing mother and daughter, she brushed her teeth, put on a hairband, and was washing her face when a knock came at the door.

"It's me," said Kaoru's voice.

Mitsuki hastily patted her face dry and opened the door, and there stood Kaoru, fully dressed with her makeup on and a long scarf around her neck. A trace of the night's exhaustion lingered around her eyes, but her expression was cheerful. After breakfast, everyone had gathered in the lounge and more or less waited for Mitsuki to appear; when she didn't come down by ten, Mr. Matsubara had suggested that Kaoru go up to check on her.

"He was worried and thought I should peek in on you."

Mitsuki explained a bit awkwardly that after staying up late she'd taken a sleeping pill and had only just now gotten up. "So, did they find the missing people?"

"My dear," said Kaoru, "*Takeru* found them." She looked abashed yet unmistakably proud. The rest of the story came pouring out.

Last night, after she stepped out of the elevator on their floor, Takeru had told her he was going down again to join the search.

The hotel staff was out scouring the vicinity of the lake by car and on foot. When he heard this, instead of joining them Takeru drove directly up the winding road to Hakone Shrine. In less than five minutes, he was out of the car; he headed through the tunnel of red torii gates and, with the aid of a flashlight, soon found the two women huddled under the eaves of a shrine building, soaking wet. The daughter was even more dazed than usual, the mother nearly frantic. He reasoned with her, calmed her down, and got them both safely into the car, then called the hotel on his cell phone just as the manager was on the point of contacting the police.

The manager would have preferred that he bring them straight back, but since they'd been out in the rain for hours, Takeru convinced him it was better to err on the side of safety and took them to the closest emergency room. The hospital decided to keep them overnight for observation, not only because they were both chilled through but also because the daughter was clearly on a drug of some kind. The manager and assistant manager, who had rushed over to escort them back, accepted this decision and returned without them.

Was it divine guidance that made her come back last night instead of staying in the Hyatt with Takeru? This thought went through Mitsuki's mind as she listened to the story, and then two figures appeared at the far end of the corridor—Mr. Matsubara and Takeru. When Kaoru failed to return, they must have grown impatient and decided to investigate. Observing that Mitsuki was still in pajamas, they halted a discreet distance from her door. She asked what everyone's plans were. The elderly couple would be staying till the day after tomorrow, it seemed, but everyone else was leaving the next day. The four of them agreed to have dinner together that night and parted ways.

Mitsuki spent the day reading *Madame Bovary* and dozed in the afternoon. After she woke up, it occurred to her that she had gone an entire year without napping. She hadn't had the time, for one thing, but her nerves would never have allowed it either. Her nap that day was sheer nectar.

That evening, the hotel furnished them with a semiprivate room in the French restaurant. In gratitude for Takeru's heroism, the hotel was picking up the tab. Kaoru and Takeru were already seated when Mr. Matsubara and Mitsuki arrived.

Seeing them, Kaoru said with unconcealed merriment, "So again today Takeru has shown he has his uses after all!" The girl's mother, she went on more seriously, had apparently been deeply touched by Takeru's kindness and overcome with relief. "This morning a nurse telephoned the hotel asking to have *him* come pick them up if he could, and of course he did." The mother then begged him to wait in their room until her brother and his wife came for them in the late afternoon.

Takeru, looking slightly embarrassed, took over. "She and her daughter are a pitiful pair."

While they waited, the daughter had slept, and the mother had talked ceaselessly in a low voice. She said that years ago her husband had died in a car crash, ramming his car into a guardrail. Her daughter, their only child, was in junior high school at the time. Her parents took them in. They weren't rich by any means, but her father's pension stretched far enough. In a few years the daughter started college. Then just after her twentieth birthday, she began behaving strangely. She was diagnosed with a difficult-to-treat brain disorder whose name Takeru hadn't been told — something perhaps inherited from the father. She dropped out of college and went on medication. Then her grandfather died, leaving the three of them dependent on a meager survivors' pension. On top of that, the grandmother's Alzheimer's began to take its toll. The strain of caregiving combined with financial worries brought the mother to the verge of a nervous breakdown. She could hardly eat or sleep. The grandmother had a care manager who offered to arrange a two-week stay in a nursing home for her so the mother could get some rest. While filling out forms, the mother had decided she simply couldn't go on. She would take one last trip with her daughter and then end both their lives. Her mother's future care she could entrust to her brother and his wife.

She'd chosen Hôtel du Lac because it was where she'd spent her honeymoon. Since coming, she'd seen her daughter innocently enjoying herself despite the haze induced by the medication and so had been wavering; but hearing the psychic's prediction had strengthened her resolve to go ahead with her plan. Her determination had peaked last night amid the storm.

As suspected, she had intended for them to drown in the lake.

"But if you think about it," said Takeru, "there's something about Lake Ashinoko that doesn't let you in."

"Yes," said Mitsuki. "All those thickets in the way, for one thing."

"Very true." Mr. Matsubara chimed in so readily that she suspected he, like her, may have looked on Lake Ashinoko with melancholic eyes more than once.

Takeru continued, looking as if he could see the surface of the lake. "The one place that looks like a jump-off spot is through that big red torii by Hakone Shrine." The only place with a pier. "But even there, out on the end of the pier, it's somehow not inviting."

The pier was too low, the waves too close. Popular suicide spots must have some sort of geographical formation that lures people to their deaths. Just standing in such a spot makes people feel an invitation to be freed from everything now, this very second . . .

As he started up his engine to go look for them, Takeru had imagined the mother standing on the end of the pier with her daughter and then suddenly getting the urge to flee. If they had headed back to the road, he figured they would have seen the steep stone steps leading to the shrine precincts and might have climbed them, and so he drove to the shrine. He shone his flashlight where there were no electric lanterns and soon found the shivering pair.

"I simply cannot believe that Takeru saved those two women," said Kaoru seriously.

Takeru turned to her with a sardonic twist of his mouth. "I didn't save them from their unhappiness."

Kaoru thought for a second. "But you saved me."

As if to keep the conversation from becoming overly sentimental, Mr. Matsubara said in a humorous tone, "He saved this hotel, too!" Everyone laughed. "Anyway," he went on, "when people reach the point of exhaustion there's no telling what they'll do."

"Very true," Mitsuki agreed, her long silver earrings swaying as she nodded.

Today she was wearing a long scarf, like Kaoru. It was her favorite, black silk finely streaked with silver. When she peered into the mirror to put on her makeup and applied silver earrings as a finishing touch, she had felt festive for the first time in quite a while. Giving herself a final check, she had thought, *Not half bad*—again for the first time in quite a while.

Just then the elderly couple came up to them. "We heard you all were leaving tomorrow, and we just wanted to say thank you and goodbye." They bowed deeply. Everyone but Kaoru laid down their napkin and scrambled to their feet, upon which the couple bowed again. The husband made a separate bow to Mr. Matsubara. "Thank you very much," he said, patting his breast pocket. "I'll be sure to give this person a call."

"By all means do," responded Mr. Matsubara warmly.

Everyone looked inquiringly at him, but he said no more. After the couple left, bowing till the very end, and they were seated again, all eyes turned to Mr. Matsubara. He looked embarrassed.

"Out with it!" Kaoru commanded.

"I just gave him a little advice, that's all."

That afternoon, he had spotted the elderly couple having sandwiches in the lounge, and since they were already on nodding terms he had gone over and introduced himself, then joined them. He'd urged them not to take sole responsibility for the debt and given them the name of a friend of his who was a lawyer. If usury was involved, they had legal recourse. Anyway, there were a number of other siblings and besides, the youngest brother had grown children, although he hadn't heard from them since the divorce. The remaining debt was actually not that huge; considering all the eldest brother had done for them, the others ought to chip in, and the estranged children could be prevailed upon too. If the family tackled the debt together, it could be repaid.

"Fortunately he agreed," concluded Mr. Matsubara.

"You did a wonderful thing," Mitsuki was the first to say. The words came from her heart. Mr. Matsubara had surely lived his life offering help to needy people he met in passing. Wakako must have been proud.

"*Bravo! Vous avez bien fait!*" Kaoru raised a glass of red wine to Mr. Matsubara, and everyone followed suit. What thoughts flitted through each one's mind? The toast offered in the hotel in the mountains of Hakone as the night deepened was aimed equally at all four of them.

# (64)

## BACK FROM THE REALM OF CLOUDS

The next morning, the four were gathered at the front desk at checkout time. As Mitsuki was arranging for her suitcase to be sent to her apartment, Kaoru's voice rang out brightly.

"We're Japanese, after all, so let's exchange business cards."

Why would Kaoru have a business card? Mitsuki wondered, but it turned out she meant everyone should exchange cards with Takeru. Mitsuki seldom used her cards, but she took out a worn old one from the back of her wallet. Her address and phone number for both work and home were on it, but not her email address. The contact information would soon be useless, but she handed it over without comment. Takeru's card, which he had apparently printed up himself, listed his occupation as "unemployed." Seeing her laugh, he laughed too, his handsome features lighting up.

Takeru and Kaoru waved from their car, taking it for granted that Mr. Matsubara would drive Mitsuki to the station. As soon as they were out of sight, he turned to her and suggested an early lunch. She agreed, and they set off for the café in the annex, which looked out on the lake. The rush of pleasure she felt embarrassed her, though she walked along with outward composure.

The menu at the lakeside café was very limited, and she had been there only once before. As she took a seat by the window, Mitsuki reflected that this was the first time she had ever sat and looked at Mr. Matsubara straight on, and also this would be his first straight look at her. When had she started to avoid sitting where the sun could strike her in the face? As luck would have it, that day she was in a seat lit all too well by the slow winter sun. Had Wakako been younger than her? The same age? Hoping that Wakako had been her elder even if only by a year, Mitsuki studied the menu.

Their conversation was desultory. It was hard to have a more involved conversation when she didn't know if she would ever see him again. The question of whether meeting again would even be appropriate—a question he might be asking himself too—inevitably cast its shadow. Even so, his calm enveloped her, and the time they spent facing each other was as warm as if she were basking in a patch of spring sun. She told him how struck she'd been by the nearness of stars in the night sky here; he told her in turn about the nearness of the sun he'd watched sink below the horizon of the flat Egyptian desert. When the bill came, he stopped her from reaching for her wallet and took out his credit card as a matter of course.

Before they stood up, Mitsuki mentioned casually, "By the way, I haven't gone through the legal formalities yet, but I did send my husband a letter of divorce."

"Good for you." He smiled and held out his card. "If I can ever be of help, call me."

Mitsuki took the small white card in both hands and then gave him a name card of her own in return. Writing her email address on it might seem a bit forward, so she refrained, which meant her card would soon be useless. But she could still contact him. The small white card in her fingers, though light, felt heavy.

The start of her solitary life.

She declined the offer of a ride to the station; she felt like walking to the bus stop and taking the bus instead. She had often studied the tourist map provided by the hotel and knew that if she kept going on the stone path around the lake she would come to the bus stop at Moto-Hakone Port. The hotel shuttle bus hadn't taken long to cover the distance, so it couldn't be far. Soon after passing the giant red concrete torii on her right, reflected in the lake, she came to a hut selling fishing tackle, followed by shops selling marquetry boxes, steamed buns, and other souvenirs. Few people were around, but she saw more and more signs of life. Places to eat offered soba noodles, ramen, sweets. Signs advertised SASHIMI RICE BOWL and other local treats at bargain prices. She felt as if she were gradually descending from the realm of clouds back to the earth.

Eventually she was well and truly back on earth. Ten days before, when the shuttle bus had come to pick her up, the pirate ship landing area had been shrouded in darkness and mist, as eerie as the dock for a ghost ship, but now in the light of day a number of shiny tourist buses were parked nearby, and the area was bustling in a perfectly ordinary way. The convenience store across the street was doing a thriving business. The fantastic night scene of ten days ago had vanished. Thrust back into the everyday, Mitsuki looked at the shining tourist buses and the noisy throng, feeling as if she had awakened from a long dream.

According to the timetable, the last bus heading to the station had just left. Resisting the impulse to get in one of the waiting taxis, she only gave them a sidelong glance and wandered aimlessly until it occurred to her to take a walk on the old highway. No one was waiting for her at home anyway. The Old Tokaido highway, planted on both sides with cedar trees four hundred years ago, ran through

Hakone, and she knew that a bit of it had been preserved as a historic site. She spread out her map and found that the starting point was close by.

Five minutes later she was standing on a peaceful road lined with giant cedars that cut off the rays of the winter sun. The trees towering on left and right were far taller and larger in circumference than she could have imagined. The trees and the deep-green moss covering their trunks brought home to her the passage of four centuries.

She felt in the surrounding air the loneliness of the old highway that had suddenly fallen into disuse after steam locomotives came along. In the old days, how many men and women of all ages must have walked here? As she in her turn walked along the old highway, the warmth of the afternoon sun and the wintry chill of the air balanced each other so well that she wished she could follow the road wherever it might lead. If she could only do that, she felt as if she would enter a time without past, present, or future, a time when she herself would disappear. All too soon the cedar-lined stretch came to an end and turned into an ordinary road. Mitsuki had no choice but to return to the present, go back, and face her life.

On the way, she saw a woman coming toward her with her arms bent at a ninety-degree angle, swinging them front and back as she approached at a good clip. She was about Mitsuki's own age—someone else who wouldn't make a good heroine in a novel. She was wearing a beat-up sweat suit and dingy sneakers. Her expression was resolute and unflinching. Undoubtedly she lived in the neighborhood and was doing her daily routine of walking for exercise. Somehow it seemed to Mitsuki that this woman was building up her strength not to care for an elderly person but rather to live out whatever time she had left. With that solitary figure, at once admirable and pathetic, imprinted on her mind, Mitsuki took the bus, the Romance Car, and the subway back to her place in Suginami Ward.

The day after she returned, she began hunting for a condominium.

She spent the next five days tramping all over the city. In the morning she would search the Internet, and in the afternoon she would visit real estate offices and be shown inexpensive properties by unenthusiastic realtors. She quickly gave up on the idea of living near her sister and started looking instead into more familiar areas: first Suginami and Setagaya wards, then gradually farther west. She began with an upper limit of 15 million yen, intending to save as much as she could, but along the way she raised it to 18 million, a little more than half of her inheritance. If the place was new and in a good location, that much would buy her a single room with a dinky kitchen and bath and a token entryway. If it was old and inconveniently located, she could have much more space. She was willing to live in an old building, but she did want a certain amount of convenience without sacrificing too much space. She found some places that were not bad deals, objectively speaking, but somehow couldn't bring herself to see them as her final abode in this life.

Perhaps the green foliage of Silkworm Forest Park near her home had spoiled her. On the way from the station to a prospective apartment, the ugliness of the road often set her face like stone. When the agent pointed out the building from a distance, her jaw clenched even more. By the time they entered the building, climbed the common stairs, and reached the common corridor, she would have lost her sense of who she was and feel as if she were living the life of a stranger. The feeling would intensify when she stepped inside the apartment, which almost always had yellowish flooring, wallpaper whose resinous surface rejected the touch of her fingertips, white fluorescent ceiling lights, and kitchen and bathroom fixtures in strangely garish colors. A small space pitilessly encapsulating Japan's 150 years of hideous modernization. If she spent a little more money, renovation was possible, and, as she had described rapturously to Natsuki over the telephone, fabrics could be transformative. But she couldn't seem to work up enough enthusiasm to plan how she might make any of the places livable. Besides, once her bookshelves, china cupboard, and desk were installed, how much room would really be left for pretty fabrics? "Pitiful!" Her sister's shriek echoed in her ears.

Worst of all, the view from the window—facing close-by concrete walls, windows, a parking lot—invariably made her want to cover her eyes. She would have to give up on organdy lace curtains and hang heavy lace ones instead. There was no other choice.

On the night of the fifth day, she flung herself down on her sofa, exhausted, and realized that all her efforts had served only to reinforce three points that had been self-evident from the start. First, she'd lived a privileged life until now. Second, she was no longer young. And third, she wasn't yet old, either.

She thought of "Happy Grampy," who came back to his wooden apartment every night with a plastic basin tucked under one arm. She had no way of knowing what sort of life he may have led in younger days, but now if he were given the chance to live in a one-room condominium with kitchen-dining area in a reinforced concrete building, he might well jump for joy. Mitsuki, however, couldn't escape a sense of having come down in the world. If she were only younger, then wherever she might live there would always be the blessing of hope, but her youth was gone. And yet she had altogether too many more years to live. The pretty things that she wanted to keep at hand, filled with memories, would have to fight for space with bulky appliances and other necessities.

She decided to see what she might be able to discard and forced her weary self to her feet. Inside the library that doubled as storage space, her eye fell on her mother's paulownia chest in the back of the room. She'd completely forgotten about it. Going closer, she pulled on the flat handles of a drawer, and the faint scent of aloeswood rose from the *Golden Demon* kimono that she'd brought home and put here. The chest was nice, but it would take up space in her new apartment. Should she persuade Natsuki to take it, although her sister had never shown much interest in kimono? That way Natsuki could have the original pair. Or should she keep it herself, abandoning the idea of buying a cupboard to hold her mother's china? She was unable to decide. One thing she couldn't do without was bookshelves. As she stood enveloped in the aroma of aloeswood, wondering what to do, the thought came to her that this was December 28—the very day when, one year ago, she'd found the tissue case like a little flower garden in Tetsuo's desk drawer. It was also the day of her mother's final fall and fractures.

The day after tomorrow, she was going to meet Natsuki in Ginza. She went over to the telephone and called her.

# 65

## A *MAKIOKA SISTERS* DAY IN GINZA

"The day after tomorrow, what do you say we make it a *Makioka Sisters* day?"

Natsuki's surprised voice sounded at the other end of the line. "You mean it?"

"Absolutely."

"A *Makioka Sisters* day" was a family expression. Based on the Tanizaki novel about the eponymous four sisters, it meant that Mitsuki, Natsuki, and their mother would go on an outing dressed up in elegant kimono. After their mother became involved with That Man they hadn't felt like having a *Makioka Sisters* day, and once he was out of the picture and their father had died, their mother's back grew so pitifully bent that it was out of the question. Now when Mitsuki suggested reviving the practice, Natsuki's response was unexpectedly sensible.

"But wearing kimono at our age will seem like a totally middle-aged fashion statement."

"Of course it will," Mitsuki said. "Who cares? We *are* totally middle-aged, and then some. Wear a semiformal or a formal one, will you?"

"Really? Why make such a big thing of it? Putting on any kimono is a production."

"It's been a long time, so why not?"

When Mitsuki used to escort their frail mother to Ginza, she had always had her hands full as caregiver, so now she wanted to take pains and make an occasion of it to revel in her freedom. In the midst of the ordeal of finding a new place to live, she wanted to let in some fresh air and revive her moping spirits.

The tea salon in the exclusive Wako Department Store was always crowded, so they met instead in the Wako coffee shop a block away. A cup of tea there cost a thousand yen, but even if she had to economize in daily life, Mitsuki intended to splurge on outings like this now and then, partly to reassure her sister that she wasn't destitute.

When she self-consciously removed her coat, revealing the five-crested formal kimono, her sister cried out in astonishment. "Don't tell me...!" Natsuki was wearing their mother's dark-blue silk crepe.

"Yes, the *Golden Demon* kimono."

"Oh wow. It must have been way too small. When did you have it altered?"

"There wasn't time. I didn't have it cleaned either. It was in perfect condition, so I decided to wear it *tsuitake*-style with the obi tied low."

"*Tsuitake?*"

Mitsuki explained that this meant wearing a kimono the way men did, without folding and tucking it up under the obi. Women hardly ever did this, especially with a formal five-crested kimono. She was a little proud of her own daring.

"See how short the sleeves are?" She spread out her arms like a kite. She had shortened the sleeves of her under-kimono so they wouldn't show. To match the kimono's formality, she was wearing a heavy obi woven lavishly with gold and silver thread—the finest of her mother's obis, one her mother had borrowed from Auntie and somehow ended up owning.

"I can't afford to have it altered, so I'm not planning to. Nowadays there's no real chance to wear a kimono like this anyway."

"Getting divorced has really made you ready to try anything." Natsuki sighed and then spoke in her usual envious tone: "I'm sooo jealous."

"You are? Why?"

"Because ever since talking to you on the phone that night, I've been thinking how nice it would be to be free. To have a place all my own—just the sound of it is lovely. You know, 'a room of one's own.'"

Mitsuki started to laugh despite herself, the mounting melancholy of the past few days briefly forgotten. "So you were jealous when I married him and now you're jealous again when I'm divorcing him?"

Natsuki joined in the laughter. "That's me, always discontent. I'm hopeless." Pressing back her kimono sleeve, she stirred Campari and soda in the tall glass with a thin glass swizzle stick.

"To tell the truth," she said, "when I heard your news, I considered divorcing Yuji too."

*How ridiculous*, Mitsuki thought, and looked at her.

Natsuki went on stirring her Campari soda. She'd figured that with her share of the inheritance from their mother she could find a place to live, she said, and if she took on a few more pupils she'd be able to maintain a minimal lifestyle. Fortunately, divorce had little effect on children's marriage prospects nowadays.

Mitsuki was silent. Her sister had never bothered her head about money matters in everyday life, let alone planned ahead about pensions and the like. With her indolent nature, her intractable eye disease, and her by now ingrained taste for luxuries, she would never be able to support herself.

"But I asked myself what I would do if I *couldn't* support myself and realized that somewhere inside I was thinking I'd go back to Yuji."

"Kind of defeats the purpose."

"I know. It made me laugh." She was laughing now as she told the story.

Then she'd recalled how even when her weight ballooned from steroids, leaving her with three chins and a body that was puffy everywhere but at her fingers and toes, Yuji would tell her affectionately how charming she was, never showing any trace of a frown. She realized then what a good husband he really was.

"And that's not all." Natsuki stopped moving the swizzle stick and looked at her sister.

As Mitsuki waited for what might come next, Natsuki suddenly asked, "How's the apartment search coming, by the way?" Her tone was casual, but her eyes were probing.

"Hmm." The fanciful castle in the air she had described that night on the telephone, less than ten days before, had turned to rubble, but she wished to avoid mentioning this—not from pride, but from a desire not to disappoint Natsuki, who she knew had been entranced by the vision. She answered in as normal a voice as she could muster, "Haven't found anything very good."

Natsuki said nothing, waiting for more.

"I'm at a funny age. I mean, of course I'd like to surround myself only with things I love, but I still have to do all my own cooking, cleaning, and laundry—live a normal life. I'm not over the hill."

Natsuki looked down and went back to stirring her soda. In the old days she would have made a great show of blowing a stream of cigarette smoke sideways, but nowadays smoking meant you couldn't get a good seat in a restaurant or ride airplanes. Before anyone knew it, she had quit.

Watching the swizzle stick go round, Mitsuki continued. "So I got to thinking, and I decided to keep the paulownia chest since I can store my fabrics in it, and not buy a china cupboard after all. I can manage with the shelves over the sink." She would give back most of their mother's dishes to Natsuki, she said.

Still stirring, eyes still downcast, Natsuki slowly began to speak. "Actually there's something…" She hesitated, fingering the thin glass stick. After a short silence, she went on. "What I wanted to tell you is that I've decided to share my inheritance from Mother with you. My portion."

"No!" Mitsuki cried out softly. "I don't need your money."

Natsuki looked up. "I'm not saying all of it. It's a funny amount, but twenty-two million yen."

"I'm telling you I don't need it."

"You need it more than I do."

After deciding against divorce, she'd come up with the idea of splitting her inheritance with Mitsuki, she said, an idea that now seemed completely natural. "And when I talked it over with Yuji, you know what he said?"

Natsuki drew back her chin and looked her sister in the eye. Her expression slowly changed to one of irrepressible joy. Mitsuki waited.

"He said why not give her all of it? He said it without a moment's hesitation. You know, I've been married to the man for thirty years, and I never knew what a prince he was."

Her smile then faded, and her expression turned serious. Mitsuki too became serious. The sisters looked at each other for several moments, their eyes grave.

Yuji's words had made Natsuki realize that for thirty years she'd felt inhibited for absolutely no reason. As far as Yuji was concerned, his money was hers too. She did want to pay for a Steinway grand piano out of her inheritance and also leave herself a bit of spending money. The piano would be about 10 million yen, the spending money another 5 million. That amount subtracted from the 36.8 million left roughly 21.8 million, which was how she came up with the odd amount of 22 million yen.

"I can't take your money."

**438**

"Yes, you can." Despite the obvious unequal treatment Mitsuki had suffered as a child, she had ended up doing far more to look after their parents in their old age. Natsuki said she wanted to do what she could to make up for that imbalance as well.

"You don't have to do anything."

Various thoughts came and went in Mitsuki's mind—how true it was that she'd ended up doing so much more; how surprising it was that her flighty sister should have come up with a gesture so thoughtful; how indignant Natsuki would be if she could read her mind now. Of course the gift was unexpected and welcome. Tetsuo's face came to mind. If he'd been born to wealth like Yuji, and the situation was reversed, would he have said, "Let your sister have it all"? She strongly doubted it. The thought made her feel sad and sorry for him. She was ashamed that she had ever made light of her sister's marrying into wealth and equally ashamed that she, Natsuki, and their mother had ever looked down upon Yuji and his straightforward good sense.

Yuji probably didn't love Natsuki the way she wanted to be loved. Like most men, he probably had no idea how a woman wanted to be loved in the first place—but that, Natsuki had apparently decided, didn't matter.

Mitsuki repeated feebly, "You don't have to do this."

"I couldn't bear for you to be struggling along in a miserable hole. Please use your inheritance to buy a decent place to live. And if you had a little over twenty million extra, that would help, wouldn't it?"

As Mitsuki nodded, tears trickled down her cheeks—the first she had ever shed in her sister's presence as an adult. Pretending not to notice, Natsuki raised her empty glass in the air and ordered a refill.

For dinner they went to Imamura, a traditional *kaiseki* restaurant across the street from Wako. They hadn't been there together for several years, not since their mother stopped being able to sit at the counter. The owner ran the place exactly as his late father had done; they enjoyed the sense that as soon as they stepped inside they went back in time, becoming characters in an Ozu film. As they wielded their chopsticks, they savored the pleasure of dressing up and going out to eat fine food on fine dinnerware. After several small cupfuls of sake, held carefully in the fingertips as befitted ladies in lovely kimono, they hailed a taxi, pleasantly tipsy. Natsuki got out first. Glancing at the meter, she tried to slip Mitsuki a disproportionately large share of the fare. When Mitsuki refused it, she said, "Don't be stubborn," but in the end, knowing her sister's temperament, pressed only her fair share into her hand.

Traveling north on Ring Road 7, Mitsuki looked out on scenery she had seen countless times before from bus and taxi windows. The outlines of the buildings gradually blurred, along with the reflected glow of white, yellow, and orange lights. Before she knew it, she was crying like a child, her face crumpled.

$$\left(66\right)$$

## THE DAY THE CHERRIES BLOOMED

Mitsuki reported to Masako over the telephone the next day, New Year's Eve.

*"You're super lucky."* Remembering the words from their last conversation, she hesitated over whether to admit that, thanks to her sister, she would now be officially "rich." Masako was struggling as a single mother with a daughter suffering from an eating disorder. In the end Mitsuki decided to tell her, first because withholding the news would be a violation of their friendship, and second because Masako knew the world was unfair and so refrained from comparing herself to others. Besides, though her mother was still in vigorous health, Masako would eventually come into a small inheritance of her own.

When she had heard Mitsuki out, Masako said, "That's great."

"Isn't it?"

"It's every woman's dream. You're Cinderella — a Cinderella for our times."

"You think so?"

"Absolutely."

"With no Prince Charming?"

"That's the beauty of it. Look at you. Still a girl in your fifties, not only your mother but your husband out of the picture, and rolling in dough. You've got it made, sister."

Having had enough of marriage, Masako had no attachment to the ideal of two people growing old together like a pair of well-worn husband-and-wife rice bowls.

"To celebrate," said Mitsuki, "let's have dinner. My treat."

"Deal." Masako lowered her voice slightly. "Tetsuo wrote to me and apologized. Said to tell you he's sorry. Said he wrote you an email but you might not open it, so he asked me to tell you."

"I did open it and read it, I just didn't answer."

"Oh." A pause. "Well, have a happy New Year, this year for sure."

Toward midnight Mitsuki opened the window and heard the ringing of the temple bell at Myohoji to mark the passing of the old year. What a long journey she'd come on this year! Soon she would leave this neighborhood, never again to hear this sound—a sound that seemed to make the winter night air, warmer now than in her childhood, a bit more bracing.

In mid-January, just beyond the Inokashira line, she found a condominium she liked. The building was far from new, but it faced a spacious park, one of the city's finest, and even now in the wintertime offered a distant view of evergreens. Closer at hand, the branches of a stout maple tree reached toward her veranda, and through them she could make out the cherry trees encircling the pond. The real estate agent tried to gloss over the building's age with the term "vintage condominium," but the moment she saw the view, Mitsuki's heart leaped. She envisioned how it would look in spring, when fresh green leaves came out and sunshine poured down. The apartment, two bedrooms with a living-dining area and kitchen, was fairly large at 62.5 square meters. Better still, the owner was in a hurry to sell, so Mitsuki could afford it even if she had the interior renovated. She had to use her married name on the contract since the divorce wouldn't be official until March, when Tetsuo returned. But on her mailbox and on the door she boldly wrote KATSURA.

After that she and Natsuki held a memorial service for their mother in the restaurant in the Shinjuku Park Hyatt Hotel, where they used to celebrate each other's birthdays. She also made a farewell visit to the university and took a big box of sweets with her to Toride to say goodbye to Tetsuo's parents. When they started to apologize for his behavior, she hastily interrupted and thanked them for all they had done. She meant every word. Their other son and their daughter-in-law she thanked too, since they had been providing care for the old couple and would continue to do so.

In between such errands, she oversaw the renovation of the "vintage condominium" and, wearing gloves and a face mask to protect against dust, packed up her things in the old apartment, leaving everything she thought Tetsuo might want. Soon the plum blossoms came out, then the peach blossoms, as with mechanical speed and precision the natural world rolled toward spring.

On a day when despite the tang of winter cold the air held a foretaste of spring, she was in the library packing paperback books brown with age into cardboard boxes. She paused to look at the name of a well-known literary publisher. This was the publisher that had asked her old professor with the striking forehead to translate *Madame Bovary* a dozen years ago. No new translation had yet come out, so perhaps the project had been shelved. She had seen the editor once or twice in the professor's office but had no way of knowing if he still worked for the same publishing house. She thought about calling on the publisher once she was settled in. Unused as she was to promoting herself, the idea seemed strange, yet she could see herself doing it.

The room faced north, and winter chill clung to the walls. Mitsuki sat for a while on a filled box, her back to the cold, examining the front and back covers of various paperbacks.

The money from Natsuki had given her a condominium beyond her dreams, plus some extra cash. But she wouldn't have quite enough to manage until her pension payments started, so she needed to do more patent translations. What to do with the rest of her time she hadn't yet decided. Her health having been particularly poor over the past year, all she'd had in mind was getting well.

She looked again at the paperbacks, brown with age.

People didn't live to do what they wanted; becoming an adult was a process of learning to give up things you wanted to do. But some abandoned dreams left a persistent ache. Her failure to accept the professor's "rather nice offer" still caused her twinges of pain. Perhaps she could revive that offer even at this late date. It was *Madame Bovary*, after all. Why not translate the first few chapters, and if they came out well, take them to the publisher? The media occasionally ran stories of divorced women who lived with flair, turning their hobby into a business. She wasn't looking for a fresh start that exciting; but if she devoted herself to regaining her physical strength, her mental energy surely would rebound as well. Then she could do something. She could at least make a stab at translating the book.

A small step, yet an outrageously bold one too.

Her mother had been about this age when she took up chansons. Perhaps her mother's rejection of old age had made Mitsuki too ready to embrace it. She didn't want to resist aging the way her mother had, yet she did want to follow her soul's yearning, reach her arms to stars above. She had been given so many things that her mother had been denied—given them thanks to her mother, as often as not. The times were different, and her innate gifts were also different. Perhaps she owed it to herself to dream new dreams,

dreams that were more ambitious, more outrageously bold — *her* dreams.

Slowly she stood up.

Returning to the bedroom, she took out her wallet, found Mr. Matsubara's business card, and tore it into tiny pieces. She picked up the little mound of white paper scraps that a puff of breath would scatter, laid it on her palm, and regarded it for a few moments as a passing dream. He was a fine man, someone she could respect. Only a man of rare depth could love one woman his whole life like that. His heart belonged to Wakako: she had no desire to turn it toward herself. Wakako had died without ever singing for him. Someone who could love a woman that modest would not, in the end, love Mitsuki the way she wished to be loved…

She moved in March, just before Tetsuo came back to Japan. As soon as the movers left, she went directly to the window. Through the gossamer-thin, gold organdy curtains that she had already hung, she could see the green of the park. Drawn by the color, she opened the curtains; along with the tender green foliage, the stirrings of early spring leaped to her eyes. Around the pond, cherry trees extended long branches covered with tight buds toward the surface of the water.

Any day now the buds would burst.

When she was young, she had preferred the autumn.

In junior high she had learned the word *wakuraba*, a poetic term for blighted leaves, leaves that change color out of season. Having never experienced real adversity, she'd felt drawn to the darkness the word evoked. She hadn't cared for spring, hadn't liked fabrics with floral designs. She had even felt a slight aversion to paintings of flowers, wondering what good it did to paint beautiful things in a beautiful way. But as she grew older and more intimately acquainted with sickness and old age, as the face of adversity became familiar, little by little she had come to appreciate spring. That was why she chose posters of Monet's water lilies to put up over her father's bed in the nursing home. But not until today, here at this window, had she ever appreciated the full value of spring, the season when nature returned from nullity with fresh, vibrant colors, singing a paean to life.

Just then the doorbell rang. Natsuki had come over to help out, bringing with her some boxed lunches from Shibuya's department store. She too made straight for the window, bags in hand.

"I'm sooo jealous."

Realizing what she had said, she burst out laughing, and Mitsuki joined in with some emotion. Natsuki seemed not to have the slightest idea that she herself had made this view possible for her sister. Perhaps it was this nonchalance, this happy unselfconsciousness, that Yuji saw and cherished.

From that day on, Mitsuki slowly opened cardboard boxes.

When emptying the house in Chitose Funabashi, and again when clearing out the apartment she and Tetsuo had shared, she'd been in a rush. Now with time and room in her heart to spare, she opened the boxes packed in such a hurry: some of them had been moved twice without ever being opened. Items she was used to seeing in Chitose Funabashi or that she had until recently used in her life with Tetsuo, she was able to unpack and put away efficiently. It was different with items she hadn't seen in a while—familiar, well-loved items, some of which she hadn't really seen in decades: those she took in hand, running her fingertips over them to reacquaint herself with their texture and bending down to inhale their aroma. Her father's English-Japanese dictionary, the pages curling. Her mother's ivory earrings from her youth. A big hair ribbon Mitsuki used to wear on special family outings to Ginza...

As the days went by, she no longer bothered to find places to put things but just went on opening box after box, almost in a trance. The apartment was a mess. Half-empty boxes, rolled-up cushioning, and mementos lay everywhere, with hardly room to move about. The mementos spoke to Mitsuki of various periods in her life. Each item she unpacked sought to engage her in dialogue with the past. She found it hard to believe that on the night of the storm in Hakone, nothing but dark memories had come to her. Her memories now weren't dark, yet neither were they full of light. The simple strangeness of it all—the strangeness that she'd been granted those times in the first place, granted the privilege of being born, of being alive like this—struck her with force.

Often she lost track of time, and she'd find herself working well past midnight.

Ten days or so went by in a haze, a stretch of time with no here or now. One morning she woke up and, still short on sleep, went out into the living-dining area. Through the gold organdy curtains, she glimpsed a white cloud around the pond in the park. With a sharp intake of breath, she drew the sheer curtains, and the cloud became a cloud of blossoms. Yesterday's glorious sun had warmed the sky and the earth, bringing the cherry blossoms out all at once.

*I am happy*: in that moment, Mitsuki thought that not to be happy now would be a sin. It had been a long time, a very long time, since she could bring herself even to say the words.

"I'm happy," she said aloud and begged forgiveness of no one in particular.


**THE END**

**MINAE MIZUMURA** is one of the most important writers in Japan today. Born in Tokyo, she moved with her family to Long Island, New York, when she was twelve. She studied French literature at Yale College and Yale Graduate School. Her other novels include the Yomiuri Prize–winning *A True Novel*; *Zoku meian* (Light and Dark Continued), a sequel to the unfinished classic *Light and Dark* by Soseki Natsume; and *Shishosetsu from left to right* (An I-Novel from Left to Right), an autobiographical work. Her most recent book in English, *The Fall of Language in the Age of English*, was published in 2015 by Columbia University Press. She lives in Tokyo.

**JULIET WINTERS CARPENTER** studied Japanese language and literature at the University of Michigan and the Inter-University Center for Japanese Language Studies in Tokyo. Carpenter's translation of Kobo Abe's novel *Secret Rendezvous* won the 1980 Japan–United States Friendship Commission Prize for the Translation of Japanese Literature, and her translation of Minae Mizumura's *A True Novel* won the same prize for 2014–2015, making her the only person to have won this prestigious award twice.

*Also by*
**Minae Mizumura**

# A TRUE NOVEL

Translated from the Japanese
by Juliet Winters Carpenter

**The winner of Japan's prestigious
Yomiuri Literature Prize,
Mizumura has written a beautiful
novel, with love at its core,
that reveals, above all,
the power of storytelling.**

A remaking of Emily Brontë's *Wuthering Heights* set in postwar Japan, *A True Novel* begins in New York in the 1960s, where we meet Taro, a relentlessly ambitious Japanese immigrant trying to make his fortune. Flashbacks and multilayered stories reveal his life: an impoverished upbringing as an orphan, his eventual rise to wealth and success — despite racial and class prejudice — and an obsession with a girl from an affluent family that has haunted him all his life. *A True Novel* then widens into an examination of Japan's westernization and the emergence of a middle class.

"A riveting tale of doomed lovers set against the backdrop of postwar Japan…Mizumura's ambitious literary and cultural preoccupations do not overwhelm the sheer force of her narrative or the beauty of her writing (in an evocative translation by Juliet Winters Carpenter)…*A True Novel* makes tangible the pain and the legacy of loss…[Its] psychological acuteness, fully realized characters, and historical sweep push it out of the realm of pastiche and into something far more alluring and memorable."
—*New York Times Book Review*

# ▓ OTHER PRESS

# ▨ OTHER PRESS

*You might also enjoy these titles from our list:*

### I'LL BE RIGHT THERE by Kyung-sook Shin

**Set in 1980s South Korea, a story of how friendship, European literature, and a charismatic professor defy war, oppression, and the absurd**

"[*I'll Be Right There* is] a page-turner, such is Shin's gift for storytelling, as well as her careful cultivation of motifs." —*New York Times Book Review*

### YOUR VOICE IN MY HEAD by Emma Forrest

**A stunning memoir that explores the highs and lows of love and the heartbreak of loss**

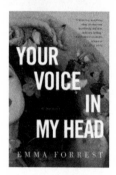

"Emma Forrest is an incredibly gifted writer... I can't remember the last time I ever read such a blistering, transfixing story of obsession, heartbreak, and slow, stubborn healing." —Elizabeth Gilbert, author of *Eat, Pray, Love*

### DROWNED by Therese Bohman

**This spellbinding novel of psychological suspense combines hothouse sensuality with ice-cold fear on every page.**

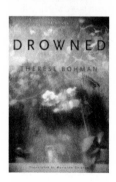

"Therese Bohman could be lumped in with the other Scandinavian authors who have taken over the mystery world since *The Girl with the Dragon Tattoo*, but her story is more quiet and nuanced, her writing lush enough to create a landscape painting with every scene." —*O, The Oprah Magazine*

*www.otherpress.com*